"I WILL REMAKE THE WORLD FOR YOU IF I MUST,"

Raymond told her. "But do not deny me. How can you say you love me and yet bear to part with me?"

"To save you hurt and shame—" Alys began.

But Raymond did not allow her to finish. Instead, he held Alys close to him and kissed her. Though she stood rigid at first, pushing at him, Alys's strength was nothing compared to his, and soon she yielded, her lips growing warm. As Raymond kissed the softness of her neck, Alys drew a shuddering breath before his mouth gently closed on hers again. . . .

WINTER SONG

is the second book of the spectacular romantic saga, the *ROYAL DYNASTY* series. Set against the lavish pageantry of medieval England, *WINTER SONG* is the passionate story of a man and woman who struggle against a world of vengeance and violence in their quest to fulfill an enduring love.

WINTER SONG

ROBERTA GELLIS

PLAYBOY PAPERBACKS

Created by the producers of
The Roselynde Chronicles,
Wagons West, and
The Kent Family Chronicles Series.

Executive Producer: Lyle Kenyon Engel

WINTER SONG

Copyright © 1982 by Roberta Gellis and Book Creations, Inc.

Cover illustration copyright © 1982 by PEI Books, Inc.

Published simultaneously in the United States and Canada by Playboy Paperbacks, New York, New York. Printed in the United States of America. Library of Congress Catalog Card Number: 82-80218.

Books are available at quantity discounts for promotional and industrial use. For further information, write to Premium Sales, Playboy Paperbacks, 1633 Broadway, New York, New York 10019.

ISBN: 0-867-21091-5

First printing September 1982.

10 9 8 7 6 5 4 3 2 1

This book is dedicated to Lyle and Marla Engel, who have been endlessly kind to me and my husband.

CHAPTER 1

****

"You do not seem to understand what I am saying, Father."
Raymond d'Aix's voice was quiet, but his pale eyes were like
glittering ice in his thin, dark face. "You cannot have me
without accepting Alys of Marlowe as my wife."

"Marriages made in haste by silly boys can be annulled,"
Alphonse d'Aix replied sharply.

"I am not married to Alys. Her father is a most upright and
honorable man. He would not even permit a betrothal between
us until your permission could be obtained," Raymond said.

Alphonse stared at his son. Raymond had always been long
and lean, and now he was painfully thin. Despite what should
have been a good night's sleep, bruised-looking patches
showed beneath his eyes. It was clear that he had traveled far
and hard with insufficient rest. He had arrived on the preceding
evening with ten guardsmen and a master-at-arms, all of them
haggard from hard riding. Little information could be gleaned
from any of them beyond the fact that they had come all the
way from England in about eighteen days, which Alphonse did
not doubt. The good horses they rode were hardly more than
scarecrows, and the men were glazed and gray with fatigue.

Raymond had wolfed down the food provided for him,
patted his hysterical mother and sisters kindly, and told his
father he had important matters to discuss with him but would
leave them to the next day, as he was half-dead for need of
sleep. Alphonse had made no objections. First, it was obvious
that Raymond was exhausted, but more than that kept Alphonse quiet. There was something different about Raymond,
something in the assurance of his voice when he said *tomorrow*, and something in the way he treated his mother and
sisters. He was kind—that had not changed—but there was
also contempt in the looks he bent on them.

This morning both the assurance and the contempt had
shown again, but they were veiled under consideration as

Raymond bade his mother—in a voice she responded to automatically—to go and rest, after she had begun to weep over the six months he had been gone without a word or a sign that he was alive. Then he had calmly announced that he wanted his father's permission to take in marriage Lady Alys of Marlowe, England. Alphonse had looked at him and said *Do not be ridiculous*—which had called forth Raymond's coldly forceful reply.

Naturally, Alphonse assumed that some wealth- and status-seeking "gentleman" with a pretty daughter had trapped Raymond into marriage. Alphonse himself was an honorable man and was glad that his son wished to honor the commitment. However, he did not consider *himself* committed, and, after all, Raymond's marriage was *his* business. He had pointed out the obvious solution—annulment—and had been stunned by Raymond's reply. There was no commitment even on Raymond's part. And, if there had been, Alphonse wondered what was the cause of the haste.

"If you have got this silly girl with child—" Alphonse began, combining the talk of marriage and the need for haste, and coming up with the usual conclusion.

"How dare you!" Raymond snarled, losing the calm that he had maintained and reaching instinctively for his sword.

He was not wearing it, but Alphonse's eyes opened wide with surprise. Barely had he time to absorb the idea that his son was so set on defending the woman's honor that he would threaten his own father than another surprise was added. Raymond lifted his hand from his hip and began to laugh.

"Earl Richard and Lady Elizabeth both specially bade me not to do just what I am doing. Please, Father, let us sit down and do you listen to the whole. When you hear, you will find that it is not so unreasonable. I have gone the wrong way about it."

"Which Earl Richard?" Alphonse asked, moving toward a chair and gesturing to Raymond to take another.

"Richard of Cornwall. Sir William is marshal of his lands and closer than a brother. Alys calls the earl 'uncle' and—"

"Richard of Cornwall approved this?" Alphonse asked, amazed.

"He approved sufficiently to ask King Henry to write you a

letter. I have not read it, of course, but I understand the king says that the union would in no way displease him."

"Why should it?" Alphonse asked angrily. He realized now that the forces arrayed against him were more considerable than he had first thought. But England was far away, and the king could not really care whether or not the marriage took place. Suddenly another question rose to Alphonse's mind. "Does Eleanor know of this?"

"Oh, yes," Raymond replied at once, his eyes glinting wickedly with humor now. "Both Queen Eleanor and Countess Sancia have written letters in Alys's favor—addressed to Mother, of course." He laughed. "So you see that both your half-sisters have turned against you, too."

"This is ridiculous," Alphonse said. "It has been said that the climate in England is so terrible that it drives men mad. I see that it has driven my sisters mad, at least. Raymond, my son, you are in love. . . . I see that. Your heart is full. No doubt the lady is perfectly beautiful and probably one of those blondes so attractive to us, who see that coloring rarely, but—"

"It is quite true, but I am not marrying Alys for her beauty of person."

"Yes, yes," Alphonse agreed quickly. "I have no doubt her soul is as gentle and delicate as a flower—"

Raymond suddenly roared with laughter, shocking his father into silence. When Raymond could speak again, he said, "Alys is marvelous, completely, but neither gentle nor"—he choked slightly, remembering some of his conversations with Alys —"nor delicate."

"Well," Alphonse hurried on, although his voice now held an uncertain note, "we will accept her character and person as perfect. But Raymond, you know one does not marry for qualities of person."

"I intend to do so, however," Raymond remarked calmly.

"You are in love," Alphonse repeated kindly. "I understand. I am sure the lady is well dowered, but—"

"No, she is not," Raymond interrupted once more, grinning. "Her dower is one small keep and its lands. Its yield is good for its size; it commands a heavily traveled road, and there are tolls, but even so—"

"Raymond, have you been having a jest at my expense?"

Alphonse bellowed. He had no time, really, to feel relief, because Raymond was shaking his head.

"No, Father. I am in dead earnest. I intend to marry Alys, though I know the match is unequal in material matters. That is not significant. Earl Richard—"

"You are mad!" Alphonse exclaimed.

Raymond nodded, grinning again. "The climate in England is *very* bad. That is true."

"This makes it even worse," Alphonse snapped, ignoring his son's levity. "But even if she had been rich as Croesus, the match would not be possible. A dower in England is of *no* value here. We do not need money. You must marry in France or Gascony so that—"

"I thank God, Father, that I am not your only child. There are Alphonse and Jeanine and Margot. You may make alliances as you like with them. Through me, you will have made a strong bond with England—"

"Stronger than my sister's marriage to the king?" Alphonse asked caustically.

Raymond bit his lip, then shrugged. "I supposed I wished to wrap the thing up in clean linen, but there is no need. I know as well as you that there can be no political advantage to the family in my marriage to Alys. The matter of dower can be arranged. Earl Richard will lend Sir William a suitable sum of money to make up a respectable dower—but I know you do not desire money. I am sorry for it, Father; however, I will not marry elsewhere, nor will I live with those who deny me the one thing of import for which I have ever asked."

"Are you threatening me?" Alphonse asked harshly.

"I do not know," Raymond replied quietly. "I am not asking for a new destrier or a new maidservant to warm my bed. My desire for Alys does not come from an ache in my loins. I am fighting for my whole life. . . ."

On the words, the eyes of father and son locked. Both remembered the last time Raymond had said those words. When his father told him he could not lead the army being sent to curb a vassal in Gascony because his mother feared for his safety, Raymond had pleaded and demanded that his mother not be allowed to make a popinjay of him. Alphonse had laughed, pointing out that it was only a little action of no importance, but Raymond countered, quite truthfully, that if a man did not learn by leading small actions, he would be of little use in major conflicts. Finally, Raymond had cried, "Can you not see that I am being toyed with as if I were a doll? Let me go and do this, Father. I am a man, not a plaything for Mother. I am fighting for my life."

That time Alphonse had made some soothing replies, but because of the near-hysterical note in his son's voice, he had been misled into thinking that Raymond would forget the matter in a few days. Alphonse had equated Raymond's behavior with his daughter's eventual calm after she had exclaimed hysterically that she would die if a suitor were disapproved. He had not even been disturbed when he learned that his son had flung out of Tour Dur in a rage, thinking Raymond would ride off his passion or work it off in hunting or rape. Even when Raymond had not returned that night, Alphonse had not worried. He believed his son was behaving like a naughty little boy, cutting off his nose to spite his face, sleeping out in a field to frighten his parents. However, a letter had come the next day to say Raymond would not return—and indeed he had not, not for six months.

"You can kill me," Raymond now continued, just as quietly, "or you can lock me up. If you do not, I will go. And this time I will not return at all, unless I bring Alys of Marlowe with me as my wife."

For a moment longer Alphonse d'Aix stared into his son's eyes, then dropped his own. He had seen his own father looking out at him from his son's face. There was no threat to him in Raymond's expression, only a determination that could not be broken by pleas or reason or time.

"Do you realize what your mother will say to this?" Alphonse asked, shifting his ground.

Imperceptibly, Raymond relaxed, hardly believing his ears. His father had yielded—so quickly, so easily. Alphonse had not yet said the formal words, but this mention of Raymond's mother was a move Raymond recognized. It was a sidestep to a new path. In the past, Raymond had often found that path a dead end, and his father's yielding becoming meaningless in the face of his mother's tears and pleading. However, Raymond was now armored against those explosions of emotionalism.

Alys had laughed at him when he described the dreadful

scenes his mother had always made. Her eyes had twinkled up at him through the abnormally long, thick lashes she had inherited from her father. "It is a woman's favorite weapon with 'soft' men," Alys had confessed merrily, after wondering aloud whether she should betray her fellow females and deprive herself of the device. "Do not pay any attention, and it will stop — or use a light slap on the cheek if you cannot wait for her to realize it is not working; that is what another woman would do. I suppose you cannot slap your mother, but you can certainly so correct your sisters' transports."

"And you, should I correct you so?" Raymond had asked, drawing Alys into his arms and kissing her.

"You will not need to," she replied so meekly after he freed her lips that Raymond looked at her suspiciously. "Papa cured me of such tricks long ago," she confessed, then giggled mischievously. "You do not think I would expose the tricks *I* use. I may not know how to direct an army, but I am not so poor a tactician as that."

But it did not seem possible to Raymond that Alys used any tricks. She appeared transparently honest to him. A more serious discussion had followed between them, in which Alys assured him that his mother did not actually feel such agony as she displayed by her shrieks and gasps. Physical fear might make a woman scream and fling herself about, Alys allowed doubtfully, but real grief or sorrow did not.

Raymond had reason to believe her. He had watched Lady Elizabeth, who had married Alys's father after years of waiting, during the days when her lover (now her husband) hung between life and death. There had been tears—slow, quiet tears—and sometimes she held her arms across her breast as if to still an unbearable pain, rocking back and forth with the agony; however, there had been no shrieks, no breast-beating, no cries calling God to witness the unnatural cruelty of her children, which was destroying her life.

Thus Raymond now saw his way clear of his mother's attempts to control him, and he smiled tightly at his father. "Mother will not like it at all, I know, but you may leave her to me."

Alphonse gaped. Never had Raymond said such a thing, nor had such a flash of amused and loving contempt crossed his face when he spoke of his mother. In the past, anxiety and desperation had been evident in Raymond's expression when he spoke of her. Now, Alphonse remembered the voice in which Raymond had forcefully directed Lady Jeannette to "go and rest" while he had this discussion, and how he had turned his back on her while his sister Jeanine supported her faltering footsteps to the door. In earlier times Raymond would have watched, perhaps even followed his mother asking if he had made her unwell.

"You mean you will tell her of this idiocy of yours, that you intend to destroy all her hopes of a Gascon alliance to extend her— our—lands there?"

"I will certainly tell her I intend to marry Alys and no other woman. As to the Gascon lands—that might be managed. Earl Richard has lands there which he ceded to his brother, the king, when he married Sancia. It might be possible to arrange for a dower for Alys in Gascony. Sir William, Alys's father, would pay King Henry out of Alys's revenues from Bix, and Alys would receive instead the revenue from the Gascon lands."

The animosity faded from Alphonse's face, and he pursed his lips. Raymond *hmmmd* with sudden thought. A very satisfactory arrangement might be made, both of them realized. King Henry could get little good out of the Gascon lands, because when the holders of the property were not corrupt, they were warring. Revenues were small and sporadic. Thus, the properties were of little value except as a base for the war against France.

If, then, Henry could be assured of a stable equivalent revenue, and not lose his right to draw on the property in times of war, he might very willingly name Raymond as vassal in his wife's right. He might, in fact, be tempted to part with a valuable stronghold because he knew and trusted Raymond and because Raymond was his wife's nephew. Moreover, Raymond had never been a vassal of Louis of France; he was, through his father, vassal to his grandfather, the count of Provence, Raymond-Berenger. This could do Henry no harm politically, since he was already bound to Provence by marriage. In addition, Raymond already held a minor property in Gascony and, through his mother, might inherit more —although it was more likely those lands would go to his younger brother, Alphonse, who was currently living at King

Louis's court. Thus, King Henry would gain a powerful and trustworthy ally in Gascony—a rare and precious thing.

From Raymond's and Alphonse's point of view, the Gascon lands would not be any burden to manage. Raymond could do it himself as long as his father was alive; after that his younger brother could spend most of his time there. As it was, Raymond often was in Gascony to oversee his mother's lands; it would be little more trouble to oversee his wife's.

"You know," Alphonse said suddenly, "I begin to like this marriage of yours much better. It will be most excellent to hold the lands directly from the king of England. If you marry a daughter of one of the Gascon houses, I would be bound to the policy of that house. This way, we will be able to make our own alliances freely as we like." He paused and bit his lip. "If this could be done, I would have no objections to the marriage . . . no . . . I would not. But can it be done?"

"I think so—that is, if I return quickly enough. The situation between the brothers—King Henry and Earl Richard —is very good, or was when I left England. That means that Henry will do whatever Richard asks, and Richard will do what Alys asks. No, that is unfair. Richard will see the value of having me as Henry's vassal. What is more, Eleanor will exert her full powers of persuasion for this. She will see the advantages therein—and the king loves her dearly."

"The advantages should be plain enough for Henry to see for himself," Alphonse remarked, surprised.

"Yes, but the king is not always governed by reason. If he should be put out of temper by a quarrel with his brother, he will seek to spite his brother's friend, Sir William, by denying what Sir William's daughter desires. I will need to be careful how I approach the subject, but yes, I think I can arrange a Gascon dower for Alys."

"Of what value?" Alphonse asked.

Raymond beckoned a manservant over. "Go ask for Arnald in the masters-at-arms' quarters, and tell him to bring me the parchment boxes he carried. Speak slowly. His French is of the north, but I warn you that if you use a saucy tone he will knock you endwise." Then Raymond turned to his father. "Alys has written out the whole thing—what is hers and what more her father could give her. I think we may depend on something very handsome from Cornwall, also; he dotes on

her. Call one of the scribes, Father, and let us see where it
would be best for the lands to lie."

Lady Jeannette had obeyed her son both times before she
realized he had twice sent her away. The first time she had told
herself he was tired and did not realize that his tone of voice
was unkind and disrespectful. She would scold him for it
lovingly, and he would say he was sorry. The second time she
had also responded instinctively, taking three or four steps
before she understood she had been sent from the room like a
wayward child. Her gasp and clutch at her heart had gained no
more response than a smile and a nod. Alphonse had been
staring at Raymond and paid her no attention either, and, when
she had tottered feebly from the hall, clinging to Jeanine's
arm, Raymond had turned his back.

In the solar, Lady Jeannette now had time to collect her
thoughts and consider how she had been hurt and slighted. Her
firstborn son, the light of her eyes, had driven her away. He
was cruel and unnatural. All his life she had striven to smooth
the path before his feet, to spare him the smallest hurt or
unhappiness, but he had always been ungrateful, rejecting the
toys she ordered for him, the musical instruments and fine
garments, in favor of swords and hunting bows, horses and
armor.

Raymond had always seemed to prefer his tutor's company,
even when that horrid man had knocked him down and bruised
him in practice combat; and, when his father had sent him
away to the household of the king of Navarre, he had not
complained but had gone willingly. She, on the contrary, had
begged and pleaded that he be sent to his grandfather,
Raymond-Berenger, where she knew he would be given
special privileges and looked after tenderly. Although Alphonse had agreed after a while, Raymond had not, insisting
he was happy in the court of Navarre.

Ungrateful, she thought. Raymond had never cared that she
might grieve or worry about him. And this last escapade,
disappearing for six months without a word and sending that
cruel letter to say it was her fault—that was monstrous! Why
should he go and fight in Gascony? Crude creatures could be
hired to do ugly, dangerous things like that. Why could

Raymond not see that it was better to stay at home and speak of poetry and philosophy, to dance, sing, and gather flowers?

Lady Jeannette wept loudly over her son's cruelty, and her daughters wept with her. They bewailed Raymond's hardness of heart, each reminding the others of incidents that had displayed his lack of consideration for their tender feelings. At last they heard his voice in the large chamber outside the solar. All of them stiffened, before emitting even louder wails as he entered—but the sound of his words came no nearer.

Their indignation grew as they heard the thin, high voices of two little girls mingling with Raymond's. He had stopped to speak with his baseborn daughters. Disgusting! Surely his mother and sisters should have precedence over the daughters of a common serf-woman elevated to a weaving woman.

Actually their indignation was wasted. Raymond did not give much thought to his bastard daughters and would not have stopped to seek them had they not run out to him. He was kindhearted, however, and had taken them in his arms to kiss and fondle, remembering with a faint pang of guilt that it had been his custom to bring them little toys and geegaws when he had been away for some time. He was apologizing for neglecting this and promising them that he would have something for them later in the day when their mother came hurriedly forward to draw them away.

"I beg your pardon, my lord," she said softly. "I was busy and did not see them run to you."

"They did no hurt," Raymond responded, but he felt somewhat awkward. He had realized as he spoke that he must get rid of Lucie before he brought Alys home. "You are looking well, Lucie," he added uneasily, wanting to say something pleasant.

Her expression changed infinitesimally. Raymond would not have noticed if he had not been wondering how to avoid hurting her more than necessary. He had never before thought about what Lucie felt, although she had been his bedmate at Tour Dur whenever he felt the need for a woman. He had first seen her when he was eighteen, some seven years before, in her father's hut on the demesne farm, and had bought her for a few copper pieces with the old man's blessing. It had not occurred to Raymond to wonder what Lucie had felt about it. He had assumed she would be grateful and overjoyed.

The assumption was quite correct. Lucie would have kissed Raymond's feet in gratitude even if he had used her harshly, for the lot of a serf-woman who has lost her man is not pleasant. To be elevated to service in the castle, even if that service included rough usage, was a miracle of good fortune. But Raymond was not cruel in his love play; he was gentle and good-humored, if somewhat indifferent.

At first that did not bother Lucie. She was so happy with the new clothing he gave her, with the fact that her stomach was full all the time, and with dry and warm lodging— compared to her previous lodging— even when she was not called to her master's bed. All she feared was that when Raymond's term of leave from his duties in the court of Navarre was over, she would be sent back to the horrors of life as a field serf. Pregnancy saved her from that fate. Raymond freely acknowledged that the child was his and directed that Lucie be taught skills that would make her useful in the castle so that his child could be fittingly raised.

The next time Raymond came home he called Lucie to his bed again, and she came gladly. However, she was more accustomed to her better condition, and she began to realize that Raymond did not "notice" her. When he needed a woman, he would seek her out and remark that she was pretty and give her a length of fabric to make an overdress or a tunic, or some trinket with which to adorn herself. At other times he could pass right by her and not even nod his head in recognition.

Naturally Lucie did not resent this; she was no one and nothing. She knew Raymond could casually order her killed instead of casually flinging her a trinket. Nonetheless, she found that she no longer dreamed about him or particularly desired that he summon her to his bed. She began to notice the men around the keep, and it warmed her heart that they obviously noticed her.

Lucie was with child again before Raymond left, and glad of it because the second babe would secure her position. The first had been only a girl; perhaps the second would be a boy. Or, if one died, the other would still bind her to the keep. However, with her belly full, it was safe to look around. Gregoire, one of the huntsmen, looked back with such longing in his eyes that Lucie was moved to comfort him.

She found in the end as much comfort as she gave. Gregoire

understood her condition; he, too, had come out of the fields by an accident of fate. He could no more be jealous of a lord than of God, nor would he have thought for a moment of refusing— or expecting Lucie to refuse—any demand a lord made. What was more wonderful to Lucie was that Gregoire was as happy to be with her, to talk to her and listen to her, when she was unable to satisfy his lust as when she had first yielded to him.

When Raymond came home again, there was only another daughter to offer him. He did not mind, but he was not much interested. He was not much interested in Lucie, either; however, his mother objected to his playing about among the maidservants, so he used Lucie when the mood moved him. There were plenty of women of the better sort in the court of Navarre who were drawn to his pale, brilliant eyes and dark skin. For all her lush beauty—and Lucie was lush now, being well fed and ten years older than Raymond—she bored him.

Raymond was so uninterested in Lucie that he had never realized that she did her best to avoid him. Both her daughters had survived—a great surprise, which she attributed to the healthier situation of the castle—and she had become a skillful weaver. Thus, she was reasonably sure she would not be cast out, even if Raymond no longer desired her. Of course, she had never dared deny him. All she dared was to keep out of his way as much as possible.

Had she been less fearful, Lucie would have achieved her heart's desire years earlier, but she had not been bred in the castle. She still saw the lords as creatures apart, superhuman, and as incomprehensible as God. So when Raymond summoned her, she came. She had conceived once more, but as soon as she missed her flux she had gone to an herb-woman who cleaned out her womb. Gregoire's get had gone the same way, but she had wept over those. Even so, she prayed Raymond would stay away. She found it harder and harder to seem willing.

This time when he said how well she looked, Lucie could not quite keep all expression from her face. She cursed herself for coming forward, but she had been afraid Raymond would be angered by the importunities of his daughters and punish them. Hastily she looked down at the little girls and sent them away, struggling to bring some welcome into her expression.

When she raised her eyes, fear almost stopped her heart. Raymond was staring at her with raised brows.

"Why did you not tell me you did not find my attentions pleasing, Lucie?" he asked.

"No," she whispered, "no—please! I—"

"Do not be frightened," Raymond hastened to assure her, much surprised by her reaction. "I am not angry. To speak the truth, I am glad. I am about to be married, and that means you must be married, also."

"I? Married?" Lucie breathed. "To whom, my lord?"

"I had not thought about it," Raymond admitted easily.

In fact, if his daughters and Lucie had not accosted him, he probably would not have remembered their existence. This notion made him rather grateful to little Fenice and Enid and to Lucie, also. He smiled at her.

"Is there someone you would like to marry, Lucie?" Raymond asked. "You have been obedient to me and have never asked for anything. I would be happy to dower you and know that you are content."

She stared at him, lips parted, desperately trying to read from his face whether this was some kind of cruel trap. But Raymond had never been cruel to her. Daring greatly, Lucie whispered, "Gregoire—the huntsman, Gregoire. He is a good man—kind."

"Gregoire . . ." Raymond shook his head, then put out his hand to catch Lucie as she grew pale as milk. "What ails you woman? I am only trying to think whether I know the man. Well, it does not matter. I suppose you can point him out." He let go of her and pulled his purse open as her color returned. "There." He put five gold pieces into her hand. "That is for you. Keep it safe. You shall have your Gregoire, although when I will have time to attend to it, I cannot guess."

Lucie watched fearfully, but there was no discontent in his face, only a look of consideration. She began to hope. If Raymond were bringing home a bride, of course he would not want his bedmate anymore. There was one problem.

"Fenice and Enid?" she asked timidly.

"They must stay here," Raymond replied. "They are my daughters. But you may see them when you like, Lucie. I will see about getting a house for you near Tour Dur so you may continue your work here during the day. But I do not know what may be available, and I must go away again almost immediately. You may have to wait a little time. Go back to your work now. I promise I will not trouble you again."

She dropped a curtsy and fled back to her loom, almost in love with Raymond again for his enormous kindness to her. It was a great relief to know she would not have to take her daughters with her. Although the most generous of men, Gregoire was uncomfortable in the presence of the little girls. They were the lord's get, and he was somewhat in awe of them. Also, indubitably, he would have resented needing to find dowers for another man's daughters if Raymond repudiated them. Then, too, Lucie loved her girls enough to be willing to part with them if that parting would be to their advantage. Great lord's daughters, even if left-handed, so to speak, might be married into the lesser nobility or to one of the rich merchants' houses. Lucie sat and thought and dreamed —Raymond, like a distant god, presiding over her fate.

CHAPTER 2

****

Raymond dismissed Lucie from his mind as swiftly as she had intruded upon it. In spite of his words of assurance to his father, he was not looking forward to the coming interview with his mother. However, he had the evidence of her obedience to his firm orders last night and this morning to reinforce Alys's earlier advice. If he faltered or showed weakness or sympathy, Alys had warned, he would be defeated. Thus, he strode into the solar with a tight mouth and an angry frown and thrust Eleanor's and Sancia's letters at her.

"Here, madame," he announced, "are letters from the queen of England and the countess of Cornwall recommending to you Alys of Marlowe, whom I intend to marry as soon as I return to England. I already have my father's agreement. The scribes are writing a contract, so do not bother to raise objections."

His treatment had the good effect of shocking his three auditors into silence. The sobbings over his cruelty were choked off by the enormity of the news and the new offense. One thing Lady Jeannette had long been determined upon was the choosing of her son's wife to suit herself.

"Who?" she gasped. "Who is this Alys? Where is Marlowe?"

"Alys is my betrothed," Raymond replied. "Marlowe is a town on the Thames in England, midway between Windsor and Oxford. Do you know more now?"

All three gaped at him, his mother and Jeanine in horror and growing rage. His younger sister Margot also knew she should be offended, but she was really more interested in Alys, who, she hoped, would add a little variety to her life. It was *very* dull in Tour Dur. Margot had hoped that she would become "eldest" daughter when Jeanine went away to be married two years ago. But Jeanine's husband had died, she had returned home since she had not produced any child, and Margot was again pushed into the background.

That might have been an enviable position in a keep where many highborn maidens were raised and trained. Under such circumstances, being "last and least" provided freedom for fun and mischief. Aix should have had just such a group of *demoiselles;* many of the lesser knights would gladly have sent their daughters to be trained. Lady Jeannette, however, said she was not strong enough, that she could barely manage her own daughters. The trouble was, Margot thought, that her mother was strong enough not to let her stray more than an arm's length from her skirt.

"Read the letters," Raymond was urging. "They will tell you more about Alys than I have time to relate."

"But Raymond," Lady Jeannette wailed, having caught her breath and gathered her thoughts, "you cannot marry a girl from England. We do not need ties to England. And what do you mean you have no time? You have just come!"

"Yes, and I will leave again as soon as Father and I decide which Gascon property we wish augmented. I believe it will be possible to have Alys's dower settled in Gascony. Her father is marshal to Richard of Cornwall and has great influence with the earl."

"Is that what decided you to marry this girl?" Lady Jeannette asked.

Then Raymond made a serious mistake. "No," he replied, his voice softening. "No. I would have taken Alys barefoot in a shift, if I could have got her no other way. I love her—"

"That is ridiculous!" Jeanine interrupted, jumping up. "Do you think you are living in the pages of a romance? Or has this little slut withheld—"

Raymond slapped her face. "You will not speak of Lady Alys in such terms," he snarled. "Alys will be mistress of Aix some day, and there is no woman in the world better fit to hold that place—or any other."

Jeanine began to scream, and Raymond slapped her again, harder, thumping her down on her stool, and threatening to give her something truly worth screaming about if she did not hold her tongue. Margot began to whimper in sympathy, but she choked off all sound when Raymond turned his glare upon her. Then he looked at his mother.

"Well, madame," he growled, "what have you to say?"

"You have been among barbarians," Lady Jeannette whispered, "and have come back a monster."

"Whatever you like, so long as you hold your tongue and treat my wife with the respect due her."

"And what of the respect due to me from my son and my son's wife?" Lady Jeannette quavered.

"You need not fear that," Raymond assured her in happy ignorance. "Alys has been properly brought up. You will find her a most dutiful daughter. I am sure you will come to love her. Indeed, it is impossible not to love Alys."

To that ridiculous statement, Lady Jeannette made no reply except a faint smile of combined bitterness and derision. Her son misread the expression completely and bent swiftly to kiss her. "There," he remarked, "now that you understand the matter of my marriage to Alys is settled and will not argue with me, I can say I am very glad to see you again." He turned to Margot and kissed her also. "You are looking very pretty, my sweet, and next to Alys you will look even prettier. She is very blond and will set off your dark eyes to perfection." Finally he stepped around his mother and stood before Jeanine. "I will forget what you said and forgive you," he remarked quietly, "if you will be careful of your tongue in the future."

"I will never forgive you," Jeanine hissed. "How dare you!"

Raymond's face tightened. "If you wish to be angry with me, Jeanine, I do not care. Just remember that if you offend Alys, I will punish you in a way that will make this seem like a kiss of love."

She sniffed, and he raised his hand again. The sniffles stopped abruptly. Lady Jeannette had absorbed Raymond's mistake and this byplay with his sister in silence. She was not clever but not completely a fool, either. Years of getting her way with a weak husband had led her to misjudge her son's character. He was gentle and loving rather than weak and had a strong desire to do what was right. This had led him to yield dutifully to his father's orders—thus, indirectly to his mother's —until he was driven too far. But Lady Jeannette did not realize that yet.

She had no intention at all of accepting Raymond's marriage to Alys; however, she had come to understand that her usual methods could not be used. It would be necessary to be more subtle and devious to separate her son from this succubus that had bewitched him. There was no use weeping and lamenting. The first step toward persuading her son had been taken by accident, but now Jeannette knew where she was going. Slowly she opened the letters Raymond had handed to her and pretended to peruse the contents while she planned what to say. She could really read the letters later. They might offer a hint as to how to deal with the girl herself.

But first she would try to delay that necessity or end it completely. Jeannette raised her eyes from Sancia's letter and smiled tremulously. "Indeed, Alys sounds to be a delightful girl."

The remark was rewarded by an embrace from Raymond and a kiss. "She is," he agreed.

"Yes, and virtuous, too, so I do not see why it is necessary to hurry back to England so fast. Surely Alys will be faithful, and surely she would not be so cruel as to deny your mother and sisters a few weeks of your company."

"Alys will be faithful," Raymond replied impatiently, "but it is the end of October. Here it is still summer, but north it is growing cold. If I spend the few weeks you speak of here, there will be snow in the mountains—"

"Oh, not so soon," Lady Jeannette said, "and even if it should fall early, it will melt. You look so tired, my poor darling, and you are so thin. You must stay here and regain your strength. God alone knows what you were eating among those barbarians."

"The food is barbarous enough," Raymond agreed to pacify his mother since he had no intention of agreeing to anything else she asked.

Actually Raymond had come to enjoy the large self-flavored roasts that were so much a part of the English diet. Here in the south the meat spoiled so much faster that it was necessary always to cook it more thoroughly if it was not eaten fresh-killed. Thorough cooking meant cutting the meat into smaller pieces fit for stewing, and flavoring it more strongly to disguise the taste of spoilage.

"Ah!" Lady Jeannette cried. "I will have all your favorite dishes prepared."

"As many as possible for today's dinner," Raymond laughed, "for I will not be here tomorrow."

"What! But you just said—"

"Tomorrow I must ride to Grandfather and obtain his approval."

"You? Why should you ride there? Have we no messengers?"

"Mother, I have said already that I am in great haste. I do not wish to cross the Alps when the passes are covered with snow, nor sail the narrow sea in the teeth of a winter gale."

"Then wait for spring, my beloved boy. Of course you will wait for spring. Whoever heard of a marriage contracted in such a hurry? One would think that the lady feared waiting lest—"

Raymond had been thinking exasperatedly that King Henry and Earl Richard might have already quarreled and that he would be too slow with the wings of a bird, but he knew from past experience that it was useless to mention such practicalities to his mother. She would either say with false soothing that she *knew* the king and his brother would not quarrel, or else she would say that the whole thing was unimportant and there would be another opportunity. Then the sense of what she was saying came to him.

"Mother!" he exclaimed, angry at her innuendo that Alys might be with child.

"Well, why the haste if she has nothing to hide?" Jeanine hissed.

Raymond turned on her, and she shrank back. He bowed stiffly to his mother. "Then I will say farewell, madame. I will see you again when my bride stands beside me."

"No! No!" Lady Jeannette cried. "I never meant such a thing. I . . . But Raymond, it will be thought odd. Even your grandfather will think . . . Wait! If you *must* fly back—if you cannot bear to be parted—"

"You have it right at last," Raymond interrupted coldly. "It is *I* who am in haste, not Alys."

"But Raymond, your haste does not look well for the lady. No, I know you would not choose a girl about whom there could be any doubt, but here, so far from her own place, no one knows her. What will be said—"

"I will answer with my fist or my sword! *Nothing* will be said to or about Alys."

Lady Jeannette swallowed and shrank a trifle. It was most

unlikely that anyone would say anything about *anything* while Raymond wore that expression. She had not known her son's face could look so cold and hard, so *dangerous*. Plainly the idea of keeping him at home day by day until his interest in the blond slut faded would not work. However, there was another way.

"If you would only allow me to finish a sentence, my heart," Lady Jeannette quavered. "I only want the best for you and your sweet Alys. All I wished to say was that if you are in such haste, we will have the marriage *here*. That would be best. All our vassals should be invited to the wedding of the heir. They would be *so* disappointed to miss such a celebration."

"Hmmm," Raymond responded. For the first time his mother had said something really sensible, he thought. It was true that the vassals would be disappointed. They would resent paying the *aide* owed for his marriage if they were not offered some compensation. Also, the marriage would serve as another opportunity to exact fresh oaths of homage to his father —and to himself as heir. That was important. Raymond did not think his father was likely to die soon, nor that young Alphonse would try to usurp his position, but it was a very uncertain world and a good idea indeed to have the men swear fealty directly to him. That would eliminate one more loophole for betrayal.

As these practical thoughts ran through his mind, Raymond was noting how his mother's face brightened when he paused to consider what she had said instead of rejecting it out of hand. It would be silly to deny her the pleasure of filling the keep with guests and having all new, magnificent clothing. Then Raymond wondered whether that might have been the reason she had objected to Alys. Doubtless she had been counting on impressing everyone with this marriage ever since he was a child. Well—why not? There was no reason he could not marry Alys once in England and again in France.

"Very well, Mother," Raymond agreed. "That is a very good idea. I will bring Alys home and marry her here."

"That will be wonderful! Wonderful!" Lady Jeannette cried, rising and embracing her son.

She was pleased with his consent. It did not seem possible to her that Raymond, who claimed to be so much in love, could fail to couple with the girl on the long trip from England. If

Alys refused when he asked her, he would grow angry and come to hate her; he would then believe his mother when she told him that Alys was a cold, uncaring, disobedient young woman. On the other hand, if Alys yielded, she could be painted as lascivious and unvirtuous. In either case it might be possible to make Raymond repudiate her, or—if he would not do that (Lady Jeannette was not always totally self-deceived) because of the marriage contract—Raymond would certainly have a strong distaste for her. Lady Jeannette was truly delighted.

Raymond was equally delighted. He did not care how often he married Alys. He liked parties. His father, he realized, might not be equally pleased with the expense, but he would certainly agree that the benefits—Lady Jeannette's cheerful acceptance of the marriage and the homage ceremony—would make it worthwhile. Moreover, the *aide* would cover the cost, no doubt.

Mutually content, mother and son embraced again, and, in the glow of good feeling, Raymond said, "Will you do me a favor, Mother?"

"Anything, my love," Jeannette responded.

"Will you see that the woman Lucie is married—to—to, ah, yes—Gregoire the huntsman. I know you do not know the man, I cannot recall myself just who he is—"

"Married? Why should Lucie be married? She is a good weaver, and Fenice and Enid—"

"It has nothing to do with Fenice and Enid. They can stay here in the care of the other women. As for the weaving, Lucie can come and work here each day if you like. However, I will not use her again, and there is no reason why the woman should not have a life of her own. She seems to favor this Gregoire, and I would like her to be content."

"But . . . Oh, very well, if that is what you desire."

"If it is too much trouble, Mother, I will see to it myself."

"No, no, not at all, Raymond. I will see to it. Do not give the matter another thought. I will arrange it all, I assure you. And now, since you have so little time to spend with us, do listen to the new lute song Margot has written. It is the prettiest thing imaginable."

Raymond hesitated, surprised by the eagerness his mother displayed to accommodate him. Usually she was not at all willing to do anything that would require more than one or two words to give an order. Then he told himself she was trying to make up for having displeased him, so he dutifully stifled a sigh and composed his features to an expression of pleasure. One thing Alys would never inflict on him was the duty of listening to tinkling love lyrics on a lute. She could not, as far as he knew, play a note on any instrument and had never spoken of poetry except to ridicule the "asses" who quoted it at her instead of making sensible conversation.

In the court of King Henry of England, Alys's emotions mirrored Raymond's. She, too, was wishing that no one could play a note and that poetry had never been devised. Nonetheless, Alys pretended to listen with enjoyment to the lady who was entertaining the select group in Queen Eleanor's chambers. She had been scolded with startling severity by her gentle stepmother for fidgeting and sighing during the previous "entertainment" of this type to which she had been summoned. Alys's eyes wandered from the singer to her father's second wife. There was true pleasure in Elizabeth's piquant face, and her large greenish eyes held a soft mist of tears.

Most of the others, Alys noted, allowing her eyes to roam cautiously to other faces, also responded to the sweet sentiments of the song. Was there something lacking in her? she wondered. Was she incapable of love? That thought brought Raymond to her mind, and immediately she was suffused with warmth and tenderness. Nonetheless, she had not the smallest desire to hear "sweet words like pearls fall from his lips." At least, the sweet words she wanted to hear were that Raymond's father found her dower sufficient and that it would be satisfactory for her to bring only two personal maids with her and, perhaps, a few men-at-arms.

In fact it was Raymond's complete disinclination to chant "Thou lily white / My sweet lady, bright of brow / Sweeter than a grape art thou" and similar nonsense that made him so attractive to her. If someone else began to tell her about how "sweet thy footfall, sweet thine eyes," Alys thought impatiently, she was going to forget all about Elizabeth's lecture and throw up right in the sighing swain's face. As for that idiot singing now, the words were ludicrous to Alys:

The lady said no more
Except that she sighed
And just before the end
Murmured, "God keep you, dearest friend."

That wasn't so bad, but Alys knew what was coming and struggled to restrain her giggles.

And with these final words she pressed
. Her arms hard against her breast
Fainting in agony. All trace
Of color vanished from her face.
Her heart was still, and she lay dead.

That, Alys thought, really was the outside of enough. Those sentiments would be just the best thing in the world for a man going off to war—just the thing to clear his mind so that he would be able to concentrate on protecting himself.

Then Alys had to fight harder to control laughter. It was quite likely, she thought, that any man afflicted with a lady of such sensibility would go to battle with a clearer mind or, anyway, with a sense of relief, if she dropped dead before he left. Still, there was Elizabeth with tears in her eyes listening to this nonsense. But Alys herself had seen Elizabeth send her husband, who was already weakened by previous wounds, to a desperate battle with a kiss and a smile and quiet assurances that there was no need to worry about her.

Apparently it was true that real life had little or nothing to do with these ridiculous effusions, and Elizabeth had admitted as much when she had reprimanded Alys. Nor was Elizabeth asking Alys to change her tastes, but only to seem appreciative. She was right, Alys thought, echoing the coo of admiration Queen Eleanor accorded a particularly sickening sentiment. Eleanor was a Provençal; Raymond was also a Provençal. Very likely his mother and sisters were as enamored of this nonsense as were the queen and her sister, Countess Sancia.

Alys's own eyes misted with tears, but it had nothing to do with the heartaches of the silly lover in the song. She loved Raymond, but the longer she remained at court, the more doubts she felt about being a suitable wife for him. Of course, it was delightful for a week or two to have nothing to do but read and embroider, ride out hawking, play games, and dance. But a whole life of it?

The song ended. Alys joined the others in calling compliments while she prayed that the requests she heard for an encore would be denied. By a special mercy of God—or so Alys thought of it—the king and his gentlemen entered just then, and the lady set down her lute. Henry was almost as addicted as his queen to the delights of this musical art. Had he come in while the song was in progress, he would have softly found a seat and listened while his gentlemen stole like mice along the walls so as not to interrupt. However, as they had come in after the piece was over, the mood was broken by greetings and invitations.

Alys's father strode across the room to stand by his wife. He, Alys thought caustically, rising to join them, was almost as silly as Elizabeth about songs and tales of love. Then her expression softened. Poor Papa, probably that was because he had had to wait so long before he could marry Elizabeth, whom he had loved from childhood. *If I could not have Raymond*, Alys wondered, *would I, too, begin to appreciate the sad tales of star-crossed lovers?* Somehow Alys did not think so, but her eyes were soft with tenderness and understanding as she looked at her father's peaceful, happy face.

For him, Elizabeth cured all ills, but, Alys thought as she made her way toward them, the topic the men had been discussing could not have been very pleasant. There were a good many frowns lingering on faces, and Uncle Richard—no, she must remember to call him "my lord of Cornwall" in public—looked black as thunder. He was bowing over his wife's hand, finding a smile for her, but his eyes had the suffused look Alys associated with bellows of rage and disastrously accurate, if impolite, characterizations of his brother.

Alys was concerned, knowing that the king's ill-will toward his brother could easily spread to her father and widen out to encompass Raymond and herself, also. Thus, she slowed as she passed Richard, hoping to catch a word that would give her a hint as to the cause of his displeasure. She heard nothing to the point—Sancia was telling her husband about the song just finished—but Alys's wish was granted nonetheless. Sir James d'Aldithel stepped forward from the wall, where he had decorously withdrawn to avoid intruding on his master's greeting to his wife, and bowed deeply.

"Lady Alys, may I offer you my arm?" he asked gravely.

Alys looked down at the hand extended toward her, then up at the offerer, and shook her head. "It is too sinewy. It would not make good eating at all. Nor do I fancy it as a decorative piece. Detached arms tend—"

"Lady Alys," the young man's voice grated, and he maintained gravity and dignity with considerable effort, "it is polite usage to offer a lady one's arm to escort her—as well you know."

Alys's eyes twinkled. She and Sir James were old friends. He had been one of Richard of Cornwall's squires before his knighting and had often been at Marlowe. He had not seen Alys for a number of years, however, because after he was knighted he had served the earl in a keep on the Welsh border. The admiration in his eyes when he first spoke had warned Alys that he no longer saw her as a playmate. Thus her ridiculous answer to his courtesy had been designed to make plain that she had no desire to begin a flirtation. Now his expression much better fitted her taste.

"Well," she sighed, continuing in jest, "I have aged sadly, I know. It is kind of you to offer to support my tottering footsteps the whole ten feet to where my father stands. I had not realized I had become so decrepit I could not go so far alone."

"Oh, how I would love to box your ears," Sir James whispered, leaning amorously over her as she laid her fingertips on his wrist.

"Do you not remember what befell you the last time you indulged yourself with that pleasure?" Alys asked, smiling as sweetly as an angel into James's eyes.

The only response she got that time was a choked growl. Obviously Sir James remembered how naughty Alys had neatly sewn together the ankles on every single pair of chausses he had, so that when he was called to attend his master, his feet could not be inserted properly into the garments. Possibly he could have stuffed the bottom of the chausses into his shoes, but since the top would then reach no higher than his thighs, he did not attempt it. Nor had he ever again used his superior strength to win an argument with Alys. There were other ways to accomplish that, Sir James thought, recovering his temper and uttering a deep, quite spurious sigh.

"I am sorry you find my company so distasteful," he said sadly. "I could not think of imposing it on you long enough to tell you what you were so obviously hoping to overhear."

"I do not find your company distasteful at all," Alys said hastily, tightening her grip on his wrist. "Dear, dear, Sir James, you are the very person I have been hoping and praying to see." She caught his smile of triumph and batted her eyes exaggeratedly at him. "I will even eat your horrid arm—or have it on the wall—if you insist," she offered with passionate sincerity.

Unable to help himself, Sir James burst out laughing. This drew a startled glance from the earl of Cornwall, but when he saw who was with Sir James, he smiled indulgently.

"Some day, someone will murder you, Alys," James said as he pulled her urgently farther away from his master.

"Perhaps," Alys admitted, not resisting the pull, "but not, I hope, until you satisfy my curiosity. Whatever made Uncle Richard—no, my lord of Cornwall—look so grim?"

"One cannot blame him," James muttered, before he thought. "It is the most infuriating thing that King Henry demanded that my lord give up Gascony, and now—" He became aware of Alys's wide-eyed attention, stopped abruptly, and said, "But you do not need my help at all—do you? There is no need for you to hang on my arm, of which you spoke so ill."

"No, no. It is the sweetest arm in all the world," Alys assured him. "I am sure it would cook up tender as a suckling pig. . . . No! Do not dare desert me, James. Please? Pretty please? All honey-coated . . . please?"

They were both giggling, and another head or two turned to examine them. Tactfully, they withdrew farther from the circle of older people, Alys in the lead this time. When she stopped in a window embrasure, however, she was no longer smiling.

"All jesting aside, James," she said, "I hope Richard and the king have not quarreled, especially over Gascony."

"Why especially over Gascony?" James asked, rather surprised by Alys's intensity.

"Because Raymond has lands there—oh, you do not know about Raymond. He is—there is some chance that I will marry him—Raymond d'Aix."

"Another of the queen's relatives?" James asked rather stiffly.

"Well, yes, but he is not seeking office or lands here in England, so you can stop looking like a stuffed bear," Alys replied.

"Then how does it come that you are going to marry him?"

James knew Alys was heiress to two substantial keeps. This did not make her a great prize, but, quite aside from her beauty, he would not have considered her beneath his own touch, especially not since Sir William had become Cornwall's marshal. And one could not put Alys's beauty aside; that was worth a keep in itself. She was a little small, perhaps, but everything else was perfect—the oval face set atop a long, graceful neck; a complexion of milk flushed with rose; lips like ripe, wild strawberries, full and sweet; a thin, short nose; and eyes like twin lakes, cerulean blue; all crowned by the gold of her hair. And, James reminded himself, a tongue like a viper and a spirit forged of steel that would bend for no man. He was lucky that she was already spoken for and not available.

"Raymond came . . . on a visit to England, and . . . and accompanied Papa to Wales." Alys was picking her way carefully, not wishing to lie, but unwilling to give all the facts.

"Accompanied Sir William . . . Raymond? You mean he is really d'Aix, not just from that area? *That* Raymond? But why was he acting as your father's man?"

"Oh . . . it suited his humor," Alys replied. Even to a trusted servant of Richard of Cornwall, Alys was not prepared to tell the truth—that Raymond had been sent by the king to spy on her father, and that the stratagem had backfired, Raymond having fallen in love with her.

"You mean," James said sardonically, "that it suited *your* humor."

Alys opened her mouth to deny this emphatically, and then merely looked arch. It was better for James to think Raymond had been so smitten with her that he had lingered and taken service with her father than that James seek further for the truth. Then she smiled and shrugged. "In any case, he wishes to marry me, and—"

"Who does not?" James asked wryly.

"You, for one," Alys replied tartly, then laughed. "You know me too well."

"Poor Raymond," James sighed.

It was obvious that he was jesting, and Alys laughed again, but there was a quiver of doubt in her. Did Raymond know her? Alys wondered. She had never tried to seem different from her real self, but had he been blinded by desire? He said not. He said it was not for her beauty, but also for her spirit, her skills in housewifery and leechcraft, and her courage that he loved her, but when he compared her with his own women, would he not think her coarse and common? Alys could ape the ways of the court ladies well enough that she was accepted among them, but it was an effort. She did not wish always to be under such constraint in her own home.

"Perhaps Raymond will not be so fortunate after all," Alys snapped. "I said he wished to marry me, not that the matter was settled. Papa is not happy about my going so far, and it may be that my dower—it is only Bix with no expectation of Marlowe, now that Papa has married again—will not be enough to satisfy his family. Nonetheless—"

"And what do *you* desire?" James asked curiously. He had not known that Sir William was remarried. He could imagine how such a thing would stick in Alys's craw. She was too used to ruling the roost.

"I am thinking about it," Alys said impatiently, "and it would help me if you would tell me what news has come from Gascony that has thrown everyone into gloom."

"You remember that when the king left Bordeaux last year, a truce had been arranged with King Louis?"

"Has Louis broken faith?" Alys asked, truly surprised. Henry spoke ill of the king of France, but the truth was that there was little ill to be said of him, except in spite. In fact, Louis of France was so consciously good and holy that Alys felt bored every time his name came into the conversation.

"No—no. Louis would not break a truce, not without real provocation. You know that. However, Theobold of Champagne is now king of Navarre and has claim, or so he says, to certain lands by Bayonne and Oloron–Sainte Marie—"

"I know that, James. I am no more deaf than you, and I have heard Un—the earl of Cornwall—detailing the complexities of

Gascon relationships near as often as you have. After all, he thought it would be his to rule."

"And all of us would have been better off had it been so. You know Lord Richard could have brought that province to order. Instead, it was—" He broke off as Alys squeezed his hand sharply.

She was quite right. This was not the time or place to voice such regrets, even though the king's decision was likely to cause ten years of chaos, until Prince Edward was old enough to administer the province. This knowledge was in Alys's eyes and Sir James's, but it was unwise to pursue the topic.

Sir James now continued more carefully, sticking to the news. "Theobold has chosen this moment to begin pressing his claims again. Nicholas de Molis—you know he is seneschal of Gascony?" Alys nodded and James went on, "De Molis has just sent to Henry to beg for men and money to hold back the forces of Navarre."

"But that is impossible!" Alys kept her voice low, but her eyes flashed with rage. "You know what Henry sucked out of us when he returned—scutage, carucage—and Papa was *there*. He near died there from a hurt in his thigh. You know no one will give the king a penny for Gascony."

"Of course I know it. All the lords are very angry that he stayed so long in Bordeaux last year after the fighting was over. He said he was reforming the government of the cities, and for all I know he was, but everyone says he was lounging in luxury—"

"Well," Alys pointed out, "the queen was heavy with child. I think he was afraid to travel lest it do her hurt. And after she bore little Margaret, Eleanor needed a time to recover herself and to be sure the child was doing well."

"Not every man carries his wife to war with him nor is so tender of her," James said dryly.

Alys raised her brows. "There we differ. *I* can see no wrong in that. However, I do agree that there was no need to entertain quite so lavishly while he was there, nor to support a hoard of Béarnese . . ." James snarled deep in his throat, and Alys cocked an eye at his suffused face. "Oho," she continued, "so *that* is why the seneschal needs money. Gaston of Béarn is also moving."

"The ungrateful, treacherous—"

"Careful, James," Alys said, patting his hand. "You will choke on your own spleen."

"It is a wonder poor Lord Richard did not choke on his. How often did he warn Henry to have nothing to do with that pair —bitch of a mother and cur of a son—"

"But James," Alys interrupted, paying no attention to the strictures against the dowager countess of Béarn and her son, whom it would have been difficult for King Henry to ignore, since the countess was his wife's grandmother, "can it be pure accident that the moment Theobold begins to threaten, Gaston does also?"

"They are longtime enemies, but of course it is not an accident. It is natural enough for a sneaking cur to snap only at the helpless."

"Could it be that Queen Blanche is stirring both Theobold and Gaston?" Alys asked. "I have heard that Theobold was quite—quite enamored of her. Louis would not break a truce, no, but Blanche would not care a pin for that, and very likely she would not let Louis know what she was doing. And even if he knew, Louis might look the other way. I believe—Papa has said so very often—that Louis really desires all the lands on the Continent that speak the French tongue to be under French dominion."

"That is true enough," James said. "He has swallowed Anjou and Poitou, setting his brother Alphonse to rule them."

Alys shrugged. "It has brought peace, at least."

"Perhaps, but that will not recommend Louis's rule to the Gascons," James said bitterly. "They do not desire peace and good governance. They love Henry because he is far away and does not interfere in their constant warring. But some will side with Theobold just because they have private enemies they wish to attack who claim to be loyal to King Henry. However, when that private war is over, they will break their faith with the king of Navarre as quickly as they have taken sides with him."

"I think you speak the truth," a new male voice agreed. Alys looked up and smiled a welcome at her father, and her companion bowed. "What brings you here from Wales, James?" Sir William asked.

"More bad news, really bad," James said, his face darkening still further. "Ralph and Mortimer have been cut to pieces,

Hereford's men have been driven back nearly to the border, and the army the king sent with Hubert FitzMatthew was taken by surprise and forced to take refuge in the towns after suffering heavy losses."

"Oh, God," William groaned, "Richard will spit blood over this. He has already quarreled with Henry because the king would not take the full army from Scotland to Wales."

"No," James said, "he knows what happened already. I went to him at once, as soon as I left the king. Lord Richard was angry, of course, but he told me to hold my tongue so that the news should not draw attention from Molis's need." James smiled and added, "I know he does not mean to keep anything from you, sir. Lord Richard said there would be no trouble gathering an army to fight the Welsh, but as soon as the barons knew of the defeats in Wales, they would use that as an excuse not to give help to Gascony."

"They do not need any excuse for that," Sir William pointed out caustically, "and if it were not for the fact that I have a private reason to wish Gascony quiet and well ruled, I would agree with all my heart. The devil should be given every chance to fly away with that whole province."

"You cannot mean that, William," a soft voice reproved. "Where would you get your wine if Bordeaux fell into the devil's hands?"

"This is my wife, Lady Elizabeth," Sir William said, as Sir James bowed to a tall, graceful woman with large green eyes. "I would drink ale instead," he replied to her remark, smiling.

"Perhaps," Elizabeth sighed, "but then I would have to listen to you complain about it." Her voice was so soft and her smile so sweet that what might have been a bitter gibe became an intimate caress. William laughed, but Elizabeth shook her head. "I think it more reasonable, especially in view of our private reasons to wish for peace in Gascony, to try to think of some way to help."

"Easier said than done," William said with a shrug, but he narrowed his eyes in thought as he looked down at Alys. "Raymond has lands there," he said next. "He is also of sweet tongue and equable temper—usually."

The last word came out with a grin. Raymond had not been at all equable of temper when opposition to his marriage to Alys had been suggested. He had thrown defiance into the teeth of the earl of Cornwall, saying he would wed her over the nay-say of the whole world. William repressed a sigh. Probably Raymond would succeed in gaining his father's permission. He had a gift for knowing when to threaten force and when to use persuasion. Most likely Alys would be happy —but he would lose her. William jerked his mind away from that.

"Do you think Raymond could help?" Alys asked. "His own property is small, and his father may not be overinclined to listen to his suggestions in favor of the English just now."

"As to the latter, I cannot guess," William replied. "However, as a landholder in his own right, he would have a place in the councils of the barons, and he might be thought to be speaking for his father. I am not sure, but it is something. When starvation is the alternative, rusty wheat is better than a haunch of venison that cannot be obtained."

CHAPTER 3

****

Thus, when Raymond arrived in England, he found himself more warmly welcomed by the earl of Cornwall and the king than by his prospective bride and father-by-marriage. Raymond was not much surprised by the lack of enthusiasm with which William received the news that Alphonse had agreed to his son's marriage. Naturally William would regret the fact that his one living child should spend the rest of her life so far from him; there was a good chance that after her marriage he would never see her again. Although Raymond knew that William was very fond of him, he accepted that he would not be overjoyed at losing Alys.

Raymond could not, however, accept Alys's initial reserve so philosophically. She was the first person, except for the servants, he accosted after rushing up from the bailey, and he had cried out, "I have you! My father has agreed!" and swept her into his arms and into a passionate kiss.

Her lips responded readily at first, but after far too short an embrace, in Raymond's opinion, she had pulled away, remarking dispassionately, "You look like death warmed over. Come to the fire."

"Because I half killed myself getting there and back," Raymond said lightly, but there was a note of hurt in his voice.

"There was no need for such haste as to keep you from sleeping and eating," Alys replied sharply. "Do you doubt my faith?"

"No!" Raymond exclaimed. "What is wrong, Alys? I missed you. I—"

"In God's name, do not say you count every day a year when you are not beside me," she snapped. Then, seeing the pained amazement in his face, she sighed. "Poor Raymond, forgive me. You have had a sad welcome. I am sorry. You *are* welcome, my love, truly. And I have missed you, also."

He sighed with relief, but continued to ask what was wrong,

and Alys laughed and confessed that her temper was soured by too much idleness and pleasure—and too many love songs on the lute. That made Raymond laugh also, and he said promptly that he understood completely why she had forbidden him to say that each day away from her was like a year.

"Only it *is*, Alys," he finished softly. "No matter how fast we rode or how long, it still seemed too slow, too far, until I could hold you again."

"In return for that loverlike speech, at least I have greeted you like a true 'lady'—coldly and with blame," she teased. "You would not wish me to be a coarse, common clod and say I was glad to see you," she added with a twinkle in her eyes.

"Oh, yes I would," Raymond contradicted quickly. "The coarser and commoner the better. If you really wish to please me, you will descend to the very depths of vulgarity and give me another kiss."

"Fie! Fie! You are no true loving knight. Doubtless you even have designs on my fair body—"

"I certainly have," Raymond agreed with enthusiasm.

Alys giggled. "I have a few on yours, also, but I fear not the same as yours on mine. Raymond, you stink like the garderobe. I will have a bath made ready as soon as you are warm enough. Is your servant bringing up your clothes?"

"I have outstripped them," Raymond said, beginning to laugh again. "None of the horses could keep pace with Gros Choc, and I would not wait. I have nothing but what I am standing in. If you do not like the way I smell, you will have to give me clothing."

"I am beginning to doubt that you have any clothes beyond what I give you," Alys chuckled. "And you never give them back, either."

"My mother's maids must have thrown them out, or given them to the servants," Raymond said carelessly. He was watching Alys's face closely, still amazed that no matter how beautiful he remembered her to be, she was always lovelier in actuality. An expression of anger or anxiety drew his attention from her perfect features back to what he had said. "Do you care about the clothes, Alys?" he asked. "I am very sorry. I should have thought—"

"I suppose the rich have no need to consider such things as odd tunics and shirts, but I was never rich, Raymond. We have no contract—no vows have been made. I had hoped you would have stayed longer in your home and considered again whether you wish to marry me."

"Alys, what have I done? Will you turn me away for some patched shirts and chausses? I will give you ten garments for each one lost. Good God, I see I am making you angrier with each word. What have I said?"

"Nothing wrong according to your lights, Raymond, but can you not see how unfit we are for each other? I will always worry about too-small things, things beneath your notice—"

"But you are right. One should not be wasteful. You will teach me, my love, and I will learn—"

"But it is not a question of right and wrong," Alys interrupted desperately. "In your world those garments are only fit for servants. In mine they are what is worn by better folk every day. Try to understand—"

"I do not want to understand anything, except—do you love me, Alys?"

She was silent, her eyes fixed on his thin, bitterly hurt face. "Yes," she sighed, "I do love you. If you were a poor, penniless knight, I would follow you barefoot through the world. I would cook for you and sew for you and, if need be, carry your goods on my back if you had no packhorse. But I am afraid, Raymond, afraid I will shame you."

"No!"

"You love me, and you cry no, but I do not understand your way of living. I knew no better than to send you away with those old things of Harold's. . . ."

"Alys, do not talk so silly. I was at court, wearing King Henry's clothes. I could have taken what I wanted from what he lent me. I never thought of it myself."

"Men do not think of such things. It is a woman's place to see that her man is fittingly attired."

"Nonsense!" Raymond laughed. "My mother would not think of studying my father's court cupboards. His servants—"

"Not even that!" Alys cried. "Raymond, I will go demented. What am I to do all day?"

"Whatever you wish, my love. Alys, all that matters is that you love me and I love you. Everything else will be arranged. Beloved, I swear I will remake the world for you if I must. Do not deny me. How can you say you love me and yet bear to part with me?"

"To save you hurt and shame—" she began.

But he did not allow her to finish. For answer, he seized her and kissed her. She was rigid at first, pushing at him, but her strength was nothing compared with his, and soon she yielded. Her lips grew warm, and she felt strangely lightheaded and weak. Raymond's lips had left her mouth and wandered to her chin, then under it. Alys drew a shuddering breath just before his mouth closed on hers again, and her hands, which had crept out from between them and around him to press him closer, did not move to save her wimple when Raymond began to pull at it.

"I do not wish to interrupt so warm a greeting," Sir William remarked, "but perhaps it is just as well that I do so before it grows any warmer."

Alys and Raymond jumped apart, coloring self-consciously. "I have my father's agreement for our marriage," Raymond assured his prospective father-by-marriage.

"I should hope so," William laughed. Then he sighed and put out a hand to clasp Raymond affectionately above his elbow. "That is not quite true, you know. I do not really know whether I am pleased or not. For Alys's sake, I am glad, but . . . Well, I suppose there is no help for it."

"Where is Lady Elizabeth?" Raymond asked.

Sir William smiled. "Are you delicately implying that I am greedy and want to keep my daughter, even after winning the wife I so long desired?"

"No, sir. I—" Raymond swallowed. In fact, he had thought just that.

Laughing at him, Sir William answered his question. "Elizabeth is still at Hurley—we were both there. She will be along soon. Come and sit down, my son." William paused over the words and smiled. "That has a pleasant sound—*my son.* Well, I cannot imagine your news was very welcome to your father. Just how unwelcome was it?"

"Not near so unwelcome as you think, sir," Raymond responded with a grin. "Of course, at first he near had a fit, not because the dower was inadequate—he did not even stop to ask —but because Alys's land was here in England."

"I can see that. I cannot say that I am overjoyed to have my daughter's husband a Provençal."

"But then I had a thought." Sensibly Raymond ignored William's remark, since there was no way of changing his nationality, and continued to put forth his notion of using the revenues of Bix to pay for lands ceded to Alys in Gascony.

William sat up straighter as he listened, and a pleased smile began to soften his rather grim expression. "By God," he exclaimed when Raymond was finished. "You have more than you realized. We—you, I, your father, and Alys—are like to make more out of this than you ever expected. Have you heard that Nicholas de Molis, the seneschal of Gascony, is hard beset between Theobold of Champagne and Gaston of Béarn?"

"Béarn? But surely he is King Henry's friend; Eleanor is his niece, and I heard that Henry and Gaston could scarce be parted when they were in Bordeaux. And Henry gave such gifts to Gaston as to—"

"But the gifts are used, the money spent," William interrupted caustically. "Wales is in arms. We have suffered severe losses there."

"Are you summoned?" Raymond asked eagerly. "May I go with you?"

"Raymond!" Alys exclaimed. "Do you want to get killed before we are even married?"

"I will come to no hurt," he assured her absently, his eyes still on Sir William.

"As Papa came to no hurt when he was last in Wales?" Alys snapped.

Laughter and love flooded Raymond at the anger in her voice and the bright fury in her eyes. His mother would have fainted, his sisters would be screaming, sobbing, and swooning by turns, and neither reason nor command would stop them. Alys, on the other hand, might quarrel with him and try to change his mind with reasons why it was unwise to go to war, but she would not try to bind him by his heartstrings, nor make his life a misery with moans and sobs and constant laments.

"No, love," he replied, laughing. "I certainly do not intend to be wounded if I can save myself from it, and I will also gladly—most gladly—marry you before I go. I will marry you right now, if it is your desire, and again before I go, or each day until I go—whatever you prefer."

"So I can be a widow?" Alys retorted, still angry but nearly won to laughter. She knew it was impossible to keep men from regarding war as a pleasant sport.

"Stop your nonsense, Alys," William said. "If I were summoned, I would naturally call on my son to support me, since I have no castellan for Bix yet and Hurley is now also on my hands. And you would hold your tongue and send your husband off with a light heart, as is your duty. As it is, you know quite well that the king will do nothing until after Christmas. The remnants of our armies are safe for a while, and it takes time to gather a levy."

"Good," Raymond put in. "Then Alys and I can be married and have a few months of quiet before we go."

"I think not." William pursed his lips, and then, seeing Raymond's face flush, he smiled. "I did not mean you could not marry," he amended hastily. "I meant you would have no time for quiet. Let me finish what I was about to say before that silly chit dragged us into this stupid discussion of going to war. The only reason I mentioned the Welsh problem was to point out why Henry cannot even try to get money or men to aid Molis."

"But if the seneschal is not crying wolf . . ."

"Molis is a good man. He would not cry wolf, although he himself might be deceived. We can hope that is true but not count on it."

"Then some help *must* be sent him," Raymond said, frowning.

"Yes, and I think that you may provide that help, or a little of it, anyway, and Alys and your children profit largely thereby."

"But my lands are small," Raymond pointed out, "and my mother's people are bound to the de Soler faction, who care more for their own freedom than for the feudal duties they owe the king."

"It may be possible to increase your lands substantially —well above the value of Bix. As you mentioned, those revenues are small but sure. Twenty pounds in the pocket is more easily spent than a hundred owed but never paid. At another time, Henry might not see this. He has a sanguine nature and can seldom be brought to see that long promises long delayed are unlikely ever to be fulfilled. At this point, however, he might gladly grant several properties to you for your promise to aid Molis now and support the right of the English throne in the future."

"I would take oath on that, and gladly," Raymond said. "As for my own lands and those granted to me, I could perform as I swore, but I cannot see what my sword and a few hundred men could do."

"It would be more than that. When you speak, it will be believed you speak for your father; there is no need to say yea or nay unless you are asked directly. Moreover, you, too, are related to Gaston of Béarn. . . ." William allowed his voice to drift away.

Raymond's pale eyes glittered with enthusiasm. "Yes, I see. Indeed, I see. I would know what to say, and I have no fear my father would differ from me." He jumped to his feet and began to pace about, turning suddenly and almost bumping into Alys, who had risen and was walking away. "Where do you go, love?" Raymond asked.

"As far as I can get from both of you," she replied.

"Dear heart—" Raymond began.

"Alys, my love—" her father said simultaneously.

She looked exasperatedly from one surprised face to another. "I am so glad my wedding will be of use to the king," she said, "and to the seneschal of Gascony, and to the power and purse of my husband, to everyone, in fact, save me! I am not sure I wish to be married for the purpose of providing King Henry with an army. And I am not at all sure I will have great pleasure from a wedding voyage spent alone while my husband goes to war."

"No, no. I will make time for you, I swear," Raymond teased, seizing her in his arms. "You do not understand," he continued more seriously, holding her so that she could not wriggle free or strike at him. "If I can rally enough support, there will not be any war at all. If the king of Navarre sees a campaign will cost too high, he will withdraw to wait for a more propitious time to push his claim. Truly, Alys," he said, releasing her and looking at her soberly, "I will defend myself when someone strikes at me, and I take pleasure in it, I admit, but I do not think it a good thing to stir up real war. That will not be my intention."

She sighed. "I beg your pardon. You are right, of course. If our marriage can be of help to the king, I should be glad, not spiteful. But—but I am used only to being a private person, not one whose doings affect the world at large."

"It is not easy, dearling," William said gravely. "I know it well. I struggled for years to avoid it—but that was wrong. Very wrong. I regret my selfishness. Every person who is called to such a place must accept the burden. It is a man's duty to serve God and man as best he can, and a woman's duty to support her menfolk in that service."

"Yes, Papa." She put her hand out to Raymond. "Forgive me. I will make no further trouble, if I can only master my unruly tongue."

"No, love, say what you like," Raymond urged. "You are right to protest what seems wrong to you. It never hurts a man to think twice over a plan, or to put his reasons for a thing into clear words. Only good can come of that, so long as you listen to reason—and I see that you do. I will always be eager to hear what you have to say."

"Even when it is silly?" Alys asked, her lips beginning to curve into a smile.

"Especially when it is silly," Raymond assured her, "because then I can kiss you for being a woman."

He suited the deed to the word, and Alys returned the salute good and hearty before she said she would see to his clothes and a bath, and went away. Sir William looked after his daughter for a moment before he turned his full attention to what Raymond was saying about the areas in which it would be best to have a grant of land. William had seen that Alys's eyes did not reflect the smile she had given Raymond when she left them. *Do not be a dog in the manger*, William told himself. *It is right that she should fear for the man she loves*. But it had not sounded like that kind of fear. William could not give his mind to the matter then. What Raymond was saying was of greater importance.

That night, however, he mentioned the scene to Elizabeth in pillow talk and noted that she did not answer him at once. "Do you think I am jealous of her love for him?" William asked.

"No—well, a little, dear heart," Elizabeth replied softly. "It

would not be possible to feel nothing when you see her
—whose whole heart and mind were always yours—begin to
look to another. But that cannot be what is troubling you now.
No, I have seen that Alys is not easy, and, love her though I
do, I am certainly not jealous."

"You do not think she has changed her heart and will marry
him only to keep her word? I would never—"

"Now *that* is jealousy, William," Elizabeth interrupted, "or
rather, your reluctance to lose her. You saw how she looked at
Raymond at suppertime, and later, when they sat together,
how she reached to touch him when there was no need. No,
she loves him, and loves him dear. Let it be, love. It may be
some maiden fancy that troubles her. When we have a little
peace together, I will try to speak to her and uncover her
uneasiness."

That peace was not long in coming. Raymond and William
were in such quick agreement on the terms of the marriage
contract that they rode out only two days later to propose their
notions to Richard of Cornwall, who was fortunately at
Wallingford. If he approved, they told Alys and Elizabeth,
they would go on to set the proposal before King Henry. And,
the day after they left, a messenger arrived to say that Richard
was so enthusiastic about the idea that he was going with them
to Henry.

"It is settled then," Elizabeth said. "We had better give all
our attention to finishing your clothing and preparing the linen
and furniture you will be taking. I have a feeling that the king
will seize at this like a drowning man reaches for a log. He will
want the marriage held in all haste so that Raymond may the
sooner leave for Gascony."

Alys did not reply, and Elizabeth reached out and took her
hand. "I have always loved you, Alys," Elizabeth said then.
"Partly because you were William's child and partly because I
never had a daughter. I know you love Raymond, and yet you
are not happy. Do you grieve at leaving your father and your
familiar place?"

"No." There was no hesitation in that response. "I will miss
Papa, but—no. Now that I am sure he will not be lonely, I do
not regret leaving, nor leaving Marlowe. I always knew
Marlowe was not mine."

"You do not fear coupling, do you?" Elizabeth asked. "You are small and may have some pain at first, but—"

"I am not afraid of pain," Alys snapped, and then her eyes clouded. "Not my own pain, but . . . Elizabeth, do you think I am fit to be Raymond's wife?"

"Fit? What can you mean?"

Mutely Alys drew her stepmother into Raymond's chamber and opened the clothing chest, from which she drew several items of court dress. They were of striking magnificence: a soft leather belt all chased with gold wire and studded with sapphires; a tunic all woven with gold thread in graceful arabesques and embroidered at neck and wrists with more gold and small gems and pearls; and a surcoat of brilliant blue velvet, cut and sheared so that acorns and oak leaves of gold showed brilliant against the darker sheen of the cloth. Neckband and fronts, hem and armbands, were again lavish with gold and gems.

"You mean that Raymond is rich, and we are not?" Elizabeth asked. "But he knew that."

"No, not the wealth. As you say, Raymond knew, and it seems that I will be a richer prize than either of us thought anyway. But this clothing shows the state in which he lives."

"Alys, you have just lived in such a state yourself—"

"And I hated it," Alys interrupted. "No, that is not true. It was pleasant enough for the time we were at court, but if I had to live like that always, I soon would hate it. I know I will burst into some speech or action that will shame Raymond dreadfully. He would be hurt."

"No, I think not, Alys. You are too clever for that. No one is on show always. Queen Eleanor pisses and shits like the rest of us, and doubtless quarrels with her husband and her servants, also. Merely, she does not do so in company. Well, neither do you. When you are alone with your husband, you may say and do what you like."

"And what am I to do the rest of the time? Listen to lovesick lyrics and twanging lutes?"

Elizabeth frowned at her thoughtfully. "I am not sure, my dear, but I think you should trust Raymond. Ask him what you can do to help. Tell him the truth—that idleness does not agree with you. As to the manners you must use, you need only watch carefully and take your behavior from that of the other ladies. Even if you think them silly, you must do things their way. You are the stranger, and you cannot expect everyone to change for you. Is this what you fear?"

"No—only that Raymond will be ashamed when I seem vulgar."

At that Elizabeth smiled. "You need not fear that! He will not notice, or, if he should, he is so besotted he will think your way more charming. It is only for your sake that I tell you to match yourself to your new family and friends. And remember, you have a ready defense. You *are* a stranger. No one will know whether your difference is owing to your English upbringing or to the simplicity of your father's station in the past. But do not defend your way. Do not always say, 'We did it this way.' There is no right or wrong way to do a thing, so long as it is done well."

"Is it worth it to change my whole life?" Alys asked.

"I cannot tell you that, dearling," Elizabeth replied softly. "You know you may change your mind if you wish. Your papa will even be glad if you do. Do you wish to live without Raymond?"

"No!"

"But that is your only choice. The new life with Raymond —the old one without."

Alys stared down at the magnificent garments strewn across the bed. They were scented with the herbs that lay in the chest to keep the clothes sweet and keep the moths and fleas at bay. On the chair beside her, however, lay a shirt and chausses Raymond had left to be washed, which a lazy maid had not taken away. Those garments exuded his male odor, pungently acrid. Somehow it was slightly different from her father's; it belonged only to Raymond.

Even as Alys resolved to have the skin off the maid's back for her carelessness, a quiver of sensation passed through her, as though her organs had moved by themselves within her. She needed to master an impulse to bury her face in Raymond's underthings and breathe in his scent. A pang of longing for him stabbed her.

"Heigh-ho," Alys sighed, smiling wryly. "Look at the new

Alys—a most daintified fine, fine lady, who lisps Provençal love songs and trips, delicate as a dewdrop, down a rose-strewn path. I cannot give up Raymond—thus, I suppose I must take what comes with him."

CHAPTER 4

****

In Marlowe keep, however, no one realized that a new Alys had been born. What they felt was that they were seeing a great deal too much of the old one. She seemed to be everywhere at once—harrying the maids to get on with their sewing on her new clothing, out on the farms driving the serfs and villeins to bring extra produce to the keep, insisting that the huntsmen lure game into Marlowe woods by putting out salt and fodder. It was as if, having decided to take the plunge, she wanted it over and done with as soon as possible.

Swift as Alys's preparations were, they were barely in time. The king, as Elizabeth had guessed, leapt at the suggestion brought by his brother. He was delighted with Raymond's idea for a multitude of reasons: Henry loved doing favors; he particularly enjoyed doing favors for his wife's relatives, whose polished manners and tastes for literature and art he found far more congenial than those of many of his own nobility, who were more interested in cattle and crops than the ethereal lift of the arches and spires of Westminster Abbey. Better still, Henry liked doing favors that cost him nothing and were highly unlikely to have repercussions from his brother and the other barons. In this case, Richard had suggested the arrangement, and, considering the condition of Gascony, none of Henry's barons wanted anything to do with it. They would be indifferent to the granting of lands in that uneasy province. Best of all, Henry liked to make a profit out of doing a favor, and it was certain this time that he would do so.

In exchange for four estates—two of which were rich properties indeed but were in the area contested by Gaston of Béarn, a third which was small and whose overlordship was contested by the vicomte de Marsan, and a fourth which was not only worthless but just outside Bordeaux, where Henry expected raging violence to erupt any day—Henry would receive a large sum in hard gold and twenty pounds of good

English silver every year. He would also obtain a vassal with every practical reason to be loyal to him, as well as a blood bond reinforced by real affection for his queen.

Henry was delighted with his bargain—and so was Raymond. The two rich estates were in a fertile river valley of the northern Pyrenees; the holder of Amou and Ibos had died without direct heirs during the war Henry had waged so unsuccessfully against King Louis. The drawback to Amou, however, was that it was only about two leagues from Orthes, one of Gaston de Béarn's strongholds. While Gaston had been Henry's "dear friend," there did not seem to be any reason to appoint a strong overlord for Amou and Ibos. When Gaston turned in opposition, the problem became acute; Henry needed someone loyal in Amou if he wanted to keep control of the area. But to place there an overlord openly antagonistic to Gaston would only have precipitated open war. Raymond was the perfect compromise—it was Richard of Cornwall who had thought of it, but Henry now felt the idea was his own —because Raymond would be loyal to Henry; nonetheless, he was Gaston's great-nephew, the countess Garsenda being his grandfather's mother. It would be difficult for Gaston to object to Raymond becoming master of Amou.

The problem with Ibos was different, although it, too, was in contested territory. When the overlord had responded loyally to Henry's call for support in his war with Louis, the castellan of Ibos had cried defiance and given his homage to Raymond of Toulouse, who was lord of Tarbes nearby. Henry had done nothing to amend the situation, having more serious troubles; thus, Ibos was legally Raymond's, but whether he could put out its current holder and take control of it was his affair. At least Raymond no longer needed to worry about Raymond of Toulouse supporting his vassal. Louis had tamed that violent and ambitious man, and Raymond would not scruple to appeal to his other uncle-by-marriage for redress if Toulouse attacked him.

Of the smaller properties, which were all Raymond had hoped to obtain originally, one was contiguous with his own lands near the great keep of the vicomte de Marsan. It had been wrested from Marsan's ancestor by King Richard some sixty years earlier, but the Marsans, ancestral or modern, had never yielded their claim. Periodically one Marsan or another would remind himself and attack Benquel so that over the years the lands had yielded more bones and blood than wheat. The current holder of Marsan had not, so far, initiated any private war; however, if his men-at-arms ran a little wild on Benquel lands and dragged off a few women or burnt a farm, Marsan became afflicted by deafness and blindness to any proof or complaint. Now, since Raymond had already done fealty to Marsan for several farms near Mont de Marsan, he would lose nothing by adding Benquel to the properties held from the vicomte.

Raymond was sanguine that the feudal dues would be moderate and the loyalty would raise no problems. In the past Marsan had vacillated between supporting the comte of Toulouse and the duc de Gascogne (who was also king of England). However, Toulouse had been thoroughly curbed by Louis, and Marsan infinitely preferred a somewhat indifferent distant overlord in England to a most attentive one much closer at hand. In any future quarrel between Louis and Henry, Marsan would support Henry—unless, Raymond feared, it was clear that Louis was winning. For the next three years, however, the truce would hold; Raymond would not worry about conflicting loyalties until then.

The last minor property was Blancheforte, which was so close to Bordeaux that it was of no military significance. Any determined assault from the town would reduce the keep in a few days. For that reason, no recent holder had made any attempt to improve it. Raymond did not intend to do so either, beyond making it a comfortable residence. There were virtually no lands, those having been gobbled up by the burghers of Bordeaux years earlier; but a small demesne, enough to support the residents of the castle, existed. What was important was that the holder of the keep had the ancient duty of guarding one of the gates of Bordeaux and, therefore, the privilege of sitting on the council of the city.

Raymond had every intention of making the most of that privilege. His mother's estates of Villandrau, Durance, and Labrede were greatly affected by the tides of power that flowed back and forth between two families, de Soler and Colom. To know how the tide was flowing and to influence it, even a little, would be of infinite value.

Considering what had been accomplished as he rode back to

Marlowe, Raymond began to understand why everyone had been so disturbed about the lack of equality between Alys's fortune and his own. He was not a greedy man, nor could he love Alys any more now that she was so well dowered; he had loved her too much almost from the day they met. Nonetheless, there was a rich sense of pride added to that love when he thought of how he would say, "This is Alys of Marlowe, my wife, who brought me Amou and Ibos and Benquel and Blancheforte." Now no one would think he had been trapped by a pretty face.

Raymond did not allow that thought to color his words when he gave Alys her betrothal gift—because with the king's sanction the contracts had been written and signed, and the betrothal was formal. She looked only briefly at the jewels —hair ornament, necklet, and bracelets of sapphires and diamonds set in elaborately worked gold—and then asked about the land. Raymond laughed and embraced her. Every woman he knew would have rushed to put on the baubles and pose and preen. Only Alys understood what was really important.

It was thus with considerable enthusiasm that Raymond described the gains to Alys. Of course, he was not fool enough to imply to any woman, not even one so sensible as Alys, that her value could be increased by her property. For a reason Raymond found obscure, women seemed to demand that a man desire them for themselves alone. And he did, of course, so desire Alys. He had been quite willing to accept her with nothing, even without Bix if that had been Sir William's condition. Still, he knew Alys would be enraged if the true source of his satisfaction showed. Still, he was surprised at her reaction.

"Mine?" she said. "How can such lands be mine? Assuredly they were granted because you are nephew to the queen."

"That helped, no doubt," Raymond replied, "in that Henry felt he could trust me and, therefore, was willing to give more. However, the lands are yours—your father and your 'uncle' Richard saw to that."

A faint flicker of anger lit Raymond's eyes when he recalled those earlier deliberations, but it died quickly. When the way the lands were to be held was discussed, Raymond and Henry had expected to have a free hand with them. Richard and

William stood adamant that they were to be Alys's at her will. Naturally, her husband would administer the properties during his life and while his wife lived; however, she could will them as *she* pleased, and, if her husband should die before her, the lands would revert intact to Alys herself, not to her son or sons. Those children would be the wards of her husband's male relatives who could take them and the land from Alys, leaving her with nothing.

Henry had been startled, Raymond appalled. "Do you not trust me?" Raymond had asked furiously. "Do you think I would cheat Alys or flout her desire? Perhaps you think I will murder her, or—"

"Do you not trust Alys?" William had countered sharply. "What do you think she will do, die before you apurpose and leave the lands to displease you? Do you want her to be utterly in the power of your father or younger brother?"

That had stopped Raymond's protests. "They would treat her with kindness," he assured William, "but you are right. It is not good to be a helpless pawn without even the right to an opinion. And if some mischance should destroy my father and brother before me, God knows where the right would go. My grandfather is old and has no legitimate sons."

Somewhat similar arguments had been advanced by Richard to Henry. "Do you want Alphonse d'Aix or the heir of Raymond-Berenger to have a claim on the lands?" Richard had asked his brother. "For God's sake, Henry, they must go only to the girl. She is English and, through her father, my vassal, thus yours. The lands may be administered by Raymond. He is a good man, honest and loyal, but they must be held in the lady's name only."

Alys now noted the flicker of anger on her betrothed's countenance—she noticed everything about him these days with a piercing clarity. "Perhaps you had better explain to me just what you mean when you say the lands are mine."

Temptation flashed through Raymond. He knew he could tell Alys anything, and she would believe him. It was a trust he could not violate. No land or power was worth the ugly knowledge that he had lied to Alys, who believed in him so implicitly. He explained as clearly as he could the terms of the marriage contract. Alys wrinkled her brows in thought.

"That means that if I wish I can hire a knight and rule the

land myself, that the dependent vassals will do homage to *me*. Is that correct?"

"Yes," Raymond said somewhat stiffly.

Alys stared at him for a moment, then turned her eyes to her own fingers. She had understood him, but could not believe that what she heard was true. The shock of Raymond's flat yes, which made of her a rich and independent woman, momentarily blotted out all other responses.

"And I will sit in justice, as my father does, and as I do when I am his deputy?"

"Yes."

"And look to the accounts of the lands?"

"Yes."

Shock had given way to joy; Alys was so absorbed in her growing sense of liberation that she failed to notice the increasing coldness of Raymond's responses. She smiled brilliantly, closed her eyes, and sighed with relief.

"Thank God I will not need to sit all day sewing a fine seam," she breathed. Then her eyes snapped open. "You will have to tell me just exactly what to do and say, Raymond," she said very seriously. "I know everything will be all different in Gascony, I mean the customs and rights. You will really have to do it all at first. And you will have to convince the vassals and castellans that I am not a fool and that your sword will back my word."

Raymond burst out laughing as the chagrin he felt melted. There was no one in the world as sensible and reasonable as Alys. Of course she must seem to rule. If she did not and he should die, the legal tenure of the land would be nearly meaningless. Whereas, if the men knew and trusted her, they would protect her until her sons reached maturity or some other arrangement—Raymond could not even think "until she married again"—could be made. He agreed warmly that she would take homage and do justice and he would stand beside her to back her word in all things.

But instead of being satisfied, Alys's brow furrowed even deeper, and she asked again about the nominal worth of the lands. When Raymond replied, her breath hissed in. "The king would not lightly part with such revenues. Will you have to fight to put out the present holders?"

More than once Sir William had commented wryly that

Raymond would find there were disadvantages to the cleverness he praised so highly in Alys. This was the first time
Raymond had cause to remember that and agree. It would not,
he suspected, be the last time.

"I hope not," he temporized. "However, the sooner we are
there in our own persons to make our claim, the less chance
there will be for any contest. The king has already sent letters
to name you overlady and me as your husband; still, the
quicker we are there to take all in our hands, the better. Thus,
need and desire match perfectly for once. The sooner we
marry, the better."

"Yes, of course, but—from what you say, Amou is strong
and very rich. Ibos is also rich, and the other two of less worth
but still not to be despised. Why should the king give so much
—unless the lands are not his to give."

"They *are* his to give," Raymond said, recognizing his
defeat in trying to turn Alys's attention, "but it is a long way
from Gascony to England, and the revenue diminishes by each
hand through which it passes until it is either nothing or a debt
by the time it comes here. Thus, the twenty pounds a year from
Bix is worth more than the several hundred marks we will have
from the lands. Moreover, Earl Richard gave the king in hand
three thousand marks, which is what he would have given to
you as a wedding gift. You do not, I hope, object to its
bestowal in land."

"No, not at all!" Alys exclaimed. "How kind of Uncle
Richard! And I know that Henry is always in desperate need of
money. But, Raymond, it still seems a great deal for relatively
little. Do you truly believe the men who hold the keeps now
will yield them to you without war?"

Clever, clever—entirely too clever, Raymond thought,
looking into Alys's face and not daring to lie. After all, the
truth would become obvious as soon as they reached Gascony.
"Blancheforte is empty except for the serfs of the demesne,"
he began, "and the man who holds Benquel will not dare
contest with me because the vicomte de Marsan will come to
my support and cast him out, whereas accepting my rule will
bring peace to his lands and cost him nothing. Besides, I know
him a little—Sir Oliver is his name—and he is a good enough
man who has done his best in an impossible situation."

"I am not an idiot, Raymond," Alys said. "I was not asking you about those lands, and you know it."

Raymond grinned at her. "It never hurts to try. I do not believe in holding my neck extended to get my head chopped off. But really, love, it is not near so bad as you seem to think. Henry is certain the castellan of Amou will be overjoyed to see me. He is a Sir Conon, an older man, without heirs, and said to be both honest and honorable. He has been writing angry letters that Béarn has been threatening him and trying to obtain the revenues."

"Then you will have to fight Béarn?"

"Not an open war, anyway, and certainly not immediately. Do not forget, Alys, that Gaston is my great-uncle. I know it is silly; he is no more than twelve years my senior, but he and my grandfather are half-brothers. Garsenda was first married to Alphonse of Provence and bore him Raymond-Berenger; many years later when Alphonse died, she married the count of Béarn and bore him Gaston. I doubt he will oppose me in arms; he will try to win me with soft words and promises."

Alys examined his face carefully for a moment. He was not, she decided, telling a half-truth about Amou, but there was something . . . "Then it is the other estate, the one at Ibos, that you will need to take by force," she said.

Raymond's lips tightened. "Most probably, yes," he replied, "although it is not certain. Now that Toulouse is cast down, Sir Garnier may think better of his defiance—but truly, Alys, I hope he will not. I could not trust him. I think I would have to tell you to refuse. In any case, I think I will need to take Ibos by force."

Alys did not say that she would not refuse, even if he told her to do so. She knew she would obey, however little she liked the result of that obedience. Moreover, it was her duty and probably one of the conditions under which the estate had been granted, because Henry's reason for granting it was that Raymond should win it back from French influence.

"How likely are you to hold it if you can take it?" she asked, wondering whether she was going to have to look forward to a whole lifetime of futile war.

"There will be no trouble about that. Toulouse had no right to take Garnier's fealty, except that Tarbes is Toulouse's. Louis certainly will not press the point during the years that remain for the truce, and, even after that, I doubt he would try to unseat me. His sense of justice is very strong—and I am Margaret's nephew as well as Eleanor's, you know. Of course, Margaret is by no means as fond of me as Eleanor is, nor does Louis listen to her as Henry listens to Eleanor, but still the blood bond must mean something, and by law the land is mine —no, yours."

"*Ours*," Alys said.

Raymond smiled at her. Now his face was clear, his eyes bright with enthusiasm. Alys repressed the thought that it only took one war to kill a man and comforted herself with the conviction that Raymond understood the policies and politics of France and the duchies that surrounded it far better than she. In any case, it was stupid to worry about things months or years in the future. Raymond would take possession of the uncontested lands first and, if he had to fight for Ibos, would spend some time gathering strength. By then, perhaps God would smite Garnier dead. At least she was not to be a painted image; she would have tasks and duties.

"Have you seen any of these places?" Alys asked.

"Only Benquel. It is a shell keep, like Hurley. The country is fine and rich, but Benquel has suffered much from Marsan's looking the other way when his men raid."

"But you said—"

"That there would be no trouble—and there will be none," Raymond assured her. "As soon as I offer to do fealty—or rather that you will do fealty—to Marsan for the lands." He then explained about the history of Benquel. "Once Marsan feels his honor is satisfied," Raymond concluded, "he will see that no more damage or insult is given. He likes me. I have always paid my dues on my farms on time and have been a visitor in Mont de Marsan. Still, the sooner we come to terms, the better."

"Yes, indeed," Alys agreed. "You are right. We had better marry in haste, so that we can begin to take the lands in hand before winter makes traveling too hard. I will speak to Papa, but I do not see any reason to invite many besides Uncle Richard."

Raymond sputtered. "Alys, you are the most unromantic woman. Do you not desire that all the maidens in the kingdom should envy your good fortune?"

"What good fortune?" Alys teased. "Marrying you? Or the possibility of becoming a widow before the next year is out?"

"Marrying me, of course! I am strong, rich, handsome, polished in manners—"

"So you are," Alys agreed tenderly, throwing her arms around him and kissing him soundly. "And I do not wish to be a widow, ever."

Raymond had only been joking, of course, expecting Alys to call him a blackamoor popinjay or to say something else equally sharp. The sudden softness of her voice, the clinging of her lips, nearly overset him. He held her close, prolonging the kiss, and then bent his head to rest his cheek against her headdress.

"It is not true that I am so great a prize," Raymond said huskily, "or if it is, it is less than nothing compared with your worth, beloved. You are like the sun, Alys. When you are in sight, all other luminaries pale into insignificance. Let us marry soon, heart of my heart, not to travel before winter or for the lands, but only so that I may the sooner call you my own."

CHAPTER 5

****

Alys's proposal for a modest affair did not meet with the enthusiastic agreement she had expected from her father. When she suggested a one-day feast with only Richard and Sancia and their immediate neighbors as guests, her father sighed and smiled and told her not to be a fool. The nephew-by-marriage of the king of England could not marry in privacy. There was to be a state affair at Wallingford, and the king and queen would attend.

Despite the fact that Alys was frightened by the huge three-week-long affair that was planned, the wedding was truly joyful. This was more true than for most marriages because both bride and groom were so happy. Then also, there was no mother to sigh over the loss of her baby girl; Elizabeth loved Alys, but Elizabeth never thought of Alys as an infant. Even at five, Alys had been a strong-willed, adult-seeming child. And, although Elizabeth knew she would miss Alys, she also understood that the marriage would save both of them hurt.

Thus far so much had happened so fast that there had been no time for Alys and Elizabeth to come into conflict over the role of lady of the manor. Had Alys remained in Marlowe, such a conflict was inevitable. Since her mother's death Alys had run her father's estates and life. At that time Alys was only ten years old. To some extent, she had assumed the responsibilities even before that, because her mother had been a limp, ineffective woman. Elizabeth, too, was accustomed to being the chatelaine of the estate to a greater degree than most women because her first husband had been indifferent to the lands except as a source of income.

Now that Elizabeth had married Alys's father, both women would have needed to live in the same keep. It was right that Elizabeth should manage her husband's house, yet how could Alys step back? The servants came to her out of habit; she

61

answered their questions out of habit. Elizabeth was sweet and mild of temper, but eventually she would begin to resent this; however, if she put out her hand to take the reins of the household, Alys would not be able to keep from resenting that.

William understood this as well as Elizabeth. The only solution would have been to separate the women, but then he would have been torn apart between them. If he stayed with Elizabeth, which his heart and body demanded, his conscience would tell him that his daughter was deserted and lonely. He could never be easy or comfortable; guilt would nag and drag at him. It was this knowledge that made it possible for William to accept his daughter's marriage with gladness.

Because William was happy, so was Richard of Cornwall. He was delighted with the marriage for political reasons, but would have been distressed if his old friend had been grieved. The other guests, some of William's neighbors but mostly Richard of Cornwall's vassals, were also happy. The neighbors were glad to see Alys so well wedded and so obviously in love with her future husband; Cornwall's vassals were pleased to meet in an informal and joyful atmosphere the man they would need to obey in the earl's name, to whom they would render accounts and submit petitions.

All in all it was a marvelous wedding. The weather was not yet cold enough to imprison everyone inside Wallingford, so hunts and outside entertainments, even a small tournament, were arranged. The grains and vegetables had not yet been so long in storage as to grow musty; the cattle, pigs, and deer were still fat from summer feeding and autumn gleaning so that meats were sweet and succulent; but best of all, everyone was in so good a humor from adequate exercise and mental content that no drunken brawls broke out during the entire week it took the guests to gather from all over Richard of Cornwall's domain.

During that week, Alys and Raymond hardly exchanged a single word with each other. Alys and Elizabeth were busy arranging sleeping quarters and table positions so that no one would be offended, and Raymond was as deeply involved in entertaining the gentlemen. The situation was strangely exciting to both—the brief meeting of eyes across the hall, an even briefer touch of fingers on hand or arm or shoulder seemed to arouse more sexual tension between Alys and Raymond than an intimate kiss. Raymond found himself with a heat and pressure in his loins that made him curse the binding of his chausses and bless the looseness of his surcoat. Alys could not put a name to what she felt. Her skin was strangely tingly, and her breasts were so sensitive that she could feel every movement of her shift against her nipples. When Raymond touched her, even as a partner in a public dance, she felt hot and cold and so shy that she could not meet his eyes.

It was ridiculous to feel shy with Raymond, Alys told herself over and over. She had not forgotten how she had laughed at him, scolded him, instructed him when he first came to serve her father. Tell herself, she could; change her feelings, she could not. Each time Raymond spoke to her, she blushed and dropped her eyes—which nearly melted him with tenderness, even while it excited him still further.

By the morning of the wedding, both were quivering with eagerness and tension. Raymond's anxieties were especially peaked by his father-by-marriage. William had begun to glare and snap at him as he realized that only hours remained before his daughter was made a wife and completely removed from his control. As he helped Raymond from the ceremonial bath before dressing the groom for the ceremony, William could not help telling Raymond to be careful in his handling of her. "She is so small," William said. "In God's name, do not hurt her."

Raymond regarded his future father-by-marriage with some trepidation. "How can I help it?" he asked with mingled nervousness and irritation, rubbing himself vigorously with the drying cloth. "If you know a way to take a maidenhead that does not cause pain, tell me and I will listen."

Too anxious to be sensible, William snapped, "It is not a thing with which I am acquainted, both of my wives having been widows. But I have heard the great lords of the south are freer with their vassals' daughters—"

"They are not so free as you have heard," Raymond retorted, grabbing the shirt William held out. "But what little knowledge I have tells me there is no easy way." He drew the shirt over his head, but when his face emerged and he caught sight of William's expression, he laid a hand on his arm. "Forgive me sir. I am . . . You must know that it will give me no pleasure to hurt Alys." His voice shook.

"Nay," William replied, taking the chausses from another

gentleman's hand and rolling one leg so that Raymond could step into it. "Rather should I beg your pardon, my son. God knows you have no reason but love for desiring my daughter, and I know you to be no light ravisher of women." He helped Raymond into the garment, then embraced him, and laughed uneasily. "I see her still as a child—that is all."

It was fortunate that the king walked in at that moment, and further private conversation was impossible. Henry was in the best of tempers. He smiled largely on his brother, on two of Richard's vassals who had drawn William away, and most particularly on Raymond, his beloved wife's nephew, who had provided the opportunity for him to be both benefactor and gainer.

Having returned all greetings pleasantly, Henry drew Raymond aside. "How long do you plan to stay in England after the wedding?" he asked.

"To speak the truth," Raymond replied, "it was my first intention to go as soon as possible because the weather will shortly make passage by sea dangerous. However, if it will serve you that I stay longer, of course I will do so."

"No, no," Henry assured him. "I have no desire to keep you, and in Gascony you could do me a quiet little service."

"If I can, I will be most willing," Raymond replied. He could say nothing else, but inwardly he stiffened.

The last time Henry had asked for a "trifling service," Raymond had ended up as a spy in his betrothed's household. What caused Raymond's anxiety was that the king's charm was so great that Raymond had agreed to the dishonorable task with gaiety, as if it were all a jest. The dishonest purpose had not really made an impact on him until he had met Sir William, himself the soul of honesty and honor. Now Raymond regarded the king with considerable caution.

"I have allowed a thousand pounds to the mayor and commune of Bordeaux for the strengthening of the walls of that city," Henry said. "Since you will be of the council, will you look at this work and see if it is being properly done?"

That seemed innocent enough. Raymond opened his mouth to say, "Gladly," and instead said, "Is this not the seneschal's duty? Do you believe him to have put the money to other uses?"

"Not at all," Henry assured him. "This money did not go

through Molis's hands. It was a direct grant to the mayor and burgesses of the town. Er . . . you had not heard, perhaps, that it was necessary for me to reorder the governing of Bordeaux?"

"Bordeaux? No. I had not heard, but I suppose whatever the form of the government, I can count on the support of my mother's kinsman, Rustengo de Soler."

The king cleared his throat. "Well . . . er . . . he is no longer the mayor, but I will give you a letter to Peter Calhau that will smooth your path."

"Calhau!" Raymond echoed.

Calhau was a Colom, if not by name in every other way, and the Coloms were deadly enemies to the Solers. What the king had said meant that the power structure in Bordeaux had shifted, or been shifted by Henry, from Raymond's relatives to their enemies. The Coloms would not be very happy to see Rustengo's kinsman in possession of Blancheforte or on the town council. The king's request, then, could scarcely have anything to do with the walls. Suddenly Raymond realized that if the Solers desired to take back power, it would be most convenient for them to do so while the seneschal was busy in the south with the threat of the king of Navarre and Gaston of Béarn. But what in the world did Henry expect him to do, Raymond wondered. Every utterance he made would be regarded by Calhau with suspicion and distrust.

"It is not likely that Calhau will regard me with favor," Raymond remarked, striving to keep any reserve from his voice.

Henry smiled seraphically. "He will not wish to disoblige me and, I think, will not be so stupid as to scorn a bridge to your kinsman. A strong bridge is a useful place for meeting and settling small difficulties. Also, your kinsman will be glad to know that I have favored you with Blancheforte and a seat on the council of Bordeaux."

"Yes, of course," Raymond replied.

It was possible that Henry was thinking of shifting his influence back to the Soler faction—or wanted them to believe that the possibility existed. Most likely of all, Henry had no idea what he would want or need to do. Raymond would be a convenient conduit for information and opinion.

"I will do my best to serve you, Sire," Raymond added,

hoping that the king would not regard that as a promise, but knowing quite well that he would.

"And when you go south to Amou—" Henry began.

"Henry!" Richard of Cornwall interrupted, his voice rich with protest. "This is Raymond's wedding day. He is not finished dressing. Do you wish him to be late at the church door and break his bride's heart? Besides, how much of your instructions can you expect a bridegroom to remember?"

"I will remember," Raymond assured the king fervently, in the hope that he would be spared further discussion, which could only involve him more deeply.

The last little stratagem into which Henry had pushed him had worked out well for all concerned, but Raymond was certain that that was by a special effort of the Merciful Mother, who puts out her hand to support all well-meaning fools, himself included. He did not, however, wish to try Holy Mary's patience by falling into another imbroglio of the king's making. Thus far, Henry had no time to demand more of him than to be the grease between the grinding gears of Bordeaux politics. Even that was no easy place to be. Most often, the grease is pressed out flat and discarded.

Raymond liked Henry, but he was also aware of the king's propensity for using people and, far worse, for blaming them when his plans did not work out just as he expected. All the while that the attending gentlemen drew on his tunic and his surcoat, adjusted the magnificent gold-wired jewel-encrusted sword belt that was Richard of Cornwall's token wedding gift, then hung around him the heavy gold collar that was King Henry's token, broad enough to spread from shoulder to shoulder, Raymond mulled over the king's words. He no longer noticed William's nervousness, and his own dissipated under the pressure of the new problem.

Alys's eagerness had peaked the preceding evening. She had barely been able to restrain herself from crying out and snatching her hand away when Raymond took it. She had cried herself to sleep from pure nervousness; however, she did sleep, and when she woke, knowing that the wedding was today, this day, that she would need to wait no longer, a quiet contentment filled her. She was not at all nervous about the wedding itself, and she simply refused to think of the future, since it was now too late to worry about it. When she was dressed, she was able to smile quite naturally as Elizabeth drew her forward to the polished silver oval that showed her reflection.

Alys looked at her image with mingled amusement and satisfaction. The cloth-of-gold underdress matched almost exactly her loose hair, which was now, strange as it seemed to her, flowing freely, unconfined except for the diamond and sapphire garland that had been part of Raymond's betrothal gift. Only on a maiden's wedding day was her hair displayed —and a fine display it was, hanging in deep waves almost to her thighs and curling at the ends. Where a few shorter strands fell forward over her shoulders, they mingled with the gold thread arabesques embroidered into the rich blue velvet of the overdress.

Blue, the color of purity, Virgin Mary's color, had been chosen for this last day on which Alys would be a maid—but also because the color matched Alys's eyes. The wide arm-holes of the outer gown displayed the long, tight-buttoned sleeves of the cloth-of-gold underdress. Alys frowned. The sapphires and diamonds of Raymond's bracelets could be seen, but the handsome gold settings were not at their best on cloth-of-gold. Ah well, she thought, the work showed excellently where the necklet crossed the blue gown.

Beneath the hem were bright, red-dyed leather shoes, all gold-embroidered and set with gems to match the gold girdle that hung low on Alys's hips, both Sancia's gift, and Elizabeth was bringing the queen's present, a magnificent cloak, scarlet wool of the finest weave, lined with soft gray fur from hood to hem.

"He will be ravished," Queen Eleanor said in Alys's ear. "You need not study to see if you are perfect."

"Oh, thank you, madame," Alys murmured, "but Raymond must be accustomed to finer dress, I think. And I had no other jewels than these he gave me, but . . . I will not shame him, will I? Am I fine enough?"

"Quite fine enough, nor yet too fine," the queen assured her, laughing. "However, it was not of your clothes I spoke, you silly child. Do you not know yourself beautiful?"

Alys frowned. "I am well enough. Men like to look upon me, yes, I know it. But if Raymond takes me for that, he is the greatest fool in the world."

"You are most eager to be a wife," Eleanor said softly, remembering how frightened she had been, less than fourteen and sent to marry a man fifteen years older whom she had never seen. She had been trained for it, of course, and had expected it; she had wanted to be a queen like her sister Margaret, who had married Louis of France. Nonetheless, she had been afraid, not eagerly happy. Most girls were afraid, for their lives lay in their husbands' hands.

"Yes," Alys replied seriously. "I love Raymond, and it is sure he loves me, for I had nothing he could desire before the king's and Uncle Richard's generosity increased my dower. Why should I not be eager, since the keeping of my husband's love will be in my hands, and it is my first purpose in life to be a good wife."

"And on those most auspicious words, it is time," Elizabeth said.

Alys turned from the burnished metal mirror at once and stepped out gladly, the women falling in behind the queen and her sister. For a wonder the weather had held fair, and it was not even very cold. The church was outside the walls, but not far enough to make it worthwhile to go on horseback. The whole way was lined with people, peering from behind the men-at-arms and making a joyous noise—for they knew there would be food and wine for the taking at the castle after the wedding.

As was proper, the men were waiting. William came forward to meet his daughter. He did not want to lose her, yet it was impossible for him to damp the joy that showed in her face, and he smiled as he took her hand and led her on and up the steps to where the archbishop-elect of Canterbury, the bishop of Bath, and the bishop of London waited with Raymond, who was flanked by the king and Richard of Cornwall.

So deep had Raymond been in his consideration of what mischief Henry was brewing up that he had been only minimally aware of passing along the road and arriving at the church door. The increase in the noise as the people cheered the coming of the bride grew slowly, and therefore was not startling enough to draw his attention. It was only the movement of the men around him, as Henry and Richard made way for Alys and her father, that made him look up. His eyes fell on Alys.

At once the tenseness disappeared from Raymond's face. His smile cleared his brow, lit his eyes, and then curved his lips. His hand reached out for Alys's and hers met his halfway. Everyone within sight of them smiled; their mutual trust and joy was irresistible. Alys in particular was uplifted. She had seen that Raymond looked worried and unhappy as she came up the stairs, and for one awful moment her smile had frozen on her face and her heart plummeted. Then he had seen her, and his pleasure, the way his hand went out to her as if for relief and succor, washed out all fear and multiplied her happiness.

There were no faint or quavering voices. The archbishop-elect bellowed out the service so that the last and least on the edge of the crowd could hear, and both Alys and Raymond called their responses so that no witness could ever say there was doubt or reluctance. When they were sealed to each other, the crowd roared out their *Fiat! Fiat!* with hearty goodwill. Most were not sure why this wedding gave them so much enjoyment, since it was only distantly connected with their personal affairs. However, there were others of a more perceptive nature who realized that it was singularly pleasant to have a groom who was sincerely enthusiastic and a bride who was neither bruised, bloody, in tears, nor on the verge of fainting with terror.

All ceremonies complete, Raymond led his bride back toward Wallingford. Men and women now mingled, the king walking with his wife, Richard with Sancia, William with Elizabeth. Talk was general, and the common folk cheered with even more enthusiasm, knowing that the feast would now begin, and fell in behind the group of nobles. The gates of Wallingford would be open to all today. Carcasses of oxen, sheep, and pigs roasted in the bailey and great tuns of beer had been broached. Mountains of bread were piled on clean sheets, and casks of salt and smoked fish stood open. No one would be turned away, and no one would be hungry—for one day, at least.

Under cover of the noise, after walking some time in silence, Alys said, "You are troubled, my lord and husband. What has happened?"

"Troubled?" Raymond had been alternately glancing at his bride and around at the smiling crowd and beautiful countryside. He had honestly forgotten, for the moment, the problem posed by the king's brief conversation. "And what is this lord and husband? Have you forgot my name?"

"No," Alys sighed, "but it is so nice to say—my lord and my husband."

Raymond's fingers tightened on her hand. "So, my lady and wife . . . yes, you are right. It is nice to say."

"And it is a true thing to me," Alys insisted. "Now we are one flesh, one blood, one bone. What falls upon you, falls upon me. Do not hide trouble from me, Raymond. Share I must, will I nill I, but truly it is my desire to be one with you in trouble as in joy."

Raymond looked down into the lovely face turned up to him. So fair, so delicate—but the chin was firm and the eyes steady and fearless, and that was more important. To Raymond's mother and sisters, no word of trouble was ever said lest they be overpowered with fear, so a man needed to smile and listen to love songs and talk of tales and feastings no matter how heavy his heart. Alys's question had, by now, recalled to Raymond his unease, but already it seemed less of a problem.

"It was something the king desired I do," he said softly, "but now is no time to talk of it."

"No, indeed," Alys agreed promptly. There was a good deal of noise, but Henry was close behind them. "Only, must you answer him at once?"

"I do not know that I need answer more than I have, but it is not the answering I fear. It is what takes shape in his own mind."

"How wise you are," Alys said softly, "but if I hang on you, which is not unreasonable during this time, he will say no more."

"And I will have much pleasure." Raymond's eyes gleamed. "I give you leave to hang on me every day, here and elsewhere."

Alys had forgotten her shyness, but the glitter of her husband's eyes brought it all back. She blushed deliciously and hung her head. This naturally inspired Raymond to further teasing. For the first time in her life, Alys had no smart replies, finding herself as tongue-tied as any girl who had never met her husband before the day of her marriage. How long the sweet modesty would have lasted under continued provocation was questionable, but they had reached the keep and were greeted with fanfares, which made either teasing or reply impossible until they were seated at the tables.

Concern for the dishes wiped out any other consideration in Alys's mind for a time, but she need not have worried. Each group of cooks had outdone itself to make its particular portion of the dinner more succulent and savory than that of any other group.

First came the boars' heads, mouths propped open to show tusks and tongues, decorated with curls of pastry. The servant carrying this dish was flanked by two others, one bearing the whole haunch of an ox, swimming in a sharp sauce, and the other a rich pudding, spicy-sweet with nuts and raisins. A second set of servants followed with baked swans, roast capons, and pheasants—the swans and pheasants dressed in their own outer feathers. The third triad bore fish: baked sturgeon, boiled pike, and eels in jelly.

Good humor lent good appetite also, especially at the high table where each couple was content both with one another and with their neighbors. Eyes gleamed as each pointed to what he or she wanted; squires in their lord's colors served, and pages, also brightly dressed, ran to and fro carrying portions to be laid upon trenchers and—the height of elegance—upon silver plates. The butlers, King Henry's and Earl Richard's, poured the wine into golden and, equally precious, glass goblets. The fanfares that had accompanied the serving of the dishes quieted into more gentle music of lute and psaltery as health, long life, and many sons were wished for the bride and groom. Then all gave their attention to the food.

Delicious food makes stuffing inevitable; stuffing brings repletion. When the sound of conversation rose to a deafening level, the trumpets called again to herald the arrival of the first subtlety. *Winter Wedding*, it was called, a towering confection of pastry and crystallized honey, depicting the wedding party before the church doors. It was carried right around the hall for each table to see and enjoy before it was placed on a sideboard. At the end of the dinner, all four subtleties would be compared and praised, broken up, and distributed among the guests.

Now the minstrels in the gallery struck up a livelier tune, servitors scrambled to clear the center of the great hall, and the bride and groom rose to head the dance. In deference to full stomachs, the stately *danse au chapelet* came first, Raymond raising cheers and stampings when he kissed Alys on her lips rather than decorously on the cheek as required.

The king and queen then led *la gaillarde,* and, food having been reasonably well digested at this point, the musicians struck up a *tourdion.* Older couples hastily retreated to their seats while the younger closed ranks. The wild whirling, stamping, and leaping was for those with strong stomachs and excess energy. Mischievously, the musicians played faster and faster as the dance progressed until first one and then another, then whole groups dropped out, some sinking exhausted and laughing to the floor.

When the last couple had been vanquished and helped breathlessly to their seats, the trumpets rang out again to herald the second course. The dishes were as numerous and as elaborately served, ranging from roast venison with red currant jelly and a litter of roast suckling pigs to a sweet of honeyed fruits stiffened with sweet, wine-soaked bread. The subtlety was *Spring Increasing,* broader than it was tall, displaying rich fields with calves and lambs and a very pregnant lady, with gold hair of dandelion flower petals preserved in crystallized honey, leaning on the arm of a dark-haired attendant swain. This piece was received with shouts of acclaim and much advice on how to ensure the accuracy of the prediction.

The hilarious mood continued to welcome the jongleurs, who tumbled and climbed upon each other, juggled gilded balls and flaming torches, and performed comic acts in which the bittersweet joys of marriage were illustrated. By the time they were finished, the sun was westering and all were ready to sample the third course. The noise from the bailey, where the common folk fed, drank, sported, fought, and watched cruder players, came up through the windows and nearly overpowered the blare of the trumpets. Everyone smiled. It was nice to know the hinds were happy, also.

Sensibly, the dishes of the third course were somewhat smaller than those which preceded them, but they were neither less numerous nor less elaborate. It opened with roast peacocks, refeathered and with tails displayed, flanked by egrets and cranes. Stewed rabbits, ragout of venison, and white meat of chicken prepared in a white curd with almonds followed. Last came a variety of fish, perch and flounder and grilled herrings, all with sauces to tempt tiring palates. The subtlety was *Summer Bearing,* and showed father and mother admiring their child being suckled by a wetnurse in an orchard heavy with fruit.

The minstrels played complicated instrumental music for a while before the dancing began, and fewer couples took to the floor. Some were too heavy with food, some too dizzy or somnolent with wine. Alys was pleased that Raymond was still quite sober. There had been many cups raised to him, and he had lifted his to each toast, but there was more water than wine in his goblet, and, even so, he drank of it sparingly. He had no mind to need to be carried to his wedding bed and perhaps being incapable of doing his duty in it.

Torches were lit before the dancing ended to supplement the waning light of the short winter day. As the sun set, lamps were lit also, and a warm, golden glow suffused the hall. Except for a few, whom wine made quarrelsome and who were quietly suppressed by their more sober friends, voices had softened and movements grew more languid. There were no calls for another measure when the minstrels put up their instruments and the trumpeters came forth for the last time.

Enthusiasm for the fourth course was minimal, but the cooks had been prepared for that. Dainty dishes predominated: tiny roast birds, lark and snipe; little birds' eggs hard-boiled and set in a spicy jelly; small fritters and fancy sweetmeats and pastries. The subtlety recognized the mellow mood of the ending day and portrayed *Autumn Fulfillment*—man, wife, and cradled child beside a cheerful fire near a table laden with the fruits of autumn.

When that masterpiece of varicolored pastry had gone the round and been admired, all the others were brought forth. The cooks were summoned, and Raymond gave each a gold coin. Then the high table descended and began breaking apart the subtleties. The king seized the images of the archbishop-elect and the attendant bishops, saying that it was the only time he was likely to have the Church in his hand. William took the golden-haired bride and Elizabeth the heavily pregnant figure, for she ardently desired to give her second husband the son he needed as heir to his lands. When the high lords had chosen, the guests at large rushed upon the pastries and tore them apart.

During and after this melee, servants hastily cleared the tables and removed them. The guests mixed more freely, talking, dancing, and playing games. Eventually torches began to gutter and the lamps to burn low. Someone, Alys could never remember who, called the party to order. The men gathered around Raymond, the women about Alys. Everyone capable of doing so began to cheer and laugh. The bedding ceremony was about to begin.

CHAPTER 6

****

Alys knew what was to happen, of course, and she was certainly not ashamed of her lovely body. She was also well aware of the purpose of exposing her naked to all; it was proof that she had no hidden defect for which her husband could repudiate her. Still, she was young and, until a few months before, had been a person of little account in the world. Had she married the son of a neighboring knight, or even someone a little higher on the social scale, there would have been fewer guests, and she would have known most of them. Now it seemed that a host of strangers surrounded her, jesting, laughing, and making pointed remarks as her clothing was removed.

There were so many witnesses that they could not fit into the bedchamber, so the disrobing was carried out in the hall. It was cold, despite the best efforts of the roaring fires. Alys had begun to shiver, and Elizabeth, noting the strain on her face, had faded from her side and suggested to Richard that he keep William away. The bond of father and daughter was unusually close and sympathetic. Whereas most fathers would have been amused by the fear and embarrassment of their daughters, William would be greatly distressed. He might even interfere in some way to protect Alys, which would be unfortunate all around.

Richard was quick to take the hint and draw William away; Elizabeth, Sancia, and the queen were the ladies actively engaged in disrobing Alys. The result for Alys was that there was hardly a familiar face in the crowd around her. She was too proud and too courageous to weep aloud and hang her head like a craven, but tears stung in her eyes and the milk of her skin was deep-dyed with blushes. Thus, when the cries, "Look on your husband!" and "Look on your wife!" rang out as the naked couple was brought face to face, Alys shrank away from the unfamiliar, staring eyes into the shelter of Raymond's arms. This produced more laughter, cheers, and jests, but Alys cared little for that. She had been received in a willing, protective embrace. She now felt comforted and sustained. Although she still blushed furiously and hid her face in Raymond's shoulder, her trembling ceased.

It was this pretty picture that William saw when he was attracted by the ceremonial cries that capped the ritual and pushed his way through the crowd. Relief and gladness filled him. The trust his daughter felt in her husband and the eager yet gentle way Raymond held her augured well for Alys's future happiness. William was soothed; he could not take pleasure in the forthcoming separation, but he did not need to fear for his daughter, either. He joined his wife, the king and queen, the earl and countess of Cornwall, and several other great magnates in accompanying the bridal pair into the bedchamber, and assisted Alys into the bed with a fond pat and a low-voiced, "Be a good girl."

To which, to his delight, his daughter responded pertly, "It is too late for that."

Alys's balance had been restored by Raymond's ready, smiling reception. Protected, she had been able to recognize the friendliness in the voices and eyes of the crowd; no matter that they were strangers, they all wished her well. The final assurance that everything was just as it should be was her father's all-too-familiar admonition and the calm on his face and in his hazel eyes.

A spate of final admonitions, none as innocent as William's followed, but at last the bed curtains were drawn closed and the witnesses withdrew, leaving the couple to themselves. Raymond uttered a loud sigh and turned toward his wife. Alys's retreat into his arms had had a powerful effect on him. Her fear and shame and the trust in him she had unconsciously demonstrated roused the deepest and strongest protective instinct in Raymond.

Yet there was nothing he could do to protect her. A maiden must be broached to be a wife, and that was never easy. William's words came back to him, also. They were true; Alys was very small. He could barely see her in the dim light that filtered through the openings in the bed curtains, only a soft paleness, which was her body, and a golden gleam here and there on her cascade of hair—but even sitting he needed to look down on her.

"Alys," he said softly, "do you know what comes now?"

"You will make me your wife," she replied. "Is that what you mean?"

"Yes. To breed children, we must couple, but   . I fear I must hurt you, my love."

He could feel her nod. "Elizabeth warned me it might be so." Her voice was low, but calm. She paused, as if to consider, and then said briskly, "Very well. I am ready."

Raymond uttered a shaken laugh; he was rather shocked. "But I am not, beloved. I fear your pain more than you do, it seems. To cause you hurt . . . the thought unmans me."

She turned more fully toward him and put her arms around his neck. "I have seen the beasts couple," she remarked, "but they are always ready in season. Is there something I can do to help? In this I am very ignorant."

"And so you should be," Raymond exclaimed.

Of course, he did not desire a shrieking, struggling, terrified bride, but there were moments when Alys could be too calm and practical. Still, her body was warm and pliant against him, and although he could not see her expression, her face was raised trustfully to his. He lowered his head a few inches to bring their lips together, and Alys sighed and tightened her arms around his neck as he slipped his hands under her hair and stroked her silken skin. Raymond leaned forward, and she fell back, but his arms were around her, and he eased her down gently without breaking their embrace.

Extricating his hands and tipping himself sideways, Raymond began to touch a firm but well-developed breast, and then the soft curves of her belly, hip, and thigh. Now that his weight held them together, Alys slid one hand from his neck over his shoulder and down his back. She could feel his shaft, hard and full, pressing against her. Ignorant of elaborate technique though Alys might be, she was not so ignorant as to be unaware of what that meant. Raymond was now ready.

Knowledgeable only in the ways of beasts, Alys expected him to turn her around and mount her. She was not at all frightened. A warmth seemed to be spreading over her from the places Raymond touched with his hands and from their joined mouths. Her skin was all tingly, almost ticklish, but it generated no desire in her to laugh or flinch away. Raymond lifted his lips from hers, but before Alys could murmur a complaint, she used her breath to gasp with pleasure. His warm lips were running down her throat, pausing a moment in the hollow where her pulse beat fast and hard, moving again until they fastened on a nipple.

Involuntarily, Alys cried out softly and clutched Raymond tighter. Every sensation she had felt before was greatly heightened and, inexplicably, the sucking at her breast waked a pulsing heat between her legs. Instinct instructed ignorance; without explanation Alys knew that she had been wrong when she first said she was ready. She was not actually thinking, of course. The growing intensity of her physical sensations blocked coherent thought, but some interior process recognized that Raymond had known she was wrong, and gratitude added to her joy and confidence.

Alys was, however, crediting her husband with rather more than he deserved. It was his own pleasure rather than his knowledge of Alys's lack of readiness that was making him prolong his foreplay. Nonetheless, his pleasure did come from an awareness of Alys as a special person and thus both a recipient and giver of special pleasure.

Although Raymond had initially been transfixed by Alys's beauty and was astonished anew by it each time he saw her after an absence, quite truly his desire to spend his life with Alys did not rest on her appearance alone. And, although strength, honesty, and good sense are not what a man thinks about in bed, there still remained a sense of something different and special about her which lent an added fillip to the way she sighed and cried out and kept Raymond playing with her. He abandoned one breast for the other, running his fingers playfully up and down her body, through the curls on her mount of Venus, and down between her thighs.

Part of Raymond's pleasure in Alys's response was that she showed so much surprise as her passion increased. It was very apparent that no man had handled her before, nor had she ever experienced the sensations his hands and lips were awakening in her body. Deliciously, she did not seem to know what to do, clutching distractedly now at his head or his hands or his body, moving instinctively in response to his fingering and kissing, and uttering little moans and cries.

Since this evidence of his success in stimulating his bride's desire was equally stimulating to Raymond, it was not very long before he mounted her. She sighed with pleasure at first when he positioned himself, the preliminary touches soothing an urgent need, but his first hard thrust brought a cry of pain, and Alys's body stiffened. The abrupt change startled Raymond into a clear awareness of the realities. Moreover, he was conditioned by the situation in his family to regard noblewomen as fragile and to treat them with gentleness and consideration.

He paused and murmured, "I am sorry, dearling, sorry, but there is no other way."

As he spoke, the tension went out of Alys's body. She had been surprised by the sudden pang for she had forgotten everything while Raymond caressed her. This was the pain she had been warned of, she remembered. "Yes, my lord," she whispered, "but kiss me again."

Enthralled by her innocence, Raymond complied and also inserted a hand between their bodies to play with her breast, all the while pressing himself into her. There was an obstruction, which yielded but did not give way under the steady pressure. Raymond withdrew slowly, still caressing her. Alys's hands, which had been gripping his back, began again to stroke his sides up and down. Nibbling her lips, her throat, and again her lips, Raymond thrust hard again.

He gained some depth and this time Alys did not cry out, although she grew tense. Then her hands slid down his back and pressed him harder against her. He tried, but the pressure alone did not succeed. Raymond had a sudden horrid memory of a jest which had gone round the court of Navarre concerning a man who could not broach his bride.

He lifted his head and shoulders to give himself leverage, drew, and thrust with all the force he could muster. Alys gasped and Raymond himself uttered a pained oath, but when he came to rest he was sheathed to the hilt.

"I am seated now," he whispered to Alys, letting himself down on her gently. "The worst is over, love."

She had been breathing quick and hard, just short of sobbing, but she quieted at once. Her faith in him was touching, and despite his urge to plunge up and down in the warm ooze that now surrounded his shaft, Raymond contained himself, concentrating on caressing her and moving minimally. Alys's grip, which had become lax, tightened. She hugged him close with one arm and stroked his back or played with his hair. Finally, to Raymond's surprise, her body began to move with his.

Alys had little awareness of what she was doing, rapt as she was in her own sensations. There had never been much fear in her of coupling, and what little tension had been generated by her physical pain had been removed by Raymond's tender explanations. He had said the worst was over, and it was. The remaining soreness and stretching were soothed by the extra lubrication of her own blood, and seemed only to intensify the thrilling sensation in her loins. All the tingling that had sensitized her skin centered there now, and every touch of Raymond's hands or lips seemed to increase it.

When he drew out, Alys sought to follow the source of her pleasure. Also the easing of Raymond's weight gave her a little freedom to position herself; thus, instinctively, she served her own purposes and increased her husband's excitement. He moved more freely; Alys responded, adding a little wriggle of the hips that drew a gasp from Raymond and a little mutter of satisfaction from her. Suddenly she gripped his buttocks hard, holding him still against her while she writhed, gasping louder and louder until the deep breaths broke into sobs.

Initially startled and thinking he had hurt her again, Raymond's fast approaching climax was delayed by a few essential minutes. Alys had torn her mouth free of his to breathe, but now she turned her head toward him to kiss his cheek and chin. Her hands relaxed, ran up his body, then stroked the back of his neck. Urgency restored, Raymond began to move again, but there was less pleasure in it when Alys lay relaxed, her body flaccid.

"Move," he bade her, almost angrily. "Put your legs around me. Move."

She obeyed him instantly. Alys clutched him tight with both arms and legs, rose to meet him, wriggled against him, and kissed his shoulders since, in his final extremity, he had lifted his head and strained backward. A single cry was wrenched from him, and he fell forward. Both lay quiet.

After a few minutes, little light kisses on his cheek and ear broke Raymond's doze. "No more," he mumbled. "I am drained out."

Alys chuckled. "I will not importune you, but I cannot breathe while you lie atop me."

"Beg pardon," he sighed, rolling off.

He was asleep again before he stopped rolling, and Alys was not far behind, her rest delayed only by the time it took her to snuggle close to his warm body. One of the drawbacks Alys had found to being a small person was that her body did not generate enough heat to warm the featherbeds quickly; generally, Alys fell asleep feeling cold. It was an added pleasure of marriage to have a source of heat provided. Pressing herself firmly against Raymond's back, Alys slept also.

For several hours Raymond was too heavily asleep to be aware of anything. However, after that he started to shift his position. The attempt to turn brought him hard against Alys, who was still plastered to his back, seeking warmth. Raymond uttered a muffled oath, and Alys squeaked as his weight came down on her arm.

He jerked upright and Alys asked him why he had sat up. She had been wakened completely by the pain when Raymond bent her arm unnaturally. Not ever having shared her bed, except with a maidservant when she was so young as to be in danger of falling out, although too old for a cradle, Alys knew at once whose body was beside her. Raymond said collectedly that he needed to use the pot. Whereupon he got out of bed and suited his actions to his word.

"Do not put it back," Alys said, crawling out also.

She was frozen when she returned to bed and pressed herself passionately into her husband's arms. These were open to receive her, but as soon as they did, Raymond yelped with shock; her icy hands and feet had made contact. Then he began to laugh.

"What is it?" Alys asked.

"I am much aggrieved," he replied.

Since he was still chuckling, Alys did not feel worried by the words. "My lord and husband, how have I offended?" she asked meekly.

"I thought you desired me," Raymond said, "but it is plain that I am no more to you than a bag of hot sand."

"No, no," Alys protested with innocent gravity. "You are more than that, for sand soon grows cold and you stay warm."

"What?" Raymond cried, half teasing and half outraged. "Do you find no pleasure other than my warmth in my company?"

He was disappointed. Although tension and a long, active day had brought him to bed fatigued and his own relief had further blurred the final moments of his nuptual coupling, Raymond had carried a strong feeling of pride into sleep. It had seemed to him that Alys had shown more than compliance during their mating, and it was not every man, he told himself, who could bring a woman to joy her first time. He could not mention the matter himself, but if one should ask . . . But now it seemed it had not happened. The slight chagrin was dissipated by Alys's giggle.

"But you told me I must not importune you, my lord."

"What?" he bellowed. Alys turned her face into the pillow, her shoulders shaking, but Raymond was not deceived. He turned her back promptly and asked, "When?"

Because the bed curtains had been pushed back when they left the bed, Raymond could see Alys widen her eyes into a stare of innocence. "Why, my lord, when I only kissed you to wake you because—"

The sentence ended in another squeak as Raymond squeezed her, but as soon as she got her breath back, she continued indefatigably, "Besides, could a modest maiden—"

That time Raymond stopped her mouth with his lips. "You are maiden no longer," he said, "and as to your modesty, even when you were a maiden, I had my doubts."

"Yet in some things I *am* modest," Alys murmured, the laughter gone from her voice. "I would not know how to ask. I only know country words. Surely so precious a set of jewels must have a more elegant name."

"No," Raymond muttered, drawing breath suddenly. "Stop, Alys. You will make me too eager."

She obeyed him, but he found that the further adventures of her questing fingers were almost as stimulating, and soon they were coupled again. This time Raymond was confident about her reaction, and when they were finished he held her almost as close as while they made love. This had been true pleasure, all pleasure, he thought. No sin to confess and do penance for; no need to sneak and hide for fear of talk or a husband; and to make better best, Alys was sweeter than all. Even the most experienced whore had been unable to arouse in him the heat that Alys's innocent explorations had generated. Moreover, with her he could have exactly what *he* wanted. She had no preconceived notions; she was willing and eager to be taught what would please him.

Alys was equally content. She was not quite as ignorant as she had implied. Although they had been sorely hurried to make all ready for the wedding, Elizabeth had not failed in her duty as Alys's stepmother. She had made clear certain important facts about men and women and their differences—and tactfully provided a small pot of sweet-smelling unguent.

"Not for the first time," Elizabeth had warned. "That once you must endure whatever pain there is. Raymond loves you and believes in you, but if he slides in too soft and easy the first time, questions will be raised in his mind. The pain will not be much, but however much it is, it will be well worth bearing."

Whatever initial doubts Alys had, and they were few, she was now abundantly certain that Elizabeth had been right not only about the joy of coupling, but about other significant facts.

"I do not know when it will come to you—early, I hope," Elizabeth had said, "because you love Raymond and desire him already. I knew it not until I came to your father's bed. And that is something you must remember. For most women —for you, I am certain—there must be love in the heart before the body will render up that pleasure. It is not so for men, although I believe their pleasure may be greater where they love."

Alys had nodded wisely at that. So much she knew from her father's behavior.

"Also," Elizabeth had continued, prudently not probing the source of Alys's knowledge, "men are quicker in coming to their pleasure than women. Those who love try to hold back, but it is not easy for them and sometimes impossible. Thus, a woman should never try to prolong her joy. Take it as soon as it comes and do what you can to bring it quickly." She smiled. "You will have no loss in that. If your husband is slow, you can be blessed twice or even thrice. That is possible for women, but not for men."

So, when Alys used the pot, she had liberally anointed herself, knowing that Raymond would look politely away while she relieved herself. The way thus eased, there had been no pain, only pleasure, and because she knew the sensation she sought, it was easier to find. Alys sighed softly. Raymond's head turned toward her at once.

"Something ails you, beloved?" he asked.

"No," Alys replied, seeking and taking his hand. "I am very happy. I know it to be untrue, for life is life and never without pain, but I feel that nothing will ever ail me again. All is so perfect, Raymond, even that we should marry in winter."

That was so curious a statement that Raymond lifted himself on an elbow, the better to see Alys's face in the light that came through the bed curtain they had forgotten to pull closed. "Why is winter better than another time to marry?" he asked.

Alys's dimples appeared, and her eyes twinkled with mischief. "Because the nights are so long," she replied.

Raymond allowed himself to fall back with a groan. "Holy Mother," he protested, "why do you always say you fear I will die in war? You will kill me long before I have a chance to don arms if you are already eager for another encounter."

"That was not what I meant at all!" Alys exclaimed. "You have already given that lesson. Quite the contrary, I only meant that we would have time to sleep and restore ourselves. But . . . are you awake enough to talk, Raymond? I know that it is wrong to trouble a man after coupling, that he then desires to sleep—"

"And how do you know this?" Raymond felt a fool for the sharpness of his tone the moment the words were out. Not only her obvious virginity but Alys's every action bespoke her innocence.

She blinked with surprise but did not take offense, merely answering, "Elizabeth warned me of it. She says that even my father, who dotes upon her, will snap if she troubles him at such a time."

"It is good advice in general," Raymond agreed, suddenly realizing that women must be different. Seemingly they desired some speech after love. It was interesting, perhaps worth remembering. "But just now," he continued, "I am awake. Speak if you wish."

"I will not keep you waking long," Alys said, "but it has come into my mind that life for us will not often be as it was in my father's keep where we had around us only trusted servants. We will move from place to place while you settle the lands firmly into your hand. The keeps will be new to our governance and, mayhap, the castle folk will not love us. Moreover, the guests we have will not often be old friends whose ways and loyalties we know."

"This is certainly true," Raymond remarked, smiling, "but it is an odd thought to have in bed on your wedding night."

"Not so." Alys shook her head. "It is because of what you said to me earlier about the king. Then I wondered to myself when it would be safe for you to tell me what I must know—"

"*Must* know?" There was a slight edge to Raymond's voice. He had not taken offense when Alys seemed to be warning him of things he knew, because he was amused and because she was so sweet and warm in his arms, but this order to disclose what might be private between the king and himself was going too far.

Briefly Alys was swept with impatience over the foolish pride the sharpness of that remark betrayed, but her body still held the languor of love and her mind the memory of Raymond's gentleness when most men would have been uncaring. Just now she was willing to turn away wrath with a soft word.

"So that I will say nothing foolish if the queen or others should ask me questions, my lord."

"Yes," Raymond said, realizing he had misunderstood, "you are right."

"And truly, it seemed to me there would not be a time we could have safe from curious ears except abed."

Raymond laughed. "Now I wonder if, instead of importuning me, you wish to avoid me. There is nothing so damping to the heat of love as talk of politics."

Alys raised herself and kissed Raymond's nose. "We could leave it for after," she suggested, "as now."

"I am not sure that is better," he said wryly. "Nonetheless, what you say is good sense, and, in truth, I do not like the situation in which I have been placed. Briefly, it is this: For many years my mother's kinsmen, the de Solers, held both power and the king's favor in Bordeaux. I do not know what happened there during the war two years ago or last year while the king lingered in Gascony, because my mother opposed my going there and my father did not wish to become involved between England and France."

"That, I think, was wise," Alys said soothingly.

"At the time it seemed so to me, also, which was why I made no argument over it. Then, soon after, as you know, I came to England and had no thought of Gascony. Now, I hear, the king shifted his favor during the war. The enemies of my kinsmen hold the reins in Bordeaux and control the council that governs the city. Henry desires me to look whether the money he sent to Bordeaux for strengthening the walls has been rightly used, but that, I am sure, is only a ruse to be sure that I will approach Peter Calhau, the new mayor. In fact, Henry said he will give me a letter to Calhau, recommending me."

"But what is the sense in approaching this Calhau, or in the king's letter, if Calhau knows you to be kinsmen to his enemies? Surely you could have no influence on him."

"I do not believe it is influence the king desires. I have a feeling that violence is brewing in Bordeaux between the Coloms—that is the party to which Calhau belongs and which the king now seems to favor—and the de Solers. Perhaps Henry believes the Coloms are actually inciting the violence, thinking while they have the power they can utterly destroy the de Solers, and the king wishes that I play the spy. He would assume I would be glad to bear tales of my kinsmen's enemies. Perhaps he only wishes the Coloms to fear his favor is shifting again so that they will be the more eager to please him."

Alys wrinkled her nose with distaste.

Raymond nodded, agreeing with her unspoken opinion, and continued. "Also joined to the latter is that my kinsman Rustengo may be given hope by having me thrust into the council. If he hopes the king's favor is swinging back toward him through dissatisfaction with the Coloms, Rustengo may be less inclined to make trouble. And this would be the time to make that trouble, with the seneschal's attention fixed on Navarre's threat in the south."

"But how long could such a delusion control Rustengo?" Alys asked.

Raymond shrugged. "Who knows what is in Henry's mind—"

"If anything is," Alys remarked caustically.

"And that may also be true—I mean that the king has *no* particular purpose. After all, it was I who asked for Blancheforte. Perhaps he did not think about my de Soler connections."

"Do not believe that for a minute," Alys snapped. "Whatever else he is, Henry is no fool in that way."

"You do him an injustice, Alys," Raymond protested. "Often Henry means no harm. It may indeed be that he only hopes my presence will keep the peace. He must know Rustengo will talk to me, and I will urge him toward restraint. Really, it can profit no one to have a war in the town. I will see what I can do, but whatever the king's desire, I cannot stay long in Bordeaux. The other estates are of greater importance."

"That is true," Alys agreed. "There is nothing at Blancheforte but the demesne farm. It will not take long to put that in order."

"Put that in order?" Raymond repeated blankly.

"You said there had been no master at Blancheforte for many years. Surely *someone* has been cheating. But that is nothing to trouble you, my lord. You will have more important matters in hand than farm accounts and the stocking of a keep and the output of women servants. I only mention it at all because I will need a week or two to learn what I need to know and set all straight."

"A week or two to reorganize an estate!" Raymond burst out laughing.

"No." Alys laughed also. "You are making jest of me. The demesne lands must be much smaller than those even of Bix."

"They must be, indeed, for I cannot remember anything about them," Raymond admitted. "All I know is that there is, and has been, no profit from them."

"Well, I am not expecting to find any profit, only to see that the keep is stocked for our residence so that we do not need to buy."

"But the town is so near. Is it worth the trouble?"

Alys was silent. Then she said slowly, "I do not know, my lord. Here we come again to the difference between you and me. I tried to warn you. To me, every tenth pence is worth trouble. It is bred in my bone to buy nothing I can harvest, breed, or make. If this will shame you among your great friends . . ." Her voice shook.

"No!" Raymond cried softly. "Love, they will envy me. It is no shame. It is only strange to me that you wish to be troubled with such things. We are rich—"

"I cannot help it," Alys sobbed. "I am not fit to be a great lady. I cannot take joy in play. I must be doing."

"Then you shall do, love. Alys, do not weep. You shall do whatever gives you joy."

CHAPTER 7

****

Nothing occurred during the week spent celebrating Raymond's and Alys's wedding to damp the pleasure everyone felt in the marriage. If William was distressed by the sight of his daughter's blood on the sheets, which were removed to be stored as evidence of Alys's virginity, the feeling was dispelled by the happiness that made her eyes sparkle and her cheeks glow. There was comfort too in the absorbed, devoted attention Raymond paid to her at all times.

And Elizabeth felt she was paid in full for every effort she had made for her stepdaughter by the rare embrace Alys bestowed on her, and the grateful thanks that made clear that Alys had taken her advice and it had been fruitful.

In the great tourney that fully occupied the next two days, no one was seriously hurt, and Alys enjoyed it as much as anyone because her husband, the groom, was not permitted to fight in it. The hunts were an unqualified success, also. Raymond fortunately killed the largest boar and the widest-antlered stag. Alys, quite properly, killed nothing, but she rode with the hunt and witnessed her husband taking his prizes.

The dinners continued excellent, although not nearly so long and elaborate as the wedding feast, and the entertainment always gave pleasure. Nor did political problems obtrude to spoil Raymond's enjoyment or worry Alys. If the king had had more to say about Gascony, he seemed to have forgotten—or someone had convinced him that a wedding celebration was not the time to speak of it. `

Even the final parting between Alys and her father was eased. Elizabeth's sons, Aubery and John, had come with their masters to the wedding and were given leave to accompany their mother and stepfather home for a few weeks. Since William had long been more of a father to them than Mauger, who had sired them, it was as if his own children would be with him.

The voyage, too, was prosperous, unusually quick and easy for a winter crossing. Alys, accustomed to boats on the river, was neither afraid nor seriously seasick, except for a few hours of queasiness the first day. Nonetheless, she was very glad when the ship docked just past dawn. They came to Blancheforte before the prime, and even in the gentle, rosy light of a new day, the outer portions of the keep were far from inviting.

It was clear at a glance that this stronghold had been long neglected. The outer walls were completely unguarded, the drawbridge down, the portcullis up. The sullen and indifferent attitude of the few men-at-arms that held the place made Raymond snarl, and when they passed through into the inner bailey, Alys's eyes opened wide with surprise at the filth and the decayed condition and utter emptiness of the outbuildings.

Alys saw Raymond's head snap toward Arnald, whose eyes were also bulging at the filth and disorder. She reached out and grasped her husband's arm. "Do not bid Arnald to cast out the old guard, my lord."

"Alys, this is no time for a woman's softness. The gates were open! They did not even challenge us! Anyone could have come in—"

"I do not plead for them, my lord. I only wish to use them. They created this filth, no doubt, so they can clean it up."

"My dear wife, I do not expect you to remain in this sty," Raymond exclaimed. "My cousin Rustengo will house us with the greatest goodwill."

"I am sure he would, Raymond, but not at all sure he *should*. What can Calhau think if you come to him from Rustengo's house demanding a place on the council as the holder of Blancheforte."

Raymond mouthed an obscenity. Alys was quite right. It was one thing for him to move into Blancheforte and demand his right as holder; it would be quite another for him to live with Rustengo and still make that claim.

"But to live here! Alys, it is not fit for you, my love."

"If the roof of the keep has not fallen in, it will soon be fit," Alys replied, her eyes gleaming with enthusiasm and determination. "Do you go into the town and do your business there. Leave me most of the troop, and do not bring guests to the keep tonight, although I think we will be ready for company tomorrow, if it is necessary."

Raymond gaped at her, but she had turned her head toward

the master-at-arms and bidden him to send men to make the keep secure and to gather together and disarm the resident men-at-arms. Before Raymond could catch his breath, two more men were sent to the stables with orders to collect what grooms and servants they could find and arrange for the comfort of the horses, reporting at once if there was not sufficient feed for that day and the next.

"Alys!" Raymond protested, after she had given the abrupt orders to secure the keep.

He did not know whether he was more shocked by the way she had assumed command or the way Arnald had snapped to attention at her word and obeyed her orders. In the next moment he called to mind that the men were accustomed to obeying her. The troop of twenty, headed by Arnald, had all come from Marlowe, hand-picked by William for skill and for willingness to live out the remainder of their lives in a foreign land—and, Raymond now suspected, for their devotion to Alys herself. All were relatively young and unmarried, except two whose wives had come along also to serve as Alys's personal maids.

Irritation flicked Raymond as he wondered whether William had arranged this to be sure Alys would have protection, even from him. Then he dismissed that unworthy thought. Naturally Alys would need men who would obey her if she were to enforce her authority on strange servants and serfs. Still, for her to order the men to secure the keep was going a little far beyond wifely duty.

Her head had turned to him when he said her name. "Yes, my lord?"

"Surely the defense of the keep is my business," he snapped.

"Defense?" Her eyes widened. "Are we in some danger here, Raymond? But we are all unprepared—"

"No, of course there is no danger, at least not of an attack on Blancheforte. But to order the men to secure the place without even a question to me is not something I like."

Astonishment showed on Alys's face. "But why? I only wanted the gates closed, lest this lazy rabble run off before I could use them. My lord, why should you be troubled with such things as sweeping the floors and carting out garbage?"

She smiled tentatively. "Indeed, what do you know of such work?"

Raymond could not help laughing, although a spot of dissatisfaction remained in him. "Nothing," he agreed, "but I feel like a fifth wheel on a cart. Perhaps you will sweep me out with the rest of the useless stuff."

Alys glanced at him under her long lashes and blushed. Her look made color rise under Raymond's dark skin also, and his eyes glittered. There had been no possibility of lovemaking on the ship, unless they chose to lie together in the open on the wet and icy deck. Raymond had become accustomed, however, to relatively long periods of celibacy. In fact, since the time he had gone to Marlowe, he had hardly touched a woman except Alys. Once he considered himself in love, he would not take a mistress, and he had little taste for casual whores. Thus, previous to their marriage, Raymond had gone longer between couplings than the days they had spent on the ship without feeling pressed for relief. Now, however, he could barely restrain himself from seizing his wife and carrying her off.

Alys was even more surprised by the urgency of her desire, because she had never felt such a thing before. Even in the period just before her marriage, when she had been so uneasy, the sensation was undefined. Now she knew what she wanted, and she had to avert her eyes, lest they devour her husband with the avidity she also felt.

"Let us go in and see how bad it is," Raymond said, his voice harsh. Inside there would be private chambers and straw pallets. If there was nothing better, that must serve. Alys would not mind. He had seen her look.

He did not wait for Alys's wordless consent, but rode forward through the bailey toward the forebuilding. Here he dismounted and helped Alys down, removing his hands hastily when she was on her feet. It was a gesture dictated by the images in his mind rather than any physical thing. He could not feel her body, nor could she feel anything beyond the pressure of his touch. Both wore several layers of heavy garments covered by fur-lined cloaks. Nonetheless, Alys drew her breath in sharply.

"The stairs are sound, at least," Raymond said, striving for a natural tone of voice.

"Good," Alys replied, "but be careful you do not trip on

some offal. It seems to me that anyone here just dropped anything unwanted whenever it was decided the thing was of no use."

Although he did not answer, Raymond took Alys's advice, feeling his way carefully in the dim light that entered through the lower door. It was as well he took care. He had to kick several unidentified masses off the stair. The heavy door into the hall stood open also. As he entered, Raymond cursed. The smell was offensive even to his hardened nose and told him what he would find. Still, the sight that met his eyes and Alys's when they had passed through the short passage that pierced the walls and the second heavy door effectively damped their sexual excitement.

There were some maids and men clustered around a choked, half-dead fire burning God-knew-what at one end of the hall, but between the entrance and the fireplace was a sea of slimy, decayed rushes from which rose an intolerable stench. Here and there was faint movement, as if some horrible vermin lived inside the putrid mass.

"There will be no place for us in this garderobe," Alys said softly to Raymond. "Go you to town, my love. It seems to me that none knows of our coming. Mayhap the king's letters were delayed. If you desire a quiet word with your kinsman Rustengo, this will be the time for it, before the other party is aware you are here."

"But how can I leave you with this burden?"

Alys smiled up at him. "It is a burden I know well how to carry and will be light for me. Will you need more than two men to assure your safety?"

"I need no men to assure my safety," Raymond replied shortly. "Do you think I am a child, incapable of defending myself?"

Calling herself ten times a fool, Alys shook her head. "Forgive me. It is this place, so abandoned and uncared for. It has made me feel that the whole town and countryside are full of disorder."

"Nonsense." Now Raymond laughed at her. Although he had reacted sharply at first, he was not ill-pleased, on second thought, that his wife cared for his safety. "Unless my kinsmen have already made more mischief than I think even they desire, Bordeaux is a well-ordered town."

"Take the men anyway," Alys pleaded. "It would look ill if you came alone. It is more fitting and adds to your consequence that you be attended."

Raymond opened his mouth to say that he need put on no airs before his mother's cousin, but it occurred to him that Alys had a good point. He was no longer "young Raymond, Jeannette's son." Now he was a substantial landholder in his own right, about to take his seat on the council of Bordeaux. It would be wrong to ride through the town with twenty men-at-arms on his tail, drawing notice to himself and displaying arrogance. However, it would be equally wrong to arrive unattended and unannounced, as if he came for help and instruction.

"Very well," he replied, "but are you sure that you do not wish me to stay?"

"You will be sorely in my way." Alys touched his hand. "I will not be able to think of cleaning—or of anything but . . ." She sighed, then laughed. "Do go away, Raymond."

He laughed also. "I will take John and Wulf with me. They speak so little French, and that so foully, that they would be of no use here, and they cannot say anything amiss in Rustengo's kitchen quarters or guardroom. Shall I bring back some decent servants, my love?"

"No, not yet. There is only rough work to be done, but if your kinsman offers you dinner, stay with him."

"And leave you to starve?"

"I will not starve," Alys assured him, "but there will be nothing fit for you, my lord. I wish to serve you as you should be served. It would shame me if the first dinner I put before you as your wife were coarse and ill-cooked."

Raymond looked around him. "If you could serve any cooked meal at all, I would think it a miracle, but I will stay with Rustengo, my heart, if it will make you easier."

"But you will come home before dark?"

Again Raymond looked at the bleak hall, at the ragged, slovenly servants who had by now got to their feet and were staring toward the gentlefolk but not moving. The truth was that Raymond hated the place. It made his skin crawl; he was dying to get away, but his conscience smote him. Alys looked so small and frail.

"If you are afraid," he said, "I will not go at all."

Fear for herself had been the last thing in Alys's mind, but this time she had sense enough not to say she wanted her husband safe behind strong walls after dark. "I am not afraid," she replied, "but to be alone in so strange a place after dark . . ."

"I will not fail you," Raymond assured her, still guilty but relieved. "Only you must promise to have one or two men-at-arms with you at all times. I do not think any of these poor creatures would offer you hurt, but still do not put temptation in their way."

"No, my lord, I will not."

Raymond turned toward her as if to kiss her, but thought better of it. Instead, he smiled and moved back into the passage, shouting down for some men to come up. It was soothing that they obeyed him as swiftly as they had obeyed Alys, although he was not specifically aware of what had pleased him. Actually, he associated the feeling with leaving Blancheforte. Even if it were cleaned, he wondered whether they could ever live in the place. When Hugo and Peter had come into the hall, Raymond went down.

Alys watched him go, waiting until the sound of his steps died away. Then she swung back toward the cluster of men and women and gestured them toward her. "What is the meaning of this disgrace?" she called.

The group, which had been advancing slowly, hesitated. A few heads turned nervously as if seeking an escape route, but Alys was sure there was no other exit from the hall, except the steps that led to the floor above and the floor below, and those were only traps.

"Come you hither, and quickly," she commanded, "or my men will fetch you with bared swords."

Several of the women began to weep, and all fell to their knees as soon as they were within normal speaking distance, babbling of Master Ernaldus, the bailiff. Alys silenced them with a single furious word.

"All of you deserve to be well whipped," she snapped, "and cast out masterless to die in the cold. I do not care that no orders were given. It is your duty to keep all clean and fresh." Actually what the servants had said was that the bailiff had forbidden them to clean, but Alys simply could not believe such a wild unlikelihood. She assumed that the difference in

dialect between her Anglo-French and this southern version of
the language had caused her to misunderstand, or simply that
the servants were lying. But such a silly lie seemed unlikely,
too. She decided to ignore the problem for the moment. It was
more important to get the hall clean than to punish the pathetic
scarecrows trembling before her.

"There is one path for you to escape your just deserts," she
continued. "If this hall is swept, washed, and garnished forth
as fitting a nobleman's place before the sun drops in the west, I
may reconsider your punishment. Now get out of that muck.
You are filthy enough without further smearing yourselves."

They rose at command, and were quieter now. Although
some still wept, most seemed quite confused, addled with fear
and weakness. Alys had to ask where the rush-rakes were, and
when they were found, she ordered that a path be cleared for
her to walk to the fireplace and to the stairs to the floor above.
This done, she lifted her skirts so that the hem would not be
sullied by the mess on either side of the cleared path, and
passed to the next floor. At the stairs she paused to say sharply
that she expected to see a good clearance made by the men,
water to be brought up, and the women to have scrubbed clean
the area around the hearth before she came down again.

Above, the situation was considerably better, in that the area
was simply dusty and unused. Alys sent Hugo to fetch Arnald,
bidding him to bring up a pair of stools, if he could find usable
ones. When the master-at-arms arrived, Alys began to laugh at
his appalled expression.

"We are landed in a pretty mess, are we not?" she said.

"I have never seen the like," Arnald replied, sitting down at
her invitation and looking around curiously. "And I will say
this, my lady. Had we not been so many and armed, I think
the men-at-arms would have done us a mischief. They are ugly
and sullen, and one loudmouth threatened that Master Ernaldus
would see us turned out."

"Master Ernaldus, eh? That is the second time I have heard
his name, and I dislike it already. We will come to him
betimes. Now all I desire is to make a clearance here. Ugly and
sullen, are they? Then you think it unsafe to use them to clear
the bailey? How many are there?"

"Twelve. It is safe if they be watched by enough of my men

to prevent a surprise," Arnald said after a moment's consideration.

"And what of the grooms and other servants?" Alys asked.

"They are like these in the hall. Never have I seen such miserable creatures; not even those at Ilmer, where I went once with your father, were so bad."

That remark lent conviction to what Alys had been thinking. The people of Ilmer had been long misused by Lady Elizabeth's first husband and by that man's father. But this keep had no direct master in constant need of money so that he starved the people to wring a few more pence from the land. The king was not that kind of master; what was more, Alys knew he had not a penny's profit out of Blancheforte. Thus it must be the bailiff whose neglect or dishonesty made the men-at-arms insolent and the servants quivering lumps of fear. Alys vowed she would make certain that bailiff made no more profit, but first things came first.

"Leave Hugo in charge of about eight men, and let him see that those men-at-arms do the filthiest work. Meanwhile, do you and the remaining nine men go out on the demesne and bring in what men and women can be snatched. They will be unwilling, but pay them no mind."

She thought for a moment, then went on. "Do as little hurt as you can. Take no women heavy with child or with small babes, and leave at least one woman in each house to care for whatever children there be. Of the men, choose out the strongest. I would bid you promise them no harm will befall them, but they would not believe you. Say what you think best to them or nothing at all."

"How many will you need?"

"Twenty of each, if so many can be gleaned. But do not spend more than an hour or two searching. Oh, yes, let your men who watch the keep guard take the carters' whips and lay on freely for any slowness in labor or sullenness in looks."

"That will be a pleasure, my lady."

"Do you know whether there are any stores at all in the keep?" Alys asked next. "Is there a cookhouse and cooks?"

"A cookhouse, yes. I saw the fires. Whether the creatures around them are cooks, I cannot say. As to the stores, I will set one of the men to looking. I could do with eight to bring in the people, and, if you give me leave, I would rather that two men stayed by you. It was Lord Raymond's order, and if you should need one to run a message, I would not like you to be alone, my lady."

"If it was my lord's order, it must be done. Now, as soon as you return with the serfs, lock up the keep men-at-arms if there is a prison room on the lower floor. If none is there, you will have to chain them, or perhaps there is a storage room you could bar in some way. I would say put them to the sword, except that my lord may wish to question them."

"Most wise, my lady." Arnald was relieved. He did not think the labor that could be extracted from the rebellious men-at-arms was worth the danger they represented.

"Oh, yes. Send Edith and Bertha up, and the carters may begin to unload my bed and the chairs and cushions for my bedchamber. Nothing else at this time. I will send word when I desire the other things to be unloaded."

The maids arrived with eyes as big as saucers. Having been born and brought up in Marlowe, neither had ever seen such dirt and disorder. Both were older than Alys and could remember that when Alys's mother was alive, Marlowe did not run with the snap and crackle it had under Alys's hand, but it had been nothing like Blancheforte.

"How do they do below?" Alys asked.

"They have the windows open and are throwing out the foul rushes. Also, the place near the fire is scrubbed clean. I took the liberty of sending two men for clean water. The whole floor will need to be washed."

Bertha answered in fair French, since her mistress had spoken that language to her. Both women spoke far better French than their husbands, a natural result of being indoor servants with much greater contact with the upper classes. Before Alys could reply, Aelfric, one of the older, steadier men-at-arms, who was Edith's husband, called out for permission to enter. Alys gestured to him, but held up a hand to prevent him from speaking while she finished her business with Bertha.

"Did you have any sour looks or grumbling?" Alys asked the maid.

"No, my lady." Bertha seemed surprised. "I do not think those poor, starved creatures could give a sour look to a worm."

"Good. If you are not afraid and can bear the stink down there, go down and make sure the work is well done, and send up two women to clear this room. Edith will tell them what to do."

Privately Alys felt like laughing at Bertha's expression, in which pride and eagerness mingled with distaste. The men and women who had elected to follow Alys to France had done so out of ambition or, for the youngest of the men-at-arms, a spirit of adventure. For the two women, it meant a chance to be personal maids—which might be a curse or a blessing, depending on the character of one's mistress. But Bertha and Edith knew Alys. She might slap them when she was out of temper, but she was fair, would protect them and their children from everyone else with vigor, and was generous, within reason, with gifts of clothing and trinkets. Moreover, the work was much lighter and more enjoyable. No more scrubbing or carrying. Their only duties were to care for Alys's clothes, jewelry, and person, all of which was a pleasure.

Now it seemed there would be even more advancement. In this keep, at least, Bertha and Edith would be the chief women, directing the other servants. Alys was both pleased and amused by her maids' reactions, complimenting herself that she had chosen well among the many who wished to accompany her. Bertha seemed to draw herself up taller as she went out to the stairs, and Edith looked around at the rooms with a suddenly possessive eye. Then she hurried out after Bertha, and Alys could hear her calling down the stairs that the women should bring up kindling and firewood so that their lady's chamber should be warm.

Alys did not wait, but followed Edith out. "Then I will leave to you the care of these chambers, and whatever else can be accomplished to make this place livable," she said.

She turned to Aelfric and had to bite her lips at the smug expression of pride he was wearing. Edith and Aelfric had not been married long, and he was patting himself on the back for his choice. A woman who had her lady's ear could help her man advance, also.

"Well, is there food?" Alys asked him.

"Yes, my lady, and good quality, also. There is a fresh-killed sheep hanging and salt pork and beef and fish, turnips in plenty, and barley and corn."

"Then why do the servants look like bags of bones?" Alys wondered.

"The men-at-arms are well fed, and the cooks and their helpers, also," Aelfric remarked.

"Oh? So. They will soon be leaner," Alys promised. "Very well, let us go down and set the cooks to work."

A glance around the great hall showed that progress was being made. The mess was nearly cleared off the floor, and the women were cleaning away the more liquid and sticky filth with brushes and sand. Although she said nothing, Alys gave Bertha an approving nod. Apparently she had set some of the men to fetching water and emptying the dirty buckets in regular relays now that few of the rushes remained. The floor could be left bare to dry overnight, Alys thought, and the next day she would discover where rushes could be obtained to cover it. Fortunately no more than sweeping was necessary in the women's quarters and the main bedchamber, and there were rugs in the baggage she could use to cover the bedchamber and anteroom floors.

The musing had brought her to the cookhouses, and here things were not nearly as horrible as in the remainder of the keep. Although the place would take no prizes for cleanliness or neatness, there was no question that the kitchens and bakehouse could function. Alys ordered that potage and stew for a hundred be made at once and said what should go into the dishes. She was surprised to see the cooks' terror mount as she recounted the ingredients.

"Do you understand me?" she asked at last, remembering that Arnald had commented on the different accent with which the men-at-arms spoke.

"Yes, yes," the cook she was addressing quavered, "but . . ."

"But what?" Alys asked, keeping her tone even. She thought that any sharpness or impatience would only reduce the man to silence, and she wanted to know what was frightening him.

"To feed so many so richly . . . there will not be enough . . ." His voice trembled into silence.

"My man says there is a whole sheep and barrels of salt meats. How can there not be enough for soup and stew?"

"For—for the soldiers. It is for the soldiers."

"It is for whom *I* say," Alys snapped. "But you can tell me who has ordered the stocking of the keep in the past."

"Master Ernaldus, the bailiff."

Master Ernaldus again, Alys thought. She should have known better than to ask, for the fear was plain in the cook's face and voice. Alys made no comment, however, merely adjuring the man to get on with his work. She noted also that the cook's helpers, the only well-fed servants in the place, were all young and handsome, the boys as pretty as the girls. Obviously they were the favorites of the men-at-arms. Alys glanced over them without favor.

"Use only the best and cleanest," she ordered. "You will all taste what is set before me and my men-at-arms, and if even one of us should suffer the smallest disorder of stomach or bowels, I will have each of you whipped bloody front and back —those I do not have the heads off. Is that understood?"

That time her voice cracked like a whip, and a dead silence fell where there had been the soft sibilance of whispers. Obviously it would be necessary to have a completely new staff in the kitchen, but there should be no difficulty in that. For this one day her threat and seeing their protectors cast into the lowest level of the donjon should be enough to control them.

There was so much to do that it seemed mere minutes instead of hours before Arnald was back with his gleaning of serfs. These poor creatures looked little better than the servants in the keep. Alys burned with rage. From what she had seen, although it was winter, the land looked as if it should be as rich and fertile as Marlowe, yet the pinch of hunger showed in every man's and woman's face. There were bad years when crops failed and hunger came even to Marlowe, but the dull resignation of these people implied years of semistarvation. Their apathy was so deep that they had hardly responded to the fear of being seized.

Arnald confirmed Alys's immediate deduction. The serfs had tried to hide, but when caught had neither struggled nor tried to escape, he told her. Nor, she saw, did they make any attempt to escape now. They stood like worn-out oxen, waiting to be driven by the pain of the goad until they dropped dead. It was the grossest stupidity, Alys thought furiously, to misuse the serfs to this degree. It would take three of them to do one healthy man's work, and, at that, they would have to be

watched every minute, having become so stupid out of fear
and hunger that even if they had wanted to complete a task,
they would not be able to think how to do it.

With the substantial increase of the work force, the cleaning
process accelerated. At an hour past noon, the hall was clean,
if damp. Huge fires burned in each of the two hearths, and
trestle tables and benches had been found and set up. This last
order caused puzzled looks among the servants, and the setting
of thick slices of large rounds of bread at each place by the
baker and his assistants caused one wretch to fall on her knees
before Alys and beg for a small piece of the heel of the bread.
The others watched hopefully.

"You may have it," Alys said, "but we will all sit down to
dinner in a few minutes. My men are just bringing in those
who are working outside. Aye, yes, here is the cook."

All stood still, gaping, even when Alys waved them toward
the tables, and she told them again to sit so that the cooks'
helpers, staggering under the weight of caldrons of stew, could
serve without hindrance. One ladleful of stew was dumped on
each round of bread. It seemed very little to Alys, who was
accustomed to the well-fed servants of Marlowe putting away
soup and roast and greens as well as stew at every meal—and a
good deal more on feast days. However, she knew that if these
starved beasts ate too much, they would only be made sick.
The thick potage, rich with salt pork and barley, would be
served to each late in the afternoon. That should carry them
through the night and, hopefully, bring them back voluntarily
to work the next day.

Nonetheless, there were endless problems still to be solved:
how to find clothing for those who were to remain in the keep,
what they were to sleep on—Alys had ordered the pallets they
had been using burned—whether there was grain enough for
bread for the next morning, a million details. Alys was hardly
aware that several more hours had passed and was just
directing that straw be brought from the stables for the servants
to sleep in, when Raymond walked in on her.

"My God, what have you done?" he exclaimed.

"Is something wrong?" Alys asked.

Raymond laughed. "I almost rode out again, believing
myself to have come to the wrong place. Had I not heard our
men's execrable French, I would have done so."

Alys smiled at the compliment, but there was a sharpness in her husband's voice that warned all was not well. Since she could not believe he could be displeased to find his residence considerably improved, she assumed that he had discovered more trouble in the town.

"Come above where we can sit in comfort," she suggested, immediately abandoning all other problems.

He glanced around at the scurrying servants and nodded. In the main chamber of the women's quarters, there was equally frenetic activity. Raymond frowned, but his expression cleared when Alys led him into their own chamber and closed the door. Here was peace. A lively fire burned in the hearth, which was flanked by two cushioned chairs. There was a table with a candelabrum ready to be lit and a flask of wine with two cups. Alys took his cloak and gestured toward a chair.

"Will you drink, my lord?" she asked.

"No. I have had enough, although not so much as Rustengo would have poured down my throat if he could. You were right about bringing attendants, but it would not have helped if I had the whole troop. My mother's cousin still thinks me a child to be told to go hither and yon and repeat speeches like a witless puppet."

"Then he will be the more surprised," Alys said calmly.

"But not the more pleased. Matters are worse than I had thought, and possibly worse than Henry believed. I fear Rustengo intends to call in men from La Réole and Langdon, which the king specially forbade, and wrest back the government of Bordeaux while de Molis is engaged in the south."

"Does Rustengo think he can fight the seneschal?"

"I doubt he believes it would go so far. For one thing, if Molis and Navarre come to blows, Molis may not be strong enough to attack Bordeaux; if he should be beaten and his army destroyed, that would end the threat. And even if Molis should come in strength, I believe Rustengo thinks he could make easy terms, retiring from office himself, but having a kinsman empowered. He did not say it in plain words, but I think he was offering me that place."

"You did not agree, did you?" Alys asked anxiously.

"What would you have me do? It is your keep, after all," Raymond replied sharply.

Alys blinked. "It is *ours* while we both live," she said

softly, "mine to keep in order; yours to defend. I would have you do what is best, but only you can know that, my lord."

Raymond sighed. "Forgive me, my love. I am sorely out of temper. Now I will take that wine you offered, but water it well." As she rose to serve him, he continued. "I did not deny him outright, but he understood and, I think, regretted saying so much to me. Before I left, he spoke strongly of the ties of blood and what kinsmen owe each other."

Alys stiffened. "He will not seek to do you harm to ensure your silence?"

"Oh, no." Raymond dismissed that with a casual wave and a smile. "What troubles me is that word of this may come to Molis, who might divide his force. Between thee and me, my love, I do not care who rules Bordeaux, but if Navarre overruns the south, the claiming of your dower lands may not be so easy. So far Navarre and Molis are in the west and away from our estates, and I do not fear my uncle Gaston—he will not oppose our taking possession, although he may ask terms I will not like—but if Molis is utterly beaten, Navarre will turn to fight Béarn, and we may be swallowed on the way."

He sipped from the cup Alys handed him and stretched his long legs, obviously soothed and more at ease although he was talking of trouble. Alys held her breath. From the light in her husband's eyes, she knew he was considering going south to join the fighting. Then he sighed and shrugged.

"I could not gather enough men to help Molis without taking possession of the lands, and that would take so long that whatever is now happening will by then be already decided. No, I like it not, but for our safety, as well as to satisfy the king's will, I must bide here and do what I can to divert Rustengo from this lunacy."

Alys was so relieved that color flooded up into her face, which had been pale with fright, and she jumped up and kissed Raymond, murmuring that he was very wise. Seeing at once how her mind worked, Raymond laughed, but he held her close with an arm around her waist and put down his cup.

"The devil fly away with Rustengo and the whole city of Bordeaux," he said, "and with Amou and Ibos, also. I should have taken you direct to Tour Dur, where such stupidities would not interfere between us."

"They cannot interfere," Alys responded, allowing him to pull her against him as he rose.

In the chamber behind, the bed was ready. It had not been warmed, but Alys did not worry about that. They would warm it quickly enough themselves.

CHAPTER 8

****

Making love, though, was not the end of Alys's day. She left Raymond sleeping and came down to see that the serfs got their potage, and that those who had been dragged in were sent home. By then, Raymond was up and out on the walls of Blancheforte with Arnald, examining the condition of the defenses. Between his raving over the neglect and more talk about the problems in Bordeaux, Alys never got to tell him about her conclusions concerning Master Ernaldus, the bailiff. In the morning, Raymond went off early to present himself and his letter from the king to Peter Calhau.

Alys, of course, broke her fast with him, but she felt incomplete; she had not heard Mass. Of course, there had been no priest aboard the ship, but that situation had been so different that she had not noticed one more break in her normal routine. Here in Bordeaux it was suddenly apparent that something was missing. In Marlowe, the priest had come every morning to say Mass in the keep chapel. True, Alys did not really listen, her mind roving over the various duties of the day or other matters sadly unrelated to God. Nonetheless, she was certain that the holy words had some beneficent effect —like a magic charm to ward off ill—and today she felt the lack. Moreover, there was a chapel, and, she reminded herself, she was rich now, rich enough to support a chaplain. The chapel was all empty, except for the carvings of saints and the crucifix, but it could be refurnished—all except for the priest.

Alys told Bertha to summon the eldest of the maidservants, and when the woman came, barely able to walk for trembling, she said, "There is nothing to fear. What is your name?"

"Mary, madame," the woman whispered.

"Very well, Mary. Do you know who is the priest who said Mass before the keep was emptied?"

"It was Father Paul, but that was long ago. I think he is dead, madame. He was old."

"Does no one come now? What of Sunday? Who listens to confession and gives the viaticum to the dying?"

"No one comes." Tears rose in Mary's eyes. "Those who were strong enough walked to Saint Remy's, when the soldiers permitted it."

That was what Alys wanted to know: Saint Remy's was the church to which Blancheforte belonged. "Comfort yourself," she said to the maid. "There will soon be a priest here, I hope." She waved the maid away and sent for Arnald, thinking that it would be another busy day. When he had sketched a bow before her, she asked, "Did the serfs return?"

"Most of them did."

"Were all fed?"

Arnald grinned and nodded. The food had served its purpose, drawing those hungry beggars back despite their fear of the keep. "Yes. Bread and cheese this morning, but there will not be enough for many more days, three or four at most."

"That will be enough, I hope. I had no time to discuss the matter of buying supplies with Lord Raymond, as he had other troubles, but I hope he will give me leave to order what we need tomorrow. Now for today, there are three things that must be done. We must have rushes for the floors. See if you can find out whether Blancheforte cuts its own supply and where. If it has its own, send out a party at once to obtain them. Second, I must ride to Bordeaux to see if I can get a priest to come and say Mass. Third, I must ride over the demesne. From what I have heard, the bailiff has been wringing this place dry and keeping all for himself."

"It must be so," Arnald agreed. "There is land enough and good land, too, to stock the keep and feed the people, yet the storerooms, except for two, are not only empty, but fallen in. Thus, it is not one year's bad crops that have emptied them, but many years of neglect."

"I must see the land for myself, then, to judge what the yield should be." Alys's eyes gleamed. "I will have back from that bailiff every groat I can squeeze out of him."

"I will order the horses, my lady," Arnald said, and went to do so.

He felt a strong sense of satisfaction. Like most men-at-arms, he had never hesitated to take a woman or a chicken or pig from the serfs on occasion, but he was horrified at the condition of the people on Blancheforte's lands. It gave his profession a bad name. If the bailiff had allowed such license, he must be punished. Nor did he doubt Alys would do what she had said. Arnald knew Sir William to be a kind and just man, yet he could scythe like the grim reaper when he felt he had been cheated, and Alys was her father's daughter.

When they left, with four men beside himself to ensure Alys's safety, she gave instructions to Hugo that he was not to admit anyone—except Raymond, of course—to Blancheforte while she was gone.

"I do not care if it be the kings of England and France together," Alys said. "It will be on my head. You do not need to give your name, nor should you say more than you were bidden to hold the keep closed until your master or mistress return. Not even the party with the rushes is to be admitted. They must wait by the gates until I or Lord Raymond return."

The excursion was a great success. The priest at Saint Remy welcomed Alys almost as reverently as he would have welcomed a holy visitation after she informed him she was the new holder of Blancheforte. He had a long list of grievances: tithes not paid, personal abuse when he wished to visit the people in the keep, mistreatment of those people when they wished to come to church, and other insults. He had complained to his superiors, but nothing was done. Here an expression of anxiety crossed his face. Alys could read the thought: She was very young; perhaps the bailiff would have more power or influence than she. Alys made no promises, for she recognized that there might be more behind Master Ernaldus than she knew; however, he could no longer control Blancheforte, and she wanted a priest. This, she was promised, would be arranged.

The inspection of the demesne was equally satisfactory. Alys looked over the fields and saw how the stubble lay, which fields were fallow, and the color of the earth. The land, she judged, was rich as Marlowe's, and it had not been mistreated. Doubtless the bailiff had seen many, many years of profit to be had from it. There were vineyards, too, but Alys frowned on those; she knew nothing about grapes. Any new bailiff they appointed would need to be experienced in the culture of the vines. Finally, most interesting of all was the cattle on the common. It was a large herd, all fat, the cows with heavy udders. Obviously these animals did not belong to the ragged, starving serfs. Possibly the bailiff considered them his, but they were on her land. Alys sent a man to fetch the herdsman to her. Finding that it was as she suspected, her smile broadened. She left two men-at-arms to make sure no one tried to remove the herd and to see that they were driven up to the keep at the end of the day.

They rode back to Blancheforte then, Alys casting nervous glances at the sun and realizing she had been out longer than she had expected. She knew that what she had been doing was necessary, but she hoped that Raymond had not yet returned. Alys's limited experience told her that men liked their women to be at hand. Her father had always expected her to be ready to talk or listen or serve him first; other duties were to be fitted in as best she could. Therefore, it was with relief that she noticed carts piled high with rushes before the gate.

The waiting carts meant that Raymond was not yet at home, so Alys did not increase the pace, discussing with Arnald where it would be most convenient to pen the cattle. It was not until they were quite close that the sound of angry voices came to her. Alys had a momentary fear that Hugo had misunderstood her and would not permit her husband to enter his own keep, but in the next moment she saw that the horse on which the shouting man was mounted was not Gros Choc, Raymond's destrier.

It was a very handsome animal, however, and the cloak and hat were also fine. Alys beckoned to Arnald and touched her mare with her heels, thinking up soothing speeches. If this were Raymond's kinsman, she would need to spread a thick grease of sweet words to soothe this additional hurt. As they cantered up, Alys heard Hugo call down, "Here is my mistress now."

"So," the man said, turning on her furiously, "you gave the orders to close this keep. By what right?"

"It is mine," Alys answered calmly.

As she replied, she heard the soft slither of Arnald's sword as it came out of its sheath. There were four armed men with the enraged stranger and their hands were on their hilts, but Alys was not alarmed. Two of her men-at-arms were behind the carts of rushes; Peter and Aelfric were coming forward. With Arnald, the five men could certainly protect her for the few minutes it would take the rest of the men in the keep to rush out. It was more important to Alys that the man could not be Rustengo de Soler. Rustengo would not have needed to ask her right to close the gates of Blancheforte.

"Yours! Who are you?" the man shouted.

"I am Alys d'Aix, née Marlowe, and Blancheforte is part of my dower lands," she replied, keeping her voice from betraying irritation. If this man were some person of importance, she did not wish to cast oil on the flames of his wrath. "And who are you, sir, that you question my right to close my own gates?"

There was a brief silence while the man gaped and choked. Finally he said, "Forgive me, my lady. I could not believe it could be you. I had just come to look over the place to see . . . But you cannot be staying here. I did not expect you so soon. I have a house all furnished, most commodious and comfortable, for you in Bordeaux."

"Oh? That is most kind." Alys's voice still had no expression. "But you have not yet told me your name."

"I am so overset to see you. I do not know whether I am on my head or my heels. Do pardon me. I am your bailiff, Master Ernaldus."

"So. No wonder you were surprised that the gates were closed." That remark came out too sharply. Alys bit her lip and choked back her rage. She wanted the fly safely inside her web. "Hugo," she called, "you may open for us."

The unusually elegant appearance of the bailiff had reminded Alys of the priest's worried expression. She did not think Ernaldus could have extracted enough from Blancheforte alone to make him as rich as the horse and clothing hinted; therefore, it was possible that he had a powerful protector or protectors. The idea did not diminish Alys's determination to remove Blancheforte from his care and recover the rents he had swallowed; it merely convinced her to be cautious about how she did it.

In the meantime, groans and screeches marked the lifting of the gate bars. The gates themselves ground open and the mounted party rode in, followed by the carts. On the inner wall the portcullis was already grinding upward. Alys did her best to keep her face a mask while she stole quick glances at the bailiff. He was frowning slightly as they passed through the outer section, clearly too deep in thought to notice any change. Once in the inner bailey, however, he was shocked to see men and women cleaning and repairing the outbuildings, burning rubbish, and washing clothing and pallet covers. They had been talking and laughing, but it cut off—even motion froze —when they saw Ernaldus.

"What?" he gasped. "Who are these people?"

"My serfs," Alys replied coolly, and then added lightly, "I have a bone to pick with you, Master Ernaldus—which is not surprising since all you have left here is a bone."

As if he had not heard her, and indeed his surprise was so great that her answer might not have sunk into him, he asked, "Where are the guardsmen who were here?"

"In the prison cell of the donjon. Oh, dear, I forgot all about them. Did you remember them, Arnald?"

The master-at-arms's sword was back in its sheath. The bailiff's attendants would know from what Alys had said that to start a fight was suicide. They were four against they-knew-not-how-many. The portcullis rumbled down again, and the bailiff looked over his shoulder and swallowed convulsively. He had realized he was in a trap.

"Yes, I remembered them, my lady," Arnald replied. "They had a bucket of the filth the cook had put aside for the servants before we came yesterday, and some water."

"Good. I would not want them to die before Lord Raymond can put them to the question." Alys turned her head in time to catch the bailiff's expression, and she smiled. "Will you not come in, Master Ernaldus?" she asked sweetly. "Perhaps you would dine with us? My husband will soon be home, I believe."

"Come in? Dine?" The bailiff's eyes were protruding with a mixture of terror and horror.

Alys was enjoying herself. She might not be able to recover in gold or goods everything the bailiff had stolen, but she was already being repaid in part. She fixed the man with her wide, innocent eyes.

"Our meal will be necessarily simple," she apologized, "since Blancheforte is mysteriously without the stores it should hold, but I am sure you will understand and make allowances."

Without giving him time to reply, she turned to Arnald. "Take Master Ernaldus's men and see that they are properly entertained," she said. "Do them no hurt," she added in English, delighted to have a private language, "but keep them out of the hall."

On the words, Arnald let out a piercing whistle, and men-at-arms began to converge on the party from all sides. Ernaldus's men hesitated only a moment before they came off their horses. The odds, with the portcullis closed, were too great, even for mounted men. The bailiff sat in his saddle, dumbfound.

"Surely," Alys said sweetly, "you will not reject my hospitality, poor as it must be. There is much we must discuss, and I know my lord and husband has a great, even an urgent, desire to meet you."

It was not a statement designed to calm a man with a guilty conscience. Aelfric and Peter had dismounted during Alys's ingenuous speech. She slid down into Aelfric's arms, but Peter had to help the bailiff from his saddle. Master Ernaldus looked around desperately, but his men were halfway down the bailey, accompanied by Alys's men-at-arms. The trap had closed, and Ernaldus knew it. He had never dreamed that the holders of Blancheforte would arrive so soon. He had doubted that they would come at all, although he had taken the precaution of ordering that the place be made as filthy as possible so that they would not stay an hour if they should come. The technique had worked for years—royal inspectors taking one look and marking the place as too much trouble for too little worth.

Ernaldus could not imagine why the practice had failed this time. The keep was useless. The demesne was only enough to support Blancheforte itself when fully manned—and why man a keep that could not really be defended? Although he had made a foolish mistake by coming in, Ernaldus was not really stupid. He recognized the amusement beneath Alys's innocent words and manner and knew she was toying with him as a cat toys with a bird or mouse. He was so frightened that the massive cleanup outside, the carts of rushes, made no impression on him.

Thus, he was stunned to find all perfectly clean, smelling of nothing worse than the smoke that escaped from the fireplaces

and the resinous torches used for light at night. Master
Ernaldus had been unable to conceive why Alys should drag
him into the noisome interior of the keep unless she intended to
torture or kill him. The ordinary appearance of the place
abolished the specter of violence, and the bailiff began to
recover his self-possession and ability to think.

Bertha came running forward to take her mistress's cloak,
and Alys smiled at her with real approval, realizing that further
advances in restoring Blancheforte to a decent residence had
been made. The first bundles of rushes had been used to cover
the floor near the hearth, and the place was set with high-
backed chairs, handsomely cushioned, for Raymond and
herself. Bertha took Ernaldus's cloak, also, and tripped away
to lay both on a chest. Alys walked to the center of the room
and clapped her hands. Every servant stopped as if frozen.

"Let the tables be set for dinner," she said loudly and
clearly. "We will eat when the lord returns." Then she gestured
Ernaldus forward toward the hearth. "Bertha," she called,
"bring a stool for our guest."

The maid hesitated, then went to do as she was bidden,
though she had been surprised. Normally, a guest would be
given one of the chairs, and when Raymond came in, it would
be Alys who moved to a stool. However, it was hers to obey,
not to question her mistress's manners. When she came back
with the stool, Alys asked what had been found to embellish
their dinner.

"There was little enough, my lady," Bertha replied disdainfully, "a few scrawny chickens and a young pig. But there was
a comb of honey, so there will be a sweet. For the rest—stew
and potage, as yesterday."

Alys nodded dismissal and turned on the bailiff. "Why are
we so bare, Master Ernaldus?" she asked. Her voice had lost
its sweetness, and her eyes were hard and cold as sapphires. "I
have ridden the lands, and the fields are thick-stubbled from a
rich harvest. Where is the produce of those fields? I saw, too,
that my kine are fat, but surely they have not eaten all the corn.
And the serfs are starving, so it is not they who have kept more
than their share." Alys switched to English and snapped,
"Watch him," to Aelfric and Peter who, faithful to instruction,
had followed close on Alys's heels and now stood near her
chair.

Their hands went to their swords, and their eyes went to the
bailiff, who emitted a squawk of terror, expecting the men to
attack him, since he had no idea what the two foreign words
Alys had spoken meant.

"The produce—the wine, the corn, the roots, the fruit
—where is it?" Alys hissed, wishing to drive him to speech
while he was off balance with fear.

"S-s-sold. M-m-madame, it was not reasonable to keep—to
keep—food when there was no one to eat it."

"Ah!" Alys smiled. "I am so glad to know it was not stolen
by dishonest persons, which could have happened when the
keep was left with open gates. How came it about, Master
Ernaldus, that you retained guards so careless that my husband
and I and all our troop marched in without even a challenge
yesterday? Is this a way to watch over King Henry's possessions?"

"I—I did not know it was within my power to dismiss
them."

It was the only thing the bailiff could say, but Alys saw from
his expression that it was not true, and also that he had
recovered from the shock of fear and had realized as he said
the words that they were a perfect defense.

"They grew insolent," Ernaldus's voice was stronger and
surer. "I wrote to complain to the master of the king's
wardrobe, but I received no answer. I did not dare drive them
out without permission. And—"

"That is of little account," Alys interrupted hastily, seeing
the haven to which Ernaldus was heading and determined to
catch him before he reached it. "But there has been no yield
from Blancheforte marked in the king's accounts for many
years. It was understood that the yield supported the keep and
its people. The people are starving, the keep is near in ruins,
the money is not in the king's hands. Where is it, Master
Ernaldus?"

Cut off from the false explanation he had hoped to make,
Ernaldus glared at Alys with hatred—a single flash before he
dropped his eyes. To say he had sent the money to the king,
which he had intended, was no longer possible, and it
infuriated him to realize that Alys was utterly indifferent to his
expression. In fact, she hardly noticed; she was taken up with a
rapid calculation of the value of his horse, clothing, and

jewelry. It should be enough, she thought, even if one subtracted the value of what she must give him to wear and a lame ancient beast from the keep stable, to pay for stocking the keep for the winter and perhaps even for a few extra bushels of corn to feed the scarecrows on the demesne.

What Alys would have liked to do—what she would have done at once had she been still at Marlowe—was to instruct Arnald to take Ernaldus someplace where his screams would not disturb her and squeeze the truth out of him. But this was not possible for two reasons: Most important was that Raymond might not approve her taking an action so far from her normal sphere of activity. Not that Alys considered the correction of a dishonest bailiff outside her ordinary duties, but she was not blind or deaf to the fact that Raymond was too aware the land was hers, that she had the right—if she were mad enough to insist on it—to sit on the council of Bordeaux instead of him. He was going to be raw enough, having to explain to Calhau that he was his wife's deputy.

Then there was the question of Ernaldus's connections. Taking him apart piece by piece might annoy someone who, politically speaking, should not be annoyed. Until she could write to Uncle Richard and get the king's order to dismember Ernaldus, she would have to content herself with gentler methods. But she would get the order. King Henry did not like to be cheated, either. Alys smiled.

The smile happened to coincide with Ernaldus's reply to her previous question. Backed into a corner but not yet defeated, the bailiff had said, with an assumption of injured dignity, that the money was in his care. With untrustworthy men-at-arms in Blancheforte, it was obviously impossible to leave anything there, and, not having had an answer from the master of the wardrobe, he knew not else what to do with it.

"Then there can be no problem," Alys responded, assuming a neutral tone of voice again, as if she were satisfied. "You can return this year's yield to me, either in gold or in kind"—and she proceeded to enumerate what she calculated the keep's share of the demesne yield to be in terms of bushels of wheat, barley, and rye.

The bailiff gaped at her. "It is not so much, not by half," he protested.

Alys's eyes grew colder. She began to recite the measure of

land and the bushels per hectare. Master Ernaldus stammered objections, naming the laziness of the serfs and their dishonesty. Alys shook her head and reminded him that she had only just come in from the fields, where she had seen the thickness of the stubble and the thinness of the serfs. Then Alys smiled again and nodded.

"Of course," she said, "I realize part must be used to feed that large herd of kine, which you were doubtless afraid to slaughter, but that then brings us to the question of cheeses. Do I not remember that Bordeaux is famous for its cheese flavored with wine?"

"The kine do not belong to Blancheforte!" Ernaldus shrieked, bounding to his feet. Instantly, Peter was in front of him, his drawn sword pressed into the bailiff's breast. Ernaldus sank back on his stool, pallid again. "It does not matter," he got out, his voice choked with fury and terror. "Four are mine, and two calves."

"Very well. I suppose the herdsman will know them. He will bring them to you when you wish. I must warn you that your term as bailiff here is ended. I am not satisfied either with the condition of the keep or of the serfs on the land. It is true that they are only cattle also, but ill-cared-for cattle give poor service."

"None of it is my fault," Ernaldus whined. "I could not watch night and day. The men-at-arms took what they wished. I could not prevent it."

"I do not see that," Alys said coldly. "If *I* had been bailiff here, I would have found a way to deal with only twelve men-at-arms so that, even if I could not dismiss them, they would have done their duty and given no serious cause for complaint."

"I do not doubt it," Ernaldus snarled.

Alys smiled. "Neither do I. Then there is only the need to decide whether you wish to return the yield in gold or in kind."

Again the bailiff tensed as if to rise, but Peter, who had stepped back, raised his sword again. "Whichever you prefer," Ernaldus got out, "but you cannot expect me to do it today. I must return home and make arrangements."

"Assuredly," Alys said calmly. "You may go whenever you like. I will only ask you to leave your clothing and rings and pins and your horse and harness as a pledge of goodwill."

"Will you send me out naked?" he cried.

"Naturally not," Alys rejoined. "That would neither become you nor please me. I will furnish clothing and a horse." And when the bailiff was on his way out, she flung a final stone. "I am grieved that the inefficiency of the king's officials in the wardrobe may have caused this trouble. I will write soon to my uncle-by-marriage, the earl of Cornwall. When I do, I will beg him to bring this matter of Blancheforte's yield to the king's own notice. Thus you will doubtless obtain your just deserts swiftly and surely."

She sent Aelfric with him to bid Arnald to escort him and his men off the grounds and be sure they did not return. Then she plopped back down on her chair and breathed a sigh of relief at having got him out before Raymond came in. This made her begin to worry because her husband was late, but before she could imagine anything very bad, word came that he had entered the outer wall.

His mood was far better than it had been the previous day, and he apologized for his lateness. Alys bade Peter summon the castle folk in to eat and took Raymond to a side chamber to divest him of his cloak and armor and give him a comfortable gown which was laid ready. Peter Calhau, he told her, had greeted him far more warmly than he had expected, and seemed eager to hear every tidbit of news and gossip from the court of England, even those things that did not pertain to Bordeaux.

Alys raised her brows. "I wonder what this pleasure in your company portends," she remarked. "Is it that he is cleverer than Rustengo—no, I do not mean cleverer because, of course, Rustengo had reason to be sure of you and Calhau knew he must either charm you or declare himself in opposition to your claim."

Laughter glinted in Raymond's eyes as he led Alys back to the hall and seated her at the table. "It is you who are clever, my heart. I could never have managed to insinuate so adroitly that I was allowing myself to be flattered enough to lose sight of the true situation."

"No! I never meant any such thing," Alys protested. "You talk as if I think you a fool. I do not! I meant only what I said."

Raymond laughed outright at her vehemence. "Very well, I will believe you because it is better for my pride. But I cannot answer you. I do not yet know what Calhau's manner portends. I doubt if he himself knows. In any case, nothing of real note was said. We talked of the problems of Bordeaux—in the most general terms with no mention of the threat of unrest that may be caused by my kinsmen. It was pleasant but not important—the opening steps of the dance of power. Now, what have you been about?"

As she told him, Raymond's eyes opened wider and wider. To Alys's relief, he seemed more surprised than angry. "Was that estimate of the yield true," he asked, "or a fancy to jolt the man?"

"It was true. I may be off a few shillings' worth, but not much more."

"Then why did you not keep him here once you had him?" he asked.

"I suppose I should have," Alys admitted, "but I was afraid to go too far. He had four well-armed men with him, and his clothes and horse and trappings were so rich, it seemed to me he must have some powerful connection. What I did can be defended, but I was afraid to hold him against his will."

What Alys did not say was that she had also been afraid that Raymond, thinking the little yield of Blancheforte insignificant, might have undone everything if Ernaldus had still been there when he returned. She did not believe Raymond would have retained the man as bailiff; he was too angry about the careless way the keep had been neglected. However, he might have waved away the loss in money and produce, considering it a cheap price to pay to be rid of the bailiff without trouble.

"I do not see that holding him could make him more bitter against us," Raymond remarked, but he was smiling. "After all, I could always say that it was my silly young wife who was at fault," he teased.

"Yes, indeed," Alys agreed, but perfectly seriously. "What a fool I am. I forget no one here knows me and that you would be easily believed if you called me a fool."

"Not if they saw this keep before and after you took it in hand or heard your disquisition on the yield of produce per hectare," he chuckled. "Now I must do my share. I must find a new bailiff and, even more important, I must hire men-at-arms. They must be trained and ready by the time we leave." He paused and pursed his lips. "I think we will leave the hanging of those dogs in the prison until after the new men come. I wish it to be clear in their minds that we will not suffer laxness."

"No, nor abuse of the serfs in the keep or on the demesne," Alys said. "These people are so stupid with fear and hunger that each provides less than a third the labor one might expect."

Raymond made an irritated sound. "You have answered one question before I asked it. I was just about to tell you to have Arnald look about on the land for men suitable for training, but we have no time to waste on those so out of condition as you say these people are. I will need to hire men-at-arms. It is most awkward."

"Why?" Alys asked, surprised. "Are there no white shields in Bordeaux?"

"Too few," Raymond replied, his face growing more troubled. "Not too few for my purposes, but too few for a town this size, and from what little I have seen, I would not care to hire those men who remain free. I fear that means both Soler and Colom have been hiring men. A pox on whatever fancy made King Henry change the line of power in this town."

"But if they have hired men already, will they not come to blows very soon?" Alys asked, laying down the chicken leg she had just picked up.

"I do not know. Perhaps there is some particular cause—at least, it may be that Calhau believes that." Raymond paused and frowned. "The king may believe it, too, and that was why he was speaking of my being a bridge between my kinsmen and the Coloms. But, Alys, I am much afraid that the particular cause is only an excuse. To me, what Rustengo said implied that he does intend to seize power again."

"But there is no sense in seizing power by pure force. It will only bring the king down upon them with an excuse to fine and imprison and, in the end, remove from their hands all chance of regaining their power."

"The king is far away," Raymond reminded her. "This is not England, where troops can be levied in a few weeks. And, as I said yesterday, if Molis abandons the south to bring order to Bordeaux . . . I do not know whether it is better to try to ease matters here or leave Rustengo and Calhau to their own devices and go south at once to take hold of Amou."

"To defend it against the king of Navarre with twenty men?" Alys asked, with an effort keeping her voice from trembling.

"Oh, I would have help. Gaston would be glad to send troops to my assistance. Whether I could rid myself of them and him once the threat of Theobold of Navarre was gone is a different matter. No, I suppose I had best try to keep Rustengo quiet. But you are not eating, my love."

"I had got so interested," Alys said.

She was learning that it was more important to hide her fear from Raymond than it had been to hide it from her father. Sir William had been amused or annoyed, as his mood determined, when Alys showed anxiety for his safety. The effect on Raymond seemed to be different—and dangerous. Alys had perceived that if she betrayed fear, her husband felt it a reflection on his ability, and it seemed to drive him toward danger in an effort to prove he was capable of surmounting it. Trying to avoid showing what she felt about the idea of defending Amou, Alys moved the discussion back to their own concerns and stumbled on another of Raymond's sensibilities.

"You will know best about those matters," she said, "but to come back to the management of Blancheforte, where will we find men or a bailiff? But wait, I have a thought. Do you not have a bailiff for the farms near Marsan? And did you not tell me that those lay near to Benquel?"

"Yes, to both," Raymond replied, "but I do not see what that has to do with Blancheforte."

"Your bailiff from the farms can come here. I assume he is more honest than that toad Ernaldus. And Sir Oliver's man from Benquel can take the farms under his care. You said, I think, that he was a good man." She paused, seeing Raymond's frown. "Have I said something foolish, my lord?"

"You make easy disposition of my farms into the hands of your vassal," Raymond said.

At which point, Alys's nervousness overset her temper, and she snapped, "It is you who ever make the mark between yours and mine. To me, the lands are *ours*. When I took you as husband, you became one flesh with me in my heart and mind. If I am not so to you, I am sorry for it."

Raymond, who had not been angry at all, but merely carelessly voicing a general irritation with the added complexities of the situation generated by the bailiff's dishonesty, was startled. He placed a hand over Alys's and laughed.

"I had forgot how easily you burst into flame. You have been so meek and mild since our wedding, I thought marriage had tamed you. Indeed, you are flesh of my flesh, my love —and it is a clever thought to take the bailiff from the farms, too. In fact, *I* have an idea to add to yours. If peace is made with the vicomte de Marsan, Sir Oliver will be able to reduce the number of men-at-arms in his keep. I can take those men into my service, thus doing him a favor—for no man desires loose men-at-arms wandering his lands, nor the expense of keeping more men than he needs."

Alys leaned over and kissed her husband's cheek. "You have a very sweet temper, my lord," she murmured.

"If so, I have not shown it these last two days," Raymond admitted.

"You have had much to try your patience. I am at fault for provoking you on little things when I know you to be troubled."

"Then we are quits," Raymond said, smiling, "for surely I know better than to bring trouble made by outsiders into my home."

"Then you have been taught wrong, my husband," Alys replied, smiling also, "for it is the first purpose of a wife to be shouted at so that a man may face the world with the bile and spleen cleansed from his blood." Her eyes twinkled. "Your sweet nature has defeated me. I offered you good cause to lose your temper, and you coddled me instead."

Raymond burst out laughing. "But it is much pleasanter to coddle you than shout at you—and it soothes me just as well." Then he sobered and pushed away the sweet, which he had barely touched. "Is there something with which I can write? I would like to put this idea of *ours* to the test, and for that I must tell the vicomte de Marsan and Sir Oliver that I am here. I wrote to both from England, but there was no time to have an answer. We must hear what Marsan thinks before we can go further."

CHAPTER 9

****

The next few days were busy but peaceful. Either Rustengo's plans were not yet ripe or Raymond's arrival and reaction had made him wish to think them over. Master Ernaldus ransomed his horse and clothing for the agreed-on sum. Alys put a new herdsman in charge of the cattle—the one who had watched over the animals was too well-fed-looking for her taste; she had noted that only Ernaldus's favorites were better than walking skeletons. The kitchen staff was banished and replaced. A young priest presented himself with a letter from the priest of Saint Remy's church. Alys liked his looks and the way he blushed when she called him Father; she invited him to stay permanently as chaplain in Blancheforte if that would suit his superiors.

Word had spread across the demesne of the miracle that had taken place in the keep. The gates of Blancheforte were thronged each dawn with men and women begging for work in exchange for the good meals available. There was no grumbling here about the exactions of the lord who took serfs from their own fields to work on the master's tasks. Alys wondered briefly if a course of starvation would have done the people of Marlowe some good by teaching them how well off they were. However, she also saw that it took ten men of Blancheforte to do the work of two of Marlowe. This was not only a result of deliberate inefficiency—naturally, the first reaction to gentleness was an attempt to take advantage, which Alys cured with selected whippings and expulsions. The straining of men and women weakened by too-long semistarvation to do a normal task showed.

Nonetheless, the work of repairing pens and sheds and stables proceeded rapidly. Clearing of the gate towers was begun, and Raymond bent his attention to the walls and the instruments of war. This occasioned a small problem when Peter Calhau arrived unexpectedly. The very last thing Raymond wanted Calhau to hear was that he was strengthening the defenses of Blancheforte. Nothing, Raymond was sure, would convince the man that it was a measure taken only in case there might be trouble. Raymond was sure that Calhau would leap to the conclusion that Raymond knew of and was ready to participate in plans for the forceful return to power of de Soler.

Fortunately Alys was in the bailey, and she came running to the gate. She so bemused Peter Calhau with bitter complaints against Master Ernaldus, dragging him into the inner bailey at once to show him the decayed condition of the outbuildings, that he did not notice the unusual activity on the outer wall. Then she asked a host of eager questions about where to purchase cloth and supplies, and began to blush and beg pardon for importuning a guest. By that time her youth and beauty had had its effect and she was able to lead Calhau into the hall, seat him in state, and press wine and cakes on him —until Raymond got the work covered and got down from the walls himself.

Most probably Calhau had come to determine just what Alys's welcoming had caused him to overlook, but he could not suspect her of deception. The very modesty with which she removed herself as soon as her husband arrived to entertain his guest showed her young and artless. However, Raymond was able to convince the mayor that he did not intend to fill Blancheforte with armed men. This was partly owing to Alys's "innocent" chatter, because she had confided how much she needed of various stores, which confirmed Raymond's assertions. Also Raymond disclosed his plan of taking men from Benquel, whom Calhau knew would be neutral. In the end they parted with considerably more sincere amity than at their previous meeting.

Alys was the greatest gainer. She had realized that Ernaldus might have been telling the truth when he first said the herd of cattle did not belong to Blancheforte. When she pressed him, it would be just like him to conceal the name of the owner so that she would get in trouble for appropriating the animals. She had told Calhau of this, and he had promised to investigate the matter.

Beyond that, from Calhau's immediate eagerness to prosecute the bailiff, he had betrayed the fact that Ernaldus was probably an adherent of the Soler party. Most innocently Alys had refused that offer. Master Ernaldus, she said sweetly, had been sufficiently punished by being deprived of his place. Moreover, she remarked with spurious timidity, since he claimed to have been appointed by the king's master of the wardrobe, it was not her place to punish him. She intended, she added, to write to the earl of Cornwall an account of what Blancheforte should have yielded over the years it was in Master Ernaldus's hands. Uncle Richard would take the account to the king. If the king wished to pursue the matter, he could then do so.

When Calhau was gone, Alys and Raymond compared accounts of the visit. Raymond decided he had better visit Rustengo to tell him of Calhau's coming to Blancheforte. Not to do so would arouse grave suspicion in Rustengo if he heard of it from another source. Incidentally, Raymond said, he would complain of Ernaldus so that if Rustengo wanted to deal with the matter himself, he could. It might add to the Soler party's problems if Alys complained to the king, so he would be grateful to Raymond for asking him first.

However, in the late afternoon those plans had to be altered. A letter arrived from the vicomte de Marsan acknowledging and enthusiastically accepting Raymond's proposals. He suggested that Raymond come to Marsan as soon as possible, bringing with him Sir Oliver, so that an agreement as to the terms of enfeoffment could be reached.

"I think I should go tomorrow," Raymond said. "I do not think Bordeaux will erupt in the next few days, and telling Rustengo about Calhau can wait. My relationship with Marsan is important—Rustengo will understand that. It is possible that I will need to convince Oliver that this is the best way, and I do not wish to give Marsan too much time to think. In the first flush of pleasure at getting back what he considers his right, he is likely to be generous, which will make it possible for me to agree to his terms without argument. That will make for a good feeling between us. If Marsan has time to consider, he may begin to think of what he has lost over the years and wish to recoup."

"But we cannot leave all undone here," Alys protested. "There are not even sufficient provisions for the servants or for what men we must leave to guard our furnishings. I intended to

ride to Bordeaux with you tomorrow to buy what is necessary."

Raymond frowned. "They must make do. This business
with Marsan is more important than supplies and servants."

Alys, of course, said no more. Raymond went back to his
work on the walls, and Alys went upstairs to tell Edith and
Bertha to pack clothing for the trip. She noticed that as soon as
the maids left them, the women of the castle began to look
uncertain and draw together when they had finished the
immediate task on which they had been employed. None had
the sense or self-confidence to begin something new without
specific orders. Alys could see that she would be back where
she started, although less filth would have a chance to
accumulate, if she left Blancheforte at this time.

Thus, when she and Raymond sat down together at dinnertime, she reintroduced the subject, asking whether Raymond
believed Sir Oliver would resent him.

"It is a possibility, but I think a distant one," Raymond
answered. "It is true most vassals would rather their lords were
at a distance and not looking over their shoulders, but this is a
different case. Here Sir Oliver has long needed an overlord's
protection and has been unable to obtain it. He is threatened
and harassed by Marsan's men. I have high hopes that he will
be delighted to see me and some expectation that he will be
eager to come to terms with Marsan. My only doubt is that in
so long a conflict, sometimes personal hatred is aroused. I
must say that Marsan's letter does not sound as if that is the
case, but he is the stronger."

"I was not thinking of Sir Oliver's hatred for Marsan, but
only whether *you* can trust him, and whether, for example, it
would be safe to go to Benquel with only a few men."

"As to that, yes, I am certain it would be safe. If he hates the
vicomte, Oliver might try to convince me not to do homage to
him, but he would be mad to offer us violence. He is only a
simple knight of neither great family nor large influence."

"You are *sure*, Raymond?" Alys asked with considerable
intensity.

"My love, what do you fear?" he asked, putting an arm
around her. "Indeed, I know Sir Oliver—not very well,
perhaps, but I have guested at Benquel. He knew I was tied to
Marsan, and he did complain to me of the constant trouble he

had from that quarter, but he did *me* no hurt nor offered any insult."

Alys sighed. "Well, if you are sure it is safe to go there, my lord, then I think I will not go with you."

Raymond had opened his mouth to reason further when the sense of what Alys had said struck him. He opened his mouth again and, still wordless, closed it once more. Meanwhile, Alys was hastily explaining her purpose and assuring Raymond that she would miss him every moment, and the only reason she could endure parting with him was that she knew, from the speed with which the courier had returned, that it was no long journey to Benquel. By this time Raymond had sorted out his emotions and started to laugh.

"Alys, I do not know whether I should strangle you or beat you," he choked. "You have managed to insult me at least three separate ways in one sentence, and I am sure if I were to think about it, I would find a few more doubts about my honor, ability, and good sense."

Astonishment opened Alys's blue eyes wide. "My dear lord, if I have truly done such a thing, you should beat me, but you will have to stop laughing to do so. It is very hard to beat someone while you are laughing. And strangulation seems to me to be overly severe a punishment for an error. What did I say amiss?"

"First, you implied that I was either so much a fool or so uncaring as to take my wife into a situation of danger without adequate precaution. Next, you implied that you could preserve me from that danger rather than I you. Last, you seem to believe I intend to do homage to Marsan when it is you who must do it."

Alys began to laugh also, and hung her head in false shame. "Alas," she chuckled, "I am guilty—but only of the first crime. As to the second, far from thinking I could be of any assistance, I only wished to share your fate. And as to the third, it is no crime for a woman to trust her husband." She looked up, serious now, and asked, "Is there not some way for you to do my homage by proxy? If my confirmation is needed, I can give it when we pass Marsan to go to Amou. You did tell me that we would do so, did you not? We could stop for one night at Benquel so that I may meet Sir Oliver, and I may say whatever must be said to Marsan. Will that not do?"

Raymond had sobered and considered her suggestion seriously. "Yes." He nodded emphatically after another moment's thought. "And if you stay, we need not chance—however slim the possibility—that Rustengo's suspicion of Calhau's visit, which I am sure will come to his ears, will cause some unwanted action on his part. You can go to him tomorrow in my stead. Tell him where I have gone and why—there is no harm in Rustengo knowing the whole matter of Marsan and Benquel, and he will feel pleased that I confide my business to him. As to Calhau's visit, speak the truth, that I wanted him to know of it and to know that Calhau has still made no definite proposals nor uttered threats. No more than smooth talk passed between us. About the cattle and the bailiff, you may say what you like."

So it was decided, and Raymond departed at first light, hoping that the roads would be good enough for him to reach Benquel by dusk. He took only five men, with Hugo to lead them. To Alys's protests he replied with laughter, pointing out that no less than an army could help him if Sir Oliver meant treachery; and if he took more than five to guard against thieves and rogues, he might make trouble by implying distrust.

I must stop acting like a hen with one chick, Alys told herself severely as she set the tasks for the day. *I was not forever telling Papa to be careful. Raymond is a man grown, and in his own territory, too.* These strictures helped a little, but Alys knew she would need an absorbing concern to stop herself from fretting. Thus, as soon as she had set all to work, she changed to her richest riding dress, ordered Aelfric to keep Blancheforte closed against all intruders as Hugo had done the previous day, and rode to Bordeaux accompanied by Arnald and five men-at-arms.

They had no trouble finding their way, for Raymond's instructions had been explicit. Rustengo was waiting for her, having been prepared by a note from Raymond the day before, and Alys's meeting with him was pleasanter by far than Raymond's had been. Alys had no more to do than act the obedient wife, and she was accustomed to a stream of well-meant advice delivered in a voice of authority. So, naturally, this did not raise Alys's hackles as it had raised

Raymond's—although she had even less intention of taking any advice that did not suit her purposes.

Alys had one real surprise, however. Had she not known Rustengo was only a cousin to Raymond and not close, she would have guessed they were father and son. There was a great likeness in looks and voice between them. Alys wondered naughtily whether Raymond's mama (whom she had reason enough to think ill of from Raymond's tales) had known Rustengo too well before Raymond's conception. It was, of course, impossible—and even if it were not, it did not matter to Alys.

All that mattered to her was that she had achieved her ends. First she explained Raymond's mission and described Calhau's visit, seeing at once that Raymond had judged his kinsman correctly. From that vantage point, she managed to insinuate into Rustengo's mind the notion that Raymond's new need to be treated with deference was owing to his desire to impress her. It was a perfectly harmless bit of conceit, even endearing in a young man, that would keep Rustengo polite and encourage greater harmony between the kinsmen. Additionally, Alys suggested that Raymond's conversations with her implied that all his natural instincts were in support of the Soler party. Though Alys did not say it, Rustengo saw for himself that to *urge* Raymond to support his natural friends implied a lack of faith. Rustengo began to look thoughtful.

Alys chattered on about "Uncle Richard," correcting herself to say "the earl of Cornwall" with a deliberate blush that drew questions. These permitted her to explain—with suitable hesitations and further blushes—her relationship with Richard of Cornwall in such a way that she would not seem to be boasting. To do that, Alys knew, might throw doubt on the validity of the claim of long and enduring friendship. And yes, of course she knew the king very well, Alys replied to another question—her complexion now normal despite the lie.

"Although, perhaps, I should not say that," she went on, "for he is a most difficult man to know. I do not mean he is haughty or unapproachable, but he does not show what is in his mind, except, perhaps, to Eleanor—oh, heaven, I mean Queen Eleanor. Please forgive my unruly tongue. She is Raymond's aunt, you know—how funny that is, for she is only the elder by a month and they were playmates as children. He always speaks of her as Eleanor, and I have caught it."

"The queen has the king's ear, then?" Rustengo asked.

"Yes, and his heart, too," Alys replied ingenuously, wondering whether Rustengo's question was a trap. Eleanor had been in Bordeaux with Henry, and Rustengo must have seen the king's devotion—unless he was already out of favor and not invited. *Tread carefully,* Alys warned herself. "Sometimes King Henry is constrained to do harsh things," she continued, "but the queen wins him softly back to the best path. The thing is, like all kings—and even more so in Henry's case because he came to be king so young, only twelve—he cannot bear to be forced. To do violence against his will . . ." Alys shook her head. "He will never forgive nor forget, not even for the queen's sake. And"—she widened her eyes—"you will not betray me if I speak what is in my mind, even if it is not all . . . all flattering to the king?"

"You may be sure I will keep your confidence."

"Well, then, King Henry has such pride that he cannot bear to admit he was wrong in anything. He may know it in his heart, and then he will set about to amend the wrong, but it must come about in such a way that the world will not see he has deliberately changed his path to mend a mistake."

Alys told several anecdotes to drive home those two points: that Henry did not forget or forgive violence against him and that he resorted to devious methods to restore the correct balance when he had made a mistake. None of the stories had anything to do with Bordeaux, of course, nor even with a situation similar to that in Bordeaux—to be too pertinent, Alys thought, would be dangerous—but the stories were illustrative of Henry's set of mind, and they were quite true. Alys had a huge fund of stories about the king gleaned from his brother's discussions with her father.

Then Alys set about making sure Rustengo believed her ignorant of his plans by relating everything she had said to Master Ernaldus. "The trouble he gave me," she exclaimed. "The filth! The stench! And the people so starved that they had not the strength to clean properly. And they all say this Master Ernaldus ordered that Blancheforte be dirty and ruinous. Perhaps they were lying out of fear, but he certainly gave them no order to clean. Oh, and do forgive me, I had almost forgot to thank you for giving my husband dinner that day. It was so kind of you and a great favor to us, for there was nothing fit for him to eat."

"You should have come, also," Rustengo said, smiling with real affection and thinking that if he had seen young Raymond preening before this pretty bird of a wife, he would not have made the mistake of talking to him as if he were still a boy. "You should have come to stay with me. You would have been most welcome."

"So Raymond said. It was my fault we did not come. I was afraid to impose unannounced guests and twenty-one men also. Then, too, Blancheforte is part of my dower. It would be wrong if it were a drain on my husband's purse instead of a gain to him. And even beyond that, I do not like to be cheated. When Raymond writes to the king and queen, I will ask him to complain for me of Master Ernaldus's doing and tell them of their bailiff's dishonesty." Alys allowed an expression of spite to show on her face. "I would not take the chance of avenging myself on a servant of the king because King Henry might take offense at such presumption. But I will have my revenge nonetheless. I know King Henry. He will see that Master Ernaldus suffers for cheating him."

So Raymond writes to the king, Rustengo thought, *and sits on the council.* And, knowing Raymond, Rustengo was sure he had told the king he was kinsman to the de Solers. Henry, then, must know Raymond was unlikely to damage his own interests by telling tales of those bound to him in blood. Insensibly, Rustengo's mind took the path Alys had laid out for it to the conclusion that Henry now must regard his alliance with the Coloms as a mistake and, by giving Raymond a place in the council of Bordeaux, might be seeking a way to back out of that arrangement and to renewing his connection with the de Solers.

Rustengo had already begun to reconsider inciting massive violence in the city. Raymond had virtually refused to raise the questions that would set the spark to that action, and Rustengo did not have another suitable pawn available. Now he began to think that it might be worth a few months or a year—provided Calhau and his party made no aggressive moves against him —to work more subtly and see whether the king would place the power back in his hands where it belonged.

Not that he would sit with folded hands, of course. There was much that could be done to undermine the Coloms and make the guildsmen of the town dissatisfied with their rule. But there was no need for violence—not yet, even though the seneschal's preoccupation with Navarre made the opportunity riper, in that he could not react fully. Still, in another sense the threat from Navarre increased the danger. Violence now might be called treason in time of war. Molis would not hold the reins long. He was already bitter over the burden. A better opportunity might occur when a new man was appointed, especially if he was a fool. In any case Navarre and Béarn would not give up easily; they would cause plenty of trouble at other times.

Violence, Rustengo thought, was a weapon that could be used at any time. Moreover, it would look more natural, less suspicious, if more time had elapsed between the violence and the change of administration. It would give a chance for dissatisfaction, real and incited, to grow. Indeed, Rustengo thought, Raymond's girl-wife had a point—even though she probably did not know she had made it. Rustengo was remembering events ten years past of which he had heard from the previous seneschal, Turbeville. Henry did have a long and vindictive memory.

Rustengo had meanwhile been replying with half a mind to Alys's remarks about Master Ernaldus. Finally, when she changed to the topic of supplies for Blancheforte, Rustengo sent out with her the clerk who purchased his own supplies. After she was gone, however, the thought of Ernaldus returned to him. He did not like the man—a baseborn bastard of a cousin who had been irresponsible enough to acknowledge the child, have him raised in the household, and then not provide for him in any way. Still, Ernaldus was a connection, even though the cousin was dead. Rustengo sighed and sent a servant to tell the bailiff to come to the house as soon as possible.

Not surprisingly, Ernaldus was not at home when Rustengo's message was delivered; however, he arrived at Rustengo's house soon after dinner. With characteristic lack of tact —men of power do not need to be tactful to inferiors they do not like—Rustengo told Ernaldus that it would be wise for him to leave—not only to leave Bordeaux, but to leave Gascony.

"You will do better," Rustengo said, "where the hand of the king of England cannot reach. I think it is too late for restitution."

It had occurred to Rustengo, once he considered the problem, that this would be an excellent opportunity to rid the family altogether of a member who could only do them harm. He certainly did not want attention drawn to the bailiff's dishonesty by an attempt to buy peace. Furthermore, such an attempt might frighten away Ernaldus's other patrons so that, as head of the family, Rustengo would be saddled with the responsibility of a pauper Ernaldus.

"If you try to restore what you have stolen from the king," Rustengo continued, "others will begin to look to their accounts, and no matter how honest those are, they will be dissatisfied and believe you have robbed them."

"Lady Alys," Ernaldus hissed, so enraged that he did not even attempt to deny the theft of which he was accused.

"Yes. I have tried to reason with her," Rustengo averred most untruthfully, "but it was impossible. Moreover, she had already spoken to Calhau. You would have had to leave Bordeaux in any case. Calhau will leap at the chance to do the Solers harm by exposing you. My advice is to change all the goods and property you can for gold, take that, and go into France or Navarre. With the money in hand, you will have no trouble in establishing yourself. A change of name might help also, and an honorable reason for leaving home."

"But I did not intend to cheat them," Ernaldus groaned, hoping to find a way out in spite of what Rustengo said. "I had a fine house all readied for them in the town. I had the money ready. I told her—"

"She took it amiss that the serfs were starved," Rustengo said dryly, interrupting an outpouring he did not believe and in which he was not at all interested.

For a moment surprise blotted out Ernaldus's rage and fear. "Why?" he protested. "What does it matter? There are always more of those animals than anyone needs. Feed them, and they grow more numerous and starve in the end anyway."

"Women take notions." Rustengo was still not interested.

"But surely Lord Raymond is not such a fool," Ernaldus cried. "If I explained the matter to him—"

"In the first place, he is not in Blancheforte," Rustengo

interrupted again. "He has gone to Marsan for one or two nights. In the second place, I would not count on his support. He and Lady Alys are new-wed, and she is both rich and *very* beautiful. In the third place, it is, as I have already told you, too late. Lady Alys has already spoken to Calhau." Rustengo knew Alys had asked the mayor not to prosecute, but he had grown enamored of the idea of being rid of Ernaldus, who was boring him. "Thus, even if you could convince Lord Raymond to prevent his wife from complaining to the king or her powerful relatives, which I do not think you can do, Calhau will still certainly expose your so-called dishonesty to ingratiate himself with King Henry."

Ernaldus moaned. Rustengo looked at him without sympathy. "It would be wise for you to go and go quickly," Rustengo said, "before others hear of this matter and begin to pluck you."

It did not end there, of course. It took some while to convince Ernaldus that the protection of the family had been withdrawn, that if Calhau prosecuted him, he would not be defended to save face but thrown to the wolves. That was not the way Rustengo put it, naturally, but that was the way Ernaldus thought of it. First desperation took hold of him and he wept and pleaded, but this only made Rustengo angry.

"You are scarcely going naked into the world," he growled. "I am not totally a fool. Take your gold and find yourself a widow with a good business. If you do not go—and at that, swiftly—I will see that you trouble me no more."

Realizing that Rustengo was adamant and that further pleas or arguments would make his case worse, Ernaldus fled. At first he was so terrified at the thought of being cut loose that he could do no more than shiver. He guessed now that many he had robbed—less obviously and for smaller amounts than he had robbed Blancheforte, but robbed nonetheless—had held their tongues because he was a de Soler. But if he had to leave Gascony, that name would no longer protect him. What would he do? How would he live? He had money and goods, but not enough to support him for the rest of his life in the style to which he had been bred.

Ernaldus thought of Rustengo's advice and nearly threw up. That advice might serve for other men, but not for him. He would never have a wife and family and relations-by-marriage.

He had to stay in Gascony where his blood kin were, or he would be naked in the world. He thought of his half-brothers and shuddered. They would not stand up for him against Rustengo because they were cowards, he told himself. He would not admit that he had long ago worn out his welcome in their hearts by his behavior and demands. Always feeling "cheated" by his birth, Ernaldus had spent his life trying "to get back his own," but all he won were enemies.

He knew, however, that Rustengo's last threat was not idle. If he did not leave Bordeaux, an "accident" would befall him. But to be alone in the world? He shivered with terror, his heart pounded, and his head whirled. Then, suddenly, the world steadied. His sister—half-sister—had married and left Gascony. He ran to the room in which he did business and scrabbled among the papers. Isabel was older than he, had married and left Gascony many years before, but she had never forgotten her family, particularly the young bastard brother for whom she felt sorry.

Over the years small gifts and letters of news had come from Isabel. The news was of no interest and the gifts were of little value, but Ernaldus had always thanked his sister and replied to her letters. It cost him nothing, his replies being sent with those of his half-brothers. It came back to him that she lived at Les Baux in Provence and that she had frequently, especially in these latter years, written of her desire to see her brothers again. Or was his own desire for a safe haven deceiving him?

He found her letters and scanned the latest. No, there it was —twice, in fact. Ernaldus sighed with relief. He remembered that his sister was now a widow living with an only son, the youngest of her children. Ah, here it was. The boy (man?) would not listen to his mother—naturally not, Ernaldus thought, no sensible man would listen to a woman. Then rage flicked him; Rustengo had listened to a woman. Ernaldus made an effort to concentrate on the letter.

Isabel desired her brother's presence, it seemed, not only because she was growing older and wished to see those dear to her in her youth before she died, but because she felt her son needed the counsel of an older man. Well, well. For a while Ernaldus forgot his rage and fear. To be a trusted counselor instead of a servant barely tolerated as a gentleman would be a pleasant change. Isabel knew her half-brother was a bastard, of course, but not that his father—the old fool!—had left him nothing and that his half-brothers had virtually cast him out.

Ernaldus sat back and breathed softly. He was remembering more and more from Isabel's letters and combining it with general knowledge. Les Baux was not far from Arles, and he knew of a ship that was leaving for Arles in two days' time. Free of panic now that he had a haven and a way to reach it, Ernaldus began to plan what to do and how to salvage most of his possessions. Then he set out with great energy to put the plans into effect.

Returning home in a foul temper, for much of the worth of anything is lost in a quick, forced sale, Ernaldus opened his strongbox to throw in the money he had collected. As he withdrew his hand, it was scratched by a sharp edge. Ernaldus cursed and put his finger to his mouth. Then an even blacker frown crossed his face, and he scrabbled in the box. Coins did not have sharp edges. Almost immediately he came up with the offender—a large iron key.

For a moment when he saw the heavy metal object which had hurt him, Ernaldus's rage rose in him until he almost screamed aloud and beat the walls with his hands. He had recognized the key at once; it opened the small secret door meant to be an escape route for those in Blancheforte in the days when the keep was in use. Then, abruptly, he became still. He was to be made an outcast and driven away, was he? For what—a few paltry *louis d'or*? That was not a crime deserving of exile! He stared at the key. It could not open the way to restoring his old life, but it could open a path for revenge—a sweet, sweet revenge.

Unlike Master Ernaldus, Alys had enjoyed a delightful day. Her visit to Rustengo had been an outstanding success. She felt she had smoothed the path for a better relationship between Raymond and his kinsman and, perhaps, even planted a seed that might make him think twice about using force to oppose the Coloms. Moreover, she was certain he did not suspect that that had been her intention. In addition, between the use of Calhau's name and the company of Rustengo's steward, she had arranged to stock Blancheforte for a very reasonable sum.

Matters within the keep were also going very well. The servants no longer trembled and shrank away quite so much each time her eyes fell on them nor came near to fainting if summoned to speak to her. The young priest was even a greater prize than Alys had thought. Father François could not only read and write devotional books but keep accounts, and, for all his youth, seemed well able to judge between a malingerer's whining and a person with a real problem. Between Father François and the bailiff Raymond would bring, there seemed a good chance that Blancheforte's problems would be solved.

Alys went to bed in the best of good humors, pleasantly tired from her active day—and could not sleep! She had been aware of missing Raymond at dinnertime; Father François was too shy when she invited him to join her at table to carry on an easy conversation, but this was different. The bed was cold and empty. Alys felt so lonely for Raymond's warmth and strong arms that she could have wept. She told herself severely not to be a fool. After all, she had slept alone all of her life, except for the past few weeks. It was impossible to become so dependent on her husband's company in just a few weeks.

Raymond's day was not yet over at the time Alys had retired to bed, but it had been equally pleasant. The weather was cold but dry, and the roads better than he had expected. He had arrived in Sir Oliver's keep before dusk and had been welcomed most warmly. Beyond that, he found that most of his work had been done for him. Eager to be free of the constant annoyance of petty depredations, Sir Oliver had sent a messenger to the vicomte de Marsan as soon as he had Raymond's letter. Respectfully, Sir Oliver announced that he had a new overlord who was already beholden to Marsan.

Sir Oliver's letter had brought a most courteous reply, mentioning Raymond's proposals and graciously commending Sir Oliver's past behavior in the face of provocation. That provocation would cease instantly, the vicomte wrote, and he considered with pleasure the opportunity to be on friendly terms in the future. Thus, when Raymond arrived in Benquel, a man was sent out immediately to Marsan. Within the hour he was back, bearing an invitation to ride to Marsan at the first opportunity. So it was that Raymond and Sir Oliver sat up late, discussing what terms to accept or to counteroffer and making arrangements about the men-at-arms Raymond wanted to take back with him if he and Marsan should come to an agreement.

However, when Raymond did at last go to bed, he, too, found it hard to sleep. Despite his long ride and a considerable quantity of wine, he missed his wife acutely. Sir Oliver had offered him a maidservant to warm his bed if he desired it, but without a thought Raymond had rejected the offer. He was in no physical need and found the idea somehow distasteful, particularly when coupled with the knowledge that, in a week or two, Alys would be lying beside him in that same bed.

This refusal owed nothing to the idea that his wife might be angry if she heard. The notion that Alys might feel she had a right to an opinion on such a subject never entered Raymond's head. Although he was too much of a gentleman ever to humiliate his wife, even had he not loved her, by keeping a mistress in her home—as some men did—he felt strongly that it was his decision to make. It was a wife's place to accept gratefully her husband's courtesy on such matters.

Early the next morning Raymond and Sir Oliver rode to Marsan. There everything continued as pleasantly as it had begun. Marsan's demands were well within Raymond's and Sir Oliver's limits, allowing Raymond to close with his offer without haggling. Marsan assured Sir Oliver that there would be no more attacks on his farms or serfs, or, if there should be, that swift punishment of the malefactors would follow any report of misbehavior. Even when Raymond explained the tenure of the land was his wife's, there was no hitch in the proceedings. Marsan thought it was very funny at first, but, as soon as he considered the matter seriously, he understood King Henry's reluctance to chance a double overlordship. He waved away any suggestion that a stronger assurance than Raymond's word was needed to bind the agreement.

"Whenever you chance to come by will be soon enough for your lady to do me homage," he said, still chuckling at the notion of a female vassal. "Although I must say that this will be the first time I have ever looked forward eagerly to giving a vassal the kiss of peace."

Raymond laughed also, but the words set off a wave of longing in him for Alys. It was ridiculous; he had been away from her for little over a day. As long as his mind was fixed on business, he was not conscious of missing her, but now that he saw hours of small talk ahead of him, he felt a vast impatience. It was, however, impossible to leave at once. Raymond knew he must stay for dinner and relate the news of the English court. Certainly Marsan's courtesy deserved reciprocity.

The least of Raymond's accomplishments, however, was playacting. Although he kept his face bland and his voice smooth, a certain tenseness betrayed him. Marsan knew him from previous visits. When the vicomte had extracted the information he considered important about King Henry's present policy and advisers, he cocked an inquisitive eyebrow at Raymond and asked if he were pressed for time. Raymond had no intention of making a laughingstock of himself by saying he missed his wife, but he thought immediately that the situation in Bordeaux would make a fine excuse and used it.

"Does it matter to you?" Marsan asked.

"Rustengo de Soler is my kinsman," Raymond replied, "and I would prefer that there be no further cause of dissatisfaction between him and the king. But if any action should divert the seneschal from holding back Navarre, I am like to suffer personally."

That remark made both the vicomte and Sir Oliver look at Raymond with surprise. He was well pleased to explain the extent of his wife's dower lands and from there go on to the sequence of events that led to his marriage. He put himself out to make a merry tale of it, but brought it back in the end to his concern with peace in Bordeaux. This concern now seemed so reasonable that Marsan even urged him on his way as soon as dinner was over. He stopped only briefly in Benquel to gather up the twenty men-at-arms waiting for him, and Sir Oliver promised to send the bailiff after him in about a week, as soon as he had time to make up the accounts and hand over the farms.

Shortly after Raymond left Benquel, Master Ernaldus had his servants load the goods he was taking with him on the ship that was sailing for Arles. They were careful and efficient, but each man's lips moved in silent prayer. None spoke to the others, yet the prayers were identical—that the ship would sink and their master drown. Ernaldus himself went back on shore after seeing his baggage bestowed. He would return before the ship sailed, he assured the captain. That would be at dawn, with or without him, the captain warned, but Ernaldus only nodded and smiled. His business would be finished long before dawn.

It was fully dark long before compline, but Ernaldus waited until he heard the bells of the nearby abbey calling the monks to prayer before he started. On winter nights all sought their beds early for warmth. 'By this hour, the inhabitants of Blancheforte would be soundly asleep, except for the men on guard, if there were any, but they would not see him. The postern pierced through the wall that was part of the keep itself, passing by a narrow tunnel into the lowest floor of the donjon. Perhaps in times past, when Blancheforte had some purpose for attack and defense, the land around it had been kept cleared and the doorway concealed and barred as well as locked, but now brush grew to the very walls, and for fifty years no bars had been fitted to the rusted slots of that door.

By the time Ernaldus's horse was saddled, the moon was high and there was light enough on the road. A sleepy guard let him out without question at the small gate which led to the docks. Elegantly dressed gentlemen were not likely to be thieves, and anyway his work was to keep dangerous persons out. The guard went quickly back to his shelter. He did not notice that the man who had asked to leave to board a ship did not ride to the docks but along the road.

Ernaldus knew the road well. He had no trouble finding the place to turn off into a small wood. The bare branches did not block much of the moonlight, and the undergrowth was dead and brittle so that, aside from the unevenness of the ground, riding was not much more difficult than on the road. Among the last of the trees he tethered his horse. His passage had not been silent, but he did not believe the walls would be patrolled. That would be a ridiculous precaution in a time of peace where there were at most twenty men-at-arms.

His guess was quite correct, and no sound beyond the crackle of twigs and dead brush marked his walk from the wood to the wall. The only anxiety he felt was over in a few minutes when the key he held at last turned in the stiffened lock. For a minute or two he had feared it was rusted closed, and he would be deprived of his revenge. The screech of the wards gave him another moment's uneasiness, and he paused before pulling the door open; however, the sound seemed to have gone unregarded. Ernaldus entered the narrow passage, cursing the door, which had screeched even louder than the lock when he opened it.

Here it was black as pitch. Ernaldus was prepared for that. He pulled a short candle and flint and tinder from his purse and crouched to make a light. When the flame was steady, he drew the door shut, cursing again at the squeal of unoiled hinges. Still there seemed to be no reaction. Either there were no guards at all or, at the distance they were, the sound was distorted so that it seemed to have a natural cause. There was another door at the end of the passage, but this yielded to the same key. The noise sounded worse here but worried Ernaldus much less. No sound could penetrate the heavy walls and thick floors of the old keep.

Once he had the door open, he cursed emphatically. Although his candle had given adequate light in the narrow passage, the glow was swallowed up completely in the huge open space. Then Ernaldus shrugged. The small radius of candlelight would have an advantage later. He left the door open halfway and began to work his way forward cautiously. Somewhere ahead of him was an old strongroom. The cooking staff, which Alys had driven out, had come to him for help. Before he had told them to "go and be damned," since he had no further use for them, he had discovered that the strongroom had been fitted with a new door and the twelve men-at arms were imprisoned there.

Ernaldus hurried forward across the dark expanse, nearly colliding with one of the thick pillars as his confidence increased to overconfidence. That act of carelessness made him gasp with fright, for he suddenly remembered the castle wells and the fact that their covers might have rotted. He went more cautiously thereafter, eventually coming to a stone wall. Ernaldus cursed again. He had lost his way in the dark. He turned right along the wall, knowing that this was what he should have done at first. Eagerness had wasted time.

Only it had not. Just a few steps farther, his candle lit a heavy, double-barred door. Ernaldus smiled in triumph. His information had been correct. The cursed blond bitch and her husband had not thought the men-at-arms worth the cost of installing a lock. He lifted the bars and swung the door open, his lips twisting wryly when there was no rush for freedom.

Then he stepped back with a grimace. What had rushed out was a fetid stink.

"It is Master Ernaldus," he announced into the dark interior. "I have come to free you so that you may take your revenge and remove this blight. When the bitch is dead, you may have your places back, as before."

Then there was a rush through the door and a babble of voices, which Ernaldus quickly ordered into silence. He did not fear detection, but merely wished to set his plans into action with the least delay and without listening to stupid questions and complaints. He told the men quickly that Lord Raymond was gone from the keep. Most of the guards had gone with the lord, and discipline would be lax. They should be able to seize weapons and kill the few remaining castle guards without difficulty. Most important, however, they must first kill Lady Alys.

There was murmuring at this statement, a few growls of approving hatred and more weak whines from men who desired only to escape. Ernaldus had his explanation all ready. The woman must be killed first because the castle belonged to her. When she was dead, it was arranged that the property was to go back into the king's hands, not pass to her husband. Once Blancheforte belonged again to the king, Ernaldus would again be the bailiff, and thus the men would be restored to the sweet life that had been reft from them.

The woman first, because once they attacked the guards, some would surely rush to defend her, whereas if there were only women above it would be easy, even without weapons, to wring her thin, white neck. This picture was so enthralling and the men so accustomed to thinking of Ernaldus as the master of Blancheforte that they accepted his statements without question. None knew Alys had stripped him of power; they had been imprisoned before she had done that. Nor did they know of the passage by which he had entered—or if they knew, they never thought of it. All assumed that Ernaldus was a welcome guest in the keep and had stolen down from his chamber to release them.

"I will give you the candle," Ernaldus said to the leader, who had been one of those eager for revenge even before he explained why it was necessary to kill Alys. "I could get no more than the one without raising suspicion. Let each man hold to the other until you find the stair so that none be lost in the dark."

The boldest, who were most filled with hatred, lined up behind the leader eagerly, each grasping the belt or arm of the man ahead of him. The fearful and broken hung back, but as the leader moved forward and the small sphere of light cast by the candle left them in darkness, they also joined the line. To be left alone in the dark was more terrifying than to go forward.

Ernaldus alone remained, smiling to himself as the point of light from the candle moved along the wall. When it suddenly began to rise and then disappeared and no cry of consternation followed, he knew that the leader had begun to climb the stairs and turned a corner. Silently, feeling his way, Ernaldus started along the wall in the opposite direction. It seemed very long, and he was growing nervous, but he did, at last, slide into the passage through the wall past the half-open door. He pulled it shut quickly and locked it, then permitted himself to give voice to his malicious laughter.

Sweet, sweet. Revenge was truly sweet when it cost nothing. From what he had seen of Alys's men-at-arms, there would be no slackening of discipline, and he knew only a few men had gone with Raymond, not most of the troop. Those twelve idiots would be cut to pieces—but not until after the bitch herself was dead. She would be strangled in her bed before any of her men even knew she had been attacked.

CHAPTER 10

****

To her dismay, Alys found it no easier to sleep the second night she spent alone in her bed than the first. She was surprised at this, for she had fallen asleep quite soon after going to bed. However, she had awakened suddenly when she turned out of the small hollow of warmth that her body had made onto the cold sheets where Raymond should have been. She snuggled back into the warm spot, sighing with exasperation, and closed her eyes, but sleep would not come again. *Perhaps*, she thought, *it is near morning and I have slept myself out.*

Hugging the covers to her, she put out an arm and drew the bed curtain aside. From the size and drippings on the night candle, she had slept only two or three hours; there were nine or ten hours of dark still to be got through before morning. Suddenly, a very faint metallic screech came to her ears. She cocked her head, trying to associate the sound with something familiar, and thought of the noise of rusty hinges. Was it one of the gate guards entering or leaving the tower? *Those hinges should be seen to,* she thought, trying to tuck the covers tighter around herself and determinedly closing her eyes again.

A moment later, her eyes opened once more. It could not be a tower door she had heard. Those were on the other side of the keep, across the bailey. Here her chamber faced the outer wall; in fact, her chamber was part of the outer wall. Alys could have sworn that the sound came through the narrow window slit, but that was impossible. There was no door in the wall. It must have been the door at the head of the stairs. Could it have been one of the women sneaking down to the bed of a man-at-arms?

At first Alys grinned naughtily, thinking that nine or ten days of good feeding and good treatment had drawn the devil's attention to the most unlikely objects of lust. Then she frowned. Although she did not believe it likely that any person

now in Blancheforte wished her ill, it was still a dangerous
precedent to allow free passage to and from the lower floor of
the keep while she, and Raymond when he was at home, were
sleeping. Also, if a maid was stealing downstairs, it meant that
Aelfric and Edith, who slept across the entrance to the stairwell
in the great hall, had agreed to let the woman pass. This
laxness, Alys realized, could not be condoned. She could
easily understand the maids seeking to win favor with her
men-at-arms and would not blame them, but her own servants
needed no favor. If Aelfric and Edith were venal enough to
take a bribe, the matter was serious.

Alys was out of bed and into her bedrobe in an instant. She
paused only to light a candle at the night light and went swiftly
through the antechamber and out into the main room. Examination of the maidservants' beds, however, showed no one to
be missing. Several of the women woke, and Alys signaled
them to be quiet as she turned and went to the door. This was
closed as it should be. Curiously, Alys pulled it open, but it did
not make a sound. Reaching up, Alys felt the well-greased
hinge. She should have known better than to think Edith or
Bertha would have neglected the door. It would have driven
them crazy, squealing each time it was opened or closed.

Then it could not have been a door she heard, Alys told
herself. Probably it was some animal cry that distance had
distorted. Annoyed with herself, she went back to her room,
but she found herself very uneasy and reluctant to get back into
bed. Nonetheless, it was ridiculous to stand shivering in the
cold. Slowly she raised the candle to blow it out, fighting the
foolish feeling that she would be trapped once she was under
the heavy covers.

Quite unaware that their "liberator," Master Ernaldus, had
abandoned them, the twelve men slowly climbed the stairs.
They no longer held on to each other. It was too awkward on
the steep rise and was not necessary in the narrow stairwell
where a man had only to cling to the wall and feel for each step
with his feet. But these men were not in the condition they had
been when Alys had ordered that they be imprisoned. Over a
week of near total darkness and semistarvation had sapped
both their strength and their self-confidence. Hatred drove four
of them—the most stubborn and stupid of the men. The

remaining eight, a few clever enough to sense something wrong in Ernaldus's argument, the others simply broken and frightened, were already thinking only of escape. As the distance widened between the leaders and the reluctant group, one man—one of the clever ones—balked. A second touched his foot when seeking the next step and stopped, also. The first man reached back and squeezed the second warningly. The light of the candle rounded another turn and disappeared, but the afterglow showed a third and fourth shadow climbing and disappearing around the turn, also. By then, the third and fourth men of the reluctant group had come to a halt.

"This is madness," the first man whispered. "We are unarmed. Where will we find weapons?"

"Ernaldus!" the second hissed back in panic. "He is behind. If we do not obey him, he will betray us!"

"How?" the first asked. "He dare not call out and be found in our company. He cannot pass us. Where is he? Is he lost?"

The second man whispered a question down to the third, the third to the fourth, and so on to the last man. Then names were whispered back up the stairs, and it was discovered that Ernaldus was not among them. Since the first man knew the bailiff had not preceded them up the stairs and knew Master Ernaldus's nature, he promptly smelled a trap. He communicated this suspicion and received quick, nervous agreement from the others. All knew Ernaldus and leapt to the conclusion that they were to be cat's-paws for his benefit. Several of the men began to weep softly, but the first had a plan which he whispered down to the rest.

The solution was simple: They need only cross the hall to the outside stairs. In the bailey there would be sticks and small timbers which could be used as clubs in case there was a man guarding the gate. Like as not, no one would be there. What was there to guard against? Ernaldus probably had lied about the guards to make them obey him. It was Ernaldus who would benefit from the woman's death, not they. Even if there were only a few men-at-arms and they succeeded in taking back the castle, when the husband returned they would all be tortured to death for a noblewoman's murder. Better to open the gate, killing the one or two men-at-arms there—and eight of them with clubs should surely be able to do that—and flee.

Before the four who had continued to climb reached the top

floor of the keep, the fourth man realized there was no one
following him. He hastened his step and plucked the man
ahead by the tunic to report this defection. Word passed up to
the leader just before he arrived at the door to the women's
quarters. He paused only for a moment before he snarled, "It
will not take more than four of us to strangle one small
woman. You heard Master Ernaldus. The man is gone. There
are none but women above. Do you fear the maidservants of
this keep?"

One of the other men laughed coarsely. "Why kill her right
off?" he asked. "If we stuff her mouth so she cannot cry out,
we could try out whether gentlewomen are softer down there
as well as elsewhere."

The leader liked the idea well enough, but he was not quite
as stupid as the others and something told him there would be
no time to waste. He hesitated slightly as he lifted the latch of
the door, vaguely troubled that no plan had been laid out for
him to follow after the death of the woman. He made an
indeterminate growl. The man behind had been fired by his
own carnal suggestion and he took the sound to be acceptance
of it. He pushed eagerly forward, and his eagerness both
infected and shamed the leader, so that he pushed the door
open at once.

Raymond had kept men and horses to a hard pace as long as
the light lasted. When it was too dark to see the road properly,
he decreed a rest. The animals were fed and watered, and the
men chewed at rock-hard travel bread and well-smoked strips
of meat. Raymond found more delicate fare, pieces of roast
fowl and slabs of cold beef and pork, together with a stoppered
flask of wine packed by Sir Oliver's lady. Since he joined his
men around the fire they had built for warmth, he shared out a
good part of these provisions, which made for good cheer and
good feeling all around. Stomachs full, the men stretched out
to sleep until the moon rose.

The going was slower when they rode out again. Although
the horses had been rested, they were not as fresh as when they
had started. The moonlight was deceptive on the rutted road,
and no pace faster than a trot was safe. Nor was there any
need, for Raymond was not in any particular hurry. He knew
there would be a warm bed and a tender welcome for him at

whatever time he arrived. Moreover, even when the moon rose higher and the light improved, they went no faster, because Raymond was not familiar with the road. It looked very different in the dark than it had the previous day in the light, and he was afraid he would miss the turn to Blancheforte.

Despite his care, however, they did just that. Fortunately, the road curved after the turnoff, and Raymond caught a glimpse of the black rectangle of a tower against the luminous sky before they had gone far. All turned eagerly when Raymond called out. They were cold and tired and very glad to be done with their journey. It was with hearty goodwill that all shouted for admittance.

There was a light in the gate tower, but Raymond was not sanguine about the wakefulness of the guard. One on the wall and one below at the gate itself were all he had decreed. There was, after all, nothing but thieves to guard against, and no thief would attack a closed keep. Nor could sixteen men-at-arms do anything more than two against any force strong enough to dare the walls.

On the top floor of the castle, the four men who had entered the women's quarters had covered about half the distance to Alys's chamber when one of the maidservants Alys had disturbed a little earlier stirred and opened her eyes. For a moment she lay still, half asleep, watching the candle and wondering why her mistress was wandering about so restlessly this night. In the next instant she realized it was a man carrying the candle and that there were others following him. Almost simultaneously, she recognized the face of the leader. A shriek of pure terror was wrenched from her before thought could urge the silence of caution. Two other women were not yet completely asleep. Startled into sitting up, they, too, screamed. The three cries woke the other women, who also began to shriek at the sight of the devils they had thought were confined below.

With utter contempt, the leader did not even pause. One of the other men, however, shouted, "Shut your mouths," and started off toward the women's pallets to enforce his orders. Seeing him advance in their direction made several others push off their blankets and leap to their feet. Two of the women, thinking only to escape their terror, ran for the door. A second man moved to intercept them. Stupid as the four men might be, they were not so stupid as to want the menservants in the main hall warned. They had no fear of the women, whom they thought of as cowed animals, but they did not want the creatures running out into the bailey, screaming with fear, and alerting Alys's men-at-arms.

At the first shriek, Bertha, who lay in the small chamber on the other side of the anteroom from Alys's bedchamber, started awake. When the second two women cried out, she rose from her bed muttering angrily, "What the devil has started those silly hens to cackling?" The male voice made her hesitate a bare instant. Could the lord have come home? She was drawing on her outer gown even as the thought crossed her mind. Lord Raymond might desire food or drink, and she must certainly quiet those women or he would be furious. Lighting a candle from her night light, Bertha darted from her chamber.

Alys had bounded out of bed at the first scream. She had not been asleep. She had been lying quiet by force of will, calling herself a fool because she was tense with fear. The maidservant's cry, then, was almost a relief. She had known something was wrong; she had felt it. Alys had her bedrobe and slippers on before the second two shrieks rang out and her candle lit before the man's voice called for silence. Her heart leapt once with joy and relief before she realized the deep, coarse voice was not Raymond's. Terror replaced joy. Alys could not imagine from where the threat came nor how she could defend herself. If the enemy was already in her women's quarters, that meant her own men had been overpowered.

All Alys could grasp at was to bar her doors. Whatever small delay that would create might at least give her time to think. She rushed from her bedchamber with her candle in her left hand and her eating knife in her right, just as Bertha emerged from the other room. The sight of two men jolted Bertha instantaneously into fear. Although she had no time to think clearly, instinct bred by lifelong habit told her that no man but the master ever came into the women's quarters. She screamed and threw what happened to be in her hand—the candle—right into the second man's face.

The hot wax splashed his cheek, and the candlestick struck his neck. His hand flew up to ward off the missile and soothe the hurt, and grabbed the guttering candle, holding it still for a single instant before he thrust it away. But the thrusting motion came too late. In the split second he had paused, the flame ignited his grease-laden hair. He screamed, which distracted the leader's attention just long enough for Alys, with her knife, to slash the hand outstretched to seize her, and dart out through the door.

Bellowing with rage and pain, the leader ran after her, leaving the other man shrieking and beating at his hair with his hands. Bertha had frozen after she had thrown the candle, but seeing the helpless terror of the man she had set afire reduced her fear enough to allow her to act. Had the way to the door been clear, she would have run out after Alys. However, her screaming victim was now blocking her path, so she seized a small table by the legs from beside Alys's chair and swung it with all her strength at his head.

The table struck with a most satisfying *thunk*. Bertha emitted a yell of glee and rushed out, still carrying the table. The outer room was in complete chaos, full of screaming women running about like chickens with their heads off. One man was still by the door. The moment he moved, women ran toward what they hoped would be safety. Bertha could see him because the night candle placed nearby was still burning. She looked about for her mistress, but in their senseless running about, the maidservants had knocked over the two other night candles, which had, as a result, been extinguished, and the main room was totally black at the far end.

When Alys had gone out the doorway, she had paused for one instant to repeat Bertha's maneuver. Hers, unfortunately, was not equally successful. The man following her dodged easily and, still bellowing with rage, charged forward at her. Alys, however, had not run straight ahead. She had turned toward the door to the stairs, but stopped abruptly when she saw the man on guard there. Meanwhile, the man who had been pursuing her had snatched at a maidservant who crossed his path.

He held her just long enough to see that her hair was not blond, but that was long enough. While he threw the maidservant from him so that she screamed with mingled pain and relief, Alys ran past behind him toward the darkest part of the room. She almost shrieked aloud herself when a huge shadow rose before her, but she realized in time that it was one of the looms, which had been set up. She darted behind it and felt safe enough for the moment to pause, catch her breath, and look around.

Although it was very dark where she stood, Alys could see into the room moderately well because figures moved against the light of the one remaining night candle. What she saw was a revelation. Aside from the man at the door, there were only two larger figures. The women seemed to be running wild more from simple terror than from being pursued. This knowledge steadied Alys so that her mind cleared. Immediately she guessed from the stance of the man at the door that no reinforcements were expected. This would be a most unlikely eventuality if an enemy force of some kind had entered Blancheforte and had killed or captured her men-at-arms. The first place conquerors headed was the women's quarters, where the richest fabrics and the strongbox were likely to be kept.

Then Alys noticed something even more significant about the man she could see clearly. He had no weapons and was dressed in filthy rags. She realized these were not invaders —they were the prisoner men-at-arms! What a fool she had been to take for granted that all the remaining servants hated and feared those men. One of them had sneaked down and released them, or perhaps it was one of the erstwhile favorites who had returned to Blancheforte in the guise of a laborer. Fury rose in Alys, but she quelled it; rage could lead to rashness.

If only the women were not such hysterical fools, there would have been no danger at all. While any two grappled with one of the men, a third could strike him senseless from behind. If she could call out to them, order them, they might come to their senses, but it was clear that the men were not merely trying to seize any woman, they were searching for her. Suddenly someone came out of her apartment carrying something. The man Bertha had distracted? No. The form was too small. It must be Bertha herself. Perhaps the two of them could manage alone, but Alys knew she needed a better weapon than her small eating knife.

She thrust the knife into the belt of her robe and began to feel around the loom for a loose piece that might be wrenched off to serve as a club. In a minute she desisted, cursing herself for wasting time. The loom had been repaired only a few days previously under the direction of the two weaving women Alys had hired to teach (or reteach) the Blancheforte maids this work. There was no chance any of the wooden dowels would have dried and loosened. But weaving led her mind instantly to spinning. A distaff, with its standing shaft and heavy foot, would make a most excellent club.

Now the darkness, which had been a friend, became an enemy. Alys could have wept with frustration when she realized she had become disoriented and did not know where the spinning instruments were. Had they been moved back against the walls? In Marlowe that was always done, but that was because there were many more maids in Marlowe and the space was needed to lay out the sleeping pallets. Here, if the maids had not been specially instructed, they would not have moved a heap of filth from the floor.

Still, it was necessary to move, to do something quickly. Alys could see Bertha's head turning from side to side anxiously. She could not believe her mistress was among the shrieking, darting women and was looking for some stealthy movement. Alys's mind scurried round and round like a rat in a trap, but she could not think of a way to attract Bertha's attention without also attracting the two men's. The intruders had managed to grab and overcome two of the women already. She would have to find a distaff and move to attack one of the men, hoping that Bertha would rush to her assistance and that perhaps one or two of those cackling geese would also come to their senses.

Wasting no more time, Alys moved back away from the loom until she could sense the cold seeping from the stone wall. Then she went to the left, bending down and sweeping her hands gently ahead of her. With any luck at all, Bertha would instinctively have followed Marlowe practice; the distaffs and carding devices would be against the wall, and she would come in contact with one or the other quickly. Perhaps Bertha would even notice her moving.

At first, luck seemed to be with her. Only a few steps past the loom, Alys's hand came upon a carding device. She grasped at it eagerly, but it was too heavy and awkward for her purpose. Breathing curses, she went forward quickly, passing another carding device. Surely the distaffs were here, also. God could not be so cruel as to have allowed Bertha to direct the spinners be separated from the carders. No, it was not sensible.

Just as Alys told herself that, firmly repressing a dreadful urge to weep aloud, her hand struck the narrower shaft of a distaff. It rocked precariously because she had hit the side, but she grasped it before it fell. Made incautious by relief, she grabbed it in both hands and lifted. At that point Alys's luck gave out. Her elbow hit another distaff placed neatly close by, and that one struck still another. Feeling what she had done, Alys grabbed wildly for the falling distaff. Naturally she missed, merely lending impetus to the fall. Both went over with a dull clatter, while the one she had lifted dropped to the floor again with a thud.

Both men stopped and turned in the direction of the sound. They could not know who was hiding in the dark but, though neither was clever, both realized it must be a "new" person. They promptly converged toward the noise. Alys gasped with fear. She could not manage both. Her instinct was to run away, but there was nowhere to go except behind the loom, and there she would be trapped and unable to swing her weapon, such as it was. Desperately she tried to lift the distaff, only to discover the foot had caught under something and would not rise.

On the floor below, chaos also reigned. The last eight men had waited a few minutes until they believed the four ahead of them would have passed up beyond the entrance to the main hall. Then they went as quickly as they could, watching for the faint glow of the banked fire and night candles that usually marked the entry to the hall. It did not occur to them that these would not be visible. As long as they had ruled the keep, the door had always hung open.

It was pure accident that they did not end on the battlements above the building proper, because the dark and their anxiety disoriented them. The first man did not realize he had reached the main floor landing, but, in feeling for the next step, he staggered sideways, uttering a low cry and windmilling his arms. Instead of helping, this unbalanced him further, and he tilted more, so terrified that he would fall off the edge of the stairs and down the shaft of the tower that his breath caught in his throat and he could not scream. The man behind had also stepped onto the landing because all had kept close after their whispered conference. He grasped for his companion, not out of concern for him but because he had heard him cry out and wished to stifle any more noise before it gave warning.

His support prevented the first man from falling heavily against the door, but his outflung hand did touch it. The realization that there was something besides empty darkness beyond him restored his rationality, and he reached out to touch again, partly to reassure himself but also to confirm that it was wood he had felt. Assured, he turned to mutter at the men crowding up behind him, "They have closed the door."

"Is it barred?" came a fearful whisper.

"What will we do?" another whimpered.

"How did Ernaldus get out if it is barred from within?" a third cried.

He was urgently hushed, although it was not likely his voice would pierce the four-inch-thick planks that made up the door. The question, however, was most reasonable. The men, if they gave Ernaldus a thought, believed him to be skulking in the dark below, expecting them to do his dirty work for him. It never occurred to them that he was already gone.

"Perhaps he closed it so that none should hear him on the stairs," a hopeful voice suggested softly.

Encouraged by this logical answer to the preceding question, the first man lifted the latch and pushed. He barely repressed a cry of joy when the door opened, but his rejoicing was somewhat premature. The door swung barely halfway before it came in contact with an obstruction.

Because the man who opened the door wished to minimize the screech of the hinges, not knowing they had been well greased, he had moved it slowly. Thus, the edge nudged Aelfric gently, rather than striking him with force. He grunted softly and, being deeply asleep, rolled away from the pressure and toward his wife. In dangerous circumstances such a thing would never have happened, for Aelfric was a good soldier and a conscientious man. However, he slept in the doorway because it was Lord Raymond's order. By now, Aelfric knew there was no danger from the castle servants. Moreover, being newly married, he had taken full advantage of his wife's presence. In fact, he had taken more than ordinary advantage. Usually Edith slept turn-about with Bertha in the chamber across from Alys's, but Bertha's husband had gone with

Raymond. Thus, Edith had been available to her husband for an extra night.

Now, when Aelfric rolled over virtually atop her, Edith was much surprised and somewhat annoyed. She had done her duty —and enjoyed it—but she had to be awake early. She pushed Aelfric away irritably, murmuring, "Get off me, you ox. Enough is enough."

The sharp shove and Edith's voice half woke Aelfric, who tried to roll back to his original position. Naturally, he hit the door, which moved ponderously away from him and pushed against the man who was coming in. This was not the first man; he had heard Aelfric's initial grunt. Realizing a man was sleeping near the door, he had leapt through immediately, angling away so that he would not step on Aelfric. The second man, hard on his heels, had not realized at first that the door had stopped half-open because there was a human obstruction behind it. He assumed the first man had opened it no wider out of caution and was careful not to push it farther. He, too, came through quickly, wishing to avoid being pushed from behind. As he entered, however, he heard Edith's murmured remark and moved instinctively away from the sound so that he did not step on Aelfric, either.

It was the third man the door swung against. Since neither of the men who had gone before had bothered to warn him that there was someone on the other side, they being solely intent on their own escape, he shoved the door away with considerable force. This time it hit Aelfric hard, and, as he was already half-awake, he shouted and began to struggle out of his blankets and grope for the sword that lay by his side. However, the weapon had been pushed under the pallet by the first nudge of the door and was not immediately available to his hand.

On his knees, still tangled in his covers, Aelfric tried to push the door closed with one hand while searching desperately for his sword with the other. His shout and Edith's scream of fear wakened Alys's other men-at-arms, who were sleeping closer to the hearth for the warmth the banked fire offered. However, the yells also warned the freed prisoners. Since their only path of escape was through the hall, they were made desperate by discovery. The remaining five men surged forward, crowding against the door and knocking Aelfric backward. Edith screamed even louder.

The hall was dark, the light of the few night candles and the dim glow of embers from the hearth swallowed up in the immensity of the place. Nonetheless, there was enough light for Aelfric to see shadows passing him. This was not a matter of one servant trying to creep up to the women's quarters.

"Ware! Guards! To arms!" Aelfric bellowed, his voice barely overriding his wife's shrieks. As he shouted, he rolled over, trying to struggle to his feet.

The other men, already alerted by his first shout of surprise, seized their weapons and pushed away their blankets. Since all their experience told them an invasion would come from the outer door, several rushed off in that direction. It was far easier to stem an attack at the narrow passage of the entrance door, where only one or two men at a time could enter. Here they found the first few men who had come through the stairwell door desperately trying to lift the bar to escape. One was cut down at once. The others ran screaming from the threat, their shrieks mingling with those of the wounded man and Edith.

Meanwhile, Aelfric had managed to shove away his wife, who had clutched at him in her fear and further impeded his movement, and stand up. He then slammed the door shut and roared at Edith to find and bring him his sword or he would murder her quicker than any enemy would. This threat and the blow he struck her when she tried to cast herself into his arms instead of doing as he told her finally accomplished his purpose—although it was mainly because she fell on the weapon when Aelfric knocked her down. Armed, he began to shout for someone to light torches.

It was a pity that in his excitement Aelfric did not call on any particular man by name. Each of Alys's men, busy with pursuing one of the shadows who were running about seeking weapons or a place to hide, assumed that one of the other men would set the torches alight. Eventually two swords clanged together and a fight began. Fortunately, one of the men instinctively shouted his old battle cry, "Marlowe!" The other, almost at the same moment, had the presence of mind to cry, "d'Aix." Both leapt back from contact, realizing they had attacked a friend in the dark. Others took the hint, and the hall began to ring with battle shouts as well as screams.

To add to the hopeless confusion, the menservants had also wakened. Some of them began to scream and cry for mercy in their terror. A few were sensible enough to creep to the walls and crouch there out of the way, but others, frightened out of the little wits they had, began to run about. No one, of course, had thought of pushing the pallets out of the way. Some of these were accidentally kicked out toward the center of the room, and men began to trip over them, shouting in alarm.

To Raymond's pleased surprise, there was an almost immediate reply to his men's shouts for admittance. Although he was annoyed when the guard demanded identification, Raymond recognized the wisdom and necessity. After all, he had not been expected, and it was a credit to the man's training that he would not open the keep to an unseen stranger who called out a name that might not be his.

After a moment's thought, Raymond called out in English, "Sir William is the holder of Marlowe keep, and Lady Elizabeth of Hurley is his new-wed wife."

That was sufficient. The likelihood of another English speaker in the neighborhood of Bordeaux was not great, and one who would know those facts made the chance of imposture exceedingly small.

"Welcome home, my lord," the guard cried instantly, and scurried down from the tower, calling to the man below to let down the drawbridge while he unbarred the smaller gates.

This took a little time, and then the man ran forward to beg Raymond's pardon for delaying him. He had been alarmed by the large party, he explained, since his lord had left with only five men.

Raymond stopped to assure him that he was more pleased by his caution than displeased by the delay. Meanwhile, Arnald, having heard the gate guard's shouts, had pulled on his clothing and come running out of the hut where the guards who were not on duty warmed themselves or slept. He asked if Raymond would come in and sit by the fire while he sent a man to rouse the keep.

"Rouse them? What need to rouse them?" Raymond asked. "All I wish is to go to bed."

"The inner door of the forebuilding will be barred, my lord," Arnald explained.

"Against what?" Raymond asked. "Have you had some alarm?"

"No, my lord, but while you were absent from the keep I thought it better to be overcautious rather than careless." Arnald looked worried. "Lady Alys is too used to being among longtime devoted servants to think of such a thing, and I did not want to make her fearful, so I gave the order myself."

Raymond swallowed his irritation at the further delay and smiled. "It was well done not to frighten your mistress. Never mind. Give me a torch, and I will go pound on the door myself. When the new men have seen to their horses, you can bed them down in the old quarters of the men-at-arms. For this night, they will have to make do with their blankets and straw. We can get pallets stuffed and move them to the hall tomorrow."

As he walked to the forebuilding, however, the small irritation he had felt disappeared. Arnald's remark about not frightening Alys rang pleasantly in his mind. For all that she did, she was only a woman, and the master-at-arms, although he obeyed her, recognized that fact. Somehow the tacit acknowledgment of Alys's weakness made Raymond even more eager to be with her. He hurried up the outer stair and through the passage, drawing his knife from its sheath so that he could knock on the door with its hilt. As he raised it, he heard faint cries, but the faintness did not deceive him. On the other side of the door, men were shouting and screaming. No normal level of voices could penetrate those planks. Frantically, Raymond pounded on the door, shouted his name, and called on the men to let him in.

CHAPTER 11

****

The men who had run to the outer door to prevent attack had taken little part in the fighting beyond slashing at a frightened servant or a released prisoner who hoped to find the place unguarded and escape. There were just enough of these to keep the men-at-arms at their post, but they knew, even if the fact was not yet clear to some of the others, that whoever was attacking them did not come from outside the keep. Therefore, when a pounding started at the door and a voice identified itself as their master, as well as calling the names of their companions, they did not hesitate to unbar the door at once.

Raymond took one look at the chaos of yelling, dodging, running forms and knew that any orders shouted into the dark would be useless. He thrust his torch into the hand of one of the men and told him to go round the hall lighting the torches in the brackets. By coincidence, Aelfric had just managed to seize one of his fellow men-at-arms, who was pursuing a screaming, weeping servant who had not wits enough to identify himself.

"Let him go," Aelfric roared in his companion's ear. "Go thrust a torch into the fire and light all the others. We will go on like this all night if we cannot see."

Since the "enemy" had already disappeared into the dark and it was useless to pursue farther, the man-at-arms felt Aelfric's suggestion was reasonable. He had almost been wounded already by one of his own companions and had stopped himself by a hair from cutting down his own best friend when that friend bellowed his name to still another man who was ready to swing at him. In fact, it had already entered this man's mind that the only people he had found with weapons were men of his own troop.

As he began to light torches on his side of the hall, light began to blossom from others at the far end. Soon it was clear that the only armed men were those of Alys's troop, and the confusion subsided rapidly. Any servant was easily recognized by his new and relatively clean garments. These were sternly bidden to stop shrieking and were thrust away to huddle together while the filthy prisoners were surrounded, searched for, and dragged from hiding places. The man cut down near the door was dead. Several others and a few servants had been slightly wounded or bruised by falling, but there were no other bodies.

"Eight!" Raymond exclaimed. "Where are the other four?" But before anyone could answer, he realized the prisoners had come up the stairs from the lower floor. "Alys!" he roared, and ran for the stair.

Since the noise of the falling distaffs had already attracted the men in her direction, Alys did not need to worry about being quiet in freeing the one she held. She wrenched at it fiercely, stepping backward and then sideways. At the third pull, the foot came free. Meanwhile, she had been screaming for Bertha to get the other women to attack the men. It seemed to her that her voice was lost among the general shouting and crying, and she dared not move her eyes from the advancing men to see whether Bertha had heard her or had retained enough courage in the midst of the hysteria to come to her assistance.

She could not fight them both, however. Alys began to sob with panic, but it did not prevent her from lifting the distaff, foot upward, over her head. The man with the candle was foremost, and Alys fixed her eyes on him. She knew she would have only one chance. If she struck him when he was at just the right distance, the foot of the distaff would hit him. That was the only part heavy enough to fell him. If she missed and only the upright made contact, it would hardly hurt him enough to delay him.

As if she were two people inside one body, one Alys could hear her own voice screaming amid hysterical sobs. That Alys looked at the advancing candle and tried to judge its distance, but the other Alys, the one who was screaming and sobbing, could not wait.

Nearer? Let him come nearer? No! Alys struck—and missed! Now nearly mad with fear, she stepped back to raise her weapon again. With abnormal strength born of terror, Alys lifted the distaff, the man lunged forward, hand outstretched, and the distaff foot came down again, hitting true. The man dropped like a log, the candle falling from his hand, the flame dying. This was what Alys had prayed for, hoping that in the dark she would be able to run away quickly enough to escape the second man—but he was too close. Just as she let go of the distaff and turned to escape, he seized her left arm.

Alys began to shriek again with fear, but instinct brought her right hand to her knife hilt and she drew the weapon. She had half raised it to strike, utterly without thought. If she had been able to think, she would have known the gesture was hopeless, that the man's other hand must be already stretched to seize her wrist and wrench the weapon from her hand. Fear hunched her together and saved her again, for she held the knife unthinkingly close to her own body where his groping hand missed it and brushed her side. Still unthinking, Alys thrust directly forward with her one free hand to push him away as he groped at her side in the dark.

As Alys was straightening her arm, she heard a meaty thud, and her attacker pitched forward right onto the knife. He screamed; Alys staggered backward under his weight, twisting aside desperately as he released her arm to clutch at the knife in his chest. Since the attacker's fall against her knife had driven her own elbow into her midsection and knocked the breath out of her, Alys's screams had been cut off abruptly. This permitted her to hear Bertha's voice crying her name.

Although Alys could not answer, she realized the blow that had felled her attacker had been delivered by her maid. The knowledge that help was near restored her to sanity. In the next moment she found enough breath to squawk Bertha's name, and they fell into each other's arms.

Both men were stirring. The one Alys had struck was groaning and making scrabbling noises against the floor, seemingly trying to get to his feet. The other was bending double around his agony but screaming more weakly. Half-stunned by Bertha's blow, he had fallen forward onto the knife, shoving it far deeper into his body than Alys could have thrust it herself without his dead-weight momentum. But Alys and Bertha did not know how badly injured he was. They could see nothing, and the sounds of movement frightened them. Neither was willing to approach to strike again, fearing to be caught. They backed away, clinging to each other for comfort.

With the cessation of active pursuit, the maidservants had also run together. Huddled in a tight knot, their hysteria diminished. The violent shrieks died away to whimpers and sobs. Then, suddenly, the door burst inward, knocking the man standing by it flat.

"Alys!" Raymond shouted. "Alys, where are you!"

"Here. Raymond, I am here," Alys cried, letting go of Bertha and whirling around, now carelessly turning her back on the men she had feared so much.

Swift and joyful as her answer was, it was drowned in the renewed cacophony of shrieks that rose from the maids. At first the cries were merely the result of surprise on already terrified women. In the next moment, however, the man Raymond had knocked down when he opened the door started to rise. Casually, with a sidelong flick of the sword, without even turning his head and still bellowing for Alys, Raymond took off the prisoner's head. Then the maids began to scream in earnest.

Raymond turned toward them to bid them be quiet and ask for his wife, but his expression was not conducive to confidence. As one, they shrank away, emitting even louder shrieks. Fortunately, before he did more than take a few steps in their direction, a flicker of movement disturbed the darkness ahead of him. He lifted the bloody sword, but Alys was not afraid of that and ran right under it into his breast. Raymond, who had barely checked the striking movement of his weapon, gasped with shock and clutched his wife so hard she squealed with pain.

There were a few moments more of confusion while Raymond kept asking whether Alys was all right and she could not answer for lack of breath. At last, frightened by her silence, he relaxed his grip enough for her to speak. Between tears and laughter, she assured him she was no more than frightened and in the next breath warned him of the two other men.

Meanwhile, Bertha had heard Alys's initial response to her husband, even if he could not. Assured of safety and protection by the presence of the lord, she had recognized that their immediate need was to be able to see their enemies. Dropping

the small table to which she had been clinging, she followed on
Alys's heels, but not into Raymond's arms. As soon as she
could see a little, she ran quickly to the wall and found a torch,
which she thrust into the fireplace. When it blazed, she went to
light others.

The light and the fact that they finally recognized the master
who had never done them any harm quieted the maidservants.
Raymond took a torch from a holder and started toward the
back of the chamber. When Alys began to accompany him, he
shook his head.

"Stay you here, love. You will get in my way. They are
unarmed and can do *me* no harm, but if one should seize you as
a shield, I would be undone."

"They might not be completely unarmed," Alys warned.
"The distaffs might be used as clubs, and one might have my
knife."

"Neither can do any good against a sword," Raymond
assured her. "Now do as I bid you."

The voice made the words an order that Alys did not dare
disobey. She watched the halo of light surrounding Raymond,
saw the glitter as his sword blade rose and fell, and uttered a
small sigh of relief. One was dead. But where was the other?
Could he be hiding outside the range of the torchlight?
Raymond was not wearing his helmet. The mail hood would be
little protection against a smashing blow to the head.

Alys almost cried a warning as she saw Raymond stoop and
then go down on one knee. Common sense brought her hands
up to stifle the cry. If one of the men was missing, Raymond
would be watching for him, not examining the results of his
own sword stroke. Then the horrible notion came to her that
she had forgotten to tell Raymond there were two men. She
started forward when that came into her mind, but just then
Raymond rose to his feet and came back toward her.

"One did, indeed, have your knife," he said, holding it out
to her. "It was firmly planted in him. That was quite a stroke.
The hilt itself was buried. I must remember, my love, not to
make you *too* angry."

His expression was an odd mingling of pride, humor—and
distaste—but Alys was too shaken to notice. She shuddered.

"That was not my doing. I was holding the knife when
Bertha struck him from behind. He fell onto it."

"Oh. Did Bertha brain the other one, also? I finished him, but I think he would have died, anyway."

"No," Alys said with a satisfaction that showed in her voice, "that was my doing. I hit him with the foot of a distaff."

"No wonder you warned me." Raymond could not help laughing. "I had no idea that spinning was so dangerous an activity."

Alys laughed shakily, too. "Only when the spinner is desperate," she said.

By then all the wall torches were ablaze, and Alys could see the bloody shambles. She was no longer afraid, but her mind was still numb with shock. She could not really take in the meaning of what she saw, but it offended her. She turned on the maids, silent now but still huddled together.

"I never saw such useless creatures in my life," she exclaimed, "running about like silly hens and squawking instead of defending yourselves. Now get to work, and clear up this mess. Carry the bodies down to the men below, and scrub the blood off the floor—and quickly, or whatever you feared those men would do to you will be a pleasure compared with what I will do."

"Is it not natural they should be afraid?" Raymond asked.

"Of course it is natural," Alys replied sharply. "I was frightened out of my wits myself, but that did not make me run about screaming. There were only four of them. If two women—"

"Four!" Raymond exclaimed. "Where is the fourth?"

"I do not know," Alys replied, looking about nervously. "Bertha threw her candle at him in the antechamber. Perhaps he is hiding there or—"

"Stay!" Raymond interrupted again, lifting the torch he was holding and going forward.

Fear gripped Alys once more. She knew that there were many things in the fully furnished antechamber and bedchamber that could be used as weapons. However, before she had a chance to think further, she heard Raymond exclaim in horror or disgust. She ran in and gasped with shock. The fourth man was there, just beyond the door, but he was no danger to anyone.

His body was a blackened ruin. The burning hair had set the filthy, grease-laden tunic afire while the man lay unconscious.

Possibly the pain had roused him and he had tried to crawl for help, but all he had accomplished was to allow the flames to envelop him completely. Whether he was dead or again unconscious neither Alys nor Raymond knew, but it was not worth considering. Raymond made sure with one sword stroke. Alys shrank back, shuddering.

The gesture soothed her husband, who knew he should be glad she had managed to protect herself. If she had not had the courage to fight back, he might have come too late to save her from rape or death. Nonetheless, he found himself uneasy. Alys had said she was "frightened out of her wits," but it was clearly not true. She had wits enough left to fell one man and plan to repulse another with her knife. And she was calm enough, the emergency being over, to castigate her maids for lack of courage and order them to clean up the "mess" —sounding as if dead bodies and blood were no more than a heap of garbage spilled on the floor.

Even while he moved to seek the fourth man, Raymond had been wondering what he had married. True, he had been fed too full of shrinking violets who found a summer breeze too rough for endurance, but he had not planned to take a tigress to his bosom. Alys's cry of horror and shuddering retreat erased that image, at least partially, from his mind. She was so small, and now that he was looking at her rather than for an enemy, he saw her face was pale and her eyes enormous. Hastily Raymond thrust the torch he carried into a wall bracket and pulled Alys toward him into a protective embrace.

She tried to bury her face against him, but there was no warm comfort to be found in his steel-clad body. She lifted her head. "Who let them out?" she asked, and then in a higher, more nervous voice, "How does it come that you are here in the middle of the night? Did your meeting go ill? Are you pursued? Is there an enemy—"

"No, love, no," Raymond soothed. "There is no enemy, and my business went very well, indeed. I do not yet know how the prisoners escaped. I am here . . ." He hesitated. At another time he would have told the truth, but he felt foolish confessing a weak sentimentality to a woman who had nearly killed two men. "Matters were settled between Oliver and Marsan," he went on, "and I did not wish to linger lest anyone have second thoughts. Let them grow accustomed to the new state of affairs. Then if there are rough edges, I will try to smooth them away."

His prevarication, however, was a waste of time. Once Raymond had assured her there was no new emergency, Alys remembered she had guessed there was a disloyal servant and she barely heard the remainder of his statement.

"It must have been one of the servants," she said. "But I do not know how anyone could get by Aelfric at night. Perhaps someone hid below during the day."

"Perhaps," Raymond agreed, and shrugged. "We will discover the truth tomorrow."

"But they are all dead," Alys pointed out, looking worried.

Raymond was surprised, then realized she was speaking of the four men who had invaded the women's quarters. "The other eight were trapped in the hall below," he said. Suddenly that struck him funny and he started to laugh, squeezing Alys against him. "Down below are ten or twelve men-at-arms, all well trained and armed with swords, and they managed to kill one man and wound a few harmless servants. Up here, two women, unarmed, near killed four. Alys, you are turning the world upside down."

She smiled somewhat tremulously but did not answer, and after chuckling over his joke a little longer, Raymond let her go.

"I must go down and see to the bestowal and guarding of those we caught. I do not want them loose again."

"No," Alys agreed, "and let us hang them tomorrow. I do not think I will be at peace now until they are dead."

"We will see," Raymond temporized.

He was more interested in discovering how the escape had been contrived and who had contrived it than in the deaths of the seven men. Although he would not say so to Alys, Raymond knew that the danger would not be diminished by executing those men if there was a clever traitor inside the walls. He murmured some further comforting words and told Alys to go back to bed. He would be with her as soon as he could be.

Actually, it was nearly an hour before he returned. In the main room, the women were still removing the last traces of bloody death from the floor, but his and Alys's chamber was completely in order, and his wife sat beside the renewed fire with wine and cakes at hand, waiting to remove his armor. Once again pleasure and uneasiness mingled in Raymond. It was a delight not to need to soothe a screaming, fainting woman, to be himself tended in smiling calm, unarmed and wrapped in a warmed robe, and offered refreshment. Nonetheless, it did not seem *right*. After such an experience a *proper* woman should be prostrate, hysterical. Alys's behavior was so unfeminine that Raymond found himself strangely reluctant to go to bed with her. It was not that he had forgotten that her strength was what had drawn him to her at first—but then she was Marlowe's daughter. It was different now that she was his wife.

"I took each man aside," he said hastily, trying to push his uneasiness out of his mind, "and each told the same tale—that the bailiff Ernaldus had set them free."

"No!" Alys exclaimed. "It is impossible. Arnald has been by the gate since you left, watching who came and went. He would not have admitted Ernaldus—at least, not without asking me. Could the men have been deceived about who it was in the dark?"

"More likely it is a story they concerted together to shield their ally," Raymond said, "but I will get the truth from them."

Alys made no reply to that, staring into the fire while Raymond finished his wine. He sipped it slowly at first, then realized that delaying the inevitable was stupid, and tossed the remainder off in several long swallows.

"And so to bed," he said, with slightly more emphasis than necessary. "It is very late."

Alys rose with alacrity. In the time that Raymond had been below, the numbness in her mind had worn off, and horror and fear had coursed over her in waves. It was only with the greatest difficulty that she had restrained herself from running down after her husband and clinging to him. The relief she felt when he joined her had made it possible for her to smile at him and perform her duties, but when he spoke of getting the truth from the prisoners, her sense of horror had returned. That meant torture. Alys hated it, but would not say a word against it; the prisoners deserved it, and it was necessary that the truth be discovered.

In bed she flung herself on Raymond and gripped him frantically. The gesture was unfortunate, bringing into Raymond's well-educated mind visions of harpy claws clutching at helpless prey. He stiffened slightly and then said, "It was a long ride, Alys. I am tired."

The remark seemed totally irrelevant to Alys; there was nothing in what she desired that required any effort on Raymond's part. The idea of making love after the horrors she had seen and experienced had not entered her mind. All Alys was aware of was that her husband was lying flat with his arms at his sides, and she wanted those arms around her.

"Hold me. Hold me," she insisted.

Reluctantly Raymond brought one arm around her waist, the other around her shoulders. He was distressed, worried because he felt no stirring of passion despite the fact that Alys lay nearly atop him. Embarrassed by the fact that he found himself incapable of satisfying what he thought was her desire, he said more sharply, "I am tired. Let me be."

All Alys could think was that her weight was troubling her husband. She slid herself off him and instead pressed herself to his side. When his arms began to slip away, however, she protested, and he continued to embrace her. Alys wished that Raymond would hold her more firmly. There was some comfort to be found in the warmth of his body and the simple weight of his arms, but not the full sense of security she needed.

Alys was not a self-effacing girl. She had always been too important to her father and too well treated by him to feel a need to shrink herself into insignificance. However, she was also well trained. For all his love and indulgence, William had not really spoiled her. She knew that it was wrong to demand attention from a tired, irritable man. She thought, too, that Raymond was not looking forward to the questioning of the prisoners. It was most reasonable he should wish to lose himself in sleep.

Still, the flaccid way his arms rested on her and the slight tilt of his body away from hers sent the wrong message to her jumping nerves. She could not rest. The strength of her grip on Raymond was not enough. She needed an answering grip to assure her of protection. In the meantime, faint sounds made their way to her from the main chamber. She knew that the noises were made by the maidservants finishing their cleaning and settling back to sleep, but the knowledge did nothing to soothe her. She kept remembering the faint, strange sounds that had awakened her before the prisoners had broken in. Alys began to shiver, and tears began to roll down her cheeks.

Raymond ground his teeth, thinking she was trembling with passion and crying with frustration at his rejection. If he could have satisfied her, he would have done so, but he was cold as a stone, and his incapacity only further enraged him.

"What the devil ails you?" he snarled. "Can you not leave me to sleep?"

"I am sorry, my lord," Alys whispered, stifling sobs. "I did not mean to disturb you. I cannot help it. I am so frightened."

"Frightened! Of what?"

"I am sorry to be so silly," she whimpered. "I know the danger is passed, but . . ." Her voice broke in sobs. "But it was so horrible . . . those men . . . and all the blood . . . and they chased me in the dark . . . and . . ."

"Alys, Alys." Raymond turned and pulled her against him. "What a fool I am! My poor little love. You were so quiet, and you smiled at me. I had no idea you were afraid."

He held her tight, rocking her in his arms, kissing the tears from her face, murmuring comfort. In a few minutes the shivering and the tears stopped, but her frantic grip had not relaxed and Raymond continued to rock her while her sobs diminished to little catches of breath. Then her hands loosened, and she nestled her head into his shoulder, sighing thanks and another soft apology for troubling him.

But now Raymond was troubled in another way. The rhythmic rocking had pressed Alys's breasts to his chest in a regular, suggestive pattern and one of her legs had slipped between his thighs, rubbing back and forth against his genitals. He was hard and ready now, but Alys seemed unaware. She lay against him limply, breathing shallowly and somewhat unevenly. Raymond was reasonably sure she had fallen asleep. He was not surprised; sudden sleep was a not uncommon result of relief after fear and exertion. He hesitated, wondering whether he should allow her to sleep, but his need was urgent.

With the arm supporting Alys's neck, Raymond lifted her face and kissed her lips. He passed his other hand down over her body, caressing her breast, belly, hip, and thigh. She did not push his hand away or turn her head from his lips, but she did not respond, either, other than by a faint murmur.

Raymond could not decide whether it was a protest at being disturbed or a sleepy acquiescence. He thought of waking her completely by more drastic methods, but then he wondered what it would be like to take a sleeping woman. Would she remember at all? Would she think she had been dreaming?

Softly, Raymond removed his arm from under his wife's neck and laid her flat. She twitched and murmured, and Raymond paused. He did not want her to wake now. Her limp helplessness was exciting to him. He spread her legs carefully, just as carefully positioned himself, and began a slow insertion. It was not as easy or as smooth as usual. Raymond had to stop, draw, and press inward several times, and twice Alys tried to twist away, so that he had to lie flat atop her to hold her still.

Once he was well seated, Raymond found movement somewhat easier, but the whole thing was rapidly becoming a grave disappointment. The sensation was not as pleasurable as when Alys was moist and ready; he missed her passionate response, the extra thrill when the wriggle of her body under his caused contact with a specially sensitive area, the touch of exploring hands that tickled, stroked, scratched tenderly. Also the limp flaccidity of her body had ceased to please him. There was something unpleasantly reminiscent of the corpses he had touched, and, even when that image was erased, Raymond felt vaguely guilty, as if he had committed a sneaking act of dishonesty. That notion was ridiculous because a man had a right to use his wife any way he wished—to beat her or kill her, not to mention taking his pleasure of her any way he desired—but the knowledge did not dispel the uneasy discomfort.

Now, however, Raymond was caught in a quandary. Friction had generated too great a physical sensation to permit him to withdraw, but his dissatisfaction with himself was preventing him from relaxing enough to come to climax. His first response was to move furiously, and he thought he would succeed, but he was soon exhausted. His movements slowed, stopped, and he lay still for a few seconds, sobbing with frustration and anxiety. This had never happened to him before.

Had Raymond not been so self-absorbed, he would have wondered how any woman could sleep through the violent activity of the last few minutes. Alys, of course, had not. When he began to plunge, her blue eyes opened wide with astonishment. Even before that she had been vaguely aware of Raymond's handling. She was still to some degree in shock and very exhausted herself, and could not respond either to welcome him or reject him. However, as he entered her and began to move, she became increasingly aware and, at first, both indignant and frightened.

Alys knew as well as Raymond that she was her husband's chattel. She knew a husband had the right to do anything he wanted to or with his wife, but Alys had never thought Raymond would use *her* without her consent and compliance. Very soon, however, amusement began to replace her earlier, less pleasant emotions. It became more and more obvious that Raymond was very dissatisfied with his experiment. His eyes were closed, as was customary for him during coupling, but his face did not have its normal rapt expression of ecstasy; his brow was creased with unhappiness, his lips tight with effort.

Love and sympathy bade Alys help him; shrewdness and mischief instructed her to let him run his course. The increasing desperation of his behavior assured her that he would not again try to take advantage of her when she was helpless or unwilling. However, Alys was not having everything her own way, either. Raymond's violent activity was producing a powerful effect, and it was increasingly difficult for her to remain passive. He had very nearly tipped the scales in the balance between stubbornness and desire that was raging in Alys when he gave up and lay still.

Raymond's failure to come to climax liberated Alys. At first she did nothing, biting her lips and trying to swallow her own frustrations, thinking he had finally satisfied himself. But he did not withdraw, and Alys realized his lessoning had been more complete than she had expected. Sighing with pleasure, she turned her head and kissed her husband's neck. Raymond jerked. Thoroughly ashamed of himself and furious with himself for being ashamed, he would have pulled away despite his inflamed condition, but Alys now embraced him.

"Were you awake all the time?" he asked tightly.

"Not *all* the time," Alys murmured, stroking his back down along the spine, which she knew excited him, and moving her hips just a tiny bit from side to side.

"Then why the devil did you lie like a dead woman?" Raymond grated.

"I thought it was what you desired, my lord," Alys replied, sweetly meek.

Since her hands and lips were now adding considerably to the heat Raymond had generated in himself, he accepted her statement at face value. Mollified, he began to caress her, and to move again, slowly now, savoring the lift of her body in answer to his, the fingers that petted and scratched ever so gently at spots he had taught her were sensitive.

Alys sighed and murmured wordlessly, shifted to change the angle at which he touched her, and urged an increase in their rhythm with the contractions of her legs. The uneasy tension, the pricking, unsatisfying heat, disappeared. Raymond's brow smoothed; a familiar warmth enveloped him, spreading outward from his sheathed shaft and yet flowing back there and intensifying from the places where Alys touched him. This was right; this was perfect. Raymond surrendered to the voluptuous joy that could only be taken when it was also given.

CHAPTER 12

****

Both Alys and Raymond slept late the following morning. Indeed, the whole castle was still abed long past their usual waking hour. However, even after maids and men rolled up their pallets and made ready for the day's activity, there was no sound or movement from the great bed. Bertha peeped into her mistress's bedchamber several times but, seeing the bed curtains still closed, did not intrude. She did, however, set the maids to their work. It was a mark of how different conditions were that a few dared to grumble that they should have a day of rest after their dreadful experience. Bertha reprimanded them sharply, but in a way she was glad. A few days earlier none would have had enough spirit to grumble, even under her breath.

It was not in Bertha's power to declare a day's rest, but she would not have done so even if she could. Like Alys, she believed that no time could be wasted in renewing the spinning and weaving skills these women either had never learned or had forgotten. Money should not be wasted to purchase coarse cloth for the servants' dresses, for pallets, for horsecloths, blankets, and the like. Moreover, a quota of such products was easy to set to be finished while master and mistress were absent from a keep. The menservants' tasks could not be deferred. Hewing wood, carrying water—the men-at-arms would see those things done for their own comfort and depended on them; however, if maids did not have a quota of spinning, weaving, sewing, and embroidering, there was nothing to stop them from idling away their days.

It was the creak of the looms that woke Alys. By the time the sound reached her bedchamber, it was faint and distorted, but it reawakened the fear that carried over from the previous night. Alys sat up suddenly, and her swift movement startled Raymond awake. He pulled back the bed curtain swiftly, asking, "What is it?"

"Nothing," Alys replied, having recognized the sound as soon as she was awake. "The women are at work, and I heard the loom creaking." Still, her voice trembled slightly.

Raymond smiled and put an arm around her. "There is nothing to fear now. I am here."

She relaxed against him and nodded, smiling also. "You are my shield even when you are not by me," she told him. "It was only because I was so lonely for you that I was not murdered in my bed. I could not sleep for missing you, and every noise . . ." Her voice drifted into silence, and her fair brows knit in a frown. "Raymond," she continued quickly, "I swear I heard door hinges squeal last night. I was so sure of it that I got out of bed to check on the women, but they were all asleep."

"You cannot be sure of that," Raymond soothed. He was not displeased with Alys's apparent nervousness. It seemed to him a perfect balance between the unwomanly hardness of which he had thought her guilty the preceding night and the too-great sensibility his mother and sisters displayed. "One of them might have seen the light of your candle and run back to bed."

"Yes, but the door here does *not* squeak. The hinges are all greased. And I do not think I could have heard any other door in the keep."

"Then perhaps—" Raymond had been about to offer another comforting platitude, but he stopped abruptly and looked toward the window slit not far from the bed.

"We are on the outer wall of the keep," Alys said, confirming Raymond's unspoken thought.

"There may be a postern door!" Raymond exclaimed, releasing Alys and hopping briskly out of bed. "I should have thought of that last night."

Alys followed her husband immediately, running to the clothes chest to hand him fresh undergarments and tunic, kneeling to do up his cross garters and lace his shoes while he shrugged himself into his surcoat.

"I thought it sounded like truth those men spoke," Raymond told Alys while he dressed. "There was such bitterness in them, and they told me the bailiff was hiding on the lower floor."

Alys shuddered. "You mean he could have crept up after we were abed?"

"No, beloved." Raymond pulled her up and held her close.

"I am not so careless when I do not know all the truth. Every door was barred, and my own; new men guarded the prison room and the stair. You are safe. But a secret postern with a key in an enemy's hand is unhealthy."

"What will you do?"

Raymond kissed her forehead, patted her comfortingly, and pushed her away. "Go down and find it."

The words *Send the men down* rose to Alys's lips, but she bit them back. Raymond would be disgusted and irritated by such cowardly advice. Her father would never have done so, and her husband, she feared, was more daring and less cautious than Sir William. Moreover, the whole idea of fearing Ernaldus was ridiculous. He was of middle years and untrained in arms; Raymond could break him in two with his bare hands. She heard her husband call a cheerful answer to what must have been a question by Bertha, for the maid came in hurriedly a moment later to help her mistress dress.

"Shall I send a woman down to tell the kitchen to set the first meal?" Bertha asked.

"Has no one eaten yet?"

"The men-at-arms have broken their fast, but not the servants."

"Yes, very well," Alys said distractedly. "And see if there is some special dish to set before my lord."

She came down to the hall herself a few minutes later, finding herself listening for sounds she knew she would not hear. Her eyes were on the great rounds of cheese and loaves of coarse bread being sliced for the servants to pick up. It was just as well that the new kitchen staff did their work properly, for actually Alys saw little. She knew it was stupid to be worried, but visions persisted of an army lurking in the dark to spring out at her most precious possession.

Before long her silliness was proven. Raymond came up into the hall while the servants were still filing past the laden serving table. He made a brief detour to snatch at hunks of cheese and bread and came toward Alys, who had risen from her seat near the fire. She laughed with relief.

"Raymond! That is servants' fare. I have cold meat and a pasty ready to be warmed for you."

He shook his head. "Never mind, this will do. Just get me some wine to wash it down. We found the inner door, but it was locked. I want to find the outer and set a pair of men on guard there until I can fetch a smith from the town to make new locks and new brackets for barring the doors from within."

"It was Ernaldus, then." Alys had signaled, and Edith came to her carrying a flagon and two cups.

"I am sure of it." Raymond drank and put his cup down on the small table beside him. "While I am in Bordeaux, I will stop in to see Rustengo to lodge a complaint. If what you believe is true and Ernaldus is a connection of some kind, the family itself will wish to deal with the matter. I will not say them nay. The fewer favors I owe Calhau, the better. When I come back, we will hang those men and be done with them." He hesitated and looked at Alys, who was frowning. "They must be hanged," he said.

"Yes." There was none of the misplaced sympathy Raymond had feared in Alys's voice. "Only I hoped to make an object lesson of them for the new men-at-arms—try them for their unlawful oppression of the serfs and for allowing the keep to be open."

"It will not be necessary. The new men I have are not raw recruits, and Sir Oliver kept his men well in hand. They are not bred to such behavior. My bailiff certainly will not condone it, and you are leaving Father François here, are you not? He will report any misbehavior to us."

Alys nodded. "You are right. Shall I tell the men to build the gibbets, or do you wish to oversee that work?"

"There are seven to make," Raymond replied. "You had better start them, or we will have to delay until tomorrow. The days are short, and we are behind time already. I like justice to be swift, especially in a case like this." He paused and then asked, "Will you give the order for the hanging?"

"Yes," Alys agreed without hesitation. "It is my duty. Of course I will."

Raymond thought privately that it would have been more graceful and feminine if she had begged him to excuse her. Very likely he would then have pointed out that she must exercise her authority or it would be lost, but he felt it showed a hard streak in her to be so indifferent.

Alys, of course, gave neither the order nor the hanging itself more than a passing thought. She had condemned men to hanging before, when her father had been out of England doing military service with his overlord. A hanging was swift, and an easier death than many natural ones Alys had seen. Besides, for these men it might be a kinder death for their souls' sakes than any other. Father François would confess them and shrive them—and they would confess honestly with the fear of Divine judgment on them—and then they would die before they could sin again, so they would be saved from eternal damnation.

Although Alys did not note any change of expression on her husband's face, she experienced a vague discomfort, a subliminal awareness of his displeasure; however, she did not associate that displeasure with herself. As on the previous night, her strong conviction that her behavior was perfectly ordinary left no room for doubt. She associated the uneasiness with the preceding topic of conversation, Raymond's visit to Rustengo, and she smiled slightly, thinking that he would be better pleased with his kinsman than he expected.

This, indeed, was the case, at least insofar as Rustengo's manner to himself and his reception of Raymond's complaint. Rustengo was most properly horrified by Raymond's accusation of Ernaldus but expressed not the smallest disbelief, thanking Raymond most sincerely for bringing the matter to his attention and thus saving the family the disgrace of having a member tried and hanged by the opposition. He went in person with Raymond to try to apprehend the malefactor, explaining on the way that he had already ordered the treacherous bailiff into exile. He even apologized to Raymond for depriving him of his revenge when they learned that Ernaldus had set sail to Arles before dawn, although he confessed at the same time to relief that he was spared the duty of having the man killed.

Then, suddenly, Rustengo frowned. "Arles is your own country, is it not?"

"My grandfather's," Raymond replied. "We hold Aix to the east."

"Still . . ." Rustengo's frown deepened. "He is a sly devil and could think to do you more harm."

Raymond laughed, but there was an ugly sound to it. "A disgraced bailiff? But I—"

He stopped because Rustengo had raised a hand. The older man's brow was still furrowed, but his expression now was of puzzlement, of trying to recall something on the edge of memory.

"Wait . . . wait . . . There is something," he muttered. And then, with relief mixed with worry, "Ernaldus's sister —no, half-sister. I told you, did I not, that he was baseborn. Yes, I remember, a singularly foolish girl, but pretty, and the marriage was a good one, better than the family expected, but the man was ambitious and needed money. Yes. Give me a minute more. . . . I have it! Des Baux, that was the name."

"It would be," Raymond exclaimed with disgust. "My grandfather's most inveterate enemy. But des Baux was broken once and for all some ten years ago. The family has little left besides the one keep. I doubt they would contest with my grandfather about a baseborn relative. When I come to Provence, I will ask that this Ernaldus be sought for at Les Baux and see he is brought to justice."

Rustengo nodded. "I need not tell you how to manage. I am sure you will know what to do. However, if you need any writ of complaint from me, I will give it to you."

Rustengo's eagerness helped to set a pleasant mood. After a locksmith had been dispatched to Blancheforte, the kinsmen returned to Rustengo's house, and Raymond found him less inclined than before to give orders with the hectoring air of an elderly uncle to a foolish nephew. Not that Rustengo's opinions had changed or that he was less urgent in espousing them; however, he now spoke to Raymond as a man of power to a man of power. Since, in fact, Raymond was eager to have control of Bordeaux back in his kinsman's hands—they had differed on means rather than on ends—there was no disagreement as long as they spoke in generalities. Raymond refused to stay for dinner, however, citing the hanging of the prisoners as his excuse.

Raymond rode back to Blancheforte in a thoughtful mood. He was very glad of the change in Rustengo's manner, but its suddenness made him uneasy. Also, he was not sure whether or not to warn Alys that Ernaldus had escaped and might be going to Provence. He attended the hangings in an abstracted frame of mind, hardly noticing anything except that Alys was not so unmoved as he expected her to be. Her manner was perfect, but she seemed quieter than usual. Raymond remembered how he had misunderstood that quietness the previous night and thought that his wife was more affected by events than she permitted to show. That convinced him not to tell her about Ernaldus. There was no need to have Alys frightened. Raymond was certain that he would be able to protect her while she was in Tour Dur, now that he was forewarned. It would be better if she forgot the man existed.

Raymond would not have had time to broach the subject of Ernaldus even if he had decided to do so, for his mind was soon diverted to a more important subject. They had hardly dismissed the castlefolk, who had been summoned to watch the hangings to reinforce the authority of their masters, and turned away from the last body, still twitching on its gibbet, when the lookout in the gate tower called that two men were riding up the road. Alys went in to order the setting up of their belated dinner, and Raymond waited to greet his guests.

As it happened, the riders were not guests, but messengers with a packet of letters from Aix. Raymond had, of course, written to his father as soon as the marriage contract was signed to inform Alphonse of the rich dower he had won with Alys. He had told his father that he intended to take his future wife's property in hand before bringing her to Tour Dur because he felt that to be of paramount importance. However, Raymond discovered on reading his father's letter that this practical program did not sit well with either parent.

Lord Alphonse wanted Raymond home as soon as possible, saying that it was essential to summon the vassals to a fresh homage ceremony. Raymond's grandfather had been very ill again, he reported, and a renewal of oaths at a wedding would be of infinite value in reminding them of their duty. In addition, Alphonse wrote, Lady Jeannette had suffered agonies of disappointment and spent her days weeping over her son's lack of consideration for his womenfolk. Raymond grimaced, wondering which reason for summoning him home was more important to his father.

There was a separate letter from Lady Jeannette. Raymond now opened that. How could he drag his betrothed all over Gascony, his mother wrote. He would kill the poor girl before he married her. And, Lady Jeannette added, she was frantic, not knowing when they would arrive so that she could tell the steward when to begin preparations for the wedding. Winter

weddings were so difficult, she complained, with no fresh fruit
or vegetables to be had, no calves or lambs, and newborn
piglets very scarce. She was sick with worry. Raymond must
come at once and take the preparations in hand himself. He
should leave Alys to follow more slowly; there was no need for
her to arrive before the ceremony, but Raymond must ride
home as fast as he could.

Raymond's teeth set hard with irritation. He dismissed the
messengers to eat and rest, thrust his mother's letter impatiently into his belt, and returned to reread his father's with
more care. He now discovered that Lord Alphonse had also
covered the back of the sheet. This part of the letter was far
more to Raymond's taste. His father was passionate in his
praises of his son's cleverness in wringing so much from the
English king. He was less pleased with the arrangement that
left the property in Alys's hands but accepted it philosophically, acknowledging the reasons Raymond had given for
yielding on this point. However, he again recommended that
Raymond come to Aix as soon as possible so that the couple
could be married forthwith.

"It will be best to get the girl with child at once," Lord
Alphonse wrote, "and induce her to will the lands to the child
without delay. You can explain to her that if she survives the
bearing, she can change her will to accommodate any future
children, but that if she die in childbed without a will, the
lands will fall back into the king's hands."

A brief pang, as if an icy knife had pierced his chest, made
Raymond's hand close hard on his father's letter, crumpling it.
Alys die in childbed? Then he snorted with disbelief. What
nonsense! She was young and healthy and would have the best
and tenderest care. His father was like an old woman sometimes, starting and whimpering at every shadow. Raymond
straightened the parchment and read it to the end, snorting
again at the disquisition on the change of power in Bordeaux.
The news was a little late to be helpful to him, but his father's
recommendations on how to handle the situation fitted so well
with what Raymond had decided himself that all in all
Raymond felt quite pleased with the letter despite that stupid
part about Alys's will.

Raymond dismissed that from his mind as he climbed the
stairs to the hall. He was aware primarily of pride in having

judged so well what position he should take in the situation in
Bordeaux. Raymond knew his father had many weaknesses,
but cleverness in politics was not one of them. Lord Alphonse
was a skilled diplomat and had often won concessions for
Raymond-Berenger in conferences that he could not have won
on the field of battle. Secondly, Raymond realized that he had
forgotten completely his promise to his mother to marry Alys
at Tour Dur. He still thought it an excellent idea, and more
essential now that his grandfather's health was so uncertain,
but he wished he had told Alys at once. She might be offended
at the notion that he had allowed his parents to believe she
would travel all over Gascony with him without either the
blessings of the clergy or a suitable woman companion to
testify to her purity. Thirdly, and most immediately important,
Raymond wanted his dinner; he was starving.

That desire was to be satisfied at once. When he entered the
hall he saw all was ready and only his presence lacking for the
meal to begin. As soon as the first edge was off his appetite, he
described the contents of his parents' letters. Far from being
offended, Alys was warm in praise of his forethought in
planning a second wedding.

"It is all very well to have the contract and for us to know
that the highest prelate in England joined us, but that will mean
little to your vassals. Indeed, they must themselves witness our
marriage. I would not have thought of it, but you are very
wise, my lord. Having seen the proper ceremony with their
own eyes, they cannot ever say that your children are marked
with any stain of illegitimacy, which someone seeking to make
trouble might do, claiming that what was done so far away, in
England, might be ill done."

Another brief chill passed over Raymond at Alys's casual
mention of children. She had spoken of them before, of
course, but then the idea that she might die in the bearing had
not been forced into his mind. He ignored the unpleasant
sensation and answered lightly, "Yes, my love, but you have
forgotten one small thing. It is a bit late for you to mark the
sheets with proof of a maidenhead. How are we to explain that
with due decency for you and satisfaction for my honor?"

Alys realized he was joking and laughed. "Well, if our
eldest child is a girl, it will not matter. But if we have a
manchild, who, in due course, will be their overlord—"

"I fear we will need to confess that the wedding is not our first," Raymond interrupted, wishing she would leave the subject of children. She was so blithe and fearless, but several of Raymond's friends had lost wives in childbed, and they, too, had been young and healthy and cared for most tenderly.

"I suppose," she began slowly, and then her eyes began to twinkle. "Oh, no. I know how it may be managed, Raymond."

"Oh, you do, do you?" he exclaimed. "And where did *you* hear of such tricks?"

"Tricks?" Alys looked genuinely surprised. "I do not know any tricks, but my flux is very regular. I can tell it out on tally sticks for however many months away is needful. Then, if we set a date near the middle of my time, we would be sure to strike some blood, even should I be a day or two early or late."

Raymond burst out laughing. The assumption of a continued flux precluded getting with child and thus precluded the danger of childbirth. "There are more certain ways," he pointed out, refusing to acknowledge the relief he felt. "A bladder of chicken's blood concealed in the room or a nick with a knife where the hair grows thickest on me."

Alys leaned over and placed a light kiss on his lips. "I do not like that last notion, my lord and my husband. To endanger your jewels to prove my purity—no."

He returned her kiss in good earnest but continued to chuckle. "But it is my political purpose, not your purity, that is in question." Still, he was obviously considering the idea seriously, for after a moment he added, more soberly, "No, it will not do. Your maids will know."

"They will not speak of it if I bid them be still, but I do not think we should conceal the first marriage from your mother and father. Sooner or later you or I would mention the wedding in England. Besides, surely Queen Eleanor will write of it."

To this Raymond agreed at once; he had never intended to deceive his own family. Then his eyes lightened with inner laughter again, although he kept his expression sober. "There is another reason to tell them," he said. "If we do not, we will not be able to share a bed until we are remarried."

Alys's eyes widened. "Oh!" she exclaimed. "We will not be able to do so anyway, for if we do, all the servants in Tour Dur will know it—and we cannot stop all their mouths. But still—"

"I have lost my liking for this plan," Raymond announced,

cutting off what Alys had been about to say. But he was laughing again almost before the words were out of his mouth, and he continued, "No, perhaps I have not. There will be good sport in finding a time and place where we can slake our thirst for each other."

Alys smiled at him, but she was aware of a sudden prick of jealousy. Secure in the knowledge of her beauty, she had not until that moment considered how desirable Raymond was as a man. The easy jesting way in which he mentioned aping the devices of an illicit love affair made Alys aware that he must be familiar with those devices. She was not foolish enough to resent the women of his past, although she preferred not to think about them, but she was suddenly awake in a new way to the fact that Raymond was unusually attractive. There was a magnetism in his pale eyes, so brilliant in his dark-skinned face. There was a stamp of high breeding in his high-bridged nose and well-cut lips, an assurance of quick wits in his lively and intense expression.

Now Alys remembered that she had wanted him from the first moment she had seen him—and she had never wanted any other man. Perhaps where very dark men were more common, not every woman would be drawn so immediately or think him quite so handsome as she did, but Alys could not imagine any woman who would not respond to the sensual promise of his strong, lithe body. The past could be left buried, but what of the temptations of the future?

Unaware that he had set the seed for the birth of a monster, Raymond shrugged his shoulders. "It is something to think about, and there is no need to decide the point at once. But there is a more serious problem, Alys. My father desires that I come as soon as possible and that I send the messengers back at once with a date when we will arrive in Tour Dur. It is not fair to give the men less than a month's warning. What with the rainy spells we have in winter and the roads being bad in some places, they need time to settle their business and travel."

"That is most reasonable," Alys replied, glad to shake off the unpleasant notion of predatory women offering her husband a chance to play a game he seemed to enjoy.

"Well and good, but how can I know how long I must sit in Amou before I can come to terms with Gaston of Béarn, or how long it will take me to drive Garnier out of Ibos?"

Alys wanted to say they should leave Gaston and Garnier to their own devices, her interest in the welfare of Gascony and in the profit of Ibos being far less than her desire to keep her husband out of a war. In time she remembered that urging safety on Raymond was like setting a torch to a barrel of hot pitch—prone to cause an explosion.

Instead, she bent her head and said softly, "Only you are fit to decide whether it is truly needful to withstand Béarn or take Ibos at this time rather than another, my lord."

Raymond fished a particularly succulent piece of meat out of the bowl of ragout they were sharing and held it to his wife's lips. Alys took the tidbit offered and kissed the fingers that offered it, understanding that it was a husband's appreciation of her meekness. She thought it very clever of him to give such wordless thanks; the skill of knowing the kind of compliment that, spoken aloud, might be taken as an insult by a woman not naturally meek, however, made her uneasy. But her attention was drawn to a more healthy problem.

"Yes," Raymond said wryly, "but the truth is that I do *not* know. I wish I could be in two—no, three—places at one time. I cannot decide, for the life of me, which matter is more urgent."

Now Alys was quite accustomed to men who became caught in the ruts of their own reasoning. Richard of Cornwall was particularly prone to that failing. She had discovered an almost infallible method of jolting the sufferer onto a new track. It had its dangers, but Alys was willing to take a chance. She pursed her lips thoughtfully and then shook her head.

"If you have an idea, no matter how far-fetched, I would welcome it," Raymond urged, falling neatly into the trap Alys had laid.

"Even so, I think this will not do," Alys said very gravely. "For if you sliced yourself lengthwise, the pieces would not balance. Moreover, an arm and a leg without voice to speak or eyes to see are of no particular value, whereas a head without limbs is at a sore disadvantage. Now, crosswise, no part of you would fall over, but the center section, having neither head nor limbs—"

She stopped abruptly and began to laugh as Raymond lifted the bowl of ragout and threatened to tip the remains over her head. He had listened quite seriously for a moment and then was so stunned by what he heard that he was incapable of reacting for another few seconds.

"Raymond, do not," Alys cried, choking. "You will only ruin my dress and my wimple and then have to pay for another."

Raymond put down the bowl. "You silly goose," he said, laughing himself at the visions Alys had conjured up, but with a sense of disappointment beneath the amusement. "This is a serious matter, not a subject for jest."

He did not recognize the dichotomy that caused him at one and the same time to resent Alys's cleverness and be disappointed when she did not solve his problems for him. This blindness caused him to feel shocked when, instead of continuing to titter and jest, Alys turned completely sober. He was annoyed and delighted at the same time.

"I know it is, my lord, but I feared your mind would become fixed on the need to be in three places at once. If such a notion takes hold, the idea makes every other solution seem too weak for the purpose and, being in itself impossible, blocks every more reasonable suggestion."

One thing was sure, Raymond thought. He would never be bored by Alys. He might be infuriated, enamored, outraged, and enslaved by turns—but never bored. "Well," he admitted, "I will never be able to become fixed on that idea. The moment it comes into my head, I will see myself sliced lengthwise and crosswise—but I am still no nearer a solution. I can, of course, tell my father we will not come until summer, which will give me time to settle all my business. But, to tell the truth, Alys, I hoped to be back in Gascony by the summertime, for that is when the war, if there will be one, will reach its height. Also, to delay so long would make the second wedding a farce."

"Tell me first how long it would take to travel to Tour Dur," Alys asked, again deflecting Raymond from the primary problem. Come at sideways, a wall that could not be climbed might be circumvented.

"It is more than a hundred leagues."

"And with the baggage train we could not go more than ten leagues a day," Alys mused.

"If so far," Raymond said. "The winter rains can make a sea of mud, and I will not take you by sea in the winter. It is too dangerous."

"Then we would need two weeks for travel, but if there were some real need, Raymond, we could leave the baggage behind and halve that time—say if you had news of Amou or Ibos that made necessary your presence."

"My love, you could not ride so far and so fast," Raymond protested.

Alys looked surprised. "I would not like it, and I would be very tired, I dare say, but I am not made of crystallized honey, my lord, nor out of glass. I will not shatter nor melt in the rain. I pray you, do not consider me as a hindrance to your plans. I will make shift to fit myself to your needs."

"But the trouble is that I cannot decide what are my needs." Raymond smiled at Alys, but the sharp note in his voice betrayed his impatience with himself.

"And I cannot help you, for I know nothing of the importance of each need, but I have a question. Once Gaston of Béarn is aware that Amou and Ibos are rightfully ours, will it be needful for us to be in those keeps to prevent him from overrunning them? And another question: If there should be no war by some chance, will the seneschal release the men under arms and the mercenaries? Will the lands need to be guarded against them?"

Raymond stared at her and then lifted a sardonic brow. "Little innocent," he said wryly, "your 'ignorant' thoughts seem to be more to the point than my 'informed' ones. No, Gaston probably would not overrun Amou once I have taken —or, rather, you have taken—fealty for it. At least, he would not overrun it until he was very certain he could not win me over in some other way. And as for that other masterfully ignorant remark, I read your purpose well enough. We obviously will not need to guard against loose men-at-arms if I hire them myself for the taking of Ibos."

"I did not mean that at all," Alys protested. "You read profundities where there are none, but that is because you *do* understand and so my questions mean more to you than to me."

"Perhaps," he agreed, laughing now, "but at least one of us has answered one-third of the problem. Now I will only need to be split in half."

However, it was not necessary for Raymond to split himself at all. He went to Rustengo on the following day to deliver a

letter from his mother enclosed in the packet and found his
kinsman considerably excited over news from the south. The
king of Navarre had withdrawn—at least, he had withdrawn
his army if not his claim. Raymond asked eager questions, but
Rustengo had no more information, only the rumor that Molis
had not dismissed his army but was coming north with the
whole force.

"If he does," Raymond said blandly, "he will be pleased to
find Bordeaux so peaceful."

"Yes," Rustengo agreed cynically, a half smile lifting one
side of his mouth, "I am sure he will be pleased."

"Nor do I imagine that there will be many matters debated in
council with much heat," Raymond remarked no less cynically, adding with more sincerity, "I am very glad of it, for I
will be able to go to Aix as my father has most urgently bid
me."

"And whom will you leave as deputy to attend the council?"
Rustengo asked, abandoning his half-jesting manner also.

Raymond's eyes narrowed. "No one from the family," he
said. "That would do more harm than good, as you know,
kinsman. I think I will ask Calhau to accept my clerk, Father
François. He is not from these parts at all and must be taken as
personally neutral. I will leave him instructions on what
opinion to advance on any general matter—those of which we
have talked—and I will tell him that in any emergency he is to
consult with you."

Rustengo nodded agreement, and his smile showed how
pleased he was. He would have been somewhat less enthusiastic if he had heard Raymond's instructions to the young priest.
Raymond did, indeed, tell him to consult with Rustengo de
Soler about any matter that came up in council and would
require a vote before a letter and answer could go to and come
from Raymond. However, after the consultation, Raymond
ordered that Father François was to consider both sides of the
problem—that presented by Calhau and that presented by
Rustengo—and to advise and vote what he thought would best
promote the tranquillity and welfare of Bordeaux.

Those instructions were the last Raymond gave before he
and Alys left Blancheforte on the first leg of the long journey
to Aix. Raymond had sent his father's messengers back shortly
after he returned from his visit to Rustengo with letters

advising that he and Alys would be in Aix in six weeks' time. The next nine days had been given over to packing and instructing Raymond's bailiff in the special situation and needs of Blancheforte. An additional problem arose when Alys learned the bailiff was a widower. This meant there would be no woman to oversee the maidservants.

In addition, Alys did not like the notion of leaving the new men-at-arms virtually on their own. The bailiff was supposed to be responsible, but he had never been in charge of men-at-arms before, and Alys did not think they would respect a man who could not wield a sword. Eventually she decided to leave Edith and Aelfric at Blancheforte. Both spoke reasonably good French; both were accustomed to the ways of Marlowe and knew what would be acceptable to Alys; both would be careful and industrious, eager to make good their advancement.

Raymond thought his wife was making a great fuss over a worthless heap of masonry, but he agreed good-humoredly to let her do as she liked. Blancheforte was the first place that was truly her own, after all, and she had in a sense saved it from complete ruin. It was not surprising that it should have a special place in her heart. Also, it might be their only true home in Gascony. The other estates—Amou, Benquel, and Ibos—would all have resident vassals or castellans. Naturally, Raymond and Alys would have the right to dismiss the castellans and live on any of those estates, but that was not practical. Right or no right, he always felt uncomfortable when he moved in on a castellan for an extended period, and to dismiss an honest man who was doing his duty fairly just so one could live in the keep oneself was an injustice.

Thus, both Raymond and Alys were well content with each other and with their plans and achievements when they set out from Blancheforte. Then it was as if contentment bred more contentment. They were received at Benquel with true gladness. Sir Oliver could not sufficiently thank his new overlady for the improvement in his situation. Marsan was in his keep and took Alys's fealty with many jests and a somewhat extended kiss of peace, but he, too, gave serious assurances to Raymond of his satisfaction with the new state of affairs.

Sir Conon welcomed them to Amou with more reserve. He

was an old man, and a harsh master might assume he would soon be unable to defend the property and put him out like worthless trash. However, he was honest and determined to obey the king's writ, which he had received from the seneschal's hands some weeks earlier. Thus virtue would be rewarded. Sir Conon discovered at once that Lady Alys and her husband did not intend to do him any despite. If he needed help in the future, he would have it—say, a younger knight to lead the fighting men—but his knowledge of the people and the area was too valuable to lose.

After that, of course, he pressed them to stay, to look over everything. First Raymond inquired cautiously whether Gaston of Béarn was at Orthes, and, when he heard that Gaston was at Morlass, he agreed to stay at least a week. He wrote to his great-uncle to announce that the overlordship of Amou had passed into his wife's hands and invited him to the wedding forthcoming at Aix. He doubted that Gaston would come, the situation between himself and Navarre being what it was, and he was just as glad. The longer it was before he had to face his uncle's wooing to support his pretenses in Gascony, the longer it would be before he had to refuse.

Until that time, Raymond's letter virtually guaranteed peace between Orthes and Amou. Gaston would order no outrages committed against Raymond's wife's property until he had an opportunity to talk with Raymond and try to convert him. Of course, Raymond intended to be gone from Amou before Gaston returned to Orthes, but a piece of good fortune fell into his hands like a ripe plum. A frightened and injured man-at-arms crept into Amou begging for shelter. He had at one time served in Amou and then had gone to Ibos in the days before Sir Garnier had broken faith, when both estates were ruled by one master. This man-at-arms reported that Sir Garnier was dead—how or of what he did not know—and Ibos keep was in disarray. Various of Sir Garnier's boon companions, summoned to help him defend himself against his new overlord, were now fighting among themselves for mastery of the place.

Raymond had hardly heard him out before he ordered Alys's men and Sir Conon's to arm. They were riding out of the keep before Alys had time to draw breath, leaving her and a dozen old cripples to hold Amou. There was nothing to fear,

Raymond assured her. He would be back, he said, in a week at the most. There was no question of trying to assault or besiege Ibos with a hundred men, but if he could surprise the place, he might have it at no cost.

CHAPTER 13

****

Alys and Raymond were not alone in a run of good luck and happy spirits. Master Ernaldus, who believed Alys to be dead, found the thought of his revenge against the yellow bitch a fair compensation for his exile. She was dead, and he was not only alive but going to where he would be welcome. His half-sister was a fool, but an affectionate fool, and she had married into a powerful family—at least, they had been powerful before they challenged the count of Provence and lost. Their power, however, had not been stripped from them, only reduced. It was said the count of Provence was sick unto death and that his heir was a young girl. There had been talk among the merchants, too, that the girl's powerful sisters, the queens of England and France, would not accept the terms of their father's will.

If there should be a contest and no clear authority in Provence, des Baux might regain all that had been lost; and, if he, Master Ernaldus, gave advice that aided in that recovery of power and wealth, he might profit greatly. However, this bright expectation was dimmed by two clouds. The first was the danger of a winter passage in the Mediterranean Sea; the other was the fact that his silly sister might have invited him without her son's knowledge or permission—and he might not be welcome after all. Moreover, even if the young man had agreed, he might be even more contemptuous than the family in Bordeaux.

The smooth swiftness of the voyage eliminated the first of Master Ernaldus's fears completely and, although there was no reason for it, it went far to soothe the second. In actuality the result was much the same as if there had been some logical connection between the good voyage and the warm reception Ernaldus received. Lady Isabel fell on his neck, crying with joy, and young Sir Guillaume, although distant, was pleasant. Master Ernaldus patted his sister with seeming affection and smiled, but he would have jumped for joy if it would not have destroyed the impression he wanted to make. Within the first half-hour he had seen a clear path to a secure and probably profitable future.

From time to time as the weeks passed and Master Ernaldus entrenched himself more and more firmly in his half-sister's household, he bestowed a thought on Lady Alys. It was a pleasure to remember that she was dead, and, all in all, he was grateful to her. Because of her meddling, he was better situated than ever in his life; he had respect and a measure of power. He was not making much money now because he was establishing a reputation for inflexible honesty, but he was not in need of money—all his living expenses were covered by Guillaume des Baux—and he would make more and more profit as he became better established. Yes, Lady Alys had done him a good turn, but she had not meant to and he had repaid her as best befitted those who interfere. He hoped she had not died too cleanly.

Alys, of course, had never given Ernaldus another thought. Raymond had held to his decision not to mention the man's escape or the fact that the bailiff might be in Provence, not so very far from Aix. Even if Raymond had told her, at the moment Ernaldus would have been the least of her worries. She had more pressing problems, and now she was racked with acute anxiety. To her, Raymond's statement that there was nothing to fear was the kind of stupid irrelevance all men uttered to pacify their womenfolk. It gave her no comfort. Fortunately she had no chance to terrify herself by imagining every kind of fatal event, no matter how unlikely, that could overtake a person. Not an hour after Raymond and Sir Conon pounded out of Amou, the answer to Raymond's letter to his great-uncle came—Gaston of Béarn arrived in person.

Alys met her unwelcome guest with a babble of false relief at his coming, liberally intermingled with complaints at the lack of consideration her husband had shown for her by leaving her alone in Amou. Naturally, Gaston asked, as soon as he found a space in her flow of words, where her husband and Sir Conon had gone. This gave Alys cause to burst out anew into tears—which nervousness and worry made quite genuine—and admit that she had been so offended when she learned she was to be deserted, left alone in a strange keep in a strange country, that she had not listened and did not know where they were.

Gaston sipped his wine and interjected soothing remarks. Now Alys dried her tears and let her speech run down. She did not want to drive him away yet, because it would be too easy for him to find out where Raymond had gone, by sending out men to ask along the roads which way a large troop had passed. Finally she begged him to stay, commenting on the cold, the shortness of the winter day, and her expectation that her husband would soon be back. The last reason interested Gaston, and he did not refuse the invitation. He had nothing in particular to do in Orthes, having come specially to see Raymond.

When Gaston stayed a second night, however, without specific invitation, Alys understood that he intended to wait for Raymond to return. This, Alys knew, would annoy her husband, who wanted to avoid his great-uncle, at least until she and Raymond returned in the summer. Now she wanted to be rid of Gaston. Whatever happened at Ibos must have already happened, and Raymond would soon come back or order her to come to him.

Thus, by the third afternoon, Alys was complaining freely, wondering aloud—and far too frequently—where Raymond could be, and asking fretfully how he could be so cruel as to leave her so long without a word. Then she began to weep, bemoaning her sad fate so far from home and friends. She began to appeal to Gaston to use his authority to force Raymond to take more care of her. In his eyes she could see a strong impulse to smack her face and tell her to behave herself. Alys fondly hoped he would yield to the impulse. If he hit her, she could have hysterics in earnest and truly make Amou unbearable.

Neither had to go that far, however. With the shrill whining ringing in his ears, Gaston reminded himself that Orthes was only one league from Amou. There was no need for him to endure this torture from a woman whom his great-nephew must have been a lunatic to marry, dowry or no dowry. He could go to Orthes and ride back each day—or, rather, send a messenger each day—to discover when Raymond did return.

That would be soon enough to hear Alys's voice again, if he could not convince Raymond to come to Orthes.

When Gaston told her he had to leave, Alys alternately shrieked with rage and sobbed with self-pity until he was out of the gates. Her device ran against only one snag, and that was of her own making. The act almost came to a too-early and disastrous end before she got Gaston out. In an effort to be sure he would not return personally, Alys had screamed a furious demand to be taken to Orthes and not be left alone. The expression of horror that crossed Gaston's face before he controlled himself and tried to explain that he could not do such a thing nearly caused Alys's undoing. She began to laugh, and nearly had to choke herself to pretend she was sobbing.

And it was all for nothing, too! That was the funniest part. Not long after Gaston had been driven away, Arnald with ten of Alys's men and about half of the regular garrison of Amou rode in. All was well, Arnald assured her, handing over a letter from Raymond. There had been a little fighting, but Lord Raymond had taken no hurt. The reason Raymond himself had not returned to escort her, Arnald explained, was that he felt reasonably certain that Gaston would have come back to Orthes to talk to him. What the letter said was that Raymond had already set out for Aix; Alys was to follow more slowly with the baggage carts.

Alys might not have thought anything funny if Raymond's letter had stated the true facts, but it was only for Gaston's eyes in case he had sat down in Amou to wait. Actually, Arnald told her, Lord Raymond was waiting for her at Ibos. Alys laughed and laughed; she had made a foul reputation for herself, all for nothing. Well, it served her right for thinking herself so clever and failing to trust her husband, who, she should have known, understood his great-uncle and was capable of handling his own affairs. Nonetheless, it was funny to remember Gaston's expression.

Raymond agreed heartily that she had got what she deserved when he heard the story. The only thing he complained about was that she had probably ruined his reputation as well as her own. "For he will think me either an idiot, to be sucked into marriage with a pretty face, or so greedy that I do not care what wife I have so long as she brought a rich dower."

But since neither impression would do him any harm in dealing with Gaston of Béarn in the future, Raymond was amused. Amou and Ibos, too, would be safe, at least from Gaston, until Raymond returned to Gascony from Aix. The management of Ibos, which would need considerable reform, Raymond put into Sir Conon's hands, setting Sir Conon's nephew, a Sir Bertrand, to care for Amou for the few months. Still, they stayed nearly a week in Ibos, Raymond riding out with Sir Conon to examine the land while Alys struggled with the accounts—or lack of accounts—that Sir Garnier had kept.

She discovered that the situation of the commoners on the land was midway between that of the serf and the free villein. Although bound to the land, serfs' dues here were paid in kind and in money rather than by labor, and all the towns were free. Alys frowned, then shrugged. If that was the way it was, she would have to put up with it. Since she alone could not change the customs of the land, she would have to live within them.

Alys was happy as a lark when they set out for Aix. All her dower lands were safely in hand, and she no longer feared the meeting with Raymond's family. Indeed, Alys thought she understood Raymond's mother and sisters well. Raymond spoke freely of them, originally with resentment and lately with affection and a half-hidden contempt. When she first understood Raymond's status, Alys had been terrified by the thought of his female relatives. It was possible for him to be contemptuous, but she would be in the position of a portionless daughter, and her life could be made a hell.

Now that her dowry was so greatly expanded, she was no longer afraid. Partly it was the confidence that her experiences in Blancheforte, Marsan, Amou, and Ibos had given her. More, however, it was the knowledge that she had a home —several homes, if she wished to command them—of her own. It would still be necessary to play the role of a meek daughter while in Tour Dur, but they would not stay long there, Alys was sure. Raymond might love his parents, but Alys realized from his reaction to Rustengo's manner that he, no more than she, wished to take second position below the roast. Raymond was growing too used to command without needing anyone's yea-say.

Thus, no matter what the difficulties of the journey, Alys's mood remained good. Raymond, who had been a little apprehensive of the effect of prolonged travel in winter on even so hardy a woman as his wife, was also happy. Oddly, his very contentment raised a dim shadow from time to time. As Alys grew more precious, every threat to her well-being, no matter how distant or tenuous, grew more irritating. Every so often, Raymond would remember that the closer they drew to Provence, the closer they drew to the man who had tried to take Alys's life. Then he would dismiss the irritating idea, reminding himself that he would attend to Ernaldus and that Alys would not be out from under his own eyes while she was in Provence.

Lord Alphonse was proud of Raymond when he heard the whiplash crack of his son's voice giving orders in the courtyard of Tour Dur shortly after their arrival there. Marriage seemed to have done Raymond good. A moment later Alphonse heard the clear, imperious tones of a woman giving orders with no less assurance. He crossed hurriedly toward the cortege in time to see his son lift down from her horse a small creature, surely a child, toward whom a larger woman hurried. A child? Surely Raymond had said his wife was a maiden, not a widow.

Before the thought was complete, he was embracing Raymond, and the "child" was drawn forward and presented as "my lady and wife, Alys of Marlowe." She dropped a deep curtsy, right down to the ground, and murmured sweetly of her pleasure in meeting Raymond's father, but when Alphonse took her hand, her head came up and her eyes met his without shyness, with the friendly curiosity of a boy who knows he is welcome. Alys had never had any doubts about her ability to win the favor of Raymond's father.

Between his astonishment at her small size and the bold glance, the formal speech of welcome Alphonse had prepared went out of his head. He said, "You are well come, Daughter. We have all been most eager to greet you."

At once, Alys dimpled into smiles, put her arms around his neck, and kissed his cheek with the confiding air of a well-loved child. "And I am most happy to meet you, Father," she said.

Alphonse was startled. The voice, not muffled by a bent head, was that which had previously been giving orders.

Nonetheless, he said, "You must be very tired, child, and very homesick also."

"Not tired," Alys chuckled. "Raymond takes such care of me, and not homesick either, because I have been too busy. Raymond has a great deal to tell you. But I am truly glad to have a new father. I *have* missed my papa."

"Have you? Is Raymond too severe?" Alphonse asked anxiously. The last time Raymond had been home he had shown a hard streak Alphonse had not previously seen in him.

Alys chuckled again. "No, you must know he is too kind for that, but one cannot play the child with a husband." Then, more seriously, she said, "Raymond is a man, and I must be a woman."

Both their eyes turned to Raymond, who was finishing his orders to the troops while Alys spoke to his father. Alphonse's eyes opened at the harsh gutturals that poured from his son's mouth. Alys explained that Raymond was speaking English. Only a few of her men spoke fluent French, and it provided less chance for misunderstanding if Raymond gave them their orders in their native tongue.

"Is he so fluent in this strange tongue?" Alphonse asked, impressed by his son's ability.

"Fluent enough for these purposes and for orders to fight," Alys said casually, "but if the matter grows complicated, such as a pleading, I attend to it."

Alphonse's eyes opened even wider at that offhand remark, but he had no time to pursue it as Raymond came back to them just then.

"I have been warning the men to behave themselves, reminding them that this is not their lady's keep and they cannot respond with blows here to laughter at their strange accent—those who have a few words of French. Let us go in. I am sure my mother and sisters are all impatience to see what I have brought home."

"They are, indeed," Alphonse agreed. "But what of the baggage? Do you want it stored?"

"I would rather that Alys set up her own apartment, Father. May we have the south tower?"

"A tower? But it will be cold and dark. Will not Lady Alys be more comfortable in a chamber above in the keep where there is more light and warmth?"

Raymond glanced at his father with considerable surprise, but he realized that Alphonse had either forgotten or simply had not thought of the special amenities of the south tower. However, this was not the place to discuss them, so he merely said, "Alys is used to her own place and her own furniture. She is not accustomed, either, to other ladies of her rank in close intimacy. She has a sharp tongue, too, my Alys. It would be well to give her breathing room. If she finds the tower too dark and cold, she will say so and we will move her."

"It cannot be darker and colder than England in winter, my lord," Alys said, her eyes shining with love and gratitude. "Where it pleases you to place me, there I will be content."

"Oh, yes, you will be content," Raymond said, grinning down at her.

Alphonse could not understand the byplay, and what Raymond said again struck him as being hard and unfeeling. "You must suit yourself in this matter, not your husband," Alphonse urged kindly. "When you see your quarters, you must feel free to change your mind if they are not to your taste."

"They are not like to be worse than what we found at Blancheforte," Alys assured him, meanwhile touching Raymond's hand, trying to show him without words that she understood what he had done was to protect her from his mother and sisters.

"Very well," Alphonse agreed doubtfully, unwilling to press the matter further. "Shall I tell the steward to have Lady Alys's things brought to the south tower?"

"Alys will see to it herself," Raymond responded without a thought. "Do not trouble yourself over us, Father. Alys will see to everything. Let us go in, or there will be a peal rung over us for our neglect."

But they could not go at once, for Alys had already moved away. Alphonse heard her snap an order to the carters to have the wains drawn to the south tower. They could then, she said, unharness the beasts and see to their comfort. Then she turned to the master-at-arms. Alphonse's mouth opened and closed. He could not conceive of his own wife addressing a carter or a man-at-arms. But before he could protest or protect her from he knew not what, she had given her orders, Arnald had bowed respectfully, Bertha had curtsied, and Alys was back beside them.

"Forgive me," she said, "if I have delayed you. I am now ready, my lord."

Raymond's lips twitched at the bemused expression on his father's face, and he urged him once again to go in. Wakened from his astonishment, Alphonse led them to the main hall where Lady Jeannette was sitting firmly in a high-backed chair with a daughter like a flanking guard to each side. Her expression, which had been grim, changed to smiling as the trio came toward her, but her daughters were not so quick to respond. Jeanine glared; Margot looked first wide-eyed and then with an inward sigh of contempt at the diminutive figure advancing between her father and brother. There would be little of interest, Margot expected, in a child with a pretty face.

For the first few minutes of stilted greetings, Margot saw nothing to change her opinion. True, it was clear as soon as Alys removed her cloak that, small as she was, she was no child. Her firm breasts swelled the front of her gown, and her golden girdle rested on provocative hips. But after Alphonse and Raymond withdrew to talk, there was nothing in her downcast eyes, her low curtsy, or the soft murmur of her voice making conventional replies to stiff questions that gave Margot any hope of amelioration of her boredom.

The first jolt of surprise came when Lady Jeannette said sweetly, "Do sit down, Alys," gesturing vaguely at the stool near her chair.

Alys glanced over her shoulder, saw that Raymond and Alphonse had established themselves in a window seat where they were engaged in earnest talk, and calmly moved to the other high-backed chair opposite that of her mother-by-marriage. It was not near the stool, but Lady Jeannette's gesture had been wide and languid, and, even if she had pointed directly, Alys thought the wife of the heir should defer only to the men of the household.

"I thank you, Mother," Alys said pointedly, sitting down on the chair and hooking a stool closer on which to rest her feet.

"By what right do you sit in my father's chair?" Jeanine snapped.

"Good gracious," Alys exclaimed raising her brows, "is it the custom here for no one to sit in the master's chair? I never heard of that except in fairy tales and legends."

"It is the custom of daughters to sit on stools before their mother," Lady Jeannette said, with poisonous kindness.

"Even the wife of the heir of the house when there is a chair empty? I am so sorry." She rose to her feet. "I will go and beg Lord Alphonse's pardon at once for my mistake."

"There is no need for that," Lady Jeannette said immediately, and from her expression Alys saw that the custom, if it existed, was of Lady Jeannette's making.

Alys had no intention of conforming to such a custom, but to reseat herself on the chair would be outright rudeness, and she did not wish to resort to that. She smiled as she shook her head. "Well, now we are met, I fear I must run away, for just now I have no more time for talk. Could you tell me, please, at what time dinner is served here? Raymond said it was later than I am accustomed—"

"Do you expect us to move our time forward for you?" Jeanine interrupted.

"Of course not," Alys replied blandly, "but I wish to set in motion the moving of my furniture into my quarters."

"Moving? Your furniture? Your quarters?" Lady Jeannette gasped. "But is that not all arranged? And what have you to do in such matters? Raymond . . . surely Raymond . . ."

"Raymond must not be troubled with such stupidities," Alys responded, her voice sharpening for the first time. "He must be free for matters of more importance, for the doings of kings and counts, not for the arranging of chairs and beds."

"The steward arranges chairs and beds," Lady Jeannette said with honeyed contempt. "Raymond or my husband will give the order."

"But Raymond has already told Lord Alphonse that I would see to it," Alys pointed out, softening her tone. "Doubtless they have both forgot the matter already. And Raymond likes his things set in just such a way—"

"Raymond's things are already set as he likes them." This time it was Lady Jeannette who cut Alys off. "It was not necessary to bring here a load of furniture, as if we had not enough or Raymond had not a place of his own in this house." Her voice had lost its sweetness.

Alys dropped her eyes. She had thought all along that the extreme delicacy Raymond described in his female relatives was merely a façade that concealed their nasty willfulness. Her suspicion was now confirmed for everyone except the youngest sister, who had not spoken at all. All she said, however, was that Raymond had ordered their furniture and clothing carried to the south tower. This brought a small shriek from Lady Jeannette, who called for her son in shrill, quavering tones that carried to where the men were seated.

Raymond looked toward the women. He was no longer accustomed to inconsiderate demands and was annoyed by the interruption of his conversation with his father. There was an obvious hesitation before he rose and came to them. He listened to about one-quarter of his mother's tearful protest —just enough to understand what it was she was complaining about—his expression growing blacker and still more impatient. Then he cut her off with a bellow for Gervase that shook the rafters.

"I have my reasons for the south tower," he said sharply to his mother, who had been shocked into silence by the way he had shouted instead of signalling for a servant to fetch the steward. "Do not trouble your head or heart, Mother," Raymond continued. "Leave it to Alys. Leave everything to Alys. She could run this whole estate without bailiff or butler or steward and still have time to make merry with me whenever I desired."

As he spoke, he looked at his wife's lowered head and was flooded by remorse for every harsh thought he had ever had about her. He had forgotten what it was like to be unable to finish a conversation without being interrupted by female irrelevancies and complaints. Masterful as Alys might be, she never had drawn him, and never would, from important matters with silly nonsense about where he would lodge.

It was as well that Raymond did not see more of Alys's expression because her head was bowed with seeming docility. The naughty gleam of her eyes might not have informed him that she had deliberately baited his mother into a trap, but it would certainly have raised doubts in his mind about her behavior. Counting on what Raymond had told her in the past, however, Alys was quickly planning her next move. She could not permit her mother-by-marriage to become hysterical in the hall—and that, she expected, would be Lady Jeannette's reaction to Raymond's strictures. Raymond might or might not be impervious, but Alphonse would not be.

"Gervase," Raymond said, turning his back on his mother and addressing the portly steward who had come nearly running. "This is Alys of Marlowe, my betrothed wife. From this moment, her orders are as mine, to be overruled only by my father or myself—and do not come running to either of us unless she bids you turn the castle upside down. If Alys tells you to do a thing, she has a good reason."

Ignoring his mother's further gasps of outrage and surprise, Raymond went back to his father and sat down beside him again. Alphonse looked at the cluster of women with some trepidation, hearing his wife utter a strangled cry.

"You should not be so sharp with your mother," Alphonse protested. "She will make herself ill."

"Leave her to Alys," Raymond said again.

"Are you mad?" Alphonse exclaimed. "What can that child do . . ."

His voice drifted away as he saw Alys on one side and Margot on the other, lifting his wife bodily from the chair. Alys's voice rose over Lady Jeannette's sobs and Jeanine's furious protests.

"But, sweet sister," Alys insisted, blocking Jeanine's grab at her mother with her own hip and propelling Lady Jeannette away from the men and toward the stairway, "your mother must lie down. Do you not see she is unwell? She must rest and be quiet." And then to Lady Jeannette in the sweetest of tones, "Yes, he spoke cruelly, but truly he did not mean it. He is overworn from the long journey and many other annoyances. Come now and rest, Mother. Anon, when his mind is clear of man-things, he will come to you and say he is sorry."

They had got to the stairs and Alys had reached behind her and closed the door before Lady Jeannette's shock and indignation at being grabbed and hustled out of the hall had subsided sufficiently for her to release a real shriek of protest. As it smote her ears, Lady Jeannette realized it was too late. Furious, she wrested herself free from the supporting arms and turned toward the door, but Alys's hand was still on the latch.

Outrage gripped her again for a moment, but as Alys lifted her hand from the latch—almost like an invitation—Lady Jeannette realized it would be stupid to rush back into the hall screaming. The little yellow-haired bitch would pursue her, murmuring poisonous lies, and Lady Jeannette herself, if she

were weeping or screaming or fainting, would not be able to
contest anything Alys said.

Let Alys think she has won, Lady Jeannette thought, sinking
back into the supporting arms stretched out to her. She would
find herself in a different situation entirely if she tried this
again. There were other knives held up her sleeve, Lady
Jeannette told herself, that she could use to sever the bonds
that tied Raymond to this little monster. She had a way to
demonstrate to Raymond the true cruelty of this creature's
nature, and Raymond would see that he had made a mistake.
Leave it to Alys, should she? Very well, she would give Alys a
few tasks that would expose her coarseness. She would make
Raymond hate the girl so much that he would never see her or
speak to her, except to get her with child.

CHAPTER 14

****

Alphonse looked after the women with amazement, then shook his head in disbelief. Raymond had not even glanced in that direction, he noticed. He had gone back to the topic in hand, which was whether it was worthwhile to pretend the wedding at Tour Dur was the first. By this time, of course, Alphonse knew it was not.

"You promised your mother you would marry here," Alphonse had said when Raymond first raised the question. "I had not the heart to tell her you were married already."

"I am not sure what to do about that," Raymond had replied, looking at his father with wry resignation, "but I cannot imagine how you could have believed for a moment that Sir William or the earl of Cornwall would permit their pearl without price to leave the country without being wed. They took three weeks over it, from the time of arriving to the time the guests departed. The archbishop of Canterbury married us, the king and Eleanor and Sancia and Cornwall stood witness. I told you my Alys was highly valued, but I am more than willing to marry her again, and Alys, too, thinks it is wise."

It was at that point that they had been interrupted by Lady Jeannette's demands. Alphonse had started to rise with Raymond, but then sank back. Raymond had managed his mother very well the last time. Perhaps he had been hard, but he had made Lady Jeannette understand that Alphonse could not forbid the marriage so that Jeannette had not wasted her time tormenting her husband. Then Raymond's brusque behavior and Alys's removal of his wife had left Alphonse speechless. Raymond had sat down again as if the whole thing had not happened and was asking whether "our" vassals—through his bemusement Alphonse heard that word substituted for "your" —would have contacts in England who might have attended the ceremony.

"I do not know," Alphonse said vaguely, and then with

203

concern, "That order to Gervase was of rather wide permission for your wife. What if she should decide to empty the treasury or—"

"Alys?" Raymond laughed. "No! Her fault is the other way. She will pinch both a coin and a man until they do double service. If you have any doubts of your clerks, set Alys on their accounts. You should see how she made sense of the confusion that devil Garnier left in Ibos. Of course, there was no knowing where he threw the money and goods he gathered, but Sir Conon has a clean beginning and a certain knowledge of what is due and from where."

Alphonse was beginning to smile. Everything was working out so much better than he had expected. The magnificent dower had reconciled him to the marriage immediately. He could not have done nearly as well himself. And now the girl seemed to be a treasure also—a weird and wonderful treasure, but still . . .

"Will she know what to do for your mother?" Alphonse asked.

"Alys is an excellent physician," Raymond assured his father, remembering how she had treated his wounds when he had returned to Marlowe after fighting in Wales, "but I think she will divert Mother to some happier thoughts before there is need for physicking. In any case, we will hear no more of this. Alys has been taught most firmly that women's crochets must not disturb men's business."

Alphonse's eyes opened wide, and then he smiled broadly. "I can see now why you were willing to risk all to have her. If what you say is true, she would indeed be a treasure, even barefoot and in a shift." He then suggested that they move to the greater warmth and comfort of the chairs by the fire.

Perhaps Raymond was too sanguine, Alphonse thought. After all, Alys would not sleep between him and his wife, but if worse came to worst he could sleep elsewhere, and, for less than constant vapors, he was accustomed to dealing with his wife. More important was that Raymond seemed so different, so sure, so like Alphonse's own father. And he had said "our" vassals, as if he were ready to shoulder that burden. Consequently, Alphonse felt a heavy weight slide off him. Although weak, he was by no means a fool; he had served his father in diplomacy, and Raymond-Berenger's power had been what kept Alphonse d'Aix's vassals docile.

However, Raymond-Berenger had been very sick only a few months previously. He had recovered, but not completely. During the time that Raymond had been in England and Gascony, Alphonse had heard that his father had been stricken again, although not so severely as earlier in the yea.. Nonetheless, it was plain that Raymond-Berenger could not live long. Alphonse had been dreading the arrival of news that his father was dead, and had no idea how he could quell the turmoil that would follow. There was no male heir to Provence, only one unmarried daughter. Surely there would be war. Alphonse had no taste for war.

"As it happens," Alphonse said, "this wedding will be of greater importance than we had thought. You may not have heard that your grandfather is not well."

The combination of Alys's competent handling of Lady Jeannette's intrusion into his conversation and the mention of the importance of the wedding reminded Raymond of how precious a jewel Alys was. Value brought fear of loss, and suddenly Raymond thought of Ernaldus, who had tried to destroy his treasure and might be at Les Baux only a few leagues from Arles. This then was connected in his mind with his grandfather's illness and the political problems Raymond-Berenger's death would cause. Old enemies would lift their heads again, seeking excuses to take insult. It was most unfortunate, but this, Raymond realized, was not the time to demand that a relative of des Baux be given up to justice.

It was not important, he told himself. Even if Ernaldus's half-sister gave him shelter, a disgraced bailiff was nothing and nobody. Alys was safe in Tour Dur, and he would watch over her himself. He dismissed the prick of worry to consider the far greater problem of his grandfather's health.

"I knew my grandfather had been sick," Raymond said, "and—and he looked old when I went to him for quittance to marry Alys. He gave it too easily, also. I thought I would have more ado to explain why I wished to take an English wife, but he only sighed and said he supposed it was for love. When I admitted I did love Alys, but that I had other reasons as well, he said that love was reason enough and wished me happy."

"Yes." Alphonse nodded unhappily. "He has been . . . not

childish, but—but soft, and thinking in—in odd ways. He has made a will leaving all to Beatrice."

"He cannot!" Raymond exclaimed. "He cannot leave the province to his wife."

"Not to his wife," Alphonse explained, "to young Beatrice."

"To little Beatrice? But what of Margaret and Eleanor and Sancia?"

"He said they were well settled and that he did not desire that the province be divided, with each piece going to this and that far-distant overlord."

"There is sense in that," Raymond agreed thoughtfully.

"There would be sense in it if he had chosen a proper man and got her well married, but, as I said, he has grown . . . peculiar. He would not hear of her marriage, not even a betrothal, saying she was too young."

"Too young?" Raymond repeated astonished. "Beatrice is all of fourteen." Then he frowned. "Well, but even if she had been married, her sisters will not like this—particularly Margaret. She will not like it at all. All the daughers have rights as heirs general, but the queen of France, being so close, has more power."

"Not really," Alphonse remarked. "Louis keeps a tight rein on her."

"But will he not support her in this? For all his piety, Louis has the same ends in mind as his father and grandfather. He wishes to unite all the lands east of the Rhine with France, but he would not mind adding Provence to that."

"He is not so bad an overlord," Alphonse said hesitantly.

Raymond opened his mouth to make a hasty remark, then closed it and frowned. After a short silence, he said slowly, "It will make problems for me if the war between England and France should be renewed, but you are right. Louis is a good overlord. He is truly just and very patient, not prone to suspicion or hasty anger, and is quicker than most to bring help in time of need. As for the double vassalage—to Henry of England for the lands in Gascony, and to Louis for these lands —well, I will not need to face that problem for many, many years, I hope."

Alphonse smiled. He had never thought Raymond would wish to supplant him, but the affection in his son's eyes when he spoke was warming. "The truce has some years to run,"

Alphonse pointed out. "Louis will not break it. Do you think Henry is likely to renew the war?"

"It is never easy to know what Henry intends," Raymond replied somewhat sourly. "It seems he himself often does not know. The only thing I fear is that if Louis should seize Provence in the name of his wife, as Margaret is the eldest, *that* might spur Henry into action."

"I do not think Louis would do that." Alphonse shook his head. "He will not try to seize Provence by force. He will contest my father's will before the Pope . . . but there is another, easier path for him."

"Charles!" Raymond exclaimed, naming the king's youngest brother, who was still unmarried and without any large inheritance of his own. "Louis could marry Charles to Beatrice, accomplish his purpose, and still uphold the dying wish of his father-by-marriage. Yes, of course. Does Louis know of the provisions of my grandfather's will?"

"I cannot believe he does not. My father made no particular secret of it, and Louis must have had informers in his court as elsewhere." Alphonse frowned as he spoke. "My thought was the same as yours. This plan must be in the back of King Louis's mind, but I am not so happy with it. Charles is not Louis. His disposition has little sweetness now, and I think it very likely he will sour, not mellow, with time."

Raymond thought that over, tapping his fingernails on the arm of the chair. Then he cocked his head to one side. "Do you think Charles would be unkind to Beatrice?"

"I do not think he would beat her. Of course, I do not think he will be very interesting to her as a husband, either. . . . But my concern was more selfish. I feel that Charles is the kind who will interest himself too closely in his vassals' affairs, and the stronger the vassal, the more interested he will be. Also, he is . . . ambitious."

"Is that so?" Raymond mused. "I do not know Charles at all. Well, then, do you think as I do that we should, perhaps, be bound directly to King Louis? If grandfather should die, the news will come to us sooner than elsewhere. Lady Beatrice trusts you and so does Sir Romeo de Villeneuve. Hmmm. You must find time, before the contracts are written, or even discussed, to go to Louis."

Alphonse stared at his son's strong face. "You think this to be right?"

"Certainly not wrong—and it will be best for us," Raymond assured him.

"The one difficulty I see," Alphonse said, his vacillation firmed to decision by the stronger will of his son, "will be convincing Louis to take what he may believe to be his brother's due."

"He must know Charles as well as or better than you do," Raymond pointed out. "If Charles is, as you say, ambitious, Louis will be glad to curb his power a little, or so I think."

"I think so, too," Alphonse said with a touch of impatience, thinking that Raymond knew what he wanted but did not understand how to get it diplomatically. "But I need to give Louis a reason with which he can convince himself that taking our fealty is the right thing to do. Hmmm. Well, you may leave that to me. There are several paths I might follow. What troubles me more immediately is the other side to changing our fealty. What of our own vassals? Will they, too, wish to hold directly? Do you see why I began by saying this wedding is more important than we thought at first?"

"Indeed I do. God be thanked that my mother desired this." Raymond grinned at his father. "It was a most fortunate fancy. You sent out word that I was taking a wife already, I suppose."

"Yes, and I most strongly urged each to come, hinting it was not only for the festivities and witnessing, but also that it was time to take council together."

"Good. Good," Raymond approved. "Now we must make plain to them why it will be better that they remain tied to us."

"Yes, but I am not too eager to tell them outright what I think of Charles—" Alphonse began doubtfully.

"Why not?" Raymond broke in. "Pardon me, Father, I did not mean to interrupt, but to tell them of Charles's ambition —without harsh words, of course—may suit our purpose very well."

"*If* Louis takes me as vassal. But what if he does not?" Alphonse asked.

"All the more, then. Would it not be easier for Charles to swallow up one small holding at a time? If we all stand together, he will choke on so large a mouthful. Moreover, you and I will stand buffer between what is his desire and what is theirs."

That did not make Alphonse look any happier. "I would not care to oppose Charles," he said.

Raymond's eyes flashed. "He will learn a sharp lesson if he tries to bite a piece out of Aix. However, let us look on the bright side and assume Louis will accept your homage. I believe it likely he will, for Charles will not dare argue about anything until he has Beatrice hard and fast, and Louis, as we both agree, is no fool. Either way, I still feel that the more honest we are, the less trouble we will have with our men."

Alphonse sighed. "Yes."

"Then we had better be honest about the wedding in England, also," Raymond went on. "To be caught in a little lie would be a great mistake at this time."

"That is true," Alphonse agreed, looking even more worried. "On the other hand, what if they choose to take offense? There are those among them who are troublemakers. I can just hear them grumbling that they were drawn to Aix for a farce."

"There is that. We will need to straddle the truth. Let us admit I married in England and broached my bride there for the witnesses, but have kept apart from her since then for the purpose of renewing the pledge and making her truly my wife here in Aix."

"It may serve," Alphonse agreed, "but then you must not share her bed until the wedding."

"Or, at least, no one must catch me at it," Raymond agreed, laughing.

"And what will Alys think of this?" Alphonse asked with some trepidation. He had found his daughter-by-marriage's strong will useful up to this moment, but the idea of crossing her had less appeal.

"We have discussed it already," Raymond assured his father. "Anyway, that was why I asked that she be lodged in the south tower. Did you forget the secret passage that goes there?"

Alphonse threw back his head and laughed heartily. "I wondered why you were so indifferent at the loss of so pretty a wife. You are a sly dog, my son."

"When I must be," Raymond admitted, grinning. Then he sobered. "Even if so easy a solution were not available,

Father, Alys is the most sensible and reasonable woman alive. I need only explain to her what is needful and why, and she will engage in no female crochets to interfere with our political purposes."

Just after the door to the stairwell closed and Lady Jeannette realized it was too late to use her customary methods to control her son and husband, Alys was saying almost the same words to Jeanine. Raymond's eldest sister had been furious, crying, "How dare you? How dare you lay hands on my mother?"

"Lay hands?" Alys repeated, glancing over her shoulder as she and Margot supported Lady Jeannette up the stairs. "I never did! I saw that she was about to cry out, and so I took her from the hall lest she disturb your father and brother. They would have been so *angry* if a woman's weakness should interfere with their business. I would not for the world have my husband's nor my father's anger turned upon my mother if I could shield her from it."

They had reached the top of the stairs by then, and Margot steered them in the direction of her mother's apartment. Margot could not remember so thoroughly enjoying a half-hour. She still could not decide whether Alys was stupid as an owl or clever as a witch, but it did not impede her pleasure or her determination to aid and abet her sister-by-marriage if she could do so without bringing trouble on herself.

"Angry?" Now it was Jeanine who repeated a word she could hardly believe she heard. "You stupid barbarian, our menfolk are civilized, not wild animals. They are softened by a woman's tears."

Alys did not reply to this until they were in Lady Jeannette's private solar. First she had asked with soft sweetness whether the older woman wished to lie down, but Lady Jeannette said she was recovered and would sit in her chair. Then Alys procured a cup of wine for her. Finally she turned her eyes to Jeanine.

"Sister," she said smoothly, "our men are also softened by tears, but not when they are deep in a discussion of affairs of importance. I will gladly yield to your menfolk the palm for gracious manners." A smile twitched her lips. "After all, I married one. But your aunts, Queen Eleanor and Sancia, countess of Cornwall, are very content with two of our barbarians."

"How do you know the men were talking of important affairs?" Margot asked curiously. "Most of the time their talk is as idle as ours—hunting or women."

Alys smiled at her. "I know because I know my husband. He has many heavy burdens to consider, and I am certain he is very eager to hear his father's advice."

"Why should Raymond need to bother himself with such matters?" Lady Jeannette asked peevishly. "He is at last come home. He should be free to take his pleasure at his will."

"But the world does not stop because a man is in a different place," Alys pointed out. "And it takes so long for a letter to go and an answer to come. Now, when he is with his father, is the time for exchange of news and a thorough sifting of plans and counterplans."

"You seem to know a great deal about my son's business," Lady Jeannette snapped.

Alys's eyes opened wide. "Of course. I know *all* his business. Who should know it if not I? And, more particularly, as a good part of the business is mine as much as his."

"What do you mean?" Jeanine asked.

"The estates in Gascony—Blancheforte, Benquel, Amou, and Ibos—they are mine," Alys replied calmly and deliberately, blessing her father and dear, beloved Uncle Richard, who had been so wise in the manner in which the lands were bestowed.

"Do not be so stupid," Jeanine commanded. "Dower lands pass into a husband's hands."

"Not mine," Alys said, hoping Raymond never heard of this conversation. "They are settled on *me*, not entailed. I take homage of the vassals and castellans, and I sit in justice. If I die without issue—in fact, if I die without writing a will and stating how my lands are to be bestowed—the lands go back to King Henry, or, rather, to the crown of England. When I have issue, I may will the lands as I choose. Raymond explained it all to me most carefully."

"Raymond? Raymond told you this? He agreed to it?" Lady Jeannette sounded stunned.

"Of course. Why should he not? I assure you I do not plan to die without issue just to spite my husband, nor am I fool enough to contest his will in the management of my lands."

"Why do you keep speaking of Raymond as your husband?" Lady Jeannette asked pettishly.

"He *is* my husband. Did not Queen Eleanor or Sancia write of our wedding? Both of them attended me. It was a very grand affair."

"But Raymond promised he would marry you here," Lady Jeannette shrieked.

"Yes, Mother, yes," Alys soothed. "And indeed he will. Of course we must be married where your husband's vassals can see that all is done rightly and according to custom. But you cannot have thought that my father would let me out from under his eyes without first seeing me wed."

"It is good enough for royal brides to travel to their new homes unwed," Lady Jeannette cried. "Are you so much more precious?"

"Perhaps to Papa and Uncle Richard I am," Alys replied, smiling. "But I was traveling with my husband, which is not the case with royal brides." Alys laughed aloud. "I do not think, knowing us both, that Papa or Uncle Richard would take the chance of my arriving intact if we had not married."

"Shameless," Jeanine cried.

"It is not shameless to love my husband and to joy in giving him joy," Alys protested, quite shocked.

That her pleasure in coupling with Raymond was shameful had never entered Alys's mind. She knew lust was a sin, but did not associate lust with the joyful pleasure of procreation. Even the most severe and austere of priests agreed that procreation was a marital duty. Taking pleasure in it might be a sin—some priests said that *all* pleasure was a sin, even pleasure in eating and drinking and being warm and comfortable—but that was no problem. Alys regularly confessed to such pleasures, was regularly enjoined to turn her eyes to God and take pleasure only in Him, regularly given a penance of a few Aves and Paters, and regularly absolved. There was nothing more shameful in coupling than there was about eating or pissing, to Alys's way of thinking.

"When you are married—" Alys began, to be abruptly cut off.

"Silence!" Lady Jeannette ordered. "Do not corrupt my daughters with such foul talk."

Alys's mouth opened and closed. She bowed her head hastily to hide the glitter in her eyes. Corrupt, was she? Until this moment Alys had taken no offense. Lady Elizabeth had pointed out that a mother who desired to keep her son so tied to her would almost certainly resent his giving his heart and be jealous of a daughter-by-marriage. Lady Jeannette, Alys realized, was the one who was corrupt; she smeared with the filth of her mind what was innocent and beautiful. She deserved a good lesson, and Alys considered herself just the girl to give it—and to lift the claws of this harpy out of the bodies of her husband and daughters, too.

"Forgive me," Alys said meekly. "I am young. There are many things of which I am ignorant, my mother having died when I was only a child. And more than all I am ignorant of the ways of this land."

"You certainly are," Jeanine snapped.

Not as ignorant as you, Alys thought, but all she said was "I can see that my dress is not right. I hope you will instruct me, Sister, in the correct fashion."

"I?" Jeanine gasped, outraged. "I am no maid to sew for you!"

While this exchange was going on, Lady Jeannette had been thinking of Alys's innocent confession of her lust. Since Alys and Raymond were already married—and *why* had she not been informed of that?—her original plan would not work; however, it was not too late to incite in him a healthy disgust for his wife by showing that Alys was crude and lascivious. Also, it would be possible to point out to Raymond that a wife who took such pleasure in coupling would be very prone to seek that pleasure with others as well as with her husband.

It had been a mistake to expose Alys to the idea that, for a decent woman, love was of the heart and mind, a source of beautiful words and fine emotion. A true lady endured the act that made children, but that was not to be confused with love. Such a mingling was an abomination to Lady Jeannette. Procreation was for husband and wife; love was for a lady and her troubadour.

Lady Jeannette comforted herself with the assurance that Raymond knew that. He also knew that some ladies and troubadours did not confine their love to songs and glances but descended to the crudities of nature. Obviously Alys was that kind. Raymond was essentially fine, Lady Jeannette thought; he would soon sicken of this coarse animal. So much the better, then, that Alys *was* coarse. It would be easy to encourage her lustful way, perhaps even urge Alys to take a lover. Then Raymond could lock her up. But to have her advice accepted, Lady Jeannette knew she would need to gain Alys's trust, and first she must seem more friendly.

"Do not be silly, Jeanine," Lady Jeannette said, responding to Jeanine's earlier indignation. "Alys did not expect you to sew clothes for her, only to advise her on how to have the maids do them."

"Our maids?" Jeanine whined. "They are busy enough. If she brought furniture, she should have brought servants, too."

"And so I did," Alys said. "I have my maid, and I am a good needlewoman myself."

"You sew your own clothes?" Lady Jeannette asked.

But before Alys could answer, Raymond spoke her name from the doorway. "I thought you were going to tell Gervase what to do about the furniture," he said, grinning at her, "and here I find you at your favorite occupation—talking about clothes."

"Oh, how you startled me, my lord," Alys cried, then winked at him. "Clothes are not only a favorite topic but a very soothing one, just the subject for calming your mother after you were so sharp with her. And then, Lady Jeannette was very shocked to hear we were already married, after you promised that the wedding should be here."

Their eyes met, and Alys could see the relief and approval in Raymond's. She had, just as he predicted, taken care of everything, saving him the unpleasant duty of making that revelation. "There will be a wedding here, also," he hastened to agree.

"I assured our mother it would be so," Alys told him, then chuckled. "And that brought clothes to mind, my lord, for I can see that fashions here are different from those of England or Bordeaux."

Lady Jeannette had again been rendered speechless, her emotions alternating between surprise and fury. She had intended to seek Raymond out or summon him privately and weep over how cruel Alys had been to her. Instead, he had found her calmly conversing, so it was impossible to claim, as she had expected to do, that Alys had shocked her and his sisters with foul talk and had tormented her. Lady Jeannette was unused to frustration and reacted to it without thinking, which led to another mistake.

"Who gave you permission to come into these chambers?" she cried, her voice high and thin with fury.

Raymond lost his smile, and his lips set hard. "My father gave me permission," he snapped. "He rules this house, not you, madame. And I came to fetch away my wife."

"Raymond, love," Alys said softly, running to him and laying a hand on his arm. "Be kind. Your mother is hurt at your sharpness. Tell her you were not angry at her belowstairs, only annoyed at the interruption of your talk. It is long since she has seen you."

"Will it make your path easier, my love?" Raymond asked, very low.

Alys immediately dropped her eyes. "Do not think of me but of your father," she whispered.

"You are my haven and my heaven," he responded, feeling more in love than when he first decided to have Alys as his wife, no matter what barred the way. Then, more loudly, he said, "Get you to your unpacking, Alys. You know I do not like to see the chambers all disordered." His eyes passed over Jeanine's face, white and thin-lipped, to Margot's countenance, which was bright-eyed with interest. "Go you with your sister, Margot," he added, "and lend what aid you can to her. Some of the words Alys uses are different, and the servants may not understand her."

Lady Jeanette uttered a cry of protest, but Raymond shook his head at her sharply and gave Margot a gentle shove to hurry her out on Alys's heels. Then he came up close to his mother and told her softly he had something to discuss with her and with Jeanine that was not fit for Margot's ears. Raymond was not above duplicity with women where he did not consider his honor involved, and he had unconsciously absorbed a great deal of information from his conversations with Alys. His wife's last remark had been a warning, and he recognized its validity at once.

Raymond knew he would soon leave Tour Dur to return to

the Gascon properties, so his mother's reactions would affect him very little. However, his father could not leave—at least not until Raymond-Berenger recovered completely or died. In any case, Alphonse would not leave his wife for long. He was truly fond of her, truly enjoyed the singing and poetry, the games of words, chess, and chance with which Lady Jeannette whiled away the hours when she was in good spirits. He loved to go on picnics and flower gatherings when they plucked the petals into baskets for potpourri while a minstrel or their daughters sang to them. Alphonse was truly grieved when his wife wept and moaned and kept to her chamber.

Since it was for his father's sake, Raymond was willing to swallow his new-found pride in dominance and return to the old path of cajolement. This he could navigate with the skill of long experience. Moreover, he had a subject he knew would interest his mother and older sister. The notion had come to him when he decided to send Margot with Alys because his younger sister seemed open to friendliness. It would be pleasant for Alys to have a woman friend. There was one topic Raymond was sure his mother would consider unfit for Margot's ears—sex. Without the slightest intention of taking any of the advice offered, Raymond asked his mother and Jeanine whether they thought it worthwhile for the vassals' sakes to pretend Alys was still a virgin and, if so, how to go about faking the evidence.

This fascinating question so riveted their attention that Raymond's "crimes" were soon forgotten. Moreover, a marvelous revelation came to Lady Jeannette. If Raymond wished to pretend he and Alys were not married, he could not share her bed. She leapt on this with such enthusiasm that Raymond had much ado not to laugh, but he agreed to it with a pretense at reluctance. This deception was not so much to pander to his mother's obvious desire to separate him from his wife as because he did not trust Lady Jeannette to be able to hold her tongue if he admitted to her he had no intention of depriving himself of the sweets of Alys's body.

CHAPTER 15

****

Alys worried a little that Lady Jeannette might cross-question Margot about the time she spent with her sister-by-marriage, but she need not have done so. Raymond's mother had far more absorbing topics for consideration than her daughter's conversation. Jeanine and Margot had always meant little to her, except as they served her comfort, compared with her eldest son. Raymond's seeming confidence in her ideas and his return to his old manner with her as soon as Alys was gone gave her two false impressions. The first was that Raymond was still amenable to her influence; the second was that his severe manner toward her had been assumed to impress or frighten Alys. The alacrity with which Alys obeyed her husband, the lack of protest or pouting, the soft, placating voice in which she spoke to him also conveyed a false impression of fear.

Thus, Lady Jeannette came down to dinner in a far different mood than she had come down earlier in the day to greet her daughter-by-marriage. She was no longer off balance and had her campaign planned out. First, Lady Jeannette set out to show Raymond how coarse and crude his wife was, despite her small size and delicate looks. At the table she professed herself amazed at the quantity of food Alys consumed. Innocently, Alys did not realize this was an attack and agreed most cordially that she was hungry and the food was very good.

This produced a reaction, but not the one Lady Jeannette had planned. Lord Alphonse looked delighted. "Are you by chance eating for two, my dear?" he asked.

"I hope to God she is not!" Raymond exclaimed before Alys had a chance to answer. "I do not wish to need to explain a seven-months child to our vassals."

"No, no," Alphonse said. "Naturally, if Alys is with child, we will not make any pretense about the wedding, merely hold it to provide a celebration and assure the men that all forms and customs of this land have been observed."

"I am sorry, my lord," Alys put in, "but I cannot answer you, although I fear it is not so. My flux was as usual last month, and it is not yet due this month."

"Ah . . . oh . . ." Alphonse cleared his throat in some embarrassment.

Raymond guffawed. "Do not ask Alys questions if you are not prepared for frank answers, Father," he choked. "She is honest to a fault."

Their laughter seemed to show acceptance of Alys as she was, but Lady Jeannette had seen something that was certainly not amusement in Raymond's face when he protested his father's interpretation of Alys's appetite. Lady Jeannette believed her son did not wish his wife to be with child, and her heart leapt with joy. Although Raymond had given a reason for his expression, his mother refused to accept it. The only reason Lady Jeannette was willing to consider for Raymond's reluctance to father Alys's child, especially when she combined that with his seeming willingness to avoid Alys's bed, was that he was already regretting his marriage.

The pleasure this thought gave her made it possible for Lady Jeannette to restrain any comment on Alys's crudity in mentioning her flux. She was now very happy, and happiness always expressed itself in Lady Jeannette with a desire for music. Thus, when the tables were cleared and the family gathered near the hearth, Lady Jeannette graciously asked Alys to sing. She was hoping, of course, that her performance would be poor in comparison with that of her own daughters. At first she was surprised when Raymond burst out laughing as Alys shook her head.

"Do sing, my love," he urged. "You have a voice like a bird."

"The wrong kind of bird," Alys said, flashing what Lady Jeannette considered a very strange glance at Raymond. "I am sorry, Mother, I cannot sing. I have a voice like a jackdaw."

"This must be modesty." Alphonse tried to encourage her. "Your speaking voice is sweet. We are only family, my dear. You need not fear we will be critical."

Raymond's eyes glittered with amusement as Alys most seriously assured his father that she could not sing or play a note because she had never learned how. Alphonse could not understand this. All daughters of great houses were taught to sing and play.

"But, Father," Alys protested, "I am not the daughter of a great house. Your son and my Uncle Richard worked some miracle whereby my dower was made suitable to your son's rank, but I am the daughter of a simple knight. Surely Raymond told you that. I can do accounts and read and write, but my education is lacking in refinements, I fear."

Raymond was laughing again. He had never been so happy in his life. Everything was a joy, and Alys was the fount of that joy in great ways and small ones. It was a great thing to be truly independent of his parents, not in the sulky, small-boy way that had made him run off to England the preceding year, but as a man with rich estates of his own. It was a very small thing to be able to look forward to listening to his sisters' silly songs because he knew his wife, however politely she listened, would be suffering boredom as acutely as he was. Between the two extremes were a whole series of greater and lesser satisfactions, all connected to Alys.

"Your taste and talent are lacking, too," Raymond muttered through his gales of laughter.

Alys shot him a single furious glance, lowered her head, and bit her lips. She was not, of course, angry about his remark on her lack of fondness for lute music. They were at one on that subject, Alys knew. However, it was clear that the rest of Raymond's family were really devoted to that musical art. Alys felt she was making headway in gaining Alphonse's and Margot's affection, and even Lady Jeannette seemed more accepting of her. Thus she did not wish to distress or disgust them and, perhaps, destroy their tentative liking by laughing at something they loved, and thought it cruel of Raymond to add to her temptation to laugh. It would be hard enough to keep her face straight when Jeanine or Margot began sighing over some imaginary knight's bravery and some silly woman's coldness without Raymond encouraging her own sense of the ridiculous.

But Alphonse had turned on his son. "Hold your tongue!" he ordered sharply. "You should be ashamed of yourself to laugh at your wife in public for what is no fault of her own. I am shocked!"

"Oh, no, my lord, do not be angry," Alys cried. "Indeed, he speaks nothing but the truth. Both taste and talent are lacking in me. But he was not laughing at me, only at a private joke that is between us. I am not hurt or offended."

"Your sweetness of disposition is a credit to you, my dear," Alphonse said softly, glaring at Raymond, who had turned crimson and was nearly choking to death in his attempts to swallow his laughter.

Eventually he did compose himself to listen to his sisters sing, but he was several times so shaken by repressed mirth that tears filled his eyes. Alys was in a similar state. She could be seen several times, at points in the songs of particular emotion—as ladies died of fear or knights broke their hearts for love—to tremble perceptibly and wipe her eyes with the hem of her sleeve.

Each observer interpreted these reactions to suit him- or herself. Jeanine disregarded her brother completely and put down Alys's behavior to envy or chagrin, and Margot thought Raymond was distressed by his father's reprimand. It was rare, indeed, for Alphonse to speak so sharply to his eldest son, and Margot felt sorry for her brother, of whom she was fond. Alys, Margot believed, was responding to the music and the sentiment in the songs. She already liked Alys and felt she owed her a debt. Now she saw her way clear to obtain a good deal of Alys's company for herself and to do Alys a service; Margot intended to teach her sister-by-marriage to play and sing.

Alphonse understood Raymond quite clearly. He had heard his son's view on love songs to the lute and was well aware of his lack of sympathy with music and delicate sentiment. He regretted it, but associated it with Raymond's pleasure in feats of arms and accepted the fact that the brutality of the arts of war dulled fine sentiment. Concurrently, he was completely mistaken about Alys's emotion, which he felt was a mixture of sensitivity to the performance, embarrassment at her own limitations, and hurt at her husband's cruelty.

Lady Jeannette was even further afield than the others. She associated Raymond's occasional rigidity and misted eyes with a deep regret for the mistake he had made. Since she could not bear to credit Alys with enough of the softer emotions to generate envy of Jeanine's and Margot's skill, she convinced herself that the effort of controlling spite and rage were causing

Alys to cry. Thus, Lady Jeannette was delighted. Even if Alys did not have courage to quarrel with Raymond, she was sure Alys would display her anger in some unsuitable way, perhaps in hurting some weaker creature.

The events of the evening had clarified a puzzle that had been troubling Lady Jeannette. There was a dichotomy between Raymond's confidence in Alys—as evidenced in his broad-ranging order to Gervase to obey his wife and his urging that everything be left to her to do as she pleased—and his disinclination to father a child on her, plus his obvious contempt for her crude nature and upbringing. The puzzle was now resolved to Lady Jeannette's satisfaction. Raymond, she decided, regarded Alys as a servant, fit to arrange furniture and sew clothing, but not fit to bear him an heir for Aix.

Although Raymond enjoyed teasing Alys, he did not really want her to disgrace herself in front of his family. Nor did he desire to lose control of himself and spoil his mother's mood. Thus, when he saw Alys urgently biting her lips at a particularly silly effusion, in which both knight and lady perished in an excess of sentiment, Raymond decided to end their torment. As the last notes died away, he stood up abruptly.

"This is all too much for my poor Alys, atop the traveling and setting her apartment to rights and meeting my father and mother," he said. "I will take her to her rooms to rest and recover."

It seemed, in fact, all too true. Alys's shoulders were shaking, and she had her sleeve pressed firmly against her lips while tears welled from her tight-shut eyes. Alphonse rose and embraced her, murmuring soothingly, but Raymond pulled her away and pressed her against him with brutal force, burying her head under his arm.

"You are making her worse, Father," he explained when Alphonse protested angrily. His voice choked and his face rigid as if he were in a fury. "She is only overtired," he continued. "Tomorrow she will be quite well."

Raymond left quickly, sweeping Alys into his arms so that her shorter and almost certainly faltering stride would not delay them, and ignoring the cries and questions that followed them. He had been just in time, for he could feel Alys whooping in his arms as she struggled to draw breath and not howl aloud.

"Stop that," he choked. "If I give way now, I will drop you, and we will both fall down the stairs."

"Put me down," she gasped.

He did so, and they clung together for a moment, struggling with themselves. Both were aware of the danger of Alphonse following them, but fortunately Lady Jeannette had checked her husband's impulse by pointing out that his interference only seemed to make Raymond crueler. Thus, supporting one another's uneven footsteps, Alys and Raymond were able to reach the haven of the south tower. Here both collapsed.

"Monster!" Alys cried when she had breath enough. "Cruel monster! How dare you set me to laughing over those silly songs and then make all worse by sounding as if I were one of the frail flowers they lamented. If I had choked to death, you would be a murderer."

Holding his aching ribs, Raymond shook his head. "How else could I have saved us? I saw you were ready to burst, and I was also."

"It is all your fault," Alys sighed, exhausted from laughing. "I had grown quite accustomed at court. If you had not started laughing like a jackass when your mother asked me to sing, all would have been well."

"Sorry," Raymond gasped, and began to laugh again, groaning between whoops as his muscles protested. He wiped his eyes. "I do not know why it struck me so funny," he said at last. "You are so small, so sweet and delicate, you are just the type to sing such songs—and you *do* have a sweet voice. I have heard it."

Alys looked surprised. "You have heard me sing?"

"Yes, sometimes when you sew in the evening you sing, and also you sang while we rode to the slow pace of the carts."

"Country songs," Alys said, blushing.

Raymond got up from his chair and pulled her out of hers into his arms. "At least those songs do not make me laugh. They are of real things, of plowing and spinning, of the coming of spring. They are sweet to hear, Alys, when you sing as you work. I hope my speaking of it will not silence you."

She smiled at him. "Perhaps it would if I were aware of it, but even now after you have told me, I cannot really remember singing. Likely I will not realize I am doing it. Raymond, those were sweet evenings at Blancheforte."

They looked at each other, memory warm in each pair of eyes. Then Raymond sighed. "I must go, my love. We should not be alone here too long."

Alys nodded. She understood that they must give no cause for gossip until it was decided how their wedding was to be treated. "Be careful you are not seen coming back," she warned. "That would be worse than staying openly."

"Good God, I forgot!" Raymond exclaimed. "I must show you the passage. I chose this tower because it is the one with the wall passage to the keep. I will come that way."

He walked to the wall just beyond where the man-high black iron candlestick stood. Twisting uncomfortably at an unnatural angle, he trod on the stone between the clawed legs of the candlestick, which was fastened by base and shaft to the wall behind. Alys had thought nothing of that. It was a heavy piece that could injure anyone if it should fall. With his foot on the stone, Raymond pushed strongly at the wall. Creaking, a block of the masonry pivoted, showing a black hole, which Alys assumed was the passage.

"I wanted to show you so you would not be frightened." He allowed the block to pivot closed.

"Will those who know of this suspect you are visiting me?"

Raymond widened his eyes into a look of great innocence. "What a shocking thought! Would I do such a thing?" Then seeing that Alys looked uneasy, he said, "My father knows, of course. I doubt anyone else will think of it, but if there should be talk we will forgo all but the second ceremony itself." He pulled her into his arms for another kiss. "I am not willing to keep apart from you, my love—even if you cannot make lute songs."

But the comfort of her husband's presence was to be denied Alys. Raymond returned not an hour later, looking black as thunderclouds, to tell her that his mother had begged him to ride over to visit her widowed sister, Lady Catherine, who had been established by Lord Alphonse's generosity on a small estate only one league to the south.

"I will wait," Alys promised. "It does not matter if you are late returning."

Raymond's frown cleared, and he kissed her. "No, do not sit up waiting for me. You are tired, I know." He touched her face gently with a forefinger where mauve, bruised-looking patches showed beneath her eyes. "This homecoming of mine cannot have been easy for you. I know my mother was not very welcoming, and Jeanine has grown into a spiteful bitch since her husband died. Do not be discouraged, dearling. Mother will grow accustomed, even fond, after a time. She is like a spoiled child—" He broke off and laughed softly. "You told me that, and now I am telling it to you. Be patient. Mother needs a space of time to accept that a thing must be so." He sighed. "To speak the truth, this homecoming has not been so easy for me, either."

"How selfish I am," Alys said, "to urge you to break your sleep twice just for the pleasure of having you lie beside me. Indeed, you must *not* come if you are late returning home."

Raymond's grip on her tightened. "You are the delight of my life and a refreshment to my soul. It is not that I would yield a minute of lying beside you for the breaking of my sleep ten times, beloved. It is that I fear I will not be able to come at all, and you will lie awake all night waiting for me. Take Bertha to your bed, my love, if you feel strange here."

Alys hugged him back. "Oh, no. How could I be so cruel! It is Hugo's first night off duty. They are bedded in the chamber below, where Hugo can guard the door as well as enjoy his wife—not that there is anything to guard against here in Tour Dur; it is only habit. Do not worry about me. I will sleep sound."

With a moue of distaste for his duty, Raymond squeezed his wife once more. "If I can come, I will, but do not *dare* lie awake waiting. I do not want to see you still all blue beneath the eyes tomorrow. Like as not, my aunt will keep me overnight." Raymond had begun to look angry again, but then his expression softened. "Aunt Catherine *would* make you welcome, Alys, but my mother says she has been very ill and I must not put even the gentle burden of your company on her. This, of course, may be only my mother's saying, but my father seemed concerned, also. In truth, that was why I agreed to go alone this afternoon."

"I am sorry to hear of her illness," Alys said with ready sympathy. "I would be very glad to nurse her, if she would have me. Do you ask her, Raymond." Then she dimpled at her husband. "I take it she is childless, and you are the apple of her eye?"

"Not childless, but she has no son." Raymond grinned back at his wife. "I will ask about the nursing. If she will have you, I will move to her manor with you. It will be a pleasure. In truth, I owe her more than simple courtesy. She bought me my first sword, against my mother's will, and bade an old man-at-arms, who still serves her, to teach me—and that even though she knew my mother might take from her what little she had."

"But your mother was well dowered—I know, because you told me her lands when we talked about what was to come with me—and I take it Lady Catherine was the elder. How comes she to be so poor?"

"She was ill-used by her husband's family. Not that my father or brother would do the same, but it was in my mind when I agreed that you should hold your own property."

"Your father never would ill-use me!" Alys exclaimed.

"No," Raymond agreed with a smile. "He loves you dearly already. You should hear how he scolded me for misusing you." They both laughed, and he kissed her again briefly before pulling his cloak tighter. "Gros Choc will be cold," he murmured, rubbing his cheek against her hair. "I must go."

Despite Raymond's warning, Alys did not go early to bed. She sat alone by the fire, embroidering, but she was not unhappy. Mostly she thought of what Raymond had said about Jeanine—that she had soured after being forced to return home by the death of her husband. Then it occurred to her that Lady Jeannette liked to have her daughters about to serve her and be company for her. But Alys knew how hard it was to be a daughter again once one had been the mistress of a household. Perhaps Jeanine wished for a second husband.

Later Alys sent Bertha to procure wine, cold meat, and some sweet cakes. She ate a little but put most aside in case Raymond should want refreshment if he was able to come to her. By the time it was fully dark, however, she had all but given up hope of that, and when a furious winter storm broke, Alys sighed, called down to Bertha to warm the bed for her, and crept in alone. Unlike the nights at Blancheforte, she slept at once.

When Raymond had returned to the hall after carrying Alys out with so little delay and so little regret in his expression, Lady Jeannette felt her work was already complete. However, when her son showed so much reluctance to visit Lady Catherine, always a great favorite with him, and insisted he wished to take Alys with him, Lady Jeannette became doubtful again. His yielding, when she said Catherine had been ill, soothed her, but she did not like Raymond's discontented expression. Even if he did think of Alys only as a useful servant, one could grow fond of servants. It was not enough, Lady Jeannette decided, that he should not accord Alys the highest form of love. It would be best if Raymond learned to dislike his wife as well as feel contempt for her.

Lady Jeannette had planned how to accomplish this. She intended to give Raymond's two daughters into Alys's care. It was only fitting that the children be raised in their father's household and not distract their mother from her work. That would be one benefit, but Lady Jeannette was sure Alys would be resentful about having such mongrels thrust upon her. As sure as the sun would rise in the morning, that nasty blond bitch would be cruel to the children. Whatever Raymond thought of his baseborn daughters—and he seemed too fond of them for his mother's taste—he would dislike his wife very much for mistreating them.

Perhaps Lady Jeannette should have taken warning from the beginning of the hard winter's storm that night. The wind blew in angrily from the sea, howling and whining around the towers. About midnight the storm slackened, but it was apparently only gathering strength for a new onslaught. Toward dawn, rain began to fall in torrents, and one would have thought that the sun had not risen. It was nearly as dark as night when it should have been morning.

Partly out of exhaustion and partly because it was so dark, Alys slept very late. She missed Mass and breakfast before she stretched and put aside the bed curtains. Bertha was waiting, sewing by the fire, which leapt and danced and occasionally spouted gouts of smoke into the room in response to the vagaries and violence of the wind. It was clear from the maid's attitude that she had been waiting a long time.

"Good gracious," Alys murmured, looking toward one of the narrow slits, which were all the windows the tower had. "I have not slept the day through, have I?"

"No, my lady," Bertha replied, smiling. "It is not much past tierce."

"Why did you not wake me?" Alys cried, bouncing out of bed.

"My lord was here about the prime and bid me strictly not to disturb you."

"He came in and I did not wake?" For no particular reason that worried Alys.

"Not up here, my lady. Lord Raymond came in below and bade me look in on you. He said he knew you would wake if you heard his step."

Alys was both pleased and annoyed. She was glad Raymond should be so tender and considerate, but doubtless Lady Jeannette would have something to say about so slug-a-bed a daughter. Alys used the pot and washed sketchily. With the wind so strong, it was cold in the tower room despite the fire, so she dressed quickly, but with careful choice nonetheless. Although no one had said anything, Alys had seen glances cast at her well-worn traveling dress. Nor was there any need, she thought, to worry about her clothing being damaged. She would not be going to the kitchens or around the farms. Clearly the ladies of this house did not demean themselves with such duties.

By the time Alys had struggled across the bailey, she discovered that the ladies had retired to Lady Jeannette's solar, and Raymond and his father were "somewhere about the keep." Resisting the temptation to sit down by the fire and wait for her husband, Alys made her way up the stairs. She found her mother- and sisters-by-marriage typically employed. Lady Jeannette and Jeanine were playing at tables, and Margot was plucking softly on a lute and apparently copying down the notes. The scene irritated Alys so much that she needed to bite her lips to keep from shouting at those three silly women.

Alys had nothing against playing games; she enjoyed them very much and was skilled in chess, tables, and a number of others. But games were for long evenings when the day's work was finished, or to ease the impatience of a convalescent. Just then Lady Jeannette saw her and beckoned her forward with a smile.

"We thought you were afraid of the storm and had decided not to come across to us," Lady Jeannette said. "I was quite cross with Raymond for placing you so far away that we could not comfort you."

This was an interesting turnabout, Alys thought, but she only said, "What is there to fear in a storm? Perhaps if I were at sea or in the open or in a serf's flimsy hut, I would be afraid, but in the south tower I did not even know there was a storm. I am sorry to say it was sloth, not fear, that kept me away. I slept very late."

Jeanine looked up from the game board. "Do you not feel uneasy, shivery, and likely to cry for no reason?"

It was difficult to discern in the warm light of the many candles that lit the room, but Alys thought Jeanine was pale. She must be the one who feared storms. There was nothing silly in that; it was one's nature or not one's nature. Alys knew horses and dogs reacted to storms, and no one could accuse them of silly fancies.

"Sometimes I do feel that way, indeed," Alys replied sympathetically, "although in my case it is not storms that bring it on."

An expression of interest crossed Jeanine's face. She seemed about to speak again when Lady Jeannette said, "It is your move, Jeanine. You are delaying the game. Sit down, Alys."

Sit and watch them play? Alys's jaw tightened over a yawn. She glanced at Margot, but realized there would be no immediate relief from that quarter. The younger girl had smiled at her warmly when she came in and then waved a hand at what she was doing to indicate she wished to finish it.

"I think I will disturb you less if I go down to the hall," Alys said. Perhaps she could find the steward and discover what she could do to help him. The man, she had felt the previous day when he had shown gratitude, surprise, and relief that she did not expect him to oversee her unpacking, was probably overburdened.

"No, no," Lady Jeannette protested. "I have something of great interest to show you. It will be best if you wait here."

Reminding herself that she had known she would be bored to death in Tour Dur and that open rebellion over a few minutes more or less in that state was stupid, Alys walked toward a window. To reach her goal, it was necessary to pass Margot, and the girl reached up and drew Alys down on the bench with her.

"I am copying some simple music," Margot said very softly.

"Mama thinks you should learn to play. Raymond would like it very much if you could sing to him."

The first thought that came into Alys's head was that Lady Jeannette knew how much Raymond disliked formal music. Her next thought, which came almost simultaneously, was how funny Raymond would think it if she did learn. The third —and first sensible one—was that music was not a skill that could be learned in a week or a month, even if she had a talent for it. Suddenly Alys chuckled. Lady Jeannette did *not* know that Raymond only listened to his sisters' songs out of politeness. Doubtless his mother hoped he would be disgusted by Alys's singing and playing because of the sour notes and bad timing a beginner displayed.

"I could not," Alys said, equally softly. "I am so stupid and clumsy. I fear this art is not for me."

"I cannot believe that," Margot replied, smiling. "A person who is moved to tears, as you were yesterday, will learn easily and quickly. There must be a great desire in you to make music."

There was a little silence while Alys again choked on suppressed mirth. She promised herself she would murder her husband for all the trouble his warped sense of humor had brought upon her. Unfortunately, the heightened color that came into Alys's cheeks from suppressing her laughter merely served to convince Margot that Alys was fearful of her lack of ability rather than reluctant to waste valuable time on a silly pursuit. Margot murmured comfortingly to her sister-by-marriage that she was too modest, that all would be made easy and simple. And, she added as confirmation, even if Alys found the lessons difficult, they would have the pleasure of one another's company.

This last remark gave Alys enough to think about to curb her mirth. She saw at once that it would be possible to divert Margot from music and therefore agreed. Margot was beautifully dressed and was clearly fond of her, Alys thought. Thus, Margot would be just the one to advise on the remaking of her gowns to suit the Provençal style. Alys asked a question about the shaping of a sleeve, pointing to her arm and then Margot's, which were side by side.

As both their interests were engaged in the discussion of fashion, Alys's and Margot's voices rose from hushed mur-

murs to normal tones of speech. Absorbed in their conversation, neither noticed the irritated glances cast at them by Lady Jeannette. She had given Margot permission to teach Alys music for just the reason Alys had earlier deduced. There was nothing that set a music lover's teeth on edge like the display of a crude, half-learned skill by a novice performer with too much pride and too little sense. However, she had not considered that her permission would open the door to friendship between Alys and Margot. The cheerful give-and-take of the conversation annoyed Lady Jeannette. She made several wrong moves and, at last, pettishly swept her hand over the board, knocking the pieces helter-skelter.

"That is enough, Margot," she said, forcing a smile. "You are supposed to teach music, not gabble about dress. How do you expect Alys to learn anything? Finish writing the lessons now. I have something to show Alys—a charge it is time for me to transfer to her hands."

Although she rose at once, Alys was surprised. It was true that Lady Jeannette now seemed much less antagonistic, but Alys still felt the only thing her mother-by-marriage would like to give her was a dose of poison. Thus, she was sure the "charge" would be unpleasant. Alys could not imagine what it could be, and certainly she did not immediately connect it with the two little girls uncomfortably perched on stools too high for them, tightly clutching one another's hands, in a small, cold chamber off Lady Jeannette's solar. The faces of the children were pale and tear-streaked.

Alys's glance passed right over the little girls as her mind sought what "charge" could be given to her in a storage room or maid's sleeping chamber. Jewels, which she could then be accused of taking without permission? Nonsense. Margot and Jeanine had heard Lady Jeannette say she was about to give her something.

Then a slight movement by the children, a shrinking together, brought Alys's eyes back to them. The posture, the place, the tears had already added up in some subconscious part of Alys's mind to "punishment." Her own experience with being whipped and then told to sit and consider her sins had been liberal—Alys had been a very willful and mischievous little girl. Now, suddenly, Alys associated the "charge" with the punishment. It would be just like Lady Jeannette to tell the poor little creatures they were to be whipped and then make them wait and, in addition, try to make Alys do the whipping.

Alys had just got as far as thinking, *No, I will not,* when Lady Jeannette said, "This is Fenice, and this is Enid," gesturing toward the children in turn. "They are Raymond's daughters."

"Raymond's daughters!" Alys echoed. She could not believe her ears. Raymond would have told her had he been married previously.

"My son is not a eunuch, as you know," Lady Jeannette said, elated by the shock Alys displayed and misunderstanding its cause. "They are baseborn, the mother was a common serf, but they are Raymond's—or, at least, he says he believes they are—so they belong in his household."

Alys had been staring at the little girls, who were clutching each other even more tightly and struggling to repress renewed sobs. Nonetheless, she had managed to take in the contempt in Lady Jeannette's voice when she called them baseborn. Two feelings struck Alys at once: relief that Raymond had not lied about or "forgotten" to mention a previous marriage and jealousy of the children's mother. Almost instantly her mind recalled the words *"was* a common serf," fixing on the past tense and eagerly leaping to the assumption that the children's mother was dead. The fact that the younger child was at least four years of age further encouraged Alys's self-delusion.

Meanwhile, Lady Jeannette had turned angrily on Fenice and Enid, calling them stupid little sluts and ordering them to make their curtsies to their new mother. The use of the word "mother" was deliberate and emphasized; Lady Jeannette found it offensive that Alys, not nearly as highbred as she, should call *her* "mother." She was certain that Alys would feel even more violently about having lowborn bastards call her "mother."

The stools were too high for the children's short legs to reach the floor, and the poor things had been sitting on them, frozen with fear and cold, for hours. They had always been afraid of "the great ladies," having picked up their mother's terror of the nobility. They were particularly afraid of their grandmother, since Lucie had repeatedly warned them to stay out of Lady Jeannette's way—and Lady Jeannette's attitude toward them when she did come across them had done nothing to reduce their fear. Her manner of ordering them dressed in their best and telling Lucie that they were to be "taken away" by a new mother, and then of telling them that they must not make a sound or move from the stools, had, naturally, induced terror in them. They had literally moved as little as possible, so that their little legs were quite numb. In attempting to obey Lady Jeannette's harsh order, both finally tumbled down from their stools.

Whatever Alys's reaction might have been under other circumstances, this pathetic sight overcame any reservations. She leapt forward and then knelt beside the sobbing children, gathering them into her arms.

"My poor little dears," she cried. "Are you hurt? Those stools were too high for you. You shall have smaller ones. Come, loveys, do not weep. Alys will make all better. Tell Alys where you are hurt."

This softness surprised Fenice and Enid very much—for though their mother loved them, she had neither the time nor the type of personal experience that would lead her to cosseting her children. They stopped crying to look up with wonder at this soft-voiced, sweet-smelling great lady.

"There, my dears, there," Alys soothed, falling automatically into the tone of voice and words her own nurse had used with her. "There is nothing to be afraid of anymore. Alys will take good care of you." She set them on their feet and smiled at them. "You are Fenice," she said to the taller child, and was rewarded with a shy nod. "And you are Enid." The little one only stared with wide, dark eyes. "I am your papa's wife," Alys continued, "and I am sure you love your papa. I also love your papa, so I must love you, too, and I am sure you will learn to love me."

Lady Jeannette had been listening to this in blank amazement. She simply could not believe that Alys meant what she said. Tear-stained and sniffling children, even her own, had never appealed to Lady Jeannette. She had occasionally enjoyed playing with her own babies when they were happy, but had handed them back to their nurse at the first sign of whimpers. All she could think was that Alys believed *she* was fond of the creatures and wished to take them away to spite her. Alys had certainly been horrified when she first heard that

Raymond had children. It was inconceivable that Alys had changed her tune so rapidly without good reason to do so.

In a sense Lady Jeannette was correct. Alys's warmth —after she had recovered from the shock of learning that Raymond was a father—had been generated by pity. However, even as she soothed Fenice and Enid, her mind had been working on a different level from her tongue. She had seen in the children a solution to a whole series of problems. Not only would Fenice and Enid provide some antidote to boredom, but they could be used as an excuse for avoiding too much of Lady Jeannette's company or Margot's music lessons. What was more, their education could be used as a cover for almost any activity in which Alys wished to engage.

Now, rising to her feet, she took one little hand in each of hers and became aware that the children were shivering and cold as ice. Their dresses were far too thin, Alys saw, and a little too small, also. It occurred at once to Alys that the gowns might have been given or ordered by Raymond the preceding spring when he was last at home for an extended period, and being their "best," they had been clothed in these inappropriate garments to meet their new mother. What was more, the children had clearly been prepared to meet her as soon as she arrived in the morning. That meant the poor creatures had been waiting in that icy room for hours. And then, Lady Jeannette had calmly gone on playing that stupid game. . . . Before she even thought to restrain herself, Alys cast a furious glance at Lady Jeannette.

"Have they a nurse?" Alys asked icily.

The enraged glance, the icy voice, and the question about the nurse confirmed all Lady Jeannette's hopes about Alys's rage at being saddled with Raymond's lowborn get. "Of course not," Lady Jeannette replied. "Since when do serf-children have nurses?"

She almost added that their mother gave them such care as was necessary for a serf's children, when she recalled that Lucie was no longer supposed to be living in the keep. Raymond had told her to have the woman married off, but that was ridiculous. Sometimes her son was too soft—and always to the wrong people. Imagine saying that Lucie had a right to a life of her own. She was a good weaver, one of the best she had, and Lady Jeannette had no intention of losing her labors. Instead, Lucie had been told to keep out of sight.

Alys bit back an angry retort, which she knew would do no good. Not much interested in Fenice and Enid at first, she had been forced by Lady Jeannette's indifferent cruelty into active championship of the two shivering mites she was now holding close to her sides for whatever warmth they could find in her full-skirted gown. This was no time to cross Lady Jeannette, who, seeing that she did not regard the "charge" as onerous, might try to take the children back. Alys lowered her glittering eyes, fearing that too much might be read in them.

"May I ask one of the women to collect the children's clothing, then?" Alys asked. "They are cold."

"Nonsense. Serfs do not feel the cold any more than dogs. Anyway, the clothes are here."

Lady Jeannette gestured to two bundles, feeling more and more pleased with her ploy. Alys had wasted her time trying to conceal her anger, a reaction which Lady Jeannette had expected. Lady Jeannette would herself have been furious to have baseborn bastards thrust upon her. No doubt Alys would complain to Raymond. He would not like that, Lady Jeannette thought, neither the aspersions cast on his daughters nor the anger displayed toward his mother. And then, all that sweetness to the little girls. Surely that was a clean cover over ugly intentions.

Raymond feels the cold, Alys thought, *and his blood runs in these veins*. But she did not give voice to the words in her mind. She only told the children to hold to her dress while she stooped to pick up the bundles of clothing. *Raymond's blood*. The thought brought a rush of tenderness and then a prick of jealousy as she thought of the mother. But the mother was gone, and these little girls were no more threat to her, Alys knew, than she had been to Lady Elizabeth. There were many ways a man could love, and a father's fondness for his daughters did not encroach on what he felt for his wife.

"I will take them down to the hall," Alys said, "so that their noise will not disturb you."

Alys could not bring herself to say "mother" this time, but Lady Jeannette did not seem to notice the omission and merely nodded. It was well that Lady Jeannette had already implied so strongly that the children were not to *her* taste. Had she been less open, Alys would have had them change their dresses before the fire in Lady Jeannette's solar for the sake of warming them more quickly, and that would have precipitated a bitter quarrel. Alys's caution would not have been proof against her temper when she saw the bruises the edge of the stools had made on the legs of the little girls in the hours they had been forced to sit and wait.

CHAPTER 16

****

Actually the rage Alys felt at Lady Jeannette's cruelty to her helpless grandchildren produced, strangely enough, a most happy effect. Unable to vent her fury on her mother-by-marriage, Alys turned it to tenderness toward Fenice and Enid, which further melted the reserve they felt toward this very different great-lady-mother. Enid, who because she was younger was less imbued with her mother's fear of the lords, began to chatter. Fenice was quiet unless a direct question was asked her. A sense of her own unworthiness had been deeply implanted in her, but she saw that Lady Alys listened to Enid with pleasure and amusement. Fenice stood as close as she dared to this kind, beautiful "mother" and, when she thought Alys would not notice, gently touched her sleeve or dress to reassure herself that Alys was real.

It was easy to direct Enid's artless confidences. Alys discovered that the children had been taught nothing. Their speech was better than that of common serfs because they echoed the accent and vocabulary of the maids, and Fenice could do some rough sewing and knew the elements of weaving. They adored their father and were timidly fond of their grandfather. Both men were kind—whenever they noticed the children—but Alys gathered this notice came infrequently. They had been told, it seemed, never to approach either man, especially their grandfather. Enid began to explain this further, but Fenice shushed her. Alys assumed Enid had been about to admit that it was Lady Jeannette who had ordered them to keep out of the way, and the wiser, more politic Fenice had not wanted her sister to criticize their grandmother.

Alys did not press the question. Instead she smiled at Fenice, who confessed, "But sometimes we do speak to Father. He always seems glad to see us."

"I am certain he is, my loves," Alys assured them, "and you

must understand that he does not seek you out more often because his mind is filled with large, important things. But you will both see more of him now because we will all live together. When he has time, I will call you, and we will all play games."

"Play games?" Fenice echoed.

Alys laughed. "Not the kind of games you play with your sister or with the other children. These are special games, but you will enjoy them. Only I will have to teach you how to play. Then we will surprise your papa with your cleverness."

"Are we clever?" Enid asked.

"Yes, indeed, and beautiful, too," Alys said—and then felt a little surprised because she realized she had spoken the truth.

The children were very pretty, with masses of dark, curling hair—rather tangled and not as clean as it should be, but that would be easily amended. And there could be no doubt at all that Fenice was Raymond's; his light eyes, not so hard and bright, but his nonetheless, looked out of her face. Her skin, however, was quite light; not the translucent alabaster of Alys's, but a warm cream. Enid was the one with Raymond's complexion, dark and smooth, but her eyes must be her mother's, large, luminous, and soft as black velvet. *Their mother must have been beautiful,* Alys thought, with another stab of jealousy.

Emboldened by Alys's praise, Enid had just begun to say how quickly and well she would learn the new games when Raymond's voice cut across hers. "Fenice! Enid!" And after a slight pause, *"Sacre bleu,* Alys!"

The girls ran to him, and he stooped and caught one in each arm automatically, but his eyes were on Alys and his skin was a dark flushed red. It was clear enough that he was appalled by the association of his wife and his natural daughters.

Fearing he would say something that would hurt the little girls, Alys forestalled him. "Your mother gave the girls into my care, my lord," she said quickly. "And I am most happy to have them. Your mother said they belonged in your household, and I agree with that, too, with all my heart."

Conflicting emotions rippled across Raymond's face—anger and relief and embarrassment. "You . . . want them?" he stammered.

"Yes. Yes, I do. They are yours, and they are *sweet* children," Alys replied.

"But—but what will you do with them?"

"I will teach them, of course," Alys laughed. "I know just what is suitable to these daughters of yours."

Raymond looked down at the children, more aware of them than he usually was. He remembered with a guilty pang that when he had last seen them he had made a promise to give each a present "later." At the same time he was annoyed. He had something to discuss with Alys, and Fenice and Enid were in the way. Still, the adoration in their happy faces checked his impulse to send them away. Instead, he sat down in the chair opposite Alys, lifted one child to each knee, and apologized gravely for neglecting to give them the promised gifts. This time, however, he assured them there would be no mistake, because Lady Alys would remind him.

"So I will," Alys agreed.

There was warm approval in her eyes and her smile, and Raymond was at the same time pleased and uneasy. It was just like Alys to accept the girls with open arms, sweet and reasonable as she was, but he wished she had not. She would be forever attending to them when he wanted her. It was his mother's fault, not Alys's or the girls', and it was annoying that there was nothing he could do about it. He realized that Enid had said something he had not caught, but Alys was laughing and shaking her head, and Fenice was anxiously shushing her sister.

"It is not necessary," Fenice said. "The . . . she . . . the lady is the best present of all."

Her voice broke with trepidation, and she crimsoned with embarrassment because she did not know what to call Alys. But Raymond could not help being pleased, and he gave his eldest daughter an affectionate squeeze.

"You must call her Lady Alys, Fenice," he said, "and you may not realize it yet, but you never said or will say a truer thing in your life. And what did you say, little mouse, that made my wife laugh?" he asked Enid.

Enid hung her head. She had learned that if Fenice hushed her, she was generally punished for repeating what her sister had warned against.

"Enid has a logical mind and will take to accounts very

well," Alys teased, "whereas Fenice will be a marvelous peacemaker. Enid said that you could make all right by giving each of them *two* presents this time."

The girls turned frightened eyes on Alys, shocked by this betrayal, but a second later all was turned to joy as their father laughed and agreed that it would be two presents. But, he said, Alys would have to furnish one of them because she had forced him to acknowledge Enid's logic. This made Alys laugh, too, since she had already come to realize that she would need to furnish both gifts, if the girls were to get them.

Out of sight was out of mind as far as Raymond's relationship with his daughters was concerned. He was fond of them, Alys saw, but they were not to him what she had been to her father. This warned her that he would grow impatient with them at this stage. Later, when they could show him some skills, he might be more interested, but at the present time the childish prattle would be a surfeit.

"Now, my dears," Alys said, "let your father be. Go and play, but take care not to go too close to the fire."

They slid from Raymond's knees at once, accustomed as they were to a stinging slap from their busy mother if an order had to be repeated. Usually obedience went unrewarded, since it was expected, and disobedience was sharply punished, but this time each had a hearty kiss for promptly doing as they were told. Hugging their joy, they hurried behind the chairs to a private spot where they could disinter their rag babies from the center of their bundles where Lucie had hidden them.

"It is very good of you, Alys," Raymond said as soon as the children disappeared, "but there is really no reason to burden you with my—er—indiscretions. I cannot imagine what my mother was thinking of when she suggested you take them in charge."

"They will be no burden, my lord," Alys protested, smiling. "You see how good and obedient they are."

"But they still need to be . . ." Raymond hesitated, having not the least idea of what was entailed in caring for children. "They need to be washed and dressed and—and suchlike."

Alys laughed at him. "I did not propose to take on the duties of a nursemaid, Raymond. Naturally, I will employ a woman to see to such things. Until I find someone, Bertha can attend to their physical needs, and I will teach them. I suppose no one thought of it, and you were away too much, but they are dreadfully ignorant. After all, they are your daughters. Suitable matches will need to be found for them, and they will need to know the duties of a chatelaine."

"You are right," Raymond said rather blankly.

He was not disturbed by the idea of providing proper marriages for his daughters, but by the realization that he could not suggest—as he had been about to do—that they be left in their mother's care. Naturally, Lucie could not teach them anything to the purpose, and the hut of a huntsman was no place to raise them. From what Alys said, no one else had attempted to fit them for their station, either. Probably he should have realized that his mother and sisters would not have troubled themselves with teaching his daughters.

"You do not mind that they will be forever under your feet?" Raymond asked.

Then Alys saw what was making Raymond reluctant that she care for his girls. "They will not be in the way at all, my lord," she assured him. "They will have their own quarters, and I will only need to take them with me when I see to household matters so that they can learn." She smiled at him. "They will not be under *your* feet. A man has little to do with daughters—except to kiss them now and again, and tell them how pretty they are, and give them presents, of course."

That made Raymond laugh, and, since Alys never allowed the demands of her household duties to interfere when he wanted her attention, the frown smoothed from his brow, but only momentarily. He looked over his shoulder at the entryway from the lower floor, and the frown returned. Then he signaled Alys to rise, took her chair, from which he could see the doorway, and motioned that she draw a stool up close.

"I have been down in the armory with my father," he said very softly, "and I am greatly troubled. Nothing is as it should be. Weapons have been flung down anywhere, rusted and broken, and unmended armor is lying useless. If we had to call in men, there would be no arms or armor for them. I do not know what my father has been doing—beyond listening to lute songs."

"There has been peace in these lands for many years," Alys suggested diffidently.

Raymond grimaced. "Once my grandfather established him-

self and broke the power of des Baux, yes. But that is no
excuse, especially since Grandfather was so desperately ill.
And it is not as if father did not know. He spoke to me himself
of the danger of war and the doubts of our vassals." He made
another moue of distaste. "I see now why they are doubtful. It
needs a man—" He stopped speaking abruptly.

Alys put a hand on his. "You are here now, my love, and all
will go better."

"I love my father." Raymond stared down into Alys's face.
"There is no better, kinder man, but . . . When he saw the
armory, he was appalled and ashamed, but he did not order the
master-at-arms to be punished or dismissed. He—"

"Raymond," Alys interrupted, "your father is not only kind
but just. He would not punish the master-at-arms for his own
fault. Perhaps he will not say it is his fault, but in his heart he
knows it."

"So why, instead of coming with me to talk of how the
problem can be most swiftly amended, did he run above to
seek comfort from my mother and sisters?"

"Oh, Raymond, if you looked so black at me as you must
have at him, I would have run elsewhere, too."

"Not you!" he exclaimed and laughed, but only briefly.
"This armory is the least of the danger. If it was neglected, so
too must have been the men. I know it is harder for a
master-at-arms when the lord is neglectful, but this man should
have known his duty better than this, even without overseeing.
What am I to do? Order my father to punish the man or dismiss
him?"

"The master-at-arms was with you in the armory?"

"Yes, and I did not like the way he looked—as if it were not
a disgrace to him."

"Tell him that he has one chance to make all right—so many
days or weeks. You will know the time it must take. This
much, surely, you may do without your father's orders."

"Yes." Raymond gestured impatiently. "But really this is
only the tip showing. Alys, if the vassals have been neglected
as this keep has been and my grandfather should die, half of
the liegemen, more perhaps, will break away. I can fight one
or two—"

"There is no profit in fighting one's own vassals," Alys said
quickly.

She had heard the words many times on Richard of Cornwall's lips, but they had meant little to her in the days when the only vassal about whom she cared was her father. It was totally inconceivable to her that her father and her uncle Richard should come to blows for any reason at all. Now, however, the words had become more meaningful than Alys desired.

"My sage counselor." Raymond's lips twisted. "You are so right, as usual, and it is no wish of mine to do so. Yet, if they feel there is no profit in vassalage to Aix and they do not fear to be severely checked for turning away, many will try to raise themselves by swearing directly."

"To whom?" Alys asked. "The whole problem rests on your grandfather's illness."

"Not the whole problem. If our vassals felt there was a leader strong enough to bind them together and protect them from the encroachments of others—say Toulouse or Navarre—"

"There is now, is there not, my lord?" Alys broke in.

Her voice was clear and steady, although her heart was heavy at the need to urge Raymond to thrust himself forward. Nonetheless, she knew her duty. Her father had spoken to her seriously, naming his own past failing by avoiding public duties and warning her that her husband already had such duties. She must support him in those duties, Sir William had insisted, not add to Raymond's burdens by discouraging his participation in state affairs.

"I could do it." Raymond's pale eyes glowed. "And I have something to offer them, also. My father and I plan, if Raymond-Berenger should die, to ask Louis of France to take fealty from us."

"Louis!" Alys was shocked.

"It could place me in an awkward position in the future, but while my father is alive—and he has many long years ahead, I hope—it will not affect my duty to King Henry." Raymond explained the fears he and Alphonse had concerning Louis's brother Charles of Anjou and the strong probability of a marriage between that young man and Beatrice. "But I believe something more positive must be offered our vassals than political talk at a wedding."

"You must show you have picked up the reins," Alys said softly.

Raymond's brows drew together in a frown. "I do not wish to supplant my father."

"No!" Alys exclaimed, although she kept her voice low. "But if your father had other, more important duties, such as negotiating with King Louis—"

"Alys, you have it!" Raymond interrupted. "As my father's deputy, I can . . . Yes! I can ride to each major vassal, warn them of the danger, urge them to prepare, and give them hope of a good solution. My father is a master of diplomacy. They will be happy that he has gone to Louis, and, I hope, they will see in me the other side of the coin."

"I am sure they will." Alys tried not to allow her anxiety to show. She was not completely successful, for her voice shook as she asked, "But there will not be any war, will there?"

"I hope not." Raymond smiled at her, his good humor restored by the expectation of direct action that would not precipitate a conflict for power with his father. "A war is no way to ingratiate oneself with a new overlord." Then his smile diminished, and a look of doubt crossed his face. "It will mean that I must be away much of the time until our wedding. I will try to ride back for a night or two, but it may not be possible."

Alys dropped her eyes. She had remembered a remark made in the past about the freedoms southern lords took with their vassals' wives and daughters. Then she looked up and smiled at her husband. To be jealous without reason was to pave a path to misery for herself and Raymond.

"It is just as well, then, that I will have the children to occupy me. But I will miss you, Raymond. I do not sleep easy in a cold bed."

"Neither do I, my love, I assure you." He laughed and stood up. "I will go now to give that master-at-arms a bone to chew on."

Before Alys could speak, he was gone. She started up to follow him, but exerted self-restraint, telling herself not to be a fool. If Raymond meant to be unfaithful, surely he would have said nothing. To mention his own distaste for sleeping alone must only mean he meant to do so. Besides, what one does not know does not hurt, Alys warned herself. It was true that it could do her no harm if Raymond disported himself elsewhere. It should not even touch her pride. To men, such things meant little.

But old, wise saws had little effect on her, and Alys could feel herself flush with rage. She rose and walked to a window to cool her face and saw that the wind had died. It was only raining slightly, and there were pale gold streaks among the black clouds. It seemed a good time to take the children to her own quarters and establish them there, particularly as she was in no mood to make polite conversation with anyone.

Because it began to rain and blow again soon after she shepherded Fenice and Enid across to the south tower, the move was successful insofar as it protected Alys from Raymond's female relatives. Alys's mood improved while she arranged where they were to sleep and delivered the presents Raymond had promised. These were a hair ribbon for each girl —pale blue for Fenice and red for Enid—and a silver penny, which Alys promised they could spend as they liked when the weather cleared and it was possible to take them into the town.

Certainly it seemed that the children would be no trouble. After their morning of terror and the excitement of Alys's and Raymond's kindness, both little girls nodded off to sleep not long after they expressed their joy over the presents. Alys remained in her own quiet chamber until dinnertime, when she made her way back to the great hall. She stopped Gervase and ordered that a plain, simple meal be sent to the south tower for the children, then was seized upon by Margot. Since a glance at her husband showed him deep in conversation with his father, she allowed her sister-by-marriage to pull her aside.

Raising the question of new clothing and a suitable wedding dress interested Margot enough to divert her from the subject of music, and when Lady Jeannette called her younger daughter away, Alys was fortunate enough to be near the chaplain. She discussed with him the question of a governess for the little girls, a woman who could teach them the duties and manners of a gentlewoman, and a tutor who could teach them to read and do accounts in case she should be too busy to attend to such lessons herself.

This subject, with all the explanations and circumlocutions necessary to avoid saying outright that their grandmother had neglected them shamefully, carried Alys to the dinner table, where she discovered that Raymond and Alphonse had pleaded urgent business and withdrawn to eat in private. Since Raymond's seeming neglect of his new wife had put Lady Jeannette in high good humor, she was sweetly sympathetic to Alys about how women were pushed into the background and ignored. Alys made proper, if slightly absent, replies. She was thinking with intense satisfaction that Raymond would be certain to come to her that night, since he might be away for more than a week thereafter.

By the time dinner was over, the weather had finally cleared —and Alys had had enough of Lady Jeannette's conversation. She made care of the children her excuse and went back to her own quarters, assuming that Raymond would come when he had finished his talk with his father. As the hours wore away, however, she became more and more irritable. It did no good to tell herself she was being unreasonable, that she was not ignored and forgotten, that her husband was merely very busy.

A nasty little inner voice kept telling her that Raymond should not be so busy as to preclude a short visit. Knowing that she was being ridiculous, however, only made Alys more irritable. Partly out of a feeling that she could bear no more of Lady Jeannette and Jeanine, who had made several pointed remarks about how brief was a husband's attention since wives were trapped prey and not interesting, and partly out of a feeling that Raymond would notice her absence and be concerned, Alys did not go across for the evening meal. Bertha fetched suitable food for them all, and it was pleasant and cozy in the south tower.

Nonetheless, Alys found little comfort in the situation when Raymond did not come right after the meal. She guessed that his mother was holding him, either in talk or by insisting that he attend another recital of lute songs. For the first time, Alys's conviction that her grip on her husband was too strong to be weakened by Lady Jeannette's devices was shaken. Alys knew that such distractions would not have kept her from going to see why Raymond had not appeared where he was expected, and anger pricked her.

Still, Alys struggled to subdue her temper with the reminder that she herself had warned Raymond to be conciliatory toward his mother so as to spare his father Lady Jeannette's lamentations. Raymond would come as soon as he could, she told herself, and as punishment for her ill humor she set herself to unpicking the seams of a gown that she intended to resew in the style worn in Provence. Later, after the children had been sent off to bed and Raymond still had made no appearance, Alys told herself it was too late for a visit. He would wait now until the keep was asleep and only a few guards prowled the walls. Then he would come.

This assurance permitted her to finish undoing the seams of the gown and let Bertha prepare her for bed with seeming calm. Underneath the placid exterior, however, there was a hard blister of rage. Alys knew that if Raymond arrived with sweet words and apologies, all would be forgotten. If he did not come . . . but that was impossible. There would be no one and nothing to stay him—except his own unwillingness to take the trouble to stay awake and walk through the passage to her chamber. But the hours passed, and he did not come, which intensified the fury already seething inside Alys's quiet body.

From the time they parted, Raymond's day had been exactly the opposite of Alys's. Her forenoon had begun rather pleasantly and degenerated into rage and misery. Raymond's had started with rage and misery and worked its way slowly, very slowly, upward to a sense of satisfaction and accomplishment. Although when he had left Alys he had felt only a quiet determination to set things to rights—having been buoyed up by her confidence in him and her agreement with what he planned—he had been thrown into a rage by the master-at-arms, who met his orders with scarcely veiled insolence and a hand on the hilt of his sword.

Before Raymond gave it a thought, his own weapon was out. At this point, the master-at-arms retreated. To him, Raymond was no more than a boy who came and went at Tour Dur and had never before taken a serious interest in anything. Also, the master-at-arms had assumed the son was like the father—although he would have been equally surprised if he had tried to threaten Alphonse. Raymond's father was no coward, despite the fact that he was disinclined to the arts of war and preferred music.

The threat having backfired, the master-at-arms was more than willing to withdraw it. To do any harm to the son of the house would merit a punishment that was utterly unthinkable. The man was lazy and did not wish to be bothered restoring the effects of his negligence, nor did he wish to accept punishment and had thought a gesture of defiance would overawe a young man of weak character.

To his horror he found there was to be no retreat. Raymond lashed at him—contemptuously, with the flat of his blade. The master-at-arms's shriek of pain and fear attracted others to the scene. A few new men, who did not recognize Raymond and did not stop to think in their excitement, also drew weapons. Arnald, who had been watching with interest and approval as his young master blade-whipped a man who deserved it, now drew his sword and bellowed for his men to come and defend Lord Raymond.

Although there were far more men-at-arms belonging to Tour Dur's than Arnald's small troop, the well-disciplined group had seized shields and weapons and formed a ring about their master before the men of the castle, who had no leader, were aware of what was going on. Moreover, the older men-at-arms, who knew Raymond, were blocking those who wished to go to the aid of the master-at-arms. These older men were trying to explain, shouting that the attacker was Lord Raymond, Lord Alphonse's son, and therefore inviolable, no matter what he chose to do to anyone.

Unfortunately, everyone was growing more and more excited. The Englishmen, with shields locked, were stamping and shouting insults at those they thought to be traitors. Men-at-arms, who had been in distant parts of the castle, came running and, seeing the foreigners seemingly threatening their companions, rushed forward to protect their own.

The master-at-arms in the meantime had been yelling for mercy and was so frightened that he did not realize Raymond was indeed being merciful. Raymond intended to do no more than beat the man to a pulp and throw him out to live or die as he chose. Since he could have had an insolent servant drawn and quartered, Raymond considered himself generous. However, the combination of pain and terror does not lead to clear thought. In desperation, the master-at-arms drew his weapon, thinking only to defend himself. That additional defiance changed Raymond's mind.

To draw steel on one's master, except for the purpose of practice combat when ordered, was the ultimate sin; there could be no excuse for that trespass. Raymond turned his blade and began to wield it in earnest. He was not armed and had no shield, but the master-at-arms was in like case—and Raymond was not frightened, nor lazy, nor out of practice. He parried two wild swings and, when a third was launched, cut off his opponent's arm, hand, and, consequently, his sword. Having disarmed his man, Raymond hesitated for a moment, wondering whether he should cut off the other hand too, sear the stumps, and use the remaining cripple as an object lesson.

The noise surrounding him then penetrated through Raymond's concentration on his own fight. A single swift glance told the story. Angry again at the trouble the man had caused, Raymond simply stepped closer to the master-at-arms, who was on his knees keening and holding his maimed arm, and struck off his head. A single bellow in English silenced Alys's men. They remained with swords drawn at the ready, but challenges and insults were cut off. A second bellow, calling squad leaders by name, soon led to order being reestablished. There were, by this time, several wounded in addition to the dead master-at-arms. Raymond looked around at the disorder and lost his temper all over again. He flayed the Tour Dur men-at-arms for their lack of skill and lack of discipline, using language that made Arnald's eyes round with admiration, and he promised them that they would find hell a place of peace and comfort before he was through with them.

Finally Raymond ordered that all weapons be given into Arnald's care until he had a chance to harrow out the noxious growths from the true plants. Seeing that this order was being obeyed in trembling haste, Raymond ordered that the master-at-arms's body be hung in chains by the barracks, to remind the men, while the flesh dropped from the bones and the stench permeated their lodgings, of the result of negligence and disobedience. Then, still seething, he went to seek his father and relate what had happened.

Considering the circumstances, the temper he was in, and Raymond's feelings about the basic cause of all the trouble —which was his father's lack of attention—Raymond was neither respectful nor conciliatory in what he said. Since Alphonse was already defensive, being as aware as Raymond that he had neglected his duty, he flew into a rage, too. A shouting match ensued, in which ugly accusations were exchanged. However, father and son truly loved one another.

Both were so shocked by the disgusting half-truths that were flung in anger that mutual apologies and tears of repentance soon made peace.

In the quiet of emotional exhaustion that followed, a more rational examination of the problem followed. Pretenses had been stripped away in the quarrel so that Raymond and Alphonse were better able to look at the naked truth. For this time, at least, neither wished for the ameliorative platitudes with which the women would try to cover the real facts. By mutual consent they withdrew to eat together and to work out the details for a division of responsibility between them that would benefit everyone. Although both were trying hard to be honest, each was now overanxious not to hurt the other, so that it took a long time to say what had to be said.

The false dawn had already streaked the sky with pale bands that gave little light when Alphonse stood up wearily and rested his hand on Raymond's shoulder. "No, my son," he said in response to a final plea from Raymond that he believe his son was not trying to seize his father's power. "I know that is true. In the bad years, when we were threatened by Toulouse, my father fought for these lands while I parleyed for allies and made pacts and treaties. I always hated fighting. I am more than glad that you are ready and willing to take up that burden. I am only fearful of laying too great a weight on your shoulders."

"The part you give me is what I like, Father, and what I understand. If you will deal with Louis and with Charles of Anjou—if and when dealing with them becomes necessary—I will have no burden that I consider heavy. I might contrive the pact with Louis, but I know from what you have told me that Charles of Anjou and I would, at best, rub each other wrong and, at worst, come to blows. I can make us strong. I can weld the vassals together. But I fear that saying sweet words to a sour neighbor or overlord might undo me."

Alphonse produced a tired smile. "That I can do, and take pleasure in the doing also. Sleep well, my son. I will see you in the morning."

"No, you will not, for I intend to be gone by first light." Raymond stood up, stretched, and yawned.

"You are tired," Alphonse protested. "Go tomorrow."

Then he sighed and shook his head. He would have delayed

a day because he was tired, and then perhaps another because it rained, and, in the end, he might not have gone at all. Raymond was different, and he had agreed that Raymond should act as he saw fit as his deputy. Then Alphonse saw his son reach for his hauberk.

"Raymond," he protested again, "at least sleep for an hour or two. It is too dark to ride out now."

"Help me on with this, Father. I must go down and settle on a temporary master-at-arms and choose out a group to ride with me. By the time I have done that, it will be light."

Alphonse closed his mouth over another protest. It would not stop Raymond and would only annoy him. He lifted the mail shirt and slid it over Raymond's raised arms after his son had cast aside his elegant tunic and surcoat and pulled on an arming tunic of heavy homespun wool.

As his head emerged through the neck opening, Raymond said, "Alys's men will be here and may be trusted implicitly if there should be any grumbling among our people, for I will leave orders about their training that some of the lazy dogs will not like. You had better tell Alys to give them their orders—"

"Alys!" Alphonse's voice rose to a muted shriek. "What could a woman know of such things? She would faint with fear among the guardsmen."

"Not Alys," Raymond said with pride. "She will sew up their wounds, order them whipped for wrongdoing and watch the whipping, and then salve their weals with not a change in complexion or countenance. She held Marlowe for her father when he was away at war."

Alphonse was now beyond words. He simply stared as Raymond laced up his hood, pulled on a surcoat for riding, and belted his sword. His son's expression first showed a marked longing and then firmed into determination.

"I will not go to her myself," he said with a wry smile, "for I might not find the strength to leave as soon as I should. What I started to say was that if orders are to be given to the Englishmen, tell Alys and she will pass the order along. Arnald speaks fair French, but of the northern kind and most of the other men have only a word or two. Alys will speak in English; they understand that best."

Raymond was pleased with himself for having found an excuse for Alys to give the orders that would not hurt his father's feelings. The truth was that he was not sure Alys's men would obey Alphonse. Then he leaned forward, kissed his still-stunned father fondly, and strode out.

By noon Raymond had reached Gréoux, the stronghold of one of Lord Alphonse's most powerful and influential vassals, where he was greeted with considerable surprise and somewhat more warmth than he had expected. On the way, he had berated himself for forgetting to tell his father about Ernaldus, warning him to investigate carefully any stranger who came to Tour Dur, and telling him to guard Alys against such a person, but Sieur de Gréoux's greeting put it out of his mind. In fact, Raymond soon discovered that matters were not nearly as bad as he had believed. In a way he had underestimated his father. Alphonse was no warrior, but he was just and honest; his vassals had a deep affection for him and would not, under ordinary circumstances, seek to free themselves from his overlordship.

The trouble was that circumstances might become far from ordinary any day. Gréoux did not hide the fact that he had been worried. With Raymond-Berenger's health so precarious and a young, unwed girl as heiress to the province, it was impossible to say what would happen. Romeo de Villeneuve was a paragon of strength and virtue, but it would be a catastrophe for him to try to withstand by force of arms any of the large, hungry mouths that would gape to swallow Provence. This was no time for an overlord to be playing at draughts with his wife, Gréoux said, with more frankness than courtesy.

"I am not so sure of that," Raymond returned. "The count of Provence is my father's father, after all. And my father has good reason to love him. Would you have him bury his father before he is dead? What *can* he do but sit at home and wait for news?" Raymond paused, raised his expressive brows, and continued, "That does not mean he cannot think and plan, or that I, his son and deputy, cannot see to the arming and organization of the men of Aix."

"Ah."

It was an indeterminate sound that could be interpreted many ways. Raymond was reasonably sure it betokened part relief and part inquiry. "My father believes," he went on, "that we need not fear Toulouse—as long as we have the goodwill of France. Louis has crushed Toulouse too thoroughly for him to challenge anyone France favors. French favor will also, most probably, protect us from Navarre. Now Louis's queen, being eldest, has the best right to the land if the will is set aside, so that Louis would never permit Navarre to contest Beatrice's claim. Moreover, Louis has a brother most suitable in age and station to Beatrice."

"Yes," Gréoux admitted, but his voice was flat and a grimace twisted his features.

Raymond laughed. "My father looks just as you do when he speaks of Charles of Anjou."

"Is that so?" Gréoux remarked with suddenly heightened interest.

With a nod Raymond affirmed the point and then began to outline Alphonse's plan to offer homage directly to King Louis. The French were not loved in Provence, but the eastern portions had not been ravaged by the Albigensian Crusade, and Gréoux soon saw the advantages to being tied directly to Louis, especially with the free appanage of Charles of Anjou between Aix and the main holdings of France.

The discussion loosened Gréoux's reserve, and he and Raymond settled into serious talk of the moves that would have to be made in the interim period between the death of Raymond-Berenger and the acceptance by Louis of France of Alphonse's vassalage. Soon, however, dinner with the ladies of the keep interrupted the conversation. Raymond, although he tried several ploys, could not steer Gréoux's wife and unmarried sister away from the subject of Alys. Having had news of his "impending" marriage from the wedding invitation, the ladies wished to hear all about the appearance, dress, manners, and interests of Raymond's "future" wife. Raymond readily extolled Alys's beauty and her many other virtues, but he wished they would have done and allow him to return to more important matters.

In this, Raymond wronged the ladies. The wife of their overlord's heir was an important, actually a political, subject —particularly if, as was obvious, the overlord's heir was marrying for love. If such a lady was offended by a vassal's wife or sister and took a spite, the lady might cause much trouble for the vassal. Raymond never thought of this aspect of their questions and, although in one way he enjoyed talking about Alys, in another it was disturbing. He was suddenly overwhelmed by a desire to see her and touch her again, too aware that it had been several days since he had shared his wife's bed.

A combination of factors served to keep strong Raymond's desire to see Alys. For one thing, Gréoux was less than ten leagues from Aix, only about a six or seven hours' ride. Raymond remembered that he had not even bidden Alys good-bye; even the most sensible woman in the world might feel hurt by that. For another thing, Raymond felt a sharp guilt about blaming his father so bitterly for losing control over his men. Apparently Alphonse had not done so, and Raymond was very eager to admit he had been wrong, at least in part, and set his father's mind at ease.

One more factor tipped the scales completely in favor of Raymond's riding home instead of spending the night at Gréoux. The vassal offered to go himself to several smaller keeps to the east and north to explain Raymond's proposals and urge those men, although he did not think they would need much urging, to have their defenses at peak readiness. Such preparations would warn any local malcontents who thought that the death of Raymond-Berenger was an invitation to pick his province apart, that Aix was too thorny a rose to grasp at with impunity.

Gréoux's offer put Raymond's next port of call to the west. The most direct route would pass north of Aix itself, but Raymond was convinced that a mere three leagues extra would be nothing in comparison with his father's—and Alys's— pleasure. He was very tired when they started back, but also happy. The road was good, the weather fair although cold, the moon bright enough so that a moderate pace could be maintained.

Occasionally Raymond dozed in the saddle, but mostly he thought of Alys, of her cry of joy when she saw him or, more likely, of her delicious, drowsy surprise when he crept into bed beside her. He could imagine the way she would shiver in protest at his cold hands and feet but still hold him close. Sometimes he even allowed himself to envision their final pleasure when comfort deepened into passion.

CHAPTER 17

****

Alys slept hardly more than Raymond the night he sat awake talking to his father. It was most unfortunate that she had decided against going to the evening meal. If she had seen that neither Raymond nor Alphonse appeared at it, she would have realized that some very important business was being discussed and that it was that, rather than his mother's influence, that kept him from coming to her. She would not have resented that, and thus, when she heard of the fight with the master-at-arms, she would not have been further enraged by the fact that Raymond had not come himself to assure her that he was safe.

The news of the fight came to Alys as soon as she summoned Bertha in the morning. Bertha had the general story from Hugo, but it was Arnald, who was called to explain in detail what had happened, who told Alys that Raymond had left Tour Dur with a strong troop of men at dawn and was not expected back for several days.

Alys was outraged at this news. Not only had her husband spent the evening clinging to his mother's skirt, but he had not even had the courtesy to bid her farewell. Pride froze an expression of placid interest on Alys's face until she dismissed Arnald. And it was pride also that drove her to see that Fenice and Enid were dressed and to take them with her to Mass and eventually to join the family at breakfast. Alys's overburdened heart was somewhat eased at Lady Jeannette's fury and at her ability to say calmly that the reason she had brought Raymond's bastards to join the family was that they *were* part of the family.

"Fenice and Enid must learn to bear themselves seemly in gentle company, Mother," Alys said with poisonous sweetness. "You gave your granddaughters into my care, and this is what I think proper for them."

"And so it is," Alponse interjected. "Raymond's daughters must be with us now that they are old enough. How pretty they are, are they not? We will have no trouble finding them husbands."

"If it will be so easy to find a dower and husbands for baseborn bastards," Jeanine spat, "why is it so difficult to do it for me? Even English nobodies can make fine marriages, but I must wither here—"

"Jeanine!" Alphonse protested. "What are you saying? Your mother told me you had begged her not to seek another marriage for you before your grief had passed. Why did you not say you were ready to marry again?"

There was a tight silence as Jeanine turned distended eyes toward her mother. Alphonse's lips tightened as he realized his daughter must have asked her mother to tell him she wished to be married again—and Lady Jeannette had not passed along the message. Lady Jeannette took one look at her husband's face, uttered a piercing shriek, and fell back in her chair. Enid promptly began to cry, too, and Fenice, although she made no sound, turned ghostly white and began to tremble. Alys withdrew the little girls from the table. Jeanine was screaming at her mother, and Margot was standing in appalled silence, unable to decide whether she should first try to silence her sister or comfort her mother.

Alys's instinct was to take the children and run, but she felt guilty for precipitating this crisis by bringing Fenice and Enid with her. She felt sorry for Alphonse also, and wished to help him. He seemed to be the only person in the whole family, including Raymond, who was not selfish to the core. Then Alys remembered that Fenice and Enid had been raised among the women servants, and she bade them quickly run up to the women's quarters and find the woman who had taken care of them. They were to stay with her until Alys herself or Bertha came to fetch them. At this, Enid's tears stopped at once, and Fenice regained some color in her pale cheeks. Hand in hand they ran off.

Freed of her responsibility, Alys glanced around. She was much surprised to see that, although they cast glances over their shoulders now and again, the servants continued calmly to eat or to perform any duty in which they were engaged. What was even more shocking to Alys was that Gervase and the chaplain stood together talking quietly; it seemed that they were not surprised by the violence that had erupted. Alys longed to join them, but her duty was with the family.

Reluctantly, Alys returned to the fray. After gasping lamentations about the cruelty of ungrateful children and how she was always misunderstood, Lady Jeannette had worked herself into a fine state of hysterics. Margot was stroking her mother's hand, Jeanine was weeping loudly, and Alphonse was distractedly trying to calm both his wife and his elder daughter. He caught sight of Alys approaching and remembered two things simultaneously: Alys had already proved her abilities when she had whisked away and calmed his wife when just such a storm as now had broken threatened, and that Raymond had said to him, "Leave everything to Alys."

"Can you calm her?" Alphonse cried.

"Yes," Alys said, "but you will not like my methods. It is too late now for sweet words."

She did not wait for him to answer but ran to Jeanine, who had slumped into a window seat, and whispered in her ear, "You fool, go quickly to your father and draw him to a private place. Then tell him what you desire. Quickly, I say, while I make sure your mother does not thrust herself between you."

Jeanine's sobs checked, and Alys shook her.

"Quickly, I say," Alys repeated. "If you can take your father away, your mother will soon be so angry with me that she will not remember how this fray began. You will come away scot-free, I promise."

Alys now hurried back to Alphonse and urged him to discover the truth concerning his elder daughter's desires, promising that she and Margot would see to Lady Jeannette, who was still screaming piercingly and throwing herself about in her chair. Alphonse turned away from the steely glint he saw in Alys's eyes to receive his still-weeping daughter in his arms. He did not wish to think about Alys's warning that he would not like the methods she would use this time to calm Lady Jeannette.

Although he and Raymond had parted on good terms, Alphonse was still sore with the knowledge of his neglect. It was easier at this time, when the hurt was sharp and new, to cast the blame for his distaste for his duty onto his wife. He could not punish her himself, partly because he knew that he should have resisted her encouragement to idle away the days in her company. However, in a certain sense he had received the whipping he deserved, and he was willing to close his mind to the fact that Lady Jeannette was about to receive her dose of the same medicine.

In fact, Lady Jeannette's hysterics were rather more genuine this time than usual. She had been truly shocked by Jeanine's outburst. Although her daughter had mentioned more than once that she regretted the death of her husband, which deprived her of her own household and the hope of children, and that she would not be averse to another marriage, Lady Jeannette interpreted these statements in her own way. Jeanine, she thought, was a truly loving daughter. She did not wish her mother to grieve over her past unhappiness nor to fear for her future unhappiness if political necessity forced her to be given again in marriage.

Naturally a daughter would wish to remain safe and protected at her mother's side where there was no need to be at a man's beck and call. Lady Jeannette could not imagine that her demands on her daughter could be in the least onerous. She was sure Jeanine enjoyed serving her. Of course, Lady Jeannette was happy with her husband and, if another man as good and kind as Alphonse should appear, then she would have tried to have a marriage with him arranged for Jeanine. But men like Alphonse were few and far between. Certainly none like him had come to Tour Dur asking for a wife, and surely Jeanine was happier at home attending on her mother than serving the purposes of some coarse man.

Besides, if Jeanine married again, Margot would be the only one left. Then if there should be a *need* to provide a daughter for an alliance, Margot would have to be married. But that would produce a calamity: Lady Jeannette would be left alone. She had intended to protect herself from so dire a fate by choosing her sons' wives to suit herself. It would be natural for Raymond and young Alphonse to be happy with any girl she chose—and if they were not, there was nothing to stop them from taking mistresses. But Raymond had been bewitched by that succubus Alys, and young Alphonse was not ready for marriage.

Jeanine had no right to want to be married, Lady Jeannette thought. It was her duty to be happier with her mother than alone in some dreadful foreign keep. Soon Margot would "want" to be married. It was unfair. Lady Jeannette had borne the pains of childbirth to give them life. Surely their lives belonged to her. Surely they could give her their time after all she had done for them. No one cared for her. All her sacrifices were thrown aside or used without thanks. She was cruelly misused, cruelly!

Lady Jeannette's reiteration of this litany of ills, which produced the shrieks and sobs and wild gestures, was brutally interrupted by a stinging slap on the right cheek. She uttered a gasp and one more shriek, which was immediately followed by an equally stinging slap on the left cheek.

"There, now," Alys said loudly, "you feel better. You must not scream anymore or you will make yourself ill, nor throw yourself about lest you be all bruised."

A blind rage pushed all other thoughts and emotions from Lady Jeannette's mind. Air rushed into her lungs, but she had no inclination to scream. Instead her hand rose to return, more viciously, the blows that had been dealt her. Alys caught and held the raised hand, and Lady Jeannette gasped with surprise. The grip bruised her wrist; for all her small size and frail looks, Alys was far stronger than she.

Then, quite deliberately, Alys let go, saying, "You may slap me if you wish, Mother, but, indeed, I meant only kindness."

Had she thought about it, Lady Jeannette would have burst into tears again and had a perfect case to present of Alys's cruelty. But she did not think. Not only did she take more than full advantage of Alys's invitation, but she jumped to her feet, pulled off Alys's headdress, and tore at her hair. At this point, Gervase the steward and the chaplain hurried forward. Gervase interposed himself between the women, and the chaplain pulled Lady Jeannette away, saying some sharp things to her about her unnecessary violence. Margot came running across the hall bearing a cup of hot wine, which she virtually forced down her mother's throat.

As the older woman was assisted into her chair again, Alys began to rearrange her hair. Her expression was blank, but her cheeks reddened, as much from fury as from the stinging slaps. It was not, of course, the first time in her life that Alys had been beaten, but her father never slapped her face and it had been many years since he had struck her at all. Gervase asked solicitously whether she was hurt, but Alys only shook her head. She was too angry to speak. She wanted no more of this ugly game, and she looked around for her cloak.

In the background she could hear Lady Jeannette hissing with anger, saying things about her that could not have been true even if she had been steeped in corruption from birth. The chaplain was trying to quiet her, but his voice sounded shocked. Alys finally saw her cloak and started toward it, still half-blinded by rage and tears. Gervase followed anxiously, and Alys turned her head to tell him she was all right. At that moment Alphonse came out of a side chamber so close that he nearly trod on Alys. He steadied her and began to go past when he saw the marks of his wife's hands, red on Alys's white skin.

Simultaneously he heard Lady Jeannette's voice, and it was clear she was raging, not weeping. Despite the fact that the chaplain was speaking at the same time, Alphonse heard the vicious calumnies. Jeanine had just told him that her mother had said *he* was unwilling for her to marry again, that the dower, which he had given with her and which had been returned by her late husband's family because she was child-less, was needed for other purposes. For the first time in years —the first time since Raymond had been sent for fostering —Alphonse was completely out of patience and out of temper with his wife.

He marched forward, bellowing, "Jeannette!" And then, as her mouth opened to scream and her hand came up to her heart, he roared even louder. "Do not dare! Do not you dare play off those tricks on me now, or I will treat you as you deserve and beat you soundly." He turned his head toward his younger daughter, who had never seen him in such a mood and was shrinking away. "Margot, stand still! Answer my question. Do you desire to live celibate and remain with your mother?"

"Celibate? I? No!" Margot cried, shocked.

Alphonse turned back to his wife. "Why did you lie to me?" he screamed. "Only two months ago I had an opportunity to settle Jeanine most advantageously. Why did you lie and make an enemy for me instead of giving me a worthy son?"

"I did not lie," Lady Jeannette shrieked. "It is her fault, hers!" She pointed at Alys. "She has corrupted your daughters with talk of lust and independence. They were happy until that daughter of Satan—"

"Jeannette!" Alphonse roared again. "You lie!"

Alys was sickened and horrified. She had heard secondhand of such family conflicts, but had had no experience with them. She could not imagine what the outcome would be and tried desperately to think of a way to placate the combatants. Jeanine had now come from the chamber where she had been talking with her father, and joined the argument, and Margot was emboldened to defend herself from her mother's accusations. Alys began to cry with remorse for causing what she believed would be a permanent rupture in the family. Then a hand fell gently on her arm.

"Come aside, Lady Alys," Gervase said softly. "This cleansing of the air has been needed for a long time. Lady Jeanine and Lady Margot must be freed. When they have all shouted themselves hoarse, they will all weep, then embrace, and the storm will pass over, leaving all fresher behind it."

"Is this true?" Alys breathed.

"I assure you all will be well, my lady. This is not the first time, and I fear it will not be the last."

And it was true, at least insofar as the fact that everything ended in tears and kisses. In a sense, Alys was relieved, but she was also furious. She felt drained and battered, although she had only been a witness of the violent dispute, and when she was drawn forward and forced to become part of the general reconciliation, her fury grew. She tried to withdraw, but this caused a renewal of tears and apologies and faint accusations from Lady Jeannette that Alys had not *truly* forgiven her.

Bitterly Alys reminded herself that she was Raymond's wife, and she was doomed to a lifelong bond with this family. At one time it had seemed that no price was too high to pay to be joined to Raymond, but he, too, had offended her and neglected her. Nonetheless, the apologies made to her had been handsome, and it would be ugly and ungenerous to reject them, no matter how false they were at heart. Alys swallowed her rage and joined the now tender and affectionate group.

Her penance lasted right through dinner, and the knot of anger and disgust inside her made every dish she tasted sour. She was released at last by an ill-natured shaft from Lady Jeannette, who asked why Alys had not insisted on having Enid and Fenice join them at dinner. The truth was that in the turmoil Alys had completely forgotten the children, but she was not going to admit that.

"I did not wish to add a bone of contention to so sweet a meal," Alys said, "but you do well to remind me of my responsibilities. It is time for Fenice to do some lessons and for Enid to sleep for a while. If you will excuse me . . ."

There were protests, of course, and an offer to send a servant, but Alys insisted that until she had a proper governess to see to the girls, she was obliged to attend to their education herself. Eventually, irritated as well as furious, Alys got away and went up to where the women servants worked at sewing, spinning, and weaving. When she reached the chamber, Alys paused to look over the work being done. She realized that she was in a foul temper and wished to calm herself before she reclaimed Fenice and Enid. They were already too timid and upset at the change in their situation. It would be cruel if she snapped at them for what was not their fault.

Despite the emotions that seethed in her, Alys could not help being interested. She spent a little time examining the spinning process, which seemed to produce finer yarn than that spun in England. Behind her, where the looms stood, Alys suddenly heard Fenice begin to talk, Enid joining in, and both speaking with more freedom than they showed to her. That irritated her all over again, although she knew it to be natural that the children should be less in awe of the woman who had raised them than of herself. In fact, it was better that way. Nonetheless, Alys felt a sudden urgency to take them away, and, instead of calling them to her, she walked quickly in the direction of the voices.

A moment later she came upon them, both girls standing beside a woman who was obviously taking a brief rest from her work. Alys could see the scraps with which the girls had been playing strewn about as they had been dropped hastily.

"Children," she said.

The woman, whose head had been bent to listen, looked up and gasped. Then she jumped to her feet and stared about wildly, as if she wanted to run away. Alys's eyes were drawn to her by her hasty movement and in the instant she recognized that this was no nurse but the children's mother. There was Fenice's creamy complexion, Enid's rich black velvet eyes. And she was beautiful! In the same instant she realized the woman's fear could only be because she had been ordered not to allow Alys to see her. Shock froze all emotion in Alys.

"Stay," Alys said, as Lucie took a step sideways. "Are you Fenice's and Enid's mother?"

Another terrified glance right and left and the recognition that escape was impossible preceded a whispered, "Yes."

"What is your name?" Alys asked.

"Lucie, my lady."

"I had no intention of stealing your children, Lucie," Alys said, still so shocked that she was unable to react emotionally, but aware that Fenice and Enid were stiff with fear, having absorbed their mother's terror although they did not know of what she was afraid.

"No, no," Lucie whispered, going down on her knees. "I know it is best for them, and they are so happy because you are kind. My lady, I beg you, do not turn them away." She pushed the two girls forward roughly, and they both began to cry.

"Do not be so silly, Lucie," Alys said, "you are frightening your daughters. Of course I will not turn them away. Get up, do. All I meant was that I would have arranged a time for them to be with you had I known you were here. Now calm yourself, and calm the girls. They are too frightened to come with me immediately. I will send my maid Bertha for them later."

"Thank you! Thank you!" Lucie cried, weeping with relief.

Alys smiled at her mechanically and turned away. She still felt nothing beyond surprise, and when she had returned to her own room in the south tower she sat for some time staring into the fire without being aware of thinking. Still, at some level below conscious thought, her mind was working. Gathering up ideas and evidence distorted by disappointment and disgust, it sorted the bits and pieces until a whole monstrous concept, concocted out of hurt and anger and suspicion, was born.

Suddenly Alys remembered that Raymond had lied to her father and herself when he first came to Marlowe, claiming to be a poor, simple knight who needed to take service to live. From the beginning then, Alys decided, he had only intended to use them. He had never loved her, merely seen her as a tool with which to wrest a rich dower from the king.

At this moment Alys was blind to the truth—that there had not been the faintest chance of any dower larger than the small estate of Bix when Raymond first declared he loved her. She had decided that Raymond loved Lucie, had always loved her, that he only needed a gentlewoman to produce a legitimate heir, and that he had chosen her because her father was too far away to protect her.

The proof of this, she thought, was that he had rushed back into his mistress's arms as soon as Lucie was within reach. That was why he had not used the passage. That was why he had ordered Alys to live in the south tower. It was not to protect her from his mother, but to keep her from finding out he had another woman more to his taste. Surely he had told his daughters not to mention their mother and had told Lucie to hide herself. No wonder the woman had been so frightened. No wonder Raymond had been so appalled when he saw her with Fenice and Enid, so reluctant for her to take them into her care.

The contradiction between Raymond's surprise at seeing his daughters with Alys and her assumption that *he* had ordered them not to speak of Lucie did not occur to Alys in the fever of rage and pain that burned her. A flicker of logic briefly cast a gleam of doubt on the edifice of nonsense she was erecting when she wondered why Raymond had revealed the passage to her if he did not intend to use it. She doused that small flame of truth quickly in a wet blanket of misery. Naturally he did not intend to desert her bed completely. He needed a legitimate heir, and Lucie could not give him that.

The day passed in adding useless embellishments to this monster of misinterpretation. Once Alys roused herself to send Bertha to fetch the children as she had promised, but she told the maid to keep them with her, see to their supper, and put them to bed. Another time she was pulled from the morass in which she was allowing herself to sink when Bertha brought her an evening meal. But Alys would not take the hand held out to rescue her. When Bertha deliberately idled about, relaying what she thought were innocent bits of gossip about the doings of the keep, Alys told her sharply to go.

Bertha's pleasure in her new situation only compounded Alys's self-inflicted pain. Alys alternately raged and wept until she was exhausted. Since she had slept hardly at all the preceding night, she was barely able to pull off her clothes and tumble into bed before she was deeply asleep. Bertha's entry later to fold her clothing and light the night candle did not

wake her, nor, some hours after that, did the calls of the
sentries and the answering cries of Raymond's men demanding
entrance to Tour Dur. This was most unfortunate. Had Alys
wakened, it would have been apparent to her that Raymond
had stopped only long enough to take off his armor before he
came to her.

As he carried his candle through the dark passage, Raymond's mood was exactly the opposite of Alys's. This was
literally true because his euphoria was equally compounded of
true and false emotion. There were real reasons for him to be
happy, but a good part of his high spirits was owing to the fact
that he was so tired that he no longer felt it.

The first small break in Raymond's mood came when he
pushed the wall open and Alys did not stir. Somehow he had
expected that she would either be awake or that the creak of the
pivot would wake her and she would spring up to welcome him
with a cry of joy. However, he suppressed this small disappointment and went to close the door Bertha had left open in
case her mistress should call her in the night. Then he threw off
his night robe and soft slippers and crept in beside his wife. He
pulled her into his arms and, still asleep, she turned to him, but
limply and without real consciousness. That, again unfortunately, was not enough for Raymond.

All the way home he had been imagining his welcome, and
it was not working out at all as he had planned. He wanted
Alys to be glad he was there; he wanted her to appreciate that
he had ridden all the way home and given up a second night's
sleep just to be with her. Moreover, his previous experience of
making love to a somnolent wife had left a decidedly bad
impression. He shook Alys gently, then bit her ear.

"Raymond?" she mumbled.

In that first hazy moment of waking, before she remembered
her rage and anguish, Alys tightened her arms around Raymond, as if by reflex, and tried to turn her head to find his lips.
The latter gesture pulled her ear harder against his teeth.
Memory returned in the instant that she felt the slight pain. It
was nothing. If all her imagined misusage had not flooded into
her mind at once, the tiny discomfort would have acted as
Raymond intended it—as a sharp spur to passion.

Instead it seemed an ugly confirmation to Alys that Raymond would rather hurt than fondle her. She pushed him away

with all her strength, using both legs and arms. Since Raymond was not expecting this kind of violent response, he was not braced against it. Moreover, he was at the very edge of the bed because Alys had been sleeping more in the center than to the side. He slid, teetered, and fell off.

"Lecher!" Alys shrieked, sitting up and clutching the covers to her as if threatened by a ravisher. "Do not dare touch me. I am no clout to be used to wipe up your dirt and be tossed away. You will get no heir on me while your love and your pleasure belong to another woman."

Raymond listened to this while lying on the floor. He had not been hurt when he fell because thick carpets padded the planks on each side of the bed, but he was too surprised to move. When he heard Alys's accusation, he was further stunned. It was so impossibly far from reality that it did not touch him at all. Alys was his pearl without price. Another woman—it was too ridiculous! He had been as faithful as a celibate priest vowed to Holy Mary. He had probably been more faithful, he thought, for he had never even thought of another woman since he had taken Alys to his bed. He had actually refused a freely offered bedmate without a moment's hesitation. And he had never been a lecher. As a man, he had had women, but they had not been, until Alys entered his life, of great importance to him.

Raymond rose to his knees, rubbing the arm he had bruised in falling. He shoved the bed curtain farther aside so that the light of the night candle penetrated into the recess of the bed, and he stared at Alys. He was far too surprised to feel any other emotion.

"What is wrong with you?" he asked mildly. "What are you talking about?"

The mildness was a further affront. Had he been innocent, Alys reasoned, he would have been angry. "Where were you last night and the night before?" Alys screamed.

"Have you run mad?" Raymond countered, still kneeling and staring at his wife's inflamed face. She was very beautiful with her cheeks flushed and her eyes brilliant with rage. "I told you I was going to my aunt, and last night I was with my father."

"For how long?" Alys raged. "And with whom did you go to bed?"

"You *have* run mad!" There was now an edge to Raymond's voice, and he got to his feet. His shock was beginning to recede, making room for other feelings, and they were not pleasant. Still the total lack of reality in Alys's accusations armored him to some extent, for it is the truth that really hurts. "I slept alone at my aunt's manor," Raymond continued. "Do you think I would casually dishonor one of her maidens? And last night I did not go to bed at all."

"Liar!" Alys spat, hardly waiting for him to finish.

Now indignation roused Raymond. "I do not lie!" he snapped. "Why should I? What business is it of yours with whom I sleep? I would not deign to lie—"

"You yellow-bellied cur, you do lie!" Alys flung herself out of bed at an angle so that she could better confront her husband. "I have found your mistress, though you bade her hide from me, and I do not deny she must be richer meat than I am. Go to her bed! Feast well! But do not think you can throw me scraps from that feast and thus content me."

"Mistress! What mistress?" Raymond roared, the shock of hearing his wife call him a yellow-bellied cur having kept him silent just long enough for Alys to finish her tirade. "I have no mistress here nor in any other keep! And what if I had? It is not your place to tell me how to regulate my life."

"Is it not?" Alys was no longer screaming. Her voice was low, but clear and deadly cold. "Perhaps not, but I can regulate my own. I will not take between my legs a man who has so little love for me, so little sense of decency in his own behavior, that he will keep a mistress in the same house to which he brings his new-wed wife."

"I tell you I have no mistress!" Raymond bellowed, thoroughly enraged.

Now the other side of the coin was showing. Before, knowledge of his own innocence had prevented Alys's shafts from hurting him. Conversely, however, once he began to be angry, he became much more angry because he was unjustly accused.

"And I tell you I found Lucie, despite your orders to her to hide from me. I will not permit you to use me to father legal sons while you disport yourself for pleasure elsewhere."

"Permit? Who are you to permit or not permit? It is a wife's duty to bear sons no matter what her circumstances."

Alys's unwise tone of arrogance deprived Raymond of his last remaining shreds of self-control. He had not slept in forty-eight hours, and in that time he had killed a man and had a soul-shaking confrontation with his father that swung him from despair and bitterness to euphoric happiness. He had come home to share that happiness with the dearest treasure of his life, certain of a joyful and passionate greeting from her. Instead he had been rejected and foully missaid.

Disappointment, rage, and fatigue swirled together and blocked all his ability to think. There was nothing left of rational humanity in Raymond, and the frustrations and hatreds of years of dealing with his mother, of feeling helpless and controlled, exploded in him. Reacting like an animal whose prey was escaping, he struck at Alys. The blow would have felled her unconscious, but she had stepped back, frightened by the distortion of his features. Moreover, fatigue had thrown off Raymond's aim and timing.

The blow fell glancingly on Alys's shoulder but was still strong enough to knock her off her feet. She scrambled away on her knees, but Raymond on his feet was much faster. He leapt at her, hit her again, then seized her and shook her so hard that he nearly broke her neck. Alys struck back at him feebly, for the blows and the shaking had made her dizzy, but that served only to incite Raymond further. Mad with frustration and rage, he now had no real awareness of himself or Alys as people. She was only a creature that he knew he must subdue. He cast her on the bed and threw himself atop her.

Her momentary weakness past, Alys struggled fiercely. She struck and scratched at Raymond's face, but he seized her wrists. Then she made a fundamental mistake and tried to kick. Raymond's legs slipped between hers. She writhed and heaved, trying to push him off, but his weight was far more than she could lift. Actually, when Raymond struck and seized Alys, he had desired conquest, not rape. But now, of course, the form of conquest Raymond desired had been made plain to him. The twisting and plunging of Alys's body, a grotesque mockery of sexual intercourse, served to stimulate him into animal rut.

He pulled one of her arms brutally across her face so that he could seize both her wrists in one hand. With the other he reached down to position himself, but Alys tried to bite his hand; she kicked, dug a heel into the back of his knee, twisted her hips desperately to prevent him from settling his shaft properly. Her efforts were in vain and worse than vain because they only served to anger and excite Raymond more and more.

However, Alys's struggles produced one advantage. By the time Raymond impaled her, he was so inflamed that only a few thrusts brought him to climax. He was aware, in those few seconds, of Alys still writhing to free herself and screaming with hatred and revulsion, but the words, if there were words, were meaningless to him, and with the outpouring of his seed the last flicker of energy left him. He was instantly so deeply asleep that his condition differed little from unconsciousness.

Alys wrenched her wrists from her husband's relaxed grasp and heaved. He was limp, a dead weight, and she was exhausted, but her outrage would not let her rest. She pushed and twisted until at last she was free. At this point Alys was little more rational than Raymond had been. All she could think of was driving him away, and she stood gasping, looking for a weapon.

Her riding crop lay on a chest, and she ran and seized it. As she reached for it, however, the bruises on her shoulder and back twinged. That was warning enough. Alys knew that Raymond could wrench so pitiful a thing from her hand and use it on her. She needed something he could not grab. Her eyes ranged the room and suddenly she gave a small, sharp cry of joy and ran to the wall. The towers, being used far more often for storage than for living quarters, were furnished with torches. Alys took one and thrust its pitch-soaked head into the embers of the fire. When it was blazing brightly, she advanced on the bed, her lips drawn back in a feral snarl.

The curtains were still pulled back as Raymond had left them, and he lay face down, his smooth, dark-skinned back exposed. Alys lifted the hand that held the whip; and for just an instant she could not bring it down. Raymond often slept on his belly, and the sight brought back to her many sweet mornings when she had bent to kiss his back and so wake him to another happy day. If she struck him and drove him off, it would be the end of all such joy. No, it was ended anyway, she realized. She could not love a man who forced her.

The whip came down, then, as hard as she could strike. Raymond gasped and jerked. Alys struck again. He pushed himself upright, cursing. Alys stepped back out of reach and extended the blazing torch toward his face.

"Out!" she shrieked. "Out of my bed and out of my life. No man who forces a wife is fit to have one."

Raymond looked at her with glazed eyes. He had the staring look of a horse just before it falls dead of exhaustion.

"Out!" Alys repeated, sobbing with the agony of having to drive away what had been the most precious thing in her life.

CHAPTER 18

****

A servant woke Raymond at full light the next morning. He responded only slowly at first, rolling away from the hand on his shoulder and the light that struck his eyes. But he did not resist waking long because he was aware of a deep anxiety. Something was very wrong, desperately wrong. His eyes flew around the room, but the trouble was not one of place; he was in his own chamber at Tour Dur. Then his eyes fixed on the servant. The man was smiling, making an easy, commonplace remark about the weather. No, there was nothing wrong in Tour Dur itself.

And then Raymond remembered—going to Alys in the south tower and what had followed. He bade the servant go in a stifled voice and then a groan he would not have uttered under torture was wrenched from him. Although he had not had a clear conscious awareness of his actions at the time, the events in Alys's bedchamber had etched themselves onto Raymond's mind and now rose before him in a series of all-too-vivid pictures.

Raymond covered his face with his hands and wept, but outrage soon dried his tears. He had done nothing to deserve such a foul welcome, and then, seeing again in his mind's eye what he *had* done, he shuddered. Whatever Alys had said and whatever his right, he should not have forced her. Raymond was well aware that nine men out of ten would have laughed at him for being so distressed at raping his wife, would have assured him that what he had done was the correct treatment for a recalcitrant woman, possibly would have sneered at him for being too gentle. He gave lip service to such views himself, but he had been conditioned by his mother and—yes—by the years of lute songs that celebrated gentleness and submission to women—to react with self-loathing to what he had done.

Perhaps Alys deserved a good beating for her temerity, but not—not a desecration of love. Raymond tried to close his

mind to that, to Alys's shrieks of pain and hatred, casting
farther back in memory to when she had first thrust him away
because . . . because he had a mistress. It was insane. He had
never truly kept any woman except Lucie. . . . Lucie! Alys
had mentioned Lucie! Raymond groaned again. If only he had
listened then! If only he had explained that he had arranged
Lucie's marriage as soon as he became betrothed to Alys. But
now it was too late. It would be long and long before Alys let
him come close enough. . . .

"Oh, God!" he cried aloud and jumped to his feet, hastily
dragging on clothing any which way. It occurred to him that
Alys might have ordered out her men and left Tour Dur. His
father and mother called to him as he ran through the hall, but
he did not hesitate, only instinctively slowing enough on the
stairs not to break his neck. And as he tore across the bailey he
was so sick of himself that he bitterly regretted that instinctive
caution. But Alys was not gone! Arnald came running toward
Raymond when he saw his master's haste, asking what was
wrong and what were his lord's orders.

Raymond skidded to a halt, feeling ten times a fool on top of
his self-hatred. He should have known that Alys would not run
away. And then, in the depths of his misery, he did something
right and poured out the whole story to Arnald.

"Get rid of the woman Lucie at once," the English master-
at-arms said calmly. "Kill her and bury her if need be—I will
do it for you—but get rid of her."

"But I did not lie with her," Raymond snarled. "I never even
thought of her."

"I know it, and you know it, and doubtless when her temper
cools, Lady Alys may be brought to believe you, but as long as
the woman lives in the keep—"

"But she does not!" Raymond protested. "At least, she may
be in the women's quarters during the day working as a
weaver, but she is married to some huntsman and must live
with him."

"A young, beautiful woman who comes every day into the
keep?" Arnald shook his head. Raymond had not said that
Lucie was young or beautiful, but it was a natural conclusion.
A lord would scarcely take someone old or ugly to his bed.
"No, my lord, there is none such. My men have stood guard
duty with the castlefolk as you ordered. I would have heard if

such a woman came in or went out. A beautiful woman is one thing my men would see, even if the dolts overlooked a whole army."

"All right! All right," Raymond conceded. "It is possible my mother asked my father to arrange duties within the keep for the man so that Lucie would be better able to do her work and see to the children, but—"

"Then get rid of them both," Arnald interrupted, keeping to the point.

"Yes, very well, I will send them both to another place to live, but first I must send the man to Alys so that he may tell her his wife slept with him both nights." Raymond pounded his fist against his forehead. "His name. What was his name? I must know for whom to ask."

It seemed a reasonable idea, but Arnald had to conceal a smile at his young lord's distress and anxiety. If he had not known Alys's hot temper, he would have advised Raymond to leave his wife alone for a day or two and then act as if he had forgot the whole thing. But that would not work with Lady Alys; some amend would have to be made, and the husband's evidence, putting her in the wrong, would be required. Still, it was funny that Lord Raymond was so frantic he could not think of the obvious answer to any question.

"What was his name?" Raymond cried again.

"If the woman is in the keep," Arnald said, "you need only ask her."

"Good God, of course," Raymond said, and strode away, not quite running this time but at considerable speed.

Raymond need not have hurried, for Alys was still soundly asleep and likely to remain that way for some time. Although Raymond had staggered back through the passage and fallen into bed in a somnambulistic state and had slid deeper into sleep immediately, Alys had found no such quick release. For some time after he was gone, she had remained at the door, weeping bitterly. She told herself she was guarding against her husband's return, but whether she would have rejected him if he came back pleading for forgiveness was a question she did not examine. However, he did not return—neither with threats nor pleas.

This gave Alys no relief, and for a while she cried even

more. At last she roused herself as fear replaced grief. If Raymond had been so angry when she denied him and called him a liar, how much more furious would he be when he remembered how she had driven him away. Alys shivered with cold and with fear, and felt herself weakening with weariness. She knew she would have to sleep sometime, and she could not bear the thought of being taken by surprise. But if the moving stone were blocked, whatever held the mechanism of the pivot could not be released. That was easy enough. A thick splinter from the hearth hammered with the hilt of her knife into the crack jammed it effectively. Then all she needed to do was drop the heavy bar into the slots of the door and she was safe against surprise.

However, security did not improve Alys's mood at all. The idea of barricading herself against her husband was more dreadful, now that she stopped to think of it, than the idea of his vengeance. Worse yet, she was beginning to doubt the reality of the accusations she had made. Raymond's surprise at those accusations and the fact that he had ridden back in the night and come to her were beginning to make nonsense of her suspicions. She wept anew until there were no tears left and eventually, still sobbing fitfully, she slept.

When Bertha came up and found the door barred against her, she did not knock on it or call out. Lady Alys had been in a foul temper the past two days, and Bertha was happy to stay out of her mistress's way. She had no orders to wake Alys, so she would not try. She would get breakfast for herself and the children. Lady Alys would accept that as a reasonable excuse if she woke and called and Bertha was not there. Suddenly the maid paused on the stairs. Could Lady Alys's temper be owing to the children? No, not the children themselves. Lady Alys was very sweet-spoken to them and had enjoyed their company. Not the children, but . . . Then Bertha remembered Lucie's beautiful face, which she had seen when she went to fetch Fenice and Enid.

Bertha started down the steps again slowly, feeling sorry for Lucie. There was nothing she could do for the woman, and even to seem to know that Lady Alys was jealous of a serf-woman could be a personal disaster. Bertha shook her head sadly. Lord Raymond should have known better, but it was not her business. Still, she was unusually patient and tender with the two little girls while she saw to their dressing and eating.

Fenice and Enid, at least, had never been happier in their lives. They did not miss their mother much, since she had little time to bestow on them. The attention she had given to their talk on the day Alys had come upon them was an exception. Lucie had been even more terrified than her daughters by the way Lady Jeannette had suddenly snatched them away. Raymond's mother had looked so strange when she said that they were to be "taken away and given to a new mother." Moreover, Lucie's terror had been multiplied because Lady Jeannette had ordered her strictly not to show herself anywhere around the keep as long as Raymond was in Tour Dur.

Because Lucie could not even conceive of herself in competition with a lady, she did not associate this order with the possibility that Raymond's new wife could be jealous. In fact, Lady Jeannette was exactly of Lucie's mind. If she had had the smallest inkling that Alys would be jealous of Raymond's serf mistress, she would have bedecked Lucie in her own jewels and set her at the family's dinner table. Lady Jeannette did not care when Lord Alphonse occasionally slept with other women, so long as he did them no honor and never addressed to them any effusions of a romantic nature. The reason Lady Jeannette had told Lucie to keep out of Raymond's way was simple: She had thought his order to marry Lucie to Gregoire was stupid. Lucie was a good weaver. If she married the huntsman, she would soon have a hut full of brats and her weaving would suffer. If Raymond did not see Lucie, Lady Jeannette was sure he would ask no questions about her.

All Lucie could think of, for the two horror-filled days and nights after the girls were taken and she was told not to speak to Raymond, was that Lady Jeannette had decided to do away with her daughters. Now that Raymond was to be married and had the expectation of noble daughters to dower, Fenice and Enid would be considered a useless burden, she thought. Lucie would have disobeyed Lady Jeannette and gone to Raymond to beg him to save Fenice and Enid, only she knew it would be useless. Lady Jeannette would deny her story, would say the girls had been sent to another castle. However, Lucie had one hope: She had been told to pack up her daughters' clothing.

And then the girls had returned, happy as larks, bubbling

with excitement and satisfaction: They had seen Papa; he had promised *two* presents, and Lady Alys—a new mama, and so wonderful, and so kind, and so sweet-smelling, and with such yellow hair and such blue eyes, and she taught them new games, and she laughed a great deal, and she said how good they were and how pretty, and *she* had given them the presents, see, a new hair ribbon for each and—wonder of wonders—Fenice sought in her pocket and drew it forth. A whole silver penny to be spent in the town on whatever they pleased.

This excited recital, however, was not what Alys had interrupted. When she had arrived, Lucie had been trying to find out what was being planned for her daughters' futures. The girls did not understand, but they made sufficient references to Lady Alys telling them they must learn many things that ladies knew, for Lucie to believe that every hope she had cherished for Fenice and Enid was coming true. Although she knew she would lose her daughters completely, that pain was nothing in comparison with the joy she felt for their escape from the horrors of life she had known.

Thus, after Lucie had recovered from her fright at Alys's discovering her and considered what Alys had said, she set about reassuring Fenice and Enid and explaining clearly in terms they would understand what would happen. And, she told them, they were not to be afraid if they did not see her again for a long time. She would be safe and happy. They were to love Lady Alys and, above all, to be absolutely, utterly, perfectly obedient to her at all times. If they were not, the most dreadful fate would befall them. They would be punished horribly and then be cast out into utter darkness, and their mother would die of grief. All they must think of now, every minute, day and night, was how to please Lady Alys.

The threats of punishment had been terrible, but the solution to avoiding it seemed so easy that the tears the girls had begun to shed dried. Lady Alys was *very* easy to please, far easier than their mother or the other women in the hall. Though Fenice was still somewhat fearful—she was old enough to understand that appearances did not always tell the whole truth —Enid's happiness was so complete that it was contagious. Finally, when they had been taken back by Bertha and had been allowed to play and the maid had talked kindly to them during supper and when she put them to sleep, all their fears faded. By the next morning, they were happy as mice in a cheese room.

They were a little disappointed when Bertha came down and said Lady Alys was still sleeping, because they had looked forward to seeing her. However, they went cheerfully enough to Mass. There the chaplain stopped Bertha to ask for Lady Alys. Told she was still abed, he mentioned that there was a poor gentlewoman living presently on Lady Catherine's charity who, he believed, would make an excellent governess to the lord's daughters. Bertha promised to give the message to Alys as soon as she woke, and took the children with her to the kitchen to collect fresh bread and cheese and milk. They had to wait, for the servers were busy carrying food to the great hall, but eventually Bertha obtained what she wanted. As they returned toward the tower, the girls exclaimed, "Papa! There is Papa."

"No," Bertha cried, but there was no need to restrain the children. The girls had seen their father running and knew they would not be welcome when he was in a hurry.

After breakfast, Bertha dressed them warmly and told them to play outside until they were cold or she called them. She went up and tried Alys's door again, but it was still barred. A few minutes later, Enid popped her head in the door to announce that they had seen Papa again, but he was still in a hurry so they had not tried to speak to him. Bertha said absently that they were good girls, but she was frowning when she turned back to her work of stitching up, according to a new pattern, the gown Alys had unpicked the preceding day. It was very odd that Lord Raymond should not come and ask for his wife.

Lady Jeannette, on the other hand, was furious because she thought that was just what Raymond had been going to do when he ran through the room without even greeting them. She had prepared an acid remark about the effects of uxoriousness on her son's manners, but he forestalled her when he returned by saying, "I must go up to the women's quarters. I must speak to Lucie."

"Lucie!"

It was a chorus: surprise from Alphonse, shock from Lady

Jeannette, disgust from Jeanine, and simple amazement from Margot.

"I need to know the name of her husband," Raymond said impatiently.

"Husband?" Alphonse asked, puzzled. He knew Lucie had been Raymond's woman; surely he would have remembered if she had been given in marriage.

"But—" Lady Jeannette cried.

Too wrapped in his own purpose to notice either his father's confusion or his mother's trepidation, Raymond snapped bitterly, "I assure you, I will not ravage any of the women in the five minutes I need to get an answer," and he strode away without waiting for permission.

Lady Jeannette began to sniffle, and Alphonse patted her hand. He had expelled a great deal of shame and bile during the previous day's violent upheaval, and he was at present in charity with his wife. He leaned over and stroked her shoulder and spoke soothingly, but Lady Jeannette scarcely heard him. She had thought Raymond was coming back to normal—and now this!

Meanwhile, Raymond had bounded up the stairs and into the large hall in which the women worked. "Lucie!" he bellowed.

Gasps and short cries of surprise came from all over the room. Raymond stared around, but no one stood up and he could not see Lucie from where he stood.

"Damn you," he shouted, "come out here to me. All I want is to ask you a question."

Lucie was not naturally stupid. Having learned that her daughters had nothing to do with Lady Jeannette's order to keep out of Raymond's sight, it was not difficult for her to guess that the order must have something to do with this question that Raymond wished to ask her. She sat frozen at her loom.

Raymond, of course, associated her reluctance to come to him with a fear that he would wish to use her again. "Come out here," he repeated. "Do not make me come looking for you. I swear I only want to learn your husband's name, and no harm will come to him."

The last sentence made no sense to Lucie at all, but the one that preceded it allowed no further hesitation. Lucie stood up slowly. If there had been a place to hide she would have done so. Raymond, she knew, would protect her no longer, since he was about to be married, and Lady Jeannette would punish her disobedience. But there was no escape.

"What the devil ails you?" Raymond asked. "All I want is for you to tell me your husband's name. Then you can go back to work. Well?"

Lucie stood staring at him, and Raymond had to control an impulse to slap her. He wondered how he had brought himself to lie with such a stupid, fearful slave. With an effort, he softened his voice.

"I promise you," Raymond said, "I will do your man no harm. I only wish to speak with him. Just tell me his name."

"I have no husband," Lucie whispered.

"What?" Raymond roared. "Did you not tell me you wished to marry some huntsman? Did I not give you five gold pieces as dower?"

Tears poured down Lucie's face. "Do not be so angry, my lord," she pleaded. "I did tell you I wished to marry Gregoire the huntsman, and you did give me the gold pieces." She fumbled at the breast of her dress. "I have them here. Do not be so angry. Take them back if you will." She was shaking so hard that Raymond caught her arm to steady her.

"I am not angry at you," he said, but his eyes were like the blue flame at the hottest part of a fire. "Do you know how it came about that your marriage to Gregoire was not arranged?"

"No, my lord," Lucie sobbed. "I only know the day after you departed, Gregoire was sent away."

"Sent away! Where? By whom? Stop crying, you fool!"

As well as she could, Lucie choked back her sobs. "He was sent to Gordes. More I do not know, my lord."

"Gordes? A huntsman from Aix was sent to Gordes?"

Lucie only trembled, but Raymond had not expected any answer from her. His questions were rhetorical and only an expression of shock and outrage. There could be no practical reason to send a huntsman from the low-lying lands of Aix to the mountain fastness of Gordes. Also the timing was too pat: Gregoire had been sent away as soon as Raymond himself left Aix. It was clear that someone in the family had deliberately ordered Gregoire to be transferred to prevent the marriage.

"Do you still wish to marry this man?" Raymond's voice grated through gritted teeth.

"Yes," Lucie gasped.

Raymond did not reply to that, only seized Lucie by the wrist and dragged her after him down the stairs and into the great hall.

"Who ordered that Gregoire the huntsman be sent to Gordes?" Raymond thundered.

Everyone in the hall froze into position. By now all the servants knew that Raymond had slain the master-at-arms and had had his body hung in chains at the barracks. There was no longer any insolence among the guards, who walked softly and in fear and trembling. If Lord Raymond whispered, they leapt to obey. Lord Alphonse might carry the title, but all knew Lord Raymond was truly the master of Tour Dur.

At the family group where Raymond stood, shock did not breed silence. The three women let out cries of alarm, and Alphonse jumped.

"Shut your mouths, you ninnies," Raymond bellowed at his sisters, "or I will slap you sillier than you already are."

"Raymond," Alphonse protested, getting to his feet, "are you mad?"

"If I am not, it is no fault of anyone in this keep," Raymond raged. "Did *you* order Gregoire be sent to Gordes?"

"Who the devil is Gregoire?" Alphonse shouted back, losing his temper.

Raymond did not even glance at him. "Then it was *you*, madame," he snarled at his mother, his free hand working as if it were being restrained from closing on her throat. "Tell me why."

Raymond's last three words held such a threat of violence that Alphonse tried instinctively to interpose his body between his son and his wife, but he was blocked by the table. He reached out to hold Raymond; however, Raymond had not leaned over to strike or choke his mother as Alphonse feared he might. And Lady Jeannette was so frightened by her son's expression that all her tricks deserted her. She could not scream or weep or faint, and his eyes, bright and hard as steel, pierced her.

"She is the best weaver," Lady Jeannette quavered. "Why should I lose her service to satisfy a silly notion you had that she should 'have a life of her own'? She would have been with child constantly and no good to *me* with a house full of brats."

The glare in Raymond's eyes diminished. He had suspected that his mother had kept Lucie and introduced her to Alys, as she had introduced his daughters to Alys, to cause trouble between himself and his wife. The reason she had given, however, was so much in accord with her normal selfishness that he was sure it was the truth. He started to turn away, Lucie's wrist still gripped in his hand.

Lady Jeannette had seen her son's rage cool and took courage from that. She associated this latest display with outbursts engendered in the past by frustration, and mistakenly believed he had accepted her logic. "Now you have your answer," she said. "Let my weaving woman go back to her work."

Raymond spun back on his heel. "You selfish, stu—"

"Raymond!" Alphonse bellowed.

First Raymond glared at his father, but then swallowed the words he was about to say. It would do no good to finish the sentence and call his mother a stupid bitch, for it was not only Lucie's presence in the keep that had caused the trouble. His mother could not have forseen the combination of circumstances that had kept him out of Alys's bed, because he *had* intended to ride home from his aunt's manor no matter what the time. He had only told Alys he would not so that she would go to sleep. It was the storm that had prevented him. And his mother knew nothing of the political problems that had kept him talking to his father all night and had sent him off to Gréoux.

More collectedly, Raymond said, "She is not your weaving woman. I paid her father for her. She is *mine*. And now you have lost her completely, for I will take her to Gordes myself and see her married to Gregoire. You have caused me—"

Raymond cut that off sharply and turned away again. He would not think of exposing his troubles to his family, although he was not at all disturbed by having told Arnald. There was something wrong in that, he knew, but he was comfortable with Arnald in the same way he was comfortable with Alys—or had been. Raymond's mouth set in a bitter line, and he started toward the door that led to the outer stair. There was a cacophony of voices behind him, but he ignored it.

Then he heard swift steps and felt a touch on his arm. "Raymond."

It was Margot. Of them all, Raymond had a soft spot in his heart for his younger sister, especially now because she had welcomed Alys. He stopped and turned his head.

"Let poor Lucie at least fetch her cloak, Raymond," Margot pleaded. "She will freeze if you take her to the mountains in nothing but that gown."

Raymond could feel Lucie shaking, and, although he knew it was not the cold that made her tremble, he recognized the reason in what Margot said; he himself was not dressed for traveling. He hesitated nonetheless, suddenly afraid that Alys would come in. He could not bear the thought of facing her in front of his family, but then he realized it was past the time for breaking fast. She was avoiding him. That hurt him, but at the same time he was grateful.

Then he remembered his other purpose for coming home and realized he had not told his father the good news about the vassals. The joy had gone out of it; the joy had gone out of everything. Still, what was right was right. None of this was his father's fault. He let go of Lucie's wrist.

"Go get your things," he said to her, "whatever you wish to bring with you to Gordes." Then he looked at Margot. "Her clothing will not be warm enough for the mountains," he said to his sister. "See if you can find her some old furs and a bolt of warm woolen cloth. I will pay for them or furnish new if necessary." He paused and then in a softer voice said, "Thank you."

Alys was finally wakened by her hunger. She lay for a moment, staring at the bed curtains, which she had forgotten to draw, and then through the opening in them at the barred door. Then she closed her eyes, but blanking out the sight could not hold back her memories. After a while she sat up slowly.

"God help me," she whispered. "I must have been mad."

Her underlying doubt about Raymond's guilt, which had begun the night before, had been made clear during her sleep. Alys did not realize that she had been emotionally unbalanced by the strain of dealing with Lady Jeannette and her lack of experience with volatile, violent personalities. Her calm father and her outwardly placid stepmother had never exposed her to that kind of emotional eruption, and even Uncle Richard, who shouted and ranted, only raged about political matters, never personal ones.

Now with her perspective restored, every false notion about Raymond that she had embraced marched through her mind, only to be rejected. She knew Raymond had married her only for love, that he would, indeed, as he had once sworn, have taken her barefoot in a shift. Lucie was beautiful, but Alys knew in her heart that Raymond had not returned to Tour Dur to lie with her that first night or any night. Moreover, Raymond was neither unkind nor crude. If he still had a lust for Lucie, he would have established her in the town or in some other keep conveniently near. Actually, the fact that Lucie was still in Tour Dur was almost a guarantee that Raymond had no further interest in her.

Alys was so sick at heart that she could not even weep. She was frightened, too, not only of Raymond but for him. Now that her mind was clear, it was inconceivable to her that he should not have reacted with rage to being struck with a whip and driven with a burning torch as if he were a wild beast. But he had not reacted at all. He had responded to the pain and threat dully, like an animal driven beyond endurance, and there had been no sense, no recognition, in his eyes. It was as if he were asleep, except that Alys knew no one could have slept through that.

Worst of all was Alys's feeling of isolation. There was no one to whom she could turn for help or advice. If only her father or Elizabeth were near. . . . And then she shuddered. Nothing could ever convince her to tell her father or her gentle stepmother what she had done. Her father would have been as angry as Raymond—not at her objections to Raymond's keeping a mistress but at her manner of objecting. And if her father ever heard that she had sewn together a misfit garment of untruth and then had beaten her innocent husband, whom she had forced to wear it, with a whip . . . Alys shuddered again. If Raymond did not kill her first, her father would do so when Raymond sent her home in disgrace.

At that thought, Alys almost fainted. That was why Raymond had never come back to punish her. He planned to repudiate her. She had given him cause enough. She would kill herself and go to hell; she deserved it. But that, too, would injure Raymond by depriving him of her dower lands. Alys's breath caught on a hysterical sob, and she choked down her terror fiercely. Now she was weaving a noose of unreality with which to hang herself.

Slowly, Alys got off the bed and went to unbar the door. It was, in fact, highly unlikely that Raymond would repudiate her. There were too many practical reasons against it—his own vassals had been invited to their wedding and the Gascon lands were valuable . . . and perhaps he still loved her, she thought. She still loved him, even though he had misused her in a revolting way. Deserved or not, guilt or no guilt, anger and bitterness flicked Alys again when she remembered his rape. That was disgusting. She had been wrong, and he had a right to beat her—but to use her like a beast . . . . It was better not to think of that.

Yet the outrage at such treatment strengthened Alys, despite her certainty of Raymond's innocence. She was not the only one who had gone too far. She opened the door and called Bertha, experiencing a pang of fear in the moment before the maid answered that Raymond had removed her own servants and, perhaps, set a jailer over her. But before she could begin to terrify herself anew, Bertha's voice came up the stairwell. Nor was there any sign when Bertha entered the room carrying washing water that she was aware Alys had quarreled with her husband.

The maid seemed subdued, but she exclaimed quite naturally that Alys should not have barred the door because she could not get in to replenish the fire, and now it was out. Alys, who was shivering more with nerves than with cold, used the remark as an excuse to pull on her own shift and long-sleeved tunic while Bertha ran down to get coals to start the fire anew. Thus, Alys was able to hide the livid bruises remaining from Raymond's blows, and that gave her confidence enough to make a neutral remark about having slept so long. At this, Bertha's face lightened, and she began to talk in much more her usual manner. It became clear to Alys then that Bertha's wariness was only a reflection of her own bad mood the previous day.

"Oh, and my lady," Bertha chattered on, "the chaplain said to tell you that he believes he knows of a gentlewoman suitable to care for the children, not that I mind having them. They are the sweetest little birds, and no trouble at all."

"When did he speak to you about this?" Alys asked, feeling her way.

"After Mass, my lady."

It was obvious from Bertha's reply that Raymond had not been at Mass, either. Bertha would surely have mentioned it. Nor could there have been any family upheaval, for the chaplain would have known about that and not been casually speaking about Fenice and Enid. Reflecting upon this, Alys felt better. Perhaps Raymond still cared enough for her to keep secret from his family what happened. However, Alys was afraid to build her hopes too high. Should she go across to the main keep? she wondered. She shuddered at the thought, and Bertha stirred the fire, thinking Alys was cold.

"While I do my hair, get me something to eat," Alys said to her maid, knowing she could not find strength to beard the lion in his den. She could only wait for whatever would happen. "Oh," she added, "ask the chaplain to step across to me. I—"

"Alys?" Margot's voice came up the stairwell. "Are you awake? Are you well?"

Alys went rigid. Her first impulse was to run and hide from the ultimate shame of being summoned to be punished before Raymond's family. But there was nowhere to hide.

"Alys?" There was anxiety in Margot's voice.

"Come up," Alys called, pride firming her voice. "I am awake."

She heard Margot's steps hurrying up on the stairs, and stiffened her back.

"Oh! We have had such a to-do," Margot cried as she entered the room. "Did you know that Raymond had returned during the night?"

Color rushed into Alys's face. Such a question was quick proof that Raymond had said nothing to his family, but hope can freeze a throat and tongue as well as fear. Alys could not answer Margot's question. Fortunately Margot assumed the silence was an answer and, in any case, she was far more interested in telling her news than in receiving a reply. She sank dramatically into a chair and began to recount the events of the morning. As Alys listened, her eyes grew wider and wider and joy flooded her. She could hardly believe her ears and kept asking Margot to repeat what she was saying.

Margot did so with enthusiasm, thrilled at the reception she was getting. Finally, when every single word, expression, and gesture had been detailed, Margot asked, "Whatever do you think got *into* Raymond? Did you say something to him about Lucie? No, of course, you could not have done so. You had not seen her or spoken to her until after Raymond left, and you did not see him after that. Good gracious, mother is *furious!* Whyever did you sleep so late? You missed all the excitement."

CHAPTER 19

****

The day, which had started with a violent upheaval, was destined to be permanently memorable, but neither Alys nor Margot knew that yet. Bertha returned with the food she had been sent to get, and as soon as Alys swallowed enough to stay her immediate hunger, she and Margot hurried over to the great hall. After Margot had unburdened herself of her more exciting news, she remembered that she had been sent to Alys by her father. Soon after Raymond left with Lucie, Alphonse had realized that Alys had not been at Mass or at breakfast and he began to worry about her.

But when she arrived, Alys was glowing with happiness. No man in the world, she thought, was equal in goodness and generosity to her husband. It was not that Alys expected to escape his wrath or punishment. She believed he had gone away not only to remove Lucie from Tour Dur, but because he wanted to cool himself before he dealt with her. She swore to herself that she would kiss his hands when he beat her. Her joy was that he had not betrayed her, that he would not expose her to the ridicule of his mother and sisters. And, above and beyond that goodness, despite his own assertion that she had no right to protest his keeping of other women, it was clear that he never intended Lucie remain in Tour Dur. In addition, even after Alys had enraged him so unjustly, his first act was to remove the source of her anger.

Assured by her looks that nothing ailed her and by a smiling apology for her late sleeping and a promise of amendment, Alphonse did not question Alys. He could not have probed too deeply anyway. Lady Jeannette was so full of her son's mad behavior that all other subjects of conversation were impossible. In the full flush of her happiness and relief, Alys was more sympathetic to Lady Jeannette than was anyone else. She was very willing to listen to endless repetitions of what had happened.

It did not matter to Alys that these repetitions were full of Lady Jeannette's self-justification. No matter how the tale was told, it reiterated the bases of Alys's joy. First, Raymond's energy proved that, whatever his reason for not reacting to his wife's abuse, he was not ill. Second, Raymond had intended that Lucie's marriage be arranged as soon as he received his father's permission for betrothal. And third, and even more marvelous, his haste and fury showed his eagerness to remove the source of Alys's hurt and set her mind at ease. However often Lady Jeannette repeated herself and her complaints, she was telling Alys a tale of perfect love.

Alphonse was almost as much in love with his daughter-by-marriage as was his son. It seemed to him that as soon as Alys appeared, he was freed from all the unpleasant aspects of his wife's demands for his attention. Raymond's news about the faithfulness of the vassals had washed away the bitterest portion of his guilt, but enough remained that he was spurred to exert himself to fulfill his part of the bargain he had made with his son. He had wished to write some letters, but had not been able to get away from Lady Jeannette. Then Alys came —and he was free.

Jeanine's feelings toward her sister-by-marriage had also undergone a change. It was Alys who had given her the key to unlock her prison and pointed out the door. Not only had her father promised to seek a suitable marriage for her as soon as possible, but he had mentioned that the way Alys's dower was settled obviated the necessity for him to add anything to it or to Raymond's allowance. Thus, Jeanine's portion could be increased. And now, Alys was sitting patiently with Jeanine's mother, not quite agreeing that Raymond was cruel and mad but still nodding and murmuring sympathetically so that Jeanine could escape unnoticed. It was Raymond's disgusting behavior when he announced the marriage, Jeanine told herself, that had prejudiced her against Alys. She should not have blamed Alys for what Raymond had done. Alys herself had many good points.

Lady Jeannette had not been won over yet despite Alys's attention to her, but the event that would conquer her began before nightfall. The connection was not immediately apparent. No one would have guessed that particular outcome from the tragedy that preceded it.

In the late afternoon, a tired rider flogging an exhausted horse called that he had an urgent message. The name of his master brought Alphonse, looking pale and shocked, out into the bailey. And the rider's news, although it was not really unexpected, wrenched a cry of pain from Alphonse. Raymond-Berenger, his father, was dead!

Alphonse discovered in that moment that it is one thing to talk about an event and quite another to experience it. Although he had discussed his father's death calmly with Raymond, now that it had taken place he realized that he had never believed it *could* happen. He was stunned, grief-stricken, and terrified all at once. He had loved his father and depended on him. Now the whole world seemed to be collapsing and sliding away from him. Alphonse reeled, and Arnald caught him and supported him, calling over his shoulder to the nearest man-at-arms to fetch Lady Alys quickly.

Alys ran down from the women's quarters at once when called, believing at first that Alphonse had been taken ill. When she heard the cause of his faintness, however, she bade the man hurry back and have Lord Alphonse carried into the keep. This was not a time for her to intrude; comfort must be administered by those most familiar. Alys herself ran up again, trying to think of a way to present the news that would not bring on hysterics, but there was no time for long, gentle preparation. All she could do was to sink into a deep curtsy before Lady Jeannette. This was unusual enough to be a warning.

"Madame," Alys said softly. "I am the bearer of ill tidings. I beg you to be strong so that you may comfort your husband. The count of Provence is dead, and Lord Alphonse is sore stricken with grief."

There was a moment's silence, and then Lady Jeannette cried, "This day is accursed! My son mad, my father-by-marriage dead, my husband—"

"Your husband needs you, madame," Alys pleaded, praying that for once in her life Lady Jeannette would, at least temporarily, abandon her selfishness. Then Alys was stricken by a brilliant idea. "If you do not comfort Lord Alphonse and support him," she warned, "he could become ill—even himself die—of grief."

That remark hit home. If Alphonse were seriously ill or dead, Lady Jeannette realized, Raymond would rule Tour Dur; Alys would be mistress there, and Lady Jeannette herself would either be put out to a small dower manor or sink into insignificance in her own home. The selfishness that ordinarily kept Lady Jeannette at rest while everyone around her worked to support and amuse her now spurred her to activity, as Alys had intended. Lady Jeannette rose from her chair and hurried to the stairs.

Alys uttered a sigh of relief; she did not believe anyone could die of grief. If it were possible, she thought, she herself would have done so last night or when she woke this morning. However, death from grief was a convention of those ridiculous lute songs Lady Jeannette loved so much. Likely *she* believed grief could kill. In any case, she would now attend most assiduously to Lord Alphonse, and that was most important. What next? Alys wondered.

The question had been rhetorical as it rose in her mind, more an exclamation about the fact that she seemed to be living in a whirlwind for the last few days. However, as the words formed, they took on a practical context. Literally next was to inform Raymond. Down the stairs Alys ran again, just slipping out past the party that was supporting Alphonse up to his wife's bedchamber. He was weeping freely, and Lady Jeannette was murmuring comfort. Neither of them noticed her.

Snatching a cloak, Alys ran out to the bailey calling for Arnald. He was with her in a moment, asking anxiously whether they should close the keep. He had been only a small child when King John died in 1218, but he had heard many tales of the violent disorders of that time. Moreover, he was worried and startled by Lord Alphonse's collapse, unable to imagine what kind of catastrophe had overtaken them. Nothing he knew of could have caused a similar collapse in Sir William.

"No, there is no need for that," Alys assured him. "Lord Raymond has spoken to me of this already. It was not unexpected. There may be war, but not in the next few days or weeks. What is most necessary is that this news go to Lord Raymond at once. You must tell the master-at-arms—oh, good God, he is dead, too."

"There is a new man," Arnald told her.

"Very well. He must choose a trusty man who knows the way to Gordes to carry a letter to Lord Raymond. Let him come to the keep. I will go in and write the letter now."

Alys knew she should be sorry about the death of Raymond's grandfather, and in a sense she was because she knew Raymond had loved him and would be grieved. Nonetheless, she was not too distressed, aware that the death was expected and would not be the shock to her husband, who was strong, that it had been to Lord Alphonse, who had regarded his father as a support for his weakness. And, truly, it was as if God had arranged it at this moment so that she would have an excuse to write to Raymond. As that thought crossed her mind, Alys offered up a prayer to be forgiven for presumption, but she could not completely quell her happiness.

She found the chaplain and Gervase in anxious consultation with the messenger, who, it seemed, had a letter but had not time enough to deliver it before Lord Alphonse collapsed. Alys put out her hand.

"I will take it. Gervase, please see to the messenger's comfort and let him rest. I do not know whether it will be necessary to send a reply at once. It is possible that we will need to leave for Arles ourselves. Please give some thought to what might be needed for the journey. I will come to you with definite instructions as soon as I am able."

Then Alys went up to Lady Jeannette's apartment again, where she found Margot and Jeanine clinging together and weeping. For the moment Alys did not disturb them but went to listen at the bedchamber door. There she heard Lord Alphonse speaking in a broken voice of his father's many kindnesses to him and his insufficient gratitude, and, between the phrases, Lady Jeannette assuring him that he had ever been a most dutiful and loving son. His father, Lady Jeannette urged, had always desired his happiness and health, and, to be a good, dutiful son now, he must strive to accept God's will. Alys nodded and withdrew.

Nothing could be better; Lady Jeannette knew her husband best, and when it was in her interest to do so, she was the one who could best soothe him. However, Alys did not think this was a good time to precipitate another crisis by presenting a letter that might contain only details of Raymond-Berenger's death. Unfortunately, however, the letter could not just be put aside until Lord Alphonse was ready to deal with it. It might also contain important news. At Marlowe, Alys would not have hesitated an instant but would have cracked the seal, for she had always been her father's trusted deputy. In a way she had that right now, for she was the wife of the heir, and Lord Alphonse was unwell. However, she did not wish to overstep the bounds of propriety, either.

"Jeanine," she said softly, approaching the sisters. "I am sorry to intrude on your grief, but there is a letter here for your father."

Jeanine sniffed and looked at her. "Why do you tell me?"

"If this letter only tells of—of the sad bereavement," Alys told her, "then it may be put aside until your father can bear it, but if there is some matter of urgency in it, then it cannot wait upon his grief but must be acted on at once."

"You desire that *I* open a letter addressed to my father?" Jeanine gasped.

"No, as Raymond's wife, that is my responsibility," Alys replied coolly, "but I must ask you to advise me. The letter is from Sir Romeo de Villeneuve. Is he more likely to have writ of the—the sad details or of matters of business?"

"Are you going to open the letter?" Margot asked, slightly breathless.

"If Jeanine believes it is a letter of affairs—yes," Alys said firmly. "Duty cannot be delayed by grief."

"I—I do not know." Jeanine bit her lip. "Sir Romeo was judex for my grandfather, but he was also his closest adviser and companion."

"He was not solely a friend but an official of your grandfather's administration?" Alys asked.

"The most important official," Jeanine confirmed.

"Then I must see what is here," Alys said and, before either girl could speak, broke the seal. Since it was too late to stop her, and, if wrong had been done, Alys had done it, both sisters came forward eagerly. Alys held out the letter toward Jeanine. "It will be quicker if you read it. I am not completely familiar with the *langue d'oc*."

First Jeanine shrank back, but her curiosity overcame her timidity and she unrolled the parchment. At once it was clear to Alys that her act was justified. Sir Romeo confirmed the news the messenger had given and then requested that Lord

Alphonse come to Arles as quickly as possible. Both he and
Lady Beatrice, Raymond-Berenger's widow, needed Lord
Alphonse's advice and support. Alys's eyes narrowed as she
listened, remembering what Raymond had told her. She was
sure Lord Alphonse must not be trapped in Arles, and Alys
knew instinctively that Arles would be a trap for him whether
or not Sir Romeo and Lady Beatrice meant it to be. Once
Alphonse was involved in discussing young Beatrice's fate, he
might be too long delayed to make his pact with King Louis.
Lord Alphonse must go to King Louis at once, not to Arles. It
would be very useful, Alys thought, if Alphonse himself
carried the news of his father's death to the king.

"Then we must make ready to leave," Alys said.

"Make ready? Without my father's order?" Jeanine quavered.

"Do you believe Lord Alphonse would refuse Sir Romeo?"
Alys asked.

"No," Jeanine replied, "but—but he is not fit to travel. And
my mother . . ." Her voice drifted away uncertainly.

"It is too late to go today," Alys agreed, "but I believe your
father will be recovered by morning. And your mother has
enough to do in comforting him. You and Margot will know
best what should be taken to Arles. If you will be so good as to
order the maids to begin packing, I will see that Gervase makes
ready the means for transporting what we will need. And I
must send Raymond this news. Margot, would you be kind
enough to find ink and parchment so I may write to him?"

Margot, whose grief had been much dissipated by the thrill
of Alys's daring behavior and by the expectation of the
excitement of new faces and new activities at her grandfather's
obsequies, went at once to do as Alys asked. Meanwhile, Alys
stepped closer to Jeanine, ostensibly to take back the parchment, which she rolled up again.

However, she also said, in a low voice, "I imagine all the
important men in the south of France will come. Perhaps I
should not be thinking of such matters at so sad a time, sister,
but life must go on. It cannot hurt you to look about and see if
some of the gentlemen you will meet are particularly pleasing
to you."

Then, before Jeanine could reply, Alys moved toward
Margot, who was bringing forward a small writing table. This

relieved Jeanine of needing to make a horrified protest, both at thinking of her marriage at her grandfather's funeral and at the idea of "choosing" a gentleman. It would do her no good anyway, Jeanine thought bitterly; her father had never listened to her plea to marry that handsome squire . . . squire . . . what was his name? Then she frowned, jolted into honesty by the events of the past few days. The fact was that her father had been right. Jeanine was now ready to admit that she had no inclination to follow a penniless knight from tourney to tourney or to live on the charity of her parents or brother. She was not likely to make so foolish a mistake again. So, actually, it might be well worth looking at the available men. Her father would be glad to please her if she chose wisely.

With the light of determination in her eyes, Jeanine went to the door and began to call the names of the maids she needed. Then she began to discuss with Margot what they would need to take. Alys drew the parchment toward her and bowed her head over it to hide her smile. Jeanine, she was sure, would do her uttermost to assure that they left promptly. Margot's desire to go had never been in question.

The smile faded from Alys's lips as she dipped her quill. The spoken message the man-at-arms would carry would ensure a reading of her letter, no matter how angry at her Raymond was, but her purpose was to assuage that anger, and she would need to be careful what she wrote. After a formal salutation she began:

> My dear lord, I am sufficiently aware of my great fault not to have dared address you at this time if there were not great need. I know how greatly I have wronged you, and that for no reason but my own jealous fears and fancies. However, it is needful for me to explain what befell here after the news of your grandfather's death, which the messenger has already given you.

Alys looked up to think. Did she need to wrap up in fair words her opening of the letter? She thought not. Raymond knew his father. She continued writing quickly:

> With the sad news we had a letter from Sir Romeo de Villeneuve. Your father being too overcome with grief to

attend to it, I made bold to break the seal. Sir Romeo desires your father's presence at Arles as soon as may be. I do suppose this is for two purposes: first, to be sure that the only living son of the count of Provence keeps faith and does not wish to seize the whole province; and, second, for counsel on how best to preserve Provence. But, my lord, you told me already that it was all but certain Charles of Anjou must have Beatrice.

At this point Margot ran in to ask whether she should tell Bertha to start packing. Alys thanked her with real warmth; it was a thoughtfulness she had not expected. It might only be a result of Margot's eagerness to go, but even so it was a step in the right direction. She returned to her missive.

Yet, if this marriage be agreed upon before Lord Alphonse can proffer homage to King Louis, it may be that the king of France will consider the fealty of Aix to be owing to his brother Charles. Thus, it is in my mind to urge your father, in your name, to go to King Louis at once, while your mother, your sisters, and I will go to Arles.

Alys flicked the feather of the quill back and forth across her lips. She realized that if Alphonse's act was suspect, she and the other women would be hostages, but she could not see that that would matter. Sir Romeo would not do them any harm. It would be boring, but they would be released as soon as Louis's brother was betrothed to Beatrice, or sooner if Louis accepted Lord Alphonse's fealty.

Our presence will be an assurance of your father's good faith. My lord, you must do all things as you see fit, but it is my thought—which you were once kind enough to say I should not withhold from you—that we women alone will be sufficient for Sir Romeo's peace of mind. Your dealings with the vassals seem to me too important to be cut short by a council that can only result in a foregone conclusion.

She dared not go further and actually tell him to stay away, and she had said all there was to say. Yet she hated to break even the tenuous contact with Raymond that writing to him gave. There was also the question of whether, since she was in utter disgrace, Raymond would think she had intruded where she did not belong.

My lord, I dare not beg mercy for my wrong to you nor for my present acts, if they be wrong. I only desire you to know that all my duty, all my desire, my every thought is for your good.

Alys lingered over the last lines. She wanted desperately to add the word "love" but was inhibited both by the desecration Raymond had made of the most intimate demonstration of that emotion and by the fear that, knowing she had driven him to use force, he would find the word an offense. And, after all, what was love but what she had written—that all her duty, desire, and thoughts were for her husband's good.

Raymond received Alys's letter the following evening. He had only arrived in Gordes himself a few hours earlier. Although he had intended to ride straight through, disregarding the fact that mountain trails are not safe in moonlight, even when there is moonlight, he had discounted the other effects of the mountainous countryside too easily. By dusk of the preceding day, they had lost one horse, and others were failing. Lucie had fainted from pain and exhaustion, and even Gros Choc, his own destrier, was showing signs of strain.

The last fact decided Raymond that they would have to stop for the night. Even his driving need to get Lucie married and explain everything to Alys would not make him risk the well-being of his favorite destrier. And, because they stayed in the hospice of a tiny monastery, Raymond thought his jealous wife would have no cause to doubt him. Lucie was not even allowed in the building, being accommodated in one of the serfs' huts of the small farm.

Raymond had slept very well; the tranquillity of the place and of the soft-voiced brothers seemed to have seeped into his soul. He was still ashamed of having forced Alys, but the

sense of horror that had oppressed him and driven him to act
with such haste and violence was gone. Well-rested, he
understood why he had misused his wife; he knew he had been
exhausted beyond rationality. He realized that he might have
some difficulty explaining this to Alys, since he doubted she
had ever reached that stage of fatigue in which one feels
violently excited rather than tired. Nonetheless, by unfairly
accusing him, *she* had been in the wrong; she would have to
forgive him.

Being able to think clearly and with the hysterical need for
haste gone, Raymond took the opportunity to pay a brief visit
to another vassal. This confirmed his better mood. The man
was visibly delighted that a plan for defense was being
organized and that Raymond had taken direction of it into his
vigorous hands. The politics of the situation were beyond this
man, but since he said he would gladly trust Lord Alphonse to
know what was best, Raymond was well satisfied.

The castellan of Gordes was very much surprised, to say the
least, when he heard Raymond's purpose; however, he had no
objection. He liked Gregoire and said the man had settled well
to his work despite his different background. Fortunately, the
huntsman was not in the field and came promptly when
summoned, but the poor man almost fainted when he saw
Lucie. He thought his indiscretion had followed him, and he
was about to die horribly for touching the lord's woman. No
fool, Raymond guessed from Gregoire's distress that Lucie's
relationship with the man had not been as innocent as it should
have been, but his interest in Lucie had always been minimal
and his mood was too good for this to make him angry, once he
had determined that Gregoire had not come to Aix until after
Enid had been conceived.

The only thing that annoyed him was the time it took to
convince Gregoire that he was about to be married, not
hanged. Eventually, however, this was accomplished, although Raymond thought that Gregoire might be too stunned
by his good fortune to make the necessary replies to the priest.
Lucie was almost as disoriented by the journey to Gordes as
Gregoire had been by fear. She had never before ridden on a
horse, and she had been bruised and terrified by the experience. Despite these problems, however, the pair was finally
united.

Still kneeling after the final words were said, Lucie swiveled and caught at Raymond's hand. She kissed it and thanked him and begged with tears that he would be kind to Fenice and Enid. Raymond patted her carelessly, much as he would a dog, but he assured her that his daughters would be well cared for and added, suddenly remembering that she might miss them, that perhaps some day she and Gregoire could return to Aix. To that, Lucie only bowed her head. She did not wish to return to Aix if Gregoire was content with his place. Although life was strange among the mountains and she would miss her girls, she would be safe from Lady Jeannette. Besides, she would have other children, Lucie thought. Anyway, Fenice and Enid had never really seemed to belong to her. They were noble born; Gregoire's get would be all hers.

Soon after the wedding was over, the messenger from Aix arrived. Raymond's mouth tightened when he heard the news. He was truly sorry, for many reasons, that his grandfather was dead, but he was not inclined to burst into tears. What he felt most strongly at that moment was surprise that his father had acted so promptly to notify him, for the messenger reported on being questioned that he had been sent out very soon after the news came to Aix.

Naturally, Raymond did not examine the seal on the letter since he was sure who had sent it. Thus, he was again surprised to see a strange handwriting. Assuming the chaplain had written the letter for his father, Raymond skipped the salutation and looked at the body only to realize that many words seemed unfamiliar. He looked back at the salutation, and it struck him like a blow. Alys! He should have known it would be Alys who had sense enough to act quickly in a crisis. His heart filled with gratitude for a wife who, however hurt and angry, could put aside her feelings when there was grave need.

By the time he had read the opening sentences, Raymond could barely restrain himself from ordering the horses saddled and rushing back to Aix, so desperately eager was he to take Alys in his arms and comfort her, assure her he was not angry any longer. But the length of the letter restrained him. Alys was not one to waste parchment in a long lament, and a few minutes more could not matter, though it took more than a few minutes to decipher the strange spelling. Many times he had to stop and think how the words sounded in Alys's voice before he could make sense of them. Each time he did, a thrill of emotion passed over him, but the meaning of the letter soon quelled softer feelings.

Alys was right. Everything she had done was right and for the best, but Raymond was torn several ways at once. He recognized the unwritten warning that he must stay away from Arles; it was not impossible that Sir Romeo might try to seize Aix itself or other portions of his father's domains if he learned that Alphonse was on his way to King Louis. Raymond hoped that Sir Romeo either would not discover where Alphonse was going or that he would understand Alphonse had no intention of asking Louis to make *him* count of Provence because he was Raymond-Berenger's son. Sir Romeo should have sense enough, even if he did not trust Alphonse, to realize that Louis would not consider such a thing even for a moment. Still, crises warp men's judgment, and Raymond might have to protect his property by force.

Equally, Raymond knew that the arrival of every female member of the Aix family, including even the "future" wife of the heir, would go a long way to steadying Sir Romeo's judgment. And, even if Sir Romeo believed Alphonse had sent the women to Arles to cover some treachery, Sir Romeo would not do the women any harm. The worst that would happen was that he would keep them mewed up until everything was settled. Thinking further, Raymond made a faint sound of dissatisfaction. Alys was right in what she had done, but he wished she were less clear-sighted. He would far rather meet Sir Romeo's suspicions, even defend his estate by arms, than lose his wife for the months it might take to settle the affairs of Provence.

Then another thought occurred to him. Ernaldus! Raymond had completely forgotten about him in the various stresses that had filled his mind. He stood up, intending to call for pen and parchment to write a warning, and then he sat down again. To whom could he write a warning? Certainly not to Alys. She had enough on her mind without his adding fear to it. Besides, his father would not be in Tour Dur to receive his letter. As for his mother, Raymond did not even think of writing to her; she would be worse than useless. So would Jeanine, and Margot was too young. He bit his lip. Arnald wouldn't do, either, for he could not read and would automatically take any letter addressed to him to his mistress.

Then Raymond's anxiety faded. It was true that many would attend Raymond-Berenger's obsequies, but probably not des Baux. They were longtime enemies and would scorn to honor the man who had broken them. Moreover, Raymond had considerable doubt that Sir Romeo would even send notice of Raymond-Berenger's death to des Baux. Sir Romeo might well believe the information would act as a spur to rebellious activity. Thus, Ernaldus might not even know the count was dead. Besides, the bailiff almost certainly thought his plot against Alys had succeeded. He would think she had been buried in Gascony and would not be looking for her.

In any case, it was ridiculous to think that des Baux would bring a bailiff along if he intended to come to the court of the count of Provence. Thus, Raymond pushed the thought of Ernaldus out of his mind; it was insignificant in comparison with the current news. Picking up Alys's letter, he began at the beginning again, reading more easily now that he was familiar with her hand and spelling.

When he came to the final lines of the letter, however, Raymond began to bite his lower lip. He read the lines again and again. Apparently Alys believed he intended to punish her in some way, yet it was impossible for her to be ignorant of the fact that he had taken Lucie away to get her married. She knew he had gone to Gordes because she had written to him there, and assured him of her love, but . . . Raymond read the lines again. No, her love was the one thing of which she did *not* assure him. Could Alys be hoping they would be kept hostage?

Again Raymond had to subdue the impulse to rush back to Aix. This time he was dissuaded by the bitter thought that if Alys was so desperate to avoid him that she preferred months of confinement, it would do him little good to go to her. Moreover, he did not believe he could arrive before Alys got the family started for Arles. Had the journey been under his mother's or even his father's direction, he probably could have walked to Aix from Gordes and arrived in time. With Alys holding the whip, however, they would doubtless be on the road before dawn.

* * *

Raymond was not quite correct in his estimate of the time of departure, but he was not far off. Actually, although everything was packed and loaded by dawn, Alys did not expect to get the women out of Aix before tierce. She was far less worried about that than about whether she would be able to convince Alphonse to go directly to King Louis without stopping at Arles to pay his respects to his father's corpse. It was surprisingly easy, however, so easy that it seemed to Alys that she must have had Divine help.

Alys had not gone to the south tower that night and was sitting in the great hall by the fire reviewing what she had done and trying to think of what still remained to be done long after everyone else was in bed. She had just got to the disposal of Fenice and Enid: The chaplain was to take them and Bertha to Lady Catherine, who, Alys had been assured, was kindness itself. Bertha would give the girls some sense of stability, Alys hoped, and would report honestly on whether they liked Mistress Sophia.

Suddenly a flicker of movement across the hall near the chapel entrance attracted Alys's eye. She held her breath and tiptoed silently after. It was, as she had hoped, Lord Alphonse. Alys had been nearly frantic trying to think of a way to talk to him alone.

For a few minutes she listened and then gave most sincere thanks to God. Alphonse was praying quietly, not weeping. After a few minutes more, Alys entered and knelt down beside him, softly echoing the prayers for the dead. Had he been alone too long, Lord Alphonse might have slipped back into despair, but the knowledge that someone was with him steadied him. When the prayer was complete, he turned his head.

"Alys? What do you here at this hour?" Alphonse got to his feet and helped Alys to hers.

"Very little, my lord," she replied quietly. "I only wished to be near if some service were needed."

Alphonse drew her closer and kissed her forehead. "Raymond has brought a true blessing into this house," he said, "but you will be overtired, my dear. Why do you not go up and share Margot's bed? She will welcome you, I am sure."

"Perhaps I will," Alys agreed slowly, trying desperately to

think of a way to introduce the subject of his trip to King
Louis.

She knew it would be impossible to raise the subject in Lady
Jeannette's presence. Lady Jeannette would have a fit; she
would weep and plead, and Alphonse would be torn apart
before he went—if he went at all. Most dangerous would be
that Lady Jeannette might convince her husband that his
presence would be necessary for the safety of his womenfolk
during the journey. Once in Arles, Alys feared, Lord Alphonse
would not get out again. If only she could get him to leave
before Lady Jeannette woke in the morning, everything else
would be easy. Since only failure loomed on every side, Alys
decided to take the bull by the horns. She laid a hand on
Alphonse's arm.

"It is dreadful that affairs of state must press upon one at a
time of grief," she said softly, "but I must tell you that all is
packed and ready, and the men who will accompany you have
been warned. You may leave for France at first light."

Alphonse looked at her with utter blankness.

"Raymond said that you decided it would be best if you
yourself brought King Louis the news of our great loss," Alys
went on, as if she were certain that everything was settled,
"and at the same time offered him your fealty. Is this not still
urgently necessary? Raymond seemed to think that the overlordship of Charles of Anjou would be very harsh, whereas
that of King Louis would be just and merciful."

"Raymond told you . . ." Alphonse repeated uncertainly,
unsure of how much his son had revealed and also astounded
that he would discuss such matters with a woman.

Alys never gave a thought to the true cause of Alphonse's
amazement. Her mind leapt to the conclusion that Alphonse
would be hurt and angry at the revelation of his weakness and
neglect. He must not think that Raymond had mentioned that.

"He was so proud that you had found an answer to the
problem," she said hastily, "that he could not resist explaining
it to me."

"Ah."

Alys took the indeterminate sound for acceptance and
satisfaction and hurried on. "So I took the liberty of having
your manservant pack your clothing and the master-at-arms
choose ten men to accompany you. You have only to call for

your arms, and you may leave when you are ready. If you do not wish to wake your wife so early, why do you not lie down in Raymond's bed? It is all ready. I will explain the necessity to Lady Jeannette in the morning, or you may leave a letter for her."

Again Alphonse stared. He did not remember clearly the talk he had had with Raymond about offering his homage to Louis, but he did not think the possibility of his not attending his father's funeral had been mentioned. Still, he knew that such an idea would not shock Raymond. Raymond was hard, he thought, but the resentful thought was followed by a wash of shame. Raymond had ridden all the way back from Gréoux to apologize to him and tell him that the vassals were faithful despite his negligence—not that Raymond had put it that way. He had said, most handsomely, that Alphonse's good qualities had ensured the devotion of his men.

Alphonse firmed his jaw and straightened his shoulders. He would not be weak and negligent again, he told himself. If Raymond felt he must go to King Louis at once, he would go. Moreover, he knew his father would by far have preferred that he save his lands and people from hurt rather than pay respects to a dead body. After all, the soul had already fled. Alphonse vowed that he would stop at every church and abbey he passed and pay for Masses to be said for his father's soul, and would go to the bishop of Paris himself and have that high prelate pray for his father. A sense of purpose and satisfaction filled Alphonse.

"Yes," he said, "I will go. Daughter, I have been stricken by a great loss, but you have softened that blow as I would not have believed possible for a woman to do."

Impulsively, Alys kissed him. "And you have repaid me a thousand times over by your kindness for any help and service I may have given."

She led him from the chapel and helped him into Raymond's bed, holding her breath all the time lest he suddenly begin to have second thoughts. But by the time she had made up the fire, Alphonse's eyes had closed and Alys hurried back to the chapel with prayers of thanks. She was sure that the holy place had had an influence and that God or His saints had convinced Alphonse.

Still, Alys did not yet feel easy. Until she saw Alphonse ride out through the gates, she did not really draw a comfortable breath. Alphonse had a few difficult minutes at the end, when he began to worry about how his wife would be affected, but Alys reminded him of how strong Lady Jeannette had been when grief had overpowered him, and assured him that his wife would rise to the need of supporting her daughters. More sincerely, Alys promised that in case Lady Jeannette should be afflicted, she herself would care for her. Fortunately, Alphonse found this last promise sufficiently reassuring, for he kissed Alys, called her a treasure once more, and departed.

Alys was, in fact, less worried about the storm she knew would break over her head from Lady Jeannette's direction than that Alphonse would lose heart and turn back. In this, however, she was mistaken. Once on the road, Lord Alphonse was overtaken by an enormous sense of freedom. He was totally unaware of how much he had feared Raymond-Berenger, of the dread he had felt at being required to advise Lady Beatrice and Sir Romeo because, somehow, he knew his father would be listening and his advice would be wrong. Now he had a clear duty, one of which he *knew* Raymond would approve and one he knew he could perform perfectly. Alphonse was equally unaware that his son had taken his father's place.

Having waited a little while to make sure Alphonse would not come back, Alys went wearily back into the keep. She looked dully around the great hall, where servants were laying away pallets and beginning the duties of the day. Gervase hurried over to her.

"Will you break your fast, my lady?"

Alys blinked heavy eyes. She had been to Mass at lauds with Sir Alphonse, and it was perfectly in reason to eat now if she liked. But she had no desire for food and shook her head. Gervase looked at her with considerable anxiety. Alys's face was white and strained, and mauve rings circled the eyes that showed lids blued with fatigue. Never in his years of employment at Tour Dur had Gervase had a day like the one past.

When Gervase had heard the news of Raymond-Berenger's death, he had almost wished for his own. Not that he was so attached to the count of Provence, although he knew him and reckoned him a good man, but Gervase had dreaded the days that would follow. Sir Alphonse, distraught with his own grief, would be further tormented by his shrieking, fainting women. Orders would be given, then canceled, renewed, changed, and Gervase would be blamed for every failure and confusion.

However, the seemingly childlike bride-to-be of Lord Raymond had grasped the reins firmly in her small hands. Under Alys's tactful guidance, Lady Jeannette had comforted her husband instead of adding to his troubles—and both were out of the way. In addition, Lady Jeanine had shown more energy and decisiveness than Gervase ever remembered, and Lady Margot also had been actively helpful. A miracle had come to pass.

"You are overweary, my lady," Gervase murmured.

Alys smiled at him. "You, also, I fear, poor Master Gervase. You are a paragon. If not for your support, nothing would have been accomplished." She laughed tiredly. "And I would be dead, I think, instead of only tired. I thank you."

For a moment Gervase was struck dumb. He was trusted and had considerable power and a comfortable life. These things had made his position valuable, but a man hungers for more, especially praise. Sometimes Lord Alphonse or Lord Raymond would utter a casual thanks for a particular task, but from the ladies of the house—and it was too often with those that he dealt—he received only complaints. Gervase's heart swelled with satisfaction and gratitude for Alys's recognition of his service. From that hour, Alys had a devoted slave.

"It is a great pleasure to serve you, my lady," Gervase said. "You make every task easy, for you say what you desire and do not change ten times. I should rather thank you. But, indeed, you must rest."

Alys was so tired, the south tower seemed leagues distant. She glanced toward the stairs to the women's quarters, and Gervase understood at once.

"Lord Raymond's room is now empty," he suggested, "and there is a fire there."

"Oh, yes." Alys sighed with relief. "How foolish of me. I had forgot." She took a few steps and then turned back. "You had better call me when Lady Jeannette asks for Lord Alphonse."

Gervase's lips tightened, and their eyes met. He sighed. "Yes, my lady."

In Raymond's room, Alys bent automatically to pick up a tunic that had fallen to the floor. It was the one Raymond had put on without even a shirt under it when he ran out to see whether Alys had left Tour Dur, and the sweat of his exertion and anxiety had soaked the wool. The odor, Raymond's particular odor, came to Alys as she lifted the garment. It was her first chance to think about her husband in relation to herself since she sent off her letter, and she burst into tears.

She should have written she loved him! One mistake could not spoil months of tenderness and consideration. Certainly Raymond had not been himself. Something had been wrong with him. She had realized that as soon as her own sanity returned. She had herself done what was nearly unforgivable, yet Raymond had acted with love in taking Lucie away to be married. And it might be long, long weeks, even months, before she saw him again. Sobbing, Alys carried the tunic with her to the bed and wept herself to sleep holding it.

CHAPTER 20

****

Getting Alphonse off before Lady Jeannette was awake turned out to be the best move Alys could have made. It had been decided between Alys and her father-by-marriage that his destination had better be a secret for as long as possible. Weak Lord Alphonse might be, but he was no fool. He recognized readily all the suspicions that might form in Sir Romeo's mind if he heard that Raymond-Berenger's son had run posthaste to King Louis without attending his father's funeral or taking part in the discussions concerning his half-sister's fate. Whether Alphonse meant that the secret be kept from his wife, Alys did not know, but she certainly intended to keep it so since she had not the smallest hope that Lady Jeannette could or would hold her tongue.

Thus, when Gervase was finally driven to confess that Lord Alphonse had left Tour Dur and told to summon Alys, she promptly denied all knowledge of where he had gone. The fact that she had known he was leaving and had assisted him to do so brought her a vicious scolding, but Alys only widened her eyes and said, "But madame—" Alys had discovered that Lady Jeannette preferred the respectful "madame" to the affectionate "mother."

"But madame," Alys said, "how would I dare question Lord Alphonse? He said he wished to go; his clothing was ready packed and the men prepared—"

"Why were clothes packed and men prepared?" Lady Jeannette interrupted furiously.

"Because Sir Romeo de Villeneuve begged in a letter that Lord Alphonse and you, madame, come at once to Arles to advise what is best to be done in view of our tragic bereavement." It was the truth, Alys thought. She had been asked where Lord Alphonse had gone, not whom he had gone to see. Alys did not know in which castle King Louis would be found. It was true that she did not know *where* Lord Alphonse had

306

gone. And the clothes *were* packed and the men alerted because of Sir Romeo's letter.

Lady Jeannette stared into Alys's face, but she did not see her. "Do you mean," she said finally in a thin, furious voice, "that Alphonse went to Arles without us? He is mad. There is plenty of time before the funeral, and since we were, I am sure, the first to have the news of the count's death, there will be time enough to decide what to do. What was Alphonse's hurry?"

"I do not know, madame," Alys replied. "He did not tell me." That, too, was true; Alys had told Alphonse why hurry was necessary, not the other way around.

"That fool!" Lady Jeannette burst out. "Now we have no escort. How are *we* to go?"

"With respect, madame, I have twenty good men and my master-at-arms is trusty and skilled."

"But who is to tell them what to do?" Lady Jeannette wailed, and Margot and Jeanine dissolved into tears of disappointment.

Alys bit her lip. She had had a few hours of sleep but was still tired and on edge. She did not know whether to laugh at the silliness of the three or to weep over the burden of supporting and guiding them—and she did not dare do either. A flicker of anger touched her. It was ridiculous that she, hardly more than a girl, should be responsible for the three, one of whom was more than double her age and the other had been married longer than she. Then she had to bite her lips again to keep from laughing. No doubt this was God's lessoning. She had feared she would be bored to death!

"My men were well trained by my father and Raymond," Alys said to the weeping trio after a pause to steady herself. "There is no need to tell them more than that we wish to go, and I will do that."

"I can tell the moon to shine," Lady Jeannette snapped, "but that does not mean it will obey me. Men obey the orders of men, as the moon obeys the orders of God."

This time it was Alys's turn to stare. The idea that any man except Raymond, whether soldier or servant, would not immediately obey her had never entered her mind.

"My men will obey me, I assure you," Alys said. "If you will give me leave to send for Arnald, I can give him the order in your presence so that you may be assured both of his willingness and his ability."

Without much more whining, Lady Jeannette allowed herself to be persuaded into donning traveling clothing, and Alys had the satisfaction of getting her party on the road within the time she had set. Fortunately, the journey was not quite the nightmare Alys had expected. For this Alys blessed the traveling wagon, which immobilized Lady Jeannette and prevented her from complaining and giving direct orders—at least, to Alys. The fact that Alys was able to "disappear" the moment any servant from the carriage began to look for her also accounted for the journey taking no more than three days rather than five or ten. They stopped only when it was necessary to rest the animals, instead of every time the wagon hit a bump or rocked as the wheels slid in and out of ruts. Lady Jeannette was not pleased and threatened dire punishments, but it was Alys who held the whip, and no one was hurt.

After they had arrived, Alys wondered why she had tried to hurry them, aside from the fact that any journey was dangerous in that it exposed the traveler to enemies and outlaws. Naturally, Alys had known that there would be trouble when Lady Jeannette discovered her husband was not already at Arles, but Alys was not prepared for the violence of the outburst. She had expected Lady Jeannette to be furious; it had not occurred to her that her mother-by-marriage would immediately assume Lord Alphonse was dead.

In vain Alys pointed out that he had been traveling with ten good men and that it was nigh impossible that all of them should be killed. In vain she expostulated that Lord Alphonse had not been carrying anything tempting enough to make outlaws attack eleven armed men. As fast as Alys demolished one cause of terror, Lady Jeannette found another until, at last, Alys realized she was being a great fool.

Lady Jeannette might, just at first, have been really frightened. Within a short time, however, she had discovered that her transports served two purposes: They prevented anyone from questioning her directly about her husband's whereabouts and they drew attention away from the widowed Lady Beatrice to herself. In her own peculiar way, Alys figured out, Lady Jeannette was protecting herself and enjoying herself. The feeling of guilt that had tied Alys to the thankless task of soothing her mother-by-marriage dissipated, and Alys slipped away to enjoy the company of the younger women.

Several days of relative peace followed. Lady Beatrice and Sir Romeo spent much of their time together in anxious conferences, which often included Lady Jeannette. This was less because they expected any sensible advice from her than because they hoped her hysterics on arrival were a pretense and she knew where her husband was. Even after they realized that she did not know, they continued to draw her into their talk in the hope that she could provide information on Alphonse's attitude, even if she krew no specific facts.

This was quite acceptable to Alys, who was certain that neither Alphonse nor Raymond had any intention of trying to seize the whole of Provence or even a share of Raymond-Berenger's estate. Thus, anything that could be extracted from Lady Jeannette would be soothing to Sir Romeo. Alys was both hurt and relieved to be dismissed by Lady Beatrice and Sir Romeo civilly but without a flicker of interest. Her property, if it had ever been mentioned, was outside their range of interest, and she was sure Lady Jeannette had given a most unflattering view of her intelligence and abilities.

On the other hand, she found herself fully accepted by the youthful members of the party, young Beatrice, Margot, Jeanine, and the young ladies being raised in the court. To her surprise, she even found that she was a center of interest to them. At first, Alys was somewhat suspicious and reserved, wondering whether these fine young ladies were meaning to make a may-game of her. However, she soon realized that she was different, to them exotic, and a relief to their boredom.

Like a beautiful doll, Alys could be dressed all anew in the latest fashions. Alys joined wholeheartedly in this amusement as soon as she determined that no one was trying to make her ridiculous by suggesting *outré* styles or colors that did not become her. Alys's life, so different from theirs, was also a source of fascination.

While young Beatrice and the other ladies were by no means sequestered or ignorant, enough of the Moorish influence remained in these southern lands to cause women to be regarded as toys. Lady Beatrice the elder, who was a Savoyard, was herself much more like Alys than like Lady Jeannette. Lady Beatrice had always taken a relatively active part in the management of the estates and politics, particularly after her childbearing years were ended; however, she could not throw off the influence of the area completely, as the nurses and tutors who attended her daughters were mostly native.

This produced a most interesting effect. Margaret, queen of France, the eldest daughter, and Eleanor, queen of England, the next in age, had received most of Lady Beatrice's direct attention. Each was actively interested in the affairs of the world and of her husband's domain. Sancia, countess of Cornwall, the third daughter, was less aggressive than her elder sisters, partly because her nature was gentler but also because, by the time she reached the age when her attitude toward her purposes and duties was being formed, Lady Beatrice's attention had already been drawn from her nursery to wider affairs. Those were the years when her husband's hold on his province was seriously threatened, and Lady Beatrice was far more often acting as Raymond-Berenger's envoy than as a mother. Young Beatrice had already been born, but she, the last, was the least benefited by her mother's strong personality and active intelligence.

Thus, Beatrice was the most like Margot and Jeanine in that she had been taught a woman's place was to be an ornament, the jewel in a man's crown of life and the solace of his idle hours, rather than a helpmate. But there had been another influence in young Beatrice's life: her father. She had been his favorite and had absorbed a portion of his ambition and strong will.

Alys, with her exotic blond coloring and her air of assurance, was fascinating to Beatrice, but far more fascinating were the discussions of her mother and Sir Romeo, to which she was not invited. Alys thought this was a mistake, for she saw that Beatrice was ambitious and intelligent and felt it would do good for her to know the reasons behind the decision to which they came. Alys was not sure whether they excluded her because her questions and objections might impede the discussions uselessly or because they did not trust her to be discreet or because they simply forgot her, but she felt Beatrice should be prepared and never turned the subject when it came up.

On the day before the date on which the vassals were

summoned to arrive, Margot had come round to the well-worn but ever interesting topic once more. "Do you think," she asked, "that your mother and Sir Romeo have found a way to prevent your sisters from contesting the will?"

"They must," Beatrice responded sharply. "My sisters have had their portions and are great enough. It is unthinkable to break up Provence into little pieces."

"I agree," Alys said. "It would only make trouble to have a keep here and a keep there owing fealty to different overlords. I do not think either King Henry or King Louis is greedy or would wish to violate the final will of their father-by-marriage. Uncle Richard, I know, would never think of it."

"Yes, but Margaret is not likely to accept it," Margot remarked, "even if Eleanor and Sancia do not press their rights."

"They have no rights!" Beatrice exclaimed hotly. "My father left Provence to me! They are queens, or rich as queens, already. They cannot have my share."

"I am sure," Alys suggested, "that a way will be found to content Margaret also. If Beatrice were to be married to a close relation of hers, for example, the benefit to the family as a whole—"

"Margaret is a spiteful bitch," Beatrice snapped, cutting Alys off. "She would not care for anyone's benefit but her own. Margot is right. She is the one who will make trouble, and once she starts demanding her share, Eleanor and Sancia will demand theirs as well. Margaret will set Louis to insist that all the daughters should be equal or that *she* as eldest should inherit."

"Louis could not ask for the whole because that would not be acceptable to King Henry, of that I am sure," Alys said. "And there is something Louis can be offered that would be more valuable to him than his wife's quarter share. Louis has a brother who is young and not ill-looking. Do you not think the king would prefer to have Provence whole, strong, and at peace and his brother well married than to start a new war with England or open the door to King Henry to gain a foothold in Provence?"

Beatrice wrinkled her nose, and Margot said, "Charles of Anjou is a grouch."

"I have heard that he is very serious," Alys amended, giving

Margot a monitory glance, "and that he is likely to enlarge and strengthen any estate that comes to him rather than dissipate it in riotous living. That is no bad characteristic for a husband."

"He is ambitious enough," Beatrice agreed, "but the French are all dull dogs. He cannot sing or write poetry."

"That may be had anywhere," Alys pointed out.

Of course, Alys was thinking of minstrels and of the wandering troubadours who sang and played and would compose poems for anyone who had a few coins to spare. It would no more have occurred to Alys to have an *ami amoureux* than to grow horns. She knew nothing of the convention by which great ladies were permitted to surround themselves with a crowd of young men, all of whom professed willingness to die for a kiss. However, both Beatrice and Margot knew that style of life well—at least, by repute if not in actuality. Lady Beatrice was too busy and too sensible and Lady Jeannette too fearful that her daughters rather than herself might be the focus of attention, so neither encouraged a "court of love."

Beatrice considered Alys's statement. "It is true," she said. "There is most excellent reason in everything you say, but why are you so sure that Charles will be my mother's and Sir Romeo's choice? They do not love the French overmuch."

"I am not *sure*," Alys replied, unwilling to admit that Raymond had said it was to be, and, as far as Alys was concerned, if Raymond said something, it must be so. "Merely, it seemed to me the safest path for you and for Provence. Charles would not be subject to his brother, so Provence would remain free; yet Charles would incline always to support his brother, so Louis would gain by that. On the other hand, Louis would never, I think, threaten Charles and would help him in times of trouble. What is more, although Charles has lands in France, they are such as can be governed by deputies. Thus, he will be able to give his mind and time to Provence."

"Well," Beatrice confessed, "you are not the only one who has mentioned Charles to me, but I cannot say I took well to him when I saw him—and he did not even look at me."

Alys was glad she was not the only one hinting of this marriage; in fact, there was something in Beatrice's manner that implied the hint had come from her mother. She laughed at

Beatrice's remark, having previously heard the story of this meeting between Beatrice and Charles.

"Why should he look at you?" Alys asked merrily. "He was a young man of fifteen and you hardly more than a babe of nine. I assure you, dear Beatrice, he will look at you now. And fifteen is not such a good age for the male as it is for the female. A woman *is* a woman at fifteen, but a man is still half a boy, with a changing voice and legs and arms too long. You will find him better, much better, at twenty."

Naturally enough, since everyone in Provence would be affected by the outcome of Sir Romeo's and Lady Beatrice's conferences, similar discussions to the one Alys and Beatrice had were taking place in widely divergent places. The notices of Raymond-Berenger's death and the summons to attend his obsequies had been received by those to whom they were sent within the province, although it was too soon for the courts of England and France to have heard. The attitudes of those who speculated about the fate of young Beatrice were as various as the natures and intelligence of the speakers.

At the citadel of Les Baux, Master Ernaldus was thinking along unique lines. He was now a favorite with both Lady Isabel and Sir Guillaume. The former, aside from affection, felt her half-brother was having an excellent influence on her son. Sir Guillaume also thought Master Ernaldus's influence was excellent—but for widely different reasons. Sir Guillaume found that his bastard uncle not only relieved him of most of the tedious aspects of managing his estate but increased the profit from it considerably.

Moreover, Ernaldus had pointed out that the friction between Sir Guillaume and his mother came about from too much honesty. Some things were not fit for a woman's ears, Ernaldus said; in fact, most things were not. If Sir Guillaume would restrict his conversations with his mother to the weather, his attendance at church, and formal visits to neighbors—or suchlike matters—he would have less trouble with her. And, if Guillaume felt he wished to tell someone of those adventures of which his mother would not approve . . . well, his uncle was not young, but he had not forgotten his youth completely. He would even vouch that Sir Guillaume was attending to business, if he should wish to be away, and attend to the business for him.

Soon enough Ernaldus was the primary adviser and chief source of comfort to both mother and son. From both he had heard the tale of the humbling of the family of des Baux—a long lament from Lady Isabel, who swore the shame had killed her husband, and a furious denunciation of the count of Provence from Guillaume, who adduced all kinds of treachery and trickery in a feud that stretched back two generations into the preceding century. Ernaldus made the proper responses to each, soothing his half-sister and holding out vague notions of redress to her son.

Naturally the notice of Raymond-Berenger's death was received with rejoicing at Les Baux. It came to them earlier than to most others because they were little more than three leagues from Arles. First Sir Guillaume exclaimed that he would not go. It did not matter to him that he had been forced to swear fealty to Raymond-Berenger; the count was dead. It was time to break away and perhaps take a small keep or two in the neighborhood. Lady Isabel cried out in protest, but her brother led her away promising her all would be well. Guillaume thanked him for removing an impediment to his desire, but Master Ernaldus shook his head and said that, for once, he agreed with Lady Isabel.

"This is more important than a raid on a small keep," Ernaldus pointed out. "That will make your neighbors angry and wary. Let us see, instead, whether there is a way to make your father's old allies band together again and take you for their leader. It is your natural position, but your youth is against you. Give me a day or two to think."

By this time, Sir Guillaume was so accustomed to Master Ernaldus being right and smoothing his path to whatever desire he had that he did not argue. He was unaccustomed to being thwarted at all; on the other hand, the prize being offered was greater than a pretty girl or a new trinket. The idea of retaking the position his father held appealed to him strongly.

Over the next two days, Ernaldus looked more often at his young master than he usually permitted himself to do. Sir Guillaume was excited and restless, his dark eyes bright with eagerness, often pacing the hall with the light, lithe stride of the competent warrior. At such times a turn or swing would show the hard curve of his thigh against his tunic or the fullness of the pectorals on his chest.

Out of Guillaume's appearance, the idea was born. Guillaume was a handsome young man. He had all the skills and charms that could be desired by a fool of a woman. He played the lute; he sang most tunefully; he could turn as pretty a phrase as any troubadour. Why should Guillaume not have the heiress himself? The talk Ernaldus had heard from visitors to Les Baux was that the girl would most likely be offered to Charles of Anjou—and no one was happy about that.

At this point Ernaldus paused and considered that the visitors to Les Baux were old friends of the family or young companions of Sir Guillaume. They might not be expressing the general opinion. The family of des Baux had supported Raymond of Toulouse against Louis of France and Raymond-Berenger of Provence. The older friends were still smarting from the defeat, and the younger men simply desired excitement, which the accession of Charles of Anjou would definitely inhibit.

True, Ernaldus thought, but there were enough of them to hold Les Baux against a far greater army for the few months it would take to wed and bed young Beatrice and get her with child. After that, no one would try to invalidate the marriage. No matter how many armies came from France and the rest of Provence, Les Baux on its precipitous cliff, standing clear on the plain, would be impregnable. There was no chance the citadel could be taken unless it were starved out. It had not fallen in the wars that ruined its master; defeats in other battles had added up to hopelessness, and Guillaume's father had not waited to be beseiged. No matter how many attacks against the cliffs and walls of Les Baux failed, hope was gone and the older Sir Guillaume had made terms.

Yes, but this was not a question of war, Ernaldus reflected. For the few months until Beatrice showed a big belly, Les Baux could hold out easily. Ernaldus did not believe they could retain the whole province, but he did not care. A quarter of it would more than restore the fortune of Guillaume des Baux. Moreover, with the other overlords so far away and the final testament of Raymond-Berenger in favor of his youngest daughter fresh in everyone's mind, it would be possible to make inroads on the portions yielded to the other sisters.

So far Ernaldus had made no profit, aside from his gain in status, from his services to Guillaume des Baux, but if he helped the young lord to become master of Provence, there would be nearly no limit to what he could take for himself.

"My lord," Ernaldus said, rising and approaching Sir Guillaume, "I have an idea I wish to propose to you, but I must beg you to consider long and very carefully, for it is a dangerous gambit and could well bring the whole power of Europe against us. On the other hand, it would win back all your heritage and more at one stroke—if it is successful."

"I do not need to consider," Guillaume replied, almost quivering with eagerness. "Only tell me. I do not care a pin for danger."

Since the purpose of mentioning the danger first had produced exactly the result Ernaldus desired, he beckoned the young man farther away from the hearth, where Lady Isabel sat with her women and her embroidery and applied a second sly spur.

"It will have to be kept secret from your mother. She would be frightened to death—and she might feel there was some wrong in the action."

Guillaume gave an impatient shrug. "Women are always frightened and always crying out against sin."

Ernaldus smiled. He had now guarded against Guillaume backing off from an act that might be considered dishonorable. Young as Guillaume was and filled with ridiculous ideas of chivalry toward women, he might have balked at abducting the heiress—and that would be necessary because Ernaldus was sure there would not be time enough, no matter how silly the girl was, for Guillaume to enamor her sufficiently to induce her to come willingly to Les Baux. Besides, Ernaldus was certain there would be many other young men trying to attract Beatrice's attention. Guillaume might not be the one on whom she would bestow her favor.

"We have heard," Ernaldus said, "that Charles of Anjou is the most like to be offered the heiress. But Charles of Anjou is known to be dour of nature, hard, and no beauty to boot."

"And he is an accursed Frenchman," Guillaume snarled.

"Yes, that comes into my plan also, but later," Ernaldus soothed. "For now, I wish to speak of the young Lady Beatrice. Is it not a shame to throw her to such a man? I have heard she is as beautiful as her sisters and has great charm and graciousness." He held up a hand as Guillaume seemed about to speak. "I know you were at war with the father, but surely you would not war against a helpless girl. And think, are not feuds best settled by marriages?"

There was a moment's stunned silence, and then Guillaume burst into bitter laughter. "Are you mad?"

"Not at all," Ernaldus replied blandly. "You are most handsome, my lord, and blessed with those skills most appealing to ladies. Would it not be for the lady's good as well as ours that you should have her?"

"Ten or fifteen years ago, before my father's power was broken, it might have been barely possible to propose such a marriage," Guillaume snarled impatiently. "Now Lady Beatrice and Sir Romeo would not only laugh in my face but spit in it."

"My lord," Ernaldus said reproachfully, "I am not a fool. I have heard what you told me about your father's humbling. I did not intend to suggest that you put yourself forward as a suitor to the lady's mother and guardian. I was only pointing out that the young lady herself would doubtless prefer you and be happier with you."

"About that, you are probably right, but no one will care about her preference."

"Nonetheless, it might have more effect than anyone would expect," Ernaldus said, and then went on to describe his notion of Guillaume wooing Beatrice and bringing her to Les Baux.

"She would never agree," Guillaume gasped.

"It is not necessary for her to agree to come to Les Baux, but only for her to leave the keep at Arles without any large escort. She might be a little angered when you carry her away by force, but she would be thrilled by your boldness and by the ferocity of your passion. There would be time enough, once she was safe here, for you to soothe her and convince her."

Guillaume stared at Ernaldus without speaking, and, after a moment, the bailiff shrugged. "I said it might bring all Europe against us, but this keep can withstand all Europe for six or eight months. And once Lady Beatrice is married and with child, they will make terms. You may not get the whole province just at first, but you will have the rest of your life to gather it in. You will be greater than your father, greater than any des Baux before you—Lord Guillaume des Baux, comte de Provence."

Still Guillaume did not speak, but Ernaldus relaxed. The young man's eyes were burning with the light of adventure. For a time Ernaldus said no more, allowing Guillaume to revel in his dreams, flattering Guillaume into thinking that his bravado would be attractive to Beatrice. Then he said softly, "We will not be alone, you know. There are many who would rather see you—or even the devil—have Lady Beatrice, anyone so long as it is not French Charles."

Guillaume focused his eyes on Ernaldus. Then he nodded and began a discussion of the practical aspects of winning the heiress's attention, arranging her abduction, and convincing a sufficient number of his friends and his father's old supporters that he would be preferable as a husband for Beatrice than Charles of Anjou.

CHAPTER 21

****

Once the vassals of Provence began to arrive for the funeral, the council on what to do with Beatrice was broadened. It included almost everyone of importance—everyone except that young lady herself. Although Beatrice was not so foolish as to expect her word to have any weight, she felt much slighted at not being invited to listen to what was going on or even being told what had been said. The only men not included in the council were the squires and younger sons, who had accompanied their fathers—and Guillaume des Baux, who presented himself to Beatrice with angry eyes and asked whether she, too, intended to slight him when the power should be in her hands.

As much flattered as astounded by the notion that she would rule Provence, Beatrice inquired who this passionate young man was. He told her promptly and honestly, adding, somewhat less truthfully, "I was a child then. I came here in good faith, thinking the quarrel between des Baux and the counts of Provence was ended, but it was clear that I was not welcome to your mother or to Sir Romeo."

This last was true enough, but it was no particular prejudice against his family or memory of the feud that prompted the coldness of Lady Beatrice and Sir Romeo. Rather it was the passionate objections Sir Guillaume advanced against the arrangement with France that had made him unwelcome. There were some other men who felt as he did, and enough who had doubts and might be swayed against the plan to make Guillaume's arguments—no matter how little logical—dangerous.

Beatrice, who was already annoyed with her mother and Sir Romeo, put out her hand. "I am sorry for your hurt, Sir Guillaume, but I am powerless to amend it." She smiled sadly. "I am no better used than you. It is my life they are deciding, yet I am not invited to speak, nor even to listen in silence."

"They care nothing for the spirit," Guillaume cried. "How can they talk of one so lovely, so gentle and gracious, as if she were a parcel of land, a mare or a bitch, without sense or feeling."

This was a most proper and elegant effusion. Beatrice blushed and made a sad reply, which inspired Guillaume to new heights of flattery and sympathy. These eventually induced enough self-pity in Beatrice to draw tears to her eyes, upon which the young man was quite carried away and professed himself willing to die to prevent a single teardrop from falling from such exquisite eyes to mar such perfect cheeks.

Had Alys been present during this meeting she might have pointed out, with enough cleverness to make Beatrice see the humor in the exaggeration, the dangers of encouraging such attentions. However, only Margot and a few still younger ladies were in attendance on Beatrice, and they were thrilled rather than concerned over the protestations.

The following day Raymond-Berenger was interred, and Alys and Jeanine had all they could do to manage Lady Jeannette. She was not only displaying emotions she felt to be suitable to the loss of so kind a father-by-marriage but also quite honestly frightened. Two weeks had passed since they had left Aix, and no word had come either from her husband or from Raymond. As if this were not sufficiently alarming, Lady Beatrice and Sir Romeo had been asking pointed, even harsh, questions about the whereabouts and intentions of her menfolk.

It was fortunate for Alys that Jeanine was so accustomed to her mother's enlargement of every absence of her husband and her eldest son into a calamity that she did not perceive the note of genuine fear. Jeanine, however, was also concentrated on her own affairs. She had picked out several suitable unmarried males from the group that had gathered and was weighing them in her mind to present their names in proper order to her father. Once the actual crisis of the funeral was over, Jeanine left Alys to attend to Lady Jeannette; she had more important business on hand than her mother's fancies, such as discovering which of the possible gentlemen were interested in her and whether any of those who had been previously married had male heirs.

This had one good result in that Lady Jeannette became even

more resigned to Alys's place in her life. She would never like
her daughter-by-marriage; their personalities were too much at
odds. Moreover, Lady Jeannette's jealousy would be constantly inflamed by her son's less-than-tactful preference for
his wife's company and her husband's reliance on Alys's
ability. Nonetheless, she had virtually given up all designs of
active opposition to Alys by the fifth day after the interment.

On that day, Alys's attentions became unnecessary because
a messenger rode in with a packet of letters from Lord
Alphonse. There was a long report addressed to Sir Romeo that
explained what Lord Alphonse had done—except for any
mention of proffering his homage to Louis. Alphonse wrote:

> I felt that the offer for Beatrice should come from Louis
> rather than that we ask him for Charles. Thus, we confer
> the favor instead of asking for one, and the terms will be
> better. I did not, of course, discuss any substantive
> conditions, only made it clear that I will never contest my
> half-sister's claim nor my father's last testament. As for
> Beatrice's marrying, I did no more than hint that, rather
> than tear Provence apart, you and Lady Beatrice would
> like a man with connections powerful enough to discour-
> age other suitors. If we could have in addition a guarantee
> of our independence, that would be decisive. To this, the
> king made no direct reply, but his thanks were very
> warm.

What Alphonse did not write was that Louis's thanks had
been so warm that he took Alphonse's homage then and there,
praising him for his loyalty to his sister and his friendship to
France. Although the private ceremony might have had little
meaning with a king like Henry of England, Alphonse was
perfectly secure that the matter was settled. Unless he himself
did something to violate the oath, Louis would keep it—and no
argument from his brother Charles that Aix was part of
Provence would move the king from what he swore on relics.
Alphonse and Louis agreed that public swearing must be
delayed until the fate of the rest of the province was settled,
but Louis was now overlord of Aix and would protect it, even
from his own brother.

Alys had a brief note: "Beloved daughter, all is well. Send

word to my son that the matter of which we spoke is settled. I
will remain with King Louis until he decides what he wishes to
say to Lady Beatrice and Sir Romeo. A blessing on you,
treasure of my house."

Lady Jeannette had a long, tender letter of apology for
leaving her without farewell or explanations. He was afraid,
Alphonse wrote, that she would suffer too many fears over his
journey. This did not completely pacify her, but the renewed
and effusive cordiality with which she was treated by Sir
Romeo and Lady Beatrice allowed her to put aside her
complaints until she could address them to Alphonse himself.
This freed Alys, who offered up thanksgiving and went to write
to Raymond. Until Alphonse's letter came, Alys had been
afraid to write. She did not wish to draw attention to herself
and suggest to anyone's mind that she might know where her
father-by-marriage had gone.

This practical reason for his wife's silence was the only one
that did not occur to Raymond. He managed to find causes as
diverse as imprisonment in the donjon of Arles and flight back
to England, but even in his disordered state of mind he realized
that these alternatives were not likely. Raymond entertained
these foolish notions because the reason he thought most likely
was the one he was least willing to accept. He was readier to
believe that Lady Beatrice, whom he knew to be both kind and
clever, and Sir Romeo, whom he knew to be a model of reason
and justice, had lost their wits and acted irrationally and
unnaturally than believe Alys no longer loved him.

In the privacy of the castellan's chamber in Gordes, which
Raymond had commandeered when he returned there two days
earlier, he took out the letter he had received from Alys three
weeks before. It was the letter of a good wife, devoted to her
husband's interests, Raymond thought as he reread it for the
some-hundredth time, but it breathed duty, not love. He felt
there was a coldness in those final words "all my duty, all my
desire, my every thought is for your good." Raymond closed
his eyes. It was impossible that one act of stupid crudity could
kill the love Alys had shown him.

He did not believe it. Alys was too reasonable. She even
admitted she had been at fault and had caused his explosion of
temper; she had said so. Could she then withdraw her love?
Raymond told himself it was impossible, yet all his life he had

dealt with women who blew up a yawn or a sigh into a major offense and punished such offenses with coldness and rejection. Over and over he assured himself that Alys was not that sort, but that only woke a violent desire to go to her and prove it to himself.

There was also the possibility that the seeming coldness of her letter was generated by fear, but that conclusion was not very helpful. It merely reinforced the urge to rush off to Arles. Unfortunately, this was the one thing Raymond knew he must not do until he learned what reaction Sir Romeo would have to the news that Alphonse had gone to King Louis. The intense frustration generated an enormous energy in Raymond, which was expended in a more thorough examination of the state of war readiness in Aix than had been experienced since the early years of Raymond-Berenger's rule when he had come himself.

Some of the older vassals and castellans, who remembered those years, scratched their heads and muttered, unsure of whether to be glad or sorry. The total freedom they had enjoyed under Alphonse's easy rule was obviously gone, but so was the indifference and neglect. Adding one thing with another, the men decided God had been watching over them. In the good years of peace after Toulouse's downfall, they had done as they pleased; now that trouble was coming, they were blessed with a strong leader.

The general satisfaction and willingness to make ready for trouble soothed Raymond in one way but gave no further outlet to his need for action. He knew there was no profit in fighting one's own men, and he picked no quarrels. Still, he was so uneasy that some rebellion would almost have pleased him better than the compliance with which he was met. He returned to Aix and put the guard and armorers to such labor that they fell, like dead men into their beds—when they were allowed to seek them. But he dared not stay long at Aix. If Sir Romeo sent a second command to come to Arles, he did not wish to be in Aix to receive it. On the other hand, if Alys should soften and decide to write, he wanted her letter. Thus, he went to Gordes, since it was the place she had last known him to be.

Raymond thought so little of Lucie that it was not until he sat rereading Alys's old letter that he remembered why he had come to Gordes in the first place. He cursed wearily, wondering if he should leave, but Gordes had another prime advantage; there was a road—not good or well traveled, but negotiable by a troop of mounted men—going almost directly to Arles. For some time he sat staring into nothing. He had been celibate as a saint since he left Alys, which was ridiculous, a self-imposed penance. Then he laughed without mirth, thinking that Alys would never believe him if he told her. And would she even care?

As if in answer to that question, the castellan appeared in the doorway. "There is a letter from Arles, my lord, sent on from Aix."

"The seal?" Raymond asked, although what he could do if the letter was from Sir Romeo, he did not know.

"I do not know it."

"Alys!" Raymond exclaimed, more because it was what he wanted than for any other reason.

The desire was fulfilled; it was Alys's seal with the arms of Marlowe. He skipped the salutation and began with the words "I dare address you so boldly because," and his heart sank. Raymond closed his eyes, but when they opened they fell on the preceding line and he was so instantly filled with joy that he had to close his jaw hard to keep from crying out in relief. He should have begun at the beginning.

"To Lord Raymond d'Aix, my dear lord and husband," Alys wrote, adding to that formal beginning, "my dearest and most precious love." That was the boldness for which she had begged pardon. Raymond took a deep breath, restrained himself from reading the lines ten times, and got to the meat of the letter:

I dare address you so boldly because my news is so good that I hope your joy in it will lead you to forgive such freedom in a wife so imperfect. Today we have had letters from your father in France. I enclose herein his short message to me. From it I understand that Louis has either accepted his homage for Aix or has given him surety that he would do so as soon as circumstances permit. Moreover, I suppose that if Louis desired Lord Alphonse to remain with him, it can only mean that he intends your father to accompany his envoy or to carry for him to Lady Beatrice an offer for young Beatrice.

Although this deduction hardly required great perspicacity, Raymond smiled as fondly as if Alys had written a sentence worthy of the judgment of Solomon. At the next, his smile broadened:

Thus, I believe it safe now, if your work among the vassals be finished, to come here. You must do what you know to be best, but for myself nothing could be more desirable. I must not write more lest I forget my duty and urge you to forget yours, so greatly do I desire to see you.

"The clever little witch," Raymond muttered to himself, having noted the date and relished the tender closing.

At the moment no new doubts had yet entered Raymond's mind. He recognized only Alys's overt purpose. Plainly, from the hesitancy of the first lines, she still feared some punishment. Her first defense had been to include his father's brief letter to her with its "treasure of my house." Modesty would forbid her to quote the lines, so she had sent the note. Her second line of defense was to urge him to come to her. Alys knew he would find it difficult to exact any punishment in the crowded conditions of Arles without raising comment and exposing more of his private affairs than he would wish. Probably she hoped to soften him enough over the time spent in a guesting situation that he would consider whatever scolding he could find time and place to deliver as sufficient lessoning.

Raymond chuckled softly and stretched until his bones cracked, feeling loose and relaxed for the first time since he had entered Tour Dur nearly a month before. He was warm and amused, very eager to see Alys, but without the feverish feeling of urgency that made him constantly miserable when he felt he had lost her love. He wished the letter had arrived earlier so that he could have started that day, but he was not furious with impatience that it was too late to go. After sitting for a while, looking comfortably into the fire and chuckling now and again as he thought of various ways of teasing and alarming his properly remorseful wife, he went to tell the castellan that he would leave at dawn.

Just before he gave the order Raymond paused, suddenly

feeling uneasy and wondering whether there might be any other reason for Alys to urge him to come to Arles—a political reason she did not wish to state. If so, the few hours, that is, whether he arrived in Arles at daybreak rather than at evening, might make a difference. Then he remembered the frank discussion of his father's purpose in going to Louis. If she feared her letter would be opened, she would never have written that. Raymond gave the original order he had intended and put the uneasiness he felt out of his mind.

It so happened that Raymond's arrival at Arles at dawn would have saved everyone there a period of great anxiety, but it could not have averted the trouble that overtook Alys because that had happened before he received her letter. When Alys finished writing it and had sent it off with one of the men from Tour Dur, she felt particularly lighthearted. She had, indeed, planned just what Raymond had deduced, but what made her happy was the thought of seeing Raymond, not escaping punishment.

The fact that she was free of Lady Jeannette's sighs, tears, and constant demands and complaints not only increased her cheerfulness but also enabled her to seek an outlet for it. For the first time since Raymond-Berenger had been interred, Alys sought out the younger group of guests. She was welcomed with pleasure by Beatrice and with stares and in-drawn breaths of admiration from the young men. They had scarcely caught a glimpse of her previously, since most of them sedulously avoided the knot of older women.

"Thou lily-white, sweet lady, bright of brow. How sweeter than a grape art thou," one of the young men sighed.

Alys's eyes opened as wide as possible, bright blue pools dramatically surrounded with overlong, dark gold lashes. "How did you know?" she asked, sounding astounded. "*I* do not even know your name, and here you are blabbing my secrets all over the place."

"It cannot be a secret that thou art sweet as a grape, lily-white, or bright of brow. That can be seen at one glance," the young man said with determined admiration, although one could see that he was a trifle put out by being interrupted before he finished his poem.

"The grapes where I come from are tarter than crab apples," Alys said, "but that was not what I meant. If I am unwelcome to you, it would be sufficient to turn your back and not speak to me. There was no need to quote at me lines from which I fled more than two hundred leagues."

"W-what?" the poor young man stammered. He had met various responses to flattery, but this one was totally new.

"Oh, did you not know?" Alys asked innocently. "Then I beg your pardon. I see you meant no offense. I have these crochets. I am driven nearly to madness when lips are likened to strawberries or necks to those of swans. . . ." Here Alys paused and cocked her head to the side. "Although," she continued, "there would be some sense in that, you know. Only think how convenient it would be if one's neck could stretch up an arm's length and then bend down and turn right around so that one could see the small of one's back."

For perhaps two heartbeats there was a stunned silence. Then Alys slowly and deliberately lowered one lid in an exaggerated wink. It was too much for another of the young men, who burst into laughter, and then the whole group followed. Alys now went and apologized prettily to the gentleman who had first spoken to her.

"I did not mean to raise laughter at your cost," she said. "I know it is a dreadful lack in me, but I am not in the least poetical. When someone says to me 'Take thou my hand,' I see myself carrying away his hand, and I wonder what in the world I am going to do with it."

"Does it never occur to you that the hand is attached to the man?" asked the gentleman who had first laughed, adding, "I am Raymond de Villeneuve."

"And I am Alys d'Aix. As to what you said, it does not seem to have occurred to poets that a man cannot be cut up. They are forever offering you pieces of their anatomy—a heart, a tongue, a liver—although what good the poet would be without the part puzzles me. Also, it would be very messy to be carrying around a dripping heart or an oozing liver, and I think the tongue would soon dry out and look quite unlike itself and horrid."

The group around Alys was by now convulsed with mirth, the men whooping with laughter and the girls tittering into their sleeves. Beatrice laughed so hard she hiccupped, but Guillaume des Baux, who had been standing closest to Beatrice, turned on Alys with a scowl.

"Your heart is hard, madame, if you cannot feel for the suffering of a hopeless lover," he said.

Alys's fair brows rose. "My heart, sir, is a red, ugly thing just as any woman's is, no harder, no softer. If you wish to blame me with justice, rather say my temper is risible or my thoughts suspicious; that is, I like to laugh and I do not believe anyone ever died of love. It is quite remarkable to me how blooming and healthy sighing swains remain—except in their verses or tales."

"You wrong us, Lady Alys," Sir Guillaume said. "Men have died for love."

"Oh, yes, and women, too," Alys agreed. "Outraged husbands have killed wives and lovers; outraged women have killed poets who whispered in one ear while their eyes sought another victim. I said no man or woman had died *of* love."

"Who has wronged you that you are so bitter, Lady Alys?" Guillaume asked nastily.

Guillaume des Baux was very angry. In a few words, Alys seemed to have destroyed the delicate structure of romance he had been building around Beatrice. First she had laughed as heartily as—more heartily than—any of the other ladies when Alys poked fun at lovers, and then her expression had grown quite hard when Alys spoke of crimes of passion. Had Guillaume not been seduced by his own verses so that he had convinced himself that he was in love with Beatrice, he would not have been so clumsy. He had lashed out with the hope of embarrassing the sharp-tongued lady, but he should have been warned by the quickness of her repartee that she was unlikely to fall into so obvious a trap.

Alys widened her eyes to their full extent. "But sir," she protested, "do you take me for corrupt from the cradle? Or do you suggest that Queen Eleanor has so little control over the damsels entrusted to her care that I could come to such harm while under her eye? Or is it my mother-by-marriage you impugn?"

Poor Guillaume, not expecting such a flood of accusations, merely gaped, and Alys changed her expression from astonished indignation to one of merriment.

"No, no," she cried, "you must be punished for so evil a calumny. I name you to be hoodman blind."

A slight tension that had developed in the group in expectation of a quarrel dissolved into laughter. Alys had broken the romantic mood with her joking, and everyone was in the right humor for a lively game. Raymond de Villeneuve stepped forward swiftly and drew the hood of Guillaume's tunic over his head and down to his chin, obscuring his vision. Beatrice jumped up from her chair and began to turn her swain round and round so he would lose all sense of direction. The other young men hastily carried whatever furniture there was in the area to the walls. Finally Beatrice gave Guillaume a hard shove, which sent him staggering into the center of the hall.

"I do not wish—" Guillaume began furiously, intending to say he did not wish to play silly games.

He reached to lift the hood that blinded him, but someone pushed him strongly from the rear, and Beatrice cried out that he should not be so poor a sport. That remark sounded a warning, even through Guillaume's fury. He might not have been a very experienced lover, but he realized that showing himself ill-humored and spiteful, unable to take a jest when it was turned on him, would certainly not inspire admiration in any lady, especially Beatrice. So he swallowed his rage as well as he could and played the game.

He was soon rewarded for his compliance. Beatrice believed that it was for her sake, so that she should not seem foolish, that Guillaume had been so angry when Alys made the group laugh at lovers. Beatrice also suspected that Guillaume was more serious than she about the game of love they were playing. Because her conscience pricked her, she deliberately did not dodge quickly enough when the hoodman came in her direction, and he caught her.

This was only the first stage of the game. Now the hoodman needed to identify the person he had caught; if he could do so, that person would take his place as hoodman and the game would begin anew. It was not at all difficult to identify Beatrice. She was wearing a gown with a decorative edging of fur and an intricate necklace, yet Guillaume held her in his arms for quite five minutes, praising her sweet scent and the contours of her body and face, over which he kept running his fingers, before he finally gave her name and released her.

Alys did not think much about this immediately, although she had noticed Beatrice's delay. The first might have been owing to a distraction of attention; Guillaume's actions were only natural, for all young men seized the opportunity to touch and embrace a lady if they caught one. That was a good measure of the attraction the game held for adults, plus the rough joy of pushing and striking the hoodman. It was only after Beatrice had been blinded and was being pushed about —albeit a good deal more gently than Guillaume had been —that it became clear to Alys there was some special relationship between them.

Raymond de Villeneuve was holding Guillaume out of the crowd surrounding the blindfolded Beatrice and saying, "Oh, no. You must stand clear. You will let her catch you and be hoodman again just for the pleasure of having her touch you."

No wonder, Alys thought, *he was furious at me for making Beatrice laugh at love poems* She was amused and a little sorry for the young man. Poor thing, he might believe himself to be in love with Beatrice even though both must know any real relationship to be impossible. Still, that could be dangerous. Beatrice was very young, and it was possible she might be infected by the tender sentiment. It would not make any difference in what happened, but it could make her very unhappy.

Absorption in such subjects is not the best method for playing a game. Slowed by her abstraction, Alys was Beatrice's victim. She, too, was easy to recognize because she was so small. Laughing, she complained vociferously of being caught in her own trap and complained that the odds against her were unfair because she did not know the names of most of the group. However, by clever strategy she caught Raymond de Villeneuve. There was considerable laughter and many jests about how she had pursued him, encouraged by his loud assertions of his willingness to be pursued by Alys at any time she chose. Eventually these were muffled by his hood, and the game went on.

Alert now, Alys avoided recapture but also found confirmation that Guillaume was wooing Beatrice. More important, it did not seem to Alys that Beatrice was fleeing more ardently than coyness suggested. Alys was concerned, but she made, as yet, no obvious attempts to separate the pair, restraining herself to a seemingly accidental interruption now and again. However, even drawing Beatrice away to advise on a new headdress or to choose between two colors of embroidery

thread was unwise. Coupled with Alys's previous jests at the
expense of lovers and the admiration Beatrice showed for her,
Alys's attempts to fix Beatrice's attention on activities that did
not include Guillaume took on a sinister light in his eyes.

So well had Beatrice responded to his attention and so
attractive did Guillaume find her, that he had begun to hope
force would not be necessary. Now Guillaume took fright. He
told himself he could not bear to lose Beatrice and decided to
go back to his original plan. All the next day he avoided
Beatrice until he found an opportunity to draw her aside when
Alys was not in the hall. Then he told Beatrice tragically that
he must no longer force his company on her.

"I wondered to where you had disappeared," Beatrice said,
smiling. "Have you been avoiding me? I assure you there is no
need. I do not find you repulsive."

"You give me life with such kindness," Guillaume sighed,
"but I fear others read more into your mercy to a man sore
stricken in love than is good for you. I fear that, in order to part
us, restraints will be placed upon you."

"What restraints?"

"Who knows? Certainly you will be ordered never to speak
to me or even cast a glance in my direction," Guillaume
announced tragically.

Beatrice felt like saying, *Do not be so silly, my mother is not
an idiot,* but in a way she was touched by Guillaume's fear. It
was in the best tradition of courtly love that "friends" should
be separated by unfeeling husbands or parents. And, in fact,
Beatrice knew that Guillaume's love could have no fruition.
She would soon marry Charles of Anjou or some other equally
highborn man with powerful connections. Still, that had
nothing to do with love. She did have a tender feeling for
Guillaume; he had been the first to woo her.

"Well, then," she said teasingly, "you will need to sing your
love songs to someone else."

"Never!" he exclaimed passionately. "I will die! If I cannot
speak to you, I will die."

It was very romantic to hear such professions of faith.
Beatrice sighed.

"I should not have showed so openly how I felt," Guillaume
went on, encouraged by this display of sympathy. "Others

have noticed. Sooner or later, and I fear sooner, someone will make issue of my attentions to you and I will be driven away."

That statement was not so far-fetched to Beatrice. She did not fear that she would be constrained to avoid Guillaume. Such an order would be too difficult to enforce, but Guillaume might be told to leave if his wooing of her came to her mother's attention. Lady Beatrice would not like hints that her daughter was amorously inclined to come to the ears of her future husband. She was not in love with Guillaume; nor had she forgotten Alys's remark that Charles of Anjou, the most likely suitor, might be more attractive to her and she to him now that both were more mature. Nonetheless, she was touched by Guillaume's protestations, and she was doubly annoyed that her first "friend" would be driven away while she was not even included in the discussions of whom she should marry.

"I will be sorry for it," Beatrice said regretfully, "but—"

"We could avoid being parted," Guillaume interrupted eagerly. And then, as Beatrice shook her head, he cried tensely, "Do not deny me before you hear me out, I beg you. I desire your good, only your good, from the bottom of my heart. I love you more than life. I would not hurt you or cause you the smallest shame, I swear."

"But Guillaume," Beatrice protested, "you know that soon you must go, even—"

"Only listen," he pleaded, interrupting again, "that is part of my plan. I know I must go, but I will die if I cannot see you —only see you and speak to you, I do not ask more than that. Will you let me die?"

Moved by this passionate plea, Beatrice responded, "I would see you if I could, but I cannot guess how it may be arranged."

"Easily, so easily, and safely, also. I will leave at once, this very day so that any suspicion that might be raised will die, but I will not go far, only to the Abbey of Montmajour."

"Ah," Beatrice cried, "of course. Mother will allow me to go to the abbey."

The light of adventure lit her eyes. She would have to think of a reason for going to the abbey and of a reason for going there without her mother. This was just the sort of adventure to appeal to Beatrice. It was perfectly safe; the abbey was less than a league away, and she could not be blamed even if she were found in Guillaume's company. No one had told her to avoid him, and it was not her fault if he happened to be visiting the abbey at the same time as she.

"But it must seem as if we meet by accident," Guillaume warned. "God forbid you should be blamed or punished for your mercy to me. I cannot watch for you. That, I fear, would give away our stratagem. You must tell me a time and a day. Then I will contrive to be where you are, as if it were by chance."

"Yes, that would be best. Let me see—"

"Let it be soon," Guillaume interrupted. "Please let it be soon. After these days so close to your sweetness, each moment apart will be ten years in torment. Think of my suffering. Let it be soon."

It would have to be soon, Beatrice thought. A few days more must bring not only a decision about her fate but the departure of all the funeral guests. Once her mother's attention was no longer fixed on political matters, it would turn on Beatrice herself. Beatrice did not fear that; mostly it would be pleasant, but it would take up much time. A suitable wardrobe for a bride and a countess, rather than the youngest daughter of the house, would have to be planned, fitted, and made. Jewels would have to be chosen, and, once the offer of marriage was made and accepted, Beatrice knew her mother would instruct her fully about her future husband and her lands. Thus, the only possible time for a last meeting with Guillaume would be the next few days.

Beatrice thought of naming the next day, but did not wish to seem too eager. "The day after tomorrow," she said. "But it may be only to say farewell. Once the conferences are over, I fear I will be kept close making ready for my betrothal and marriage."

When she spoke, Beatrice's face was pensive. She was a little sad to think this one adventure might be her last. All unwitting, she refired Guillaume's determination. He had begun to waver over the idea of abducting so sweetly trusting a maiden, and he was concerned, too, about his honor, having promised no harm would come to her. However, her apparent sadness when speaking of her betrothal and marriage led him to believe she returned his love and, thus, regretted her need to marry elsewhere. Then why should she? Why should Beatrice not marry the man she loved and at the same time bring back all the power the des Baux had lost?

Final arrangements about time and place were made. Guillaume kissed Beatrice's hands again and again, uttering passionate thanks and declarations of love. Finally he tore himself away. He had a great deal to do, for, naturally, he did not intend to be seen at the abbey himself or to allow Beatrice to arrive there.

CHAPTER 22

****

Oddly enough, had not Alys's objections to love poems caused so much amusement, Beatrice might never have fulfilled her intention of meeting Guillaume. Raymond de Villeneuve had been so enchanted by Alys's original attitude towards poets and poetry that the younger Villeneuve described the whole scene to his father, not realizing that Sir Romeo would not see it as funny.

Sir Romeo was a wise and just man, but unfortunately his wisdom did not extend to the management of high-spirited —not to say spoiled—young ladies. Instead of carrying the tale to Lady Beatrice, who would have laughed and said such an occupation was natural to young people, Sir Romeo gave young Beatrice a sharp lecture on propriety.

Sir Romeo did not accuse Beatrice of any personal partiality; his son had not mentioned Guillaume's attentions because he did not think them dangerous and he did not wish to get Beatrice into trouble. However, Sir Romeo scolded her for allowing such behavior in her presence. Did she not realize, he said, that she was about to be betrothed? Did she want her future husband to hear she had no modesty? What might be fit for a married woman—although he did not himself approve it —was not to be countenanced for innocent maidens. And so on and so on.

Beatrice was furious. She had never liked Sir Romeo, who had always seemed to regard her as a feeble-minded doll. Normally she would have complained to her mother, who would have soothed her, but Beatrice was very much annoyed with her mother. Since her father's death, her mother seemed to have forgotten she was a living person and acted as if she were part of the estate of Provence, a mere piece of land.

Too young and too spoiled, Beatrice did not stop to consider that her mother's very real grief for her husband, which had to be suppressed to permit her to deal with political necessities, was dulling Lady Beatrice's own emotions and perceptions. All young Beatrice felt, particularly after Sir Romeo had scolded her, was that her mother did not care about her and would allow her to be misused by anyone. In comparison, Guillaume's passionate assertions of love became more attractive, and the idea of meeting him, which would throw old Romeo into a convulsion, took on a new luster.

The scolding had another ill effect. Whereas previously Beatrice would have asked openly for permission and escort, now she began to scheme to get away without telling anyone. This, she soon realized, was impractical. She would not be able to get her mare saddled and ride out all alone. Finally, she confessed her problem to Margot, who had been the most sympathetic and was a member of her family. Margot immediately suggested that Alys could arrange it, but warned Beatrice against telling the truth since she was sure Alys would not approve a clandestine assignation.

Unfortunately for everyone, the appeal was made to Alys at just the right moment. Not only was she restless from being pent up in Arles with nothing to do, but she could not stop wondering whether Raymond had received her letter and what his reaction to it would be. She seized on the suggestion with enthusiasm after she learned that the abbey was less than a league away and that the reason the girls wanted to go was to obtain some of the special cheese and wine the abbey made.

Alys was very wise for her age, but she had never been a great heiress. The danger of an abduction never entered her mind. Nor did she think of Sir Guillaume, since Beatrice did not seem in the least disturbed by his departure. Nonetheless, she might have been less gullible if half her mind had not been concentrated on her husband. Alys knew when her letter would have arrived at Aix. If Raymond happened to be there and decided to come to Arles, he could arrive sometime late in the day that Beatrice and Margot wanted to go to the abbey. Alys also knew that there was a good chance he would not be at Aix and the letter would take several days longer to get to him. Still, her eagerness to see Raymond and her anxiety about his reaction was making time hang heavy on her hands. She wanted a diversion, and this small expedition to the abbey seemed ideal.

The weather could have saved them. Had it been particularly

cold or wet, all might have preferred comfort to adventure. Instead the sky was bright with sunlight, and there was even a hint of spring in the air. Alys sent down a message to Arnald that she and two ladies would ride out for an hour or two; her mare and those of Margot and Beatrice were to be saddled.

However, Arnald did not like to leave his troop. Aelfric had been left in Blancheforte; Hugo had remained behind in Tour Dur to escort his wife, Bertha, and the two little girls to Lady Catherine's manor. He was the only other man who spoke fair French. It seemed to him that every time he left the men, a fight developed owing to misunderstandings or pure aggressiveness. He mentioned this to Alys, who said immediately that he need not come since their objective was an abbey less than a league distant. In addition, Arnald had never been guard to an heiress. Lady Alys had often ridden to Bix with only two men. An armed and mounted man was easily proof against three or four ragged thieves, and he knew the land around Arles was tame and at peace. To be on the safe side, he called out four men, the best in the troop, and told two to ride before and two behind the ladies.

The journey was very pleasant. The road wound along the river for a short way and then curved up to higher ground, but the rise was very gentle. Margot and Beatrice chattered excitedly, trying to make a plan to keep Alys from interfering with a private meeting between Beatrice and Guillaume. Since they dared not say anything direct about the subject, their discussion was obscure. Still, Alys might have guessed they had a secret—only she was thinking that Raymond would not ride as slowly as they were. If he were coming . . . if . . .

Alys's men talked idly, too. They looked about, but it was ridiculous to fear danger on this road so near a town as large as Arles. There were other travelers, not very many, but enough to make any attack unlikely; there was too great a chance another party would appear to help the victims or report the thieves. Then Lady Beatrice called out and pointed. The lead men obediently turned right into a narrower path. This was more heavily wooded and climbed more steeply, but now they were only a few minutes from the abbey.

The sudden sound of breaking brush turned pleasure to nightmare. Alys's men jerked to attention and drew their swords, but they did not shift their shields and they were not anxious. Thieves, to their minds, were poor creatures on foot. The tearing brush and branches could only be caused by large bodies. The men thought that something had startled a herd of deer that was now fleeing in panic. The swords were drawn only to ward off the creatures.

These thoughts barely had time to form, however, before the first armored man burst through the trees. Margot and Beatrice shrieked in terror, and Alys saw instantly that they had fallen into a trap. She saw her lead men engaged, heard more men coming, and screamed in English, "Flee! Flee! Do not fight. No harm will come to us. Tell them at the keep that we are taken."

For the lead men, however, this order came too late. Alys saw one already down, and the other, bleeding from several wounds, was falling. Alys had no time to see whether either of the others had broken loose, but she feared they had not. She was trying to get her mare around Margot's and Beatrice's mounts, but the animal was terrified and would not obey the rein, turning in a half-circle and balking. It was too late anyway. A man in knight's armor had ridden up to Beatrice and pulled her from her saddle, setting her before him on his own mount. Setting spurs to his horse, he rode off. Another, a man-at-arms, had seized Margot, and a third was reaching for Alys. Her hand went to her breast to pull her eating knife, but it was too late for that, too.

Alys was not frightened; she was furious. As soon as the party of men-at-arms appeared, she had guessed the intention was to abduct Beatrice, and when the knight seized Beatrice first, that guess was confirmed. Obviously no harm would be done her or Margot or the heiress, but Alys's impulse was to fight. She subdued it, knowing it was useless. Even if she could draw her knife and stab the man who held her, she would not be able to escape. There was no way she could turn the horse against the tide of other horses, and the men would pursue her and bring her back.

Most of her fury was directed against herself for her stupidity. Now she recalled glances between Margot and Beatrice, half-uttered sentences that were suddenly cut off. How could she have been so stupid as to miss the fact that they were hiding something? Then she realized it was because she had been thinking about Raymond. Oh, God! He would never forgive her for this! Never! Alys began to weep.

"No one will hurt you, lady. No one will hurt you," the man-at-arms soothed.

Alys paid him no more attention than she paid the horse that carried them. Nonetheless her tears soon ceased, dried by the heat of her rage. Those idiots! Those romantic, birdbrained lackwits! *They* had arranged this! But the shrieks and wails that came floating back to Alys were sufficient proof that neither of the girls had expected an abduction. Margot and Beatrice were silly ninnies, but what could be expected when they had been raised on lute songs about love? It was she herself who should have known better, Alys thought, sobbing again with anger and frustration, thinking she was not fit to be Raymond's wife. Had she been a great lady, she would have understood why it was important that Beatrice should not leave Arles. Raymond would despise her! He would never forgive her.

"My lady, do not fear," the man-at-arms said to her again. "No harm will come to you. There is nothing to fear. We mean no hurt."

This time the words penetrated—not that Alys had ever thought physical harm was intended, but the attempt to soothe the captives betokened consideration in the captor. This notion, plus the conviction that the ambusher knew when and where Beatrice would be traveling, created the first fruitful idea Alys had had. A romantic abduction! Guillaume des Baux! It must be Sir Guillaume who had seized them, Alys thought. Oh, she would kill that nitwit Beatrice. That young idiot Guillaume probably thought he was saving his ladylove from a fate worse than death.

It occurred to Alys at this point that Margot and Beatrice had stopped screaming. Also, although she could hear Beatrice's voice, the tones were vituperative rather than terrified. For a time Alys was quite hopeful that Guillaume, having learned he had made a mistake and that Beatrice did not wish to be saved from marriage to Charles of Anjou—or whoever else was suitable—would then return them to Arles.

Alys was correct in thinking that Sir Guillaume would be disappointed to learn that Beatrice did not welcome her abduction. He might, indeed, have acted just as Alys hoped, except that Master Ernaldus had prepared him.

* * *

"She will be very angry," Ernaldus had told Sir Guillaume. "She will call you a fool and far worse things." Master Ernaldus had been surprised and not too well pleased when he discovered that Guillaume's courting had been too effective and the young man thought himself in love, but he had quickly found an answer.

"But I—I do not wish Beatrice to be angry," Guillaume protested. "I will not do it, then."

"My lord, children—and sometimes grown men—do not wish to take the bitter draughts of medicine that will restore their health," Ernaldus had pointed out. "Often they kick and scream and strike out, and it is needful to hold them down and even stop their noses until they open their mouths so that the medicine may be poured in. This is such a case. Charles of Anjou will be a bad husband. He will treat his wife harshly, beat her, and perhaps imprison her once the power is in his hands."

"Are you sure?" Guillaume had asked, horrified. He had heard that Charles had a sour temper, but this seemed too much.

"Absolutely sure," Ernaldus had lied glibly, for he knew nothing more about Charles than what he had heard from Guillaume himself. "The middle brother, Alphonse of Poitiers, married Jeanne of Toulouse, and Rustengo de Soler, my kinsman, had close dealings with them. Alphonse disliked his brother, and Lady Jeanne said she would have taken the veil or killed herself sooner than marry Charles." And then, with fine lack of logic, Ernaldus added another lie. "And he will try to destroy you utterly because your father was unjustly accused of rebellion."

Without a thought Guillaume had accepted that as truth, and it cast a false luster of truth on the other, unrelated statements. Guillaume's father had been bitter and complained constantly of malice. And after his father's death, his mother had reinforced the idea by repeating her husband's complaints. Not given to careful analysis, Guillaume accepted what he heard.

"You must understand, my lord," Ernaldus had continued, "that the truth will have been hidden from Lady Beatrice. She, poor lamb, is only the sacrifice to the ambitions of her mother and Sir Romeo, who seek their own aggrandizement. It will take a few days to explain these things and make her understand the truth, for, naturally, she will not wish to believe that her mother and her guardian would sell her for their own purposes."

Thus, although Sir Guillaume pleaded with Beatrice and reasoned with her and tried to soothe her after he seized her, he did not yield to her furious demands to be returned to Arles. Toward the end of the ride, Guillaume changed his tone from pleadings to threats. Ernaldus had warned him that too much gentleness would merely make the lady stubborn. Women always desired to rule, the bailiff pointed out sententiously, and if Guillaume did not frighten Beatrice, she would refuse to listen to him at all and insist on having her own way.

Guillaume did not accept that advice with his usual lack of doubt. He felt that Beatrice would not be like other women and, since he thought she loved him, she would be glad he had taken her. However, when all his soft words drew only more and more angry replies from his love, Guillaume began to be very annoyed with Beatrice. He had to admit to himself that Master Ernaldus had been right yet again; Beatrice would have to be tamed by some harshness. He told her angrily to hold her tongue, and when she continued to revile him, he shook her.

"You must learn reason and who is master," he said sharply. "Had you been willing to abide by your sweet words to me—"

"You idiot! You worm!" Beatrice shrieked. "Sweet words are for play. Do you not realize that my inheritance will be reft from me by my sisters if I do not marry where there is sufficient power to still their mouths?"

"Then I will win it back!" Guillaume exclaimed.

Beatrice was so infuriated by this idiotic reply that she did not even answer in words, but merely screamed, "Take me back, you dolt, you ass, you shit! Take me back or Sir Romeo's armies will grind your bones for meal and sow salt in the fields of your demesne."

"Not while I have you!" Guillaume snarled. "How will they reach me there?"

He pointed, and Beatrice's eyes followed his hand. She stared and began to wail anew. Alys did not wail, but when she saw Les Baux, tears rained down her cheeks again. Out of the gentle rolling countryside swelled a sudden steep jumble of rock. From this base, there rose a sheer cliff, perhaps a hundred feet high, and this was topped with the high, sheer walls of a keep. Hopelessness gripped Alys, and then terror. Sooner or later the identity of Beatrice's abductor would become known, and then Raymond would come and try to take the keep to free her.

When that idea came into Alys's mind, she nearly fainted. She might not be wise in war, but she knew when a place was impregnable. Thousands and thousands might die and that fortress would remain untouched. Alys saw the defenses of the narrow track that wound up and up, turning back and forth upon itself. No more than one horse or man could climb it at a time, and there were ledges in the rock from which defenders could shoot. No attacker would survive to reach the top.

Both Margot and Beatrice were screaming again. Alys went limp, wondering if she should try to throw herself from some high place. If she were dead, Raymond might not come and be killed in an attempt to storm this place. Fortunately, common sense reasserted itself. Her death would be more likely to incite her husband than restrain him, even if he were furious and disgusted with her for falling into this trap. The only way to keep Raymond from trying to take this monstrous keep was to get out of it herself—and get Margot and Beatrice out, too.

Guillaume might have tried reason again when he saw Beatrice's reaction to Les Baux, but he really could not. She screamed and struggled so, that only a brutal grip could keep hold of her and he would have had to bellow to be heard. It seemed as if Ernaldus was always right. The bailiff had suggested that Beatrice be placed in a cell and just left there until her rage abated. When she had exhausted herself with tears and cries, Ernaldus had said, and found herself utterly powerless, she would be ripe to listen to reason.

Beyond that, Ernaldus had wanted Guillaume to thrust Beatrice into the prison cells in the lowest level of the keep. Here, however, Guillaume had drawn the line. It was unfitting for a lady, he said. Not even to induce fear would he perpetrate so shameful an act, and for such an affront to her honor and dignity, Beatrice would never forgive him. Abduction was no insult, but a cell fit for common felons and murderers—no! And for the first time, Ernaldus had seen in Guillaume's eyes the kind of contempt with which the highbred regard the baseborn when their code is infringed.

Hastily, Ernaldus had withdrawn that suggestion, but pointed out that Beatrice could not be lodged in the living quarters. If she were, her presence could not be kept secret from Guillaume's mother, which they must do at least until Lady Beatrice had agreed to marriage. Guillaume had hesitated and then agreed. His mother would be terrified by his bold move and would weep and wail. There would be enough of that after the siege had started. Guillaume had felt a thrill of excitement mixed with apprehension.

Eventually it had been decided that Beatrice should be lodged in one of the towers, named for a reason even Guillaume did not know, the Sow's Tower. Such imprisonment would not be demeaning; it was common usage for noble malefactors. They decided she should have no servants at first, and later only those Guillaume would allow her. Ernaldus had promised to see to the cleaning and furnishing of the tower since they wished to keep the matter secret as long as possible. Guillaume's position would be much stronger if he married the heiress before anyone knew where she was.

What neither Ernaldus nor Guillaume had considered was that Beatrice would bring along female companions; both had thought she would wish to hide a clandestine meeting with a lover. Instinctively Guillaume had ordered his men to seize the other women as well.

Now, however, he had no idea what to do with them. All he knew was that he could not leave his shrieking, struggling prizes in the bailey to attract every eye and ear in the keep. Thus, just before they entered, Guillaume ordered that all three women be gagged, rolled in their cloaks with the hoods drawn over their faces, and carried to the middle chamber of the Sow's Tower.

Guillaume did not stay to see the women carried into confinement, only telling Beatrice harshly after she was gagged that she had brought this rough treatment on herself. When she became reasonable, he said, she could choose her own quarters. He was really infuriated, for she had kicked him in several tender spots and bitten him when he tried to restrain her. Ernaldus was right, he fumed; let her do without her dinner. Perhaps that would lower her high stomach and teach her that his sweet words were not meant in play.

Thrust roughly into the tower chamber while still blinded by their hoods and enveloped in their tightly wound cloaks, all three fell to the floor. Margot and Beatrice, shocked by such handling and exhausted by emotion and fright, lay where they were and wept. Alys, somewhat more accustomed to bruises and having within her a fixed purpose, struggled to unwind herself from the imprisoning garment. Since she had not been bound, this was not difficult. In minutes she had freed her arms and legs from the cloak, pushed back the hood, and untied the gag.

First she ran to look out the arrow slit, and immediately drew back with a gasp of fear. The view was narrow but nonetheless chilling. Alys had never been atop a mountain peak; now she knew what it was like. The world fell away to nothing. She could not see the wall of the keep, only a thin ledge of bare rock and then, far below, what looked like moss-speckled gray and green—only Alys knew that what she had seen were the tops of trees, some bare, some evergreen, because a thin brown line, a road, ran through them.

Afraid to look again lest despair seize her, she turned her attention to Margot and Beatrice, helping them unwind and free themselves. The moment the gags were off, Alys regretted it. Shrieks pierced her ears.

"There is no way screaming can help," Alys cried furiously. "If your voices had the power of Joshua's trumpets, the walls would be down already. Since they are not, we must think of something better to do than scream."

A brief, stunned silence followed this statement. Then Beatrice shivered and began to weep softly. "What can we do better?" she sobbed. "I have already done the worst."

"Weeping cannot amend that," Alys snapped. "There is no sense in weeping over the past, and not much more sense in weeping over the future."

"But I am ruined," Beatrice cried. "The fool says he will wed me, and my sisters will tear my heritage apart because he is nothing. Can he withstand two kings and the earl of Cornwall?"

"Forced marriages can be annulled," Alys snarled. "So long as he does not get between your legs and get you with child, no harm will be done. Besides, what do you think your mother and Sir Romeo will be doing?"

"What can they do?" Beatrice wailed. "You saw this place."

Again Alys saw Raymond leading a hopeless assault on the terrible cliffs and walls. "We must escape." She forced the words through a dry throat. "We must escape."

"Are you mad?" Margot cried. "How can we escape from this place? Let Beatrice marry him. It is her fault we were taken. He will let us go once they are married."

"It is your fault, too," Beatrice shrieked. "You agreed we should go. If you had refused . . ."

Alys did not listen to the remainder of Beatrice's furious reply. Guillaume might free Margot and herself, Alys thought, but that would not stop Sir Romeo from calling up an army, and Raymond would still have to fight. She covered her face with her hands, but the image of that narrow, twisting road alternated with that of the precipitous cliffs, and on both she envisioned her husband dying, his smooth, dark body broken and bleeding. Almost in defense against this fear, the peevish faultfinding of the others finally brought her back to the troubles at hand.

"Oh, hush," Alys said wearily. "If the fault is any person's, it is mine. I am the eldest and, moreover, I have lived more in the world."

"But you did not know . . ." Beatrice wept.

"I lied to you, sister," Margot sobbed.

Alys smiled wryly while tears hung in her lower eyelashes. "You are not much steeped in vice," she sighed. "If I had not been thinking of something else, I would have guessed. But that is not important. Escape may be impossible, but we must look for a way in case one exists. At the same time, we must try to convince Sir Guillaume to release us."

Margot and Beatrice were so surprised and touched by Alys's generosity in assuming the blame when she alone was innocent of any fault that each resolved she would do her best not to cause Alys any more trouble.

"God knows I am willing," Beatrice quavered, "but I have already told him I would not have him and told him why. He is an idiot! He said he would win back for me what my sisters swallowed. Can you imagine such stupidity?"

"Well, if you do not think that is possible, are you more willing to try to steal away?" Alys asked.

"It is impossible," Beatrice said after only a moment's thought. "Even if we could get out of this room, which I am sure we could not, how would we get out of the keep without drawing notice? Do you think grooms would saddle horses on our order? Who is to escort us?"

"Beatrice," Aly said caustically, "I said *steal* away. This does not include ordering horses saddled or asking for an escort. It means finding servants' garments, if possible, or hiding ours, pretending we are serfs on an errand, hiding until it is dark, and then . . ."

Alys allowed her voice to drift away. From the horrified expressions on the faces turned to her she knew, at least for now, this path was hopeless. Margot and Beatrice would have to be much more frightened and desperate before they would make such an attempt. However, she had set the seed, and now she thought they would at least consider her plan.

In the discussion that followed, Alys learned that Guillaume did not seem at all interested in the political situation. When not spouting love poems, he talked only about hunting, fighting and gambling. Alys came to the conclusion that Guillaume really did not understand the implications of what he had done, that he probably thought all he had to do was marry Beatrice and everything would drop into his hand. As Alys was ruminating on whether this could be turned to some purpose, Beatrice broke in on her thoughts.

"Surely," Beatrice said, "it is time for dinner. Where—"

"I do not think we will get dinner," Alys interrupted sharply, annoyed, "nor supper either."

"He will starve us to death," Margot shrieked.

"Do not be ridiculous," Alys snapped. "One cannot marry a corpse. We may get hungry, and perhaps very bored with what is offered to us—mayhap no more than bread and water—but starved we will not be."

This statement brought a new chorus of wails and tears. Alys listened with what patience she could muster to the laments and impotent vituperations, and when they began to subside, she said, "Well, if a meal or two and a fine table mean so much to you, Beatrice, by all means, marry the man. I have no objections! I imagine that Guillaume will release Margot and myself to carry the happy news to Sir Romeo and your mother. You, of course, will be kept close until your belly swells. Then you may have some freedom."

Beatrice gaped, momentarily mute with fury. Then she cried, "Never! Not if I *do* starve to death!"

"Then what remains," Alys said calmly, "is to convince Sir Guillaume that this is true, and that each day he keeps us and each privation he forces on us only increase your stubbornness. *But* you must speak him fair, with calm and dignity. If you shriek and threaten, he will think that your will can be broken when you have exhausted your rage. No matter what you feel, you must not show anger."

"But what of us?" Margot sobbed. "We will starve, also."

"It will be a just punishment," Alys responded bitterly, "on you for mischief and on me for stupidity." Then she went on to describe what Beatrice must say to show Guillaume that marriage to her would not only gain him nothing but cause him the loss of what he already had. "You must make Guillaume believe Louis will swallow the province and that would breed utter destruction for him. Obviously, Louis could not allow the true heiress or her husband to retain any power anywhere."

"Would King Louis kill his own sister-by-marriage?" Margot breathed.

Alys cast her an infuriated glance, but this time Margot's silliness did not overset Beatrice. "No," she said, "of course not. He is a good man. We would only be held, probably in his court with seeming honor, but closely watched." Beatrice's lips moved as if something sour was in her mouth. "I think I had rather starve. From what Margaret says, Louis's court is so holy—and so dull—one dies of ennui. I will do what you say, Alys. I will, indeed."

CHAPTER 23

****

Sir Guillaume was totally inexperienced in deeds of villainy. He had remembered to order the men who had helped him with the abduction to hold their tongues, and he had sense enough not to name the victim to them. However, it had not occurred to him to conceal his colors and arms nor to order his men to make certain Alys's guards were dead and that all the horses were gathered up. Thus, when three horses bolted, no one pursued them. It was not long before one bloodstained animal, no longer frightened, wandered into the abbey lands. The lay brother who first saw the horse cried out in surprise, and others came running. As soon as the beast was caught, they saw the blood on it and realized the blood was fresh.

Informed of this, the good brothers set out at once up and down the track that led to the abbey, and the party that went south came upon Alys's men. For one they were too late, but the others lived. Having bound up the guardsmen's wounds, the brothers carried them back to the abbey and into the infirmary, where they dosed them with syrup of poppies so they would feel the pain less and sleep. A party of lay brothers was sent for the dead body, which was decently laid out.

More than this, the good brothers could not do. No one recognized the men or the arms they bore, and all three babbled at them in an unknown tongue. Not knowing what else to do, the infirmarian and his helpers said, "Yes, yes," soothingly. The men seemed much relieved at this, and the infirmarian was delighted that he had appeased his patients, who allowed themselves to sink into sleep. The infirmarian had no idea that the babbling was meant to convey an urgent message concerning the daughter of one of their great benefactors or that "yes" was one of the few words of the *langue d'oc* these men understood, so they had taken his "yes, yes" to mean their message had been transmitted.

* * *

It was not until dinnertime that Lady Beatrice first discovered her daughter missing. Aside from a mild annoyance, she did not give the fact much heed, thinking the girl was engaged somewhere with friends and did not wish to interrupt her amusement. She sent several servants off to seek her daughter and sat down to eat. One by one the servants returned to say they could not find young Beatrice, and Lady Beatrice became alarmed.

At this point, Lady Jeannette woke up to the fact that Alys and Margot were also missing. At first this allayed the alarm, for it seemed obvious that the three must be together. Moreover, when a further investigation revealed that Alys had told Arnald they were going to Montmajour Abbey, Lady Beatrice relaxed. She was angry that her daughter had not asked her permission or left a message for her, but she was not worried. Even when the servant who had questioned Arnald mentioned that Alys's master-at-arms had expected his mistress back before dinner, Lady Beatrice merely shook her head.

"They have stuffed themselves with cheese and wine and have forgotten the time," she said.

Still, shortly after she had finished eating, she began to feel concerned again. The girls could not have failed to notice the prayers at sext. They should have started home by then at the latest, and, even if they idled on the way, they should have reached Arles by now. A knight of the household was sent off.

It was unfortunate that Lady Beatrice was so generous a contributor to the abbey. The knight of her household was brought directly to the abbot—who had not yet been informed of the body or the men in the infirmary. The prior would report this at the regular time for business since it did not seem to him to be an emergency directly affecting the abbey, and all that could be done for the men had been done for them. The abbot assured Lady Beatrice's knight with perfect certainty that neither her daughter nor her daughter's friends had visited the abbey that day.

The knight did not stay longer than necessary to ask the abbot to keep secret his search for Beatrice, which the abbot promised to do. As the knight galloped back to Arles, he passed a lone man-at-arms riding toward the abbey, but he was worried sick and paid the man no mind.

* * *

Arnald had been worried long before Lady Beatrice. He knew that if Lady Alys said she would be back for dinner, either she would return or she would send a message saying she would be late. What held him back from action was that he did not know where the abbey was, and he did not know to whom to report his mistress's absence. One thing was sure, he would not go near Lady Jeannette. He knew she would be worse than useless.

Then the servant came with questions, and Arnald had felt considerable relief. Thereafter, he had warned his men to be ready to ride out. He was quite sure he would be sent to find out what had happened to Lady Alys as soon as the servant passed on his message. However, no such order came. First, Arnald gnashed his teeth, cursing the slowness and inefficiency of these southerners. Then he comforted himself for a time by telling himself that a message must have come to Lady Beatrice and no one had bothered to tell him about it.

This was very likely. Lady Alys would not forget to ask that he be informed, but no one would think that important, and her message to him might be considerably delayed in transmission or even forgotten. Nonetheless, he felt uneasy, and he began to ask about among the other masters-at-arms where the abbey was and how to get there. As the afternoon waned, Arnald's uneasiness increased. He could not send out the troop without orders, but there was nothing to stop him from taking an hour off to make an offering for his soul's sake. He told the men he would hang the first one who started a fight in his absence, and he set off.

The abbot might be ignorant of the wounded men and the body, but the event was the most exciting thing that had happened in months to the lay brothers. There was not one of the younger group who had not found some excuse to peep into both the mortuary and the infirmary. Since Arnald was nobody of importance, a lay brother was sufficient to collect his offering. But the moment the lay brother saw Arnald's arms, he recognized them as the same as those of the dead and wounded found on the road.

A very few minutes after the recognition, Arnald was in the infirmary trying to question his men. This, after a moment, the infirmarian discouraged firmly, saying the men were too deep

in the grip of the poppy syrup to be wakened or to make sense
if they should waken. Nor would the infirmarian give any
estimate of the time when they could make sense, other than it
would be several hours. Half-mad with anxiety, all Arnald
could think of was to ride back to Arles and tell Lady Beatrice
that someone had killed and wounded his men and, almost
certainly, made off with her daughter, his mistress, and Lord
Raymond's sister. In his haste and his fear, Arnald neglected
to tell the infirmarian to withhold the next dose of opiate until
he could question his men.

The trouble was that Lady Beatrice had come to the same
conclusion as Arnald without evidence of her own. She was
frantic and appalled, torn between the need to question
everyone to discover the whereabouts of Beatrice and the need
to hide the fact that her daughter was missing. In the stress of
the moment, she denied herself to everyone—which, of
course, included Arnald.

Frustrated in his attempts to report what he knew to Lady
Beatrice, Arnald rode back to the abbey, which he managed to
enter just before the gates closed for the night. Unfortunately,
he could not gain admittance to the infirmary. The infirmarian
realized that Arnald was frantic,- but his duty was to his
patients. He did not know who Lady Alys was, and in his
distress for his mistress, Arnald failed to mention that Lady
Beatrice's daughter was with Lady Alys.

Meanwhile, the abbot had finally heard about the dead and
wounded men. He was appalled, immediately making the
connection between the report of Beatrice's unexplained absence and the injured men-at-arms. His horror was not only
over the probable abduction of the heiress but over the fact that
he had not told the knight that there were wounded men in the
infirmary. The fact that he had been ignorant, he was much
afraid, would do little to appease Lady Beatrice.

Thus, he was greatly relieved when the infirmarian told him
that the wounded men had been escorting a Lady Alys, not
young Lady Beatrice. The knight had not mentioned Lady
Alys or Margot by name, since they were of no concern to
him. The abbot breathed a sigh of relief. Two abductions on
the road to the abbey in one day simply did not seem possible
to that worthy man. He was certain that young Beatrice had
gone in a completely different direction, merely saying the

abbey was her destination to allay suspicion. He prayed earnestly for the safety and well-being of that naughty girl, but he was deeply grateful that his abbey was not involved.

It was full morning before Arnald was finally able to speak to his men. They were horrified when they learned that the message they had tried to convey had not been understood, but they told him what had happened as quickly and clearly as they could. This was not particularly quickly or clearly since all were very weak and fevered and occasionally their wits wandered. Unfortunately, even what they told Arnald did not mean much to him since he was unfamiliar with the arms and colors of the nobles of Provence. However, at the moment he was satisfied, certain that someone in Arles would be able to identify them.

Despite Beatrice's assurances, Alys had little faith that she would perform what she promised. She became quite exasperated with both girls, who, as the day wore on, could think of nothing beyond their hunger and thirst and sat bewailing it to each other. All Alys's attempts to divert their minds to a more useful activity, such as searching for a way out, were in vain. Escape was impossible, they moaned, and they were too weak with hunger to do anything.

More for something to do than for any other reason, Alys tried the door. The great bars on the inside, designed to keep enemies who had invaded the bailey from coming up into the tower and thus getting onto the walls, had, of course, been removed. Alys expected that new bars had been fastened on the outside, but she had not heard them fall into place after she was thrown down. Nonetheless, when she lifted the latch and pushed on the door, Alys nearly fell out on the small landing and down the stairs because she had been so certain the door would *not* open.

She stood for a moment, clinging to latch and frame and gasping with shock, and soon Beatrice and Margot began to scream. Alys gestured fiercely at them to be still, although she did not know why she bothered. Had there been guards below, they would have been warned already. She waited for the shouts, for feet to pound up the stairs, for the flicker of a torch's glow, but all was still and dark. After a few moments, Alys shrugged and felt for the stair with her foot. There was

only the dimmest twilight left in the chamber so that the stairs
to the totally unlighted chamber below were black as pitch.

Alys asked herself a hundred questions about why the door
was left unbarred, all except whether it was a simple oversight,
because that would mean escape was possible. However, the
forbidden question answered itself. The door to the outside
was firmly locked. Alys felt one sharp pang of disappointment
and then laughed softly at herself. Guillaume was a young
fool, either romantic or greedy or both, but he was not a total
idiot.

Or was he? It would be easy, Alys thought, to hide in the
dark and push Guillaume down the stairs, but instantly she
realized that was not true. Whoever came would bring light,
and that would expose anyone lying in wait. Nor would it do
any good to escape from the tower now. Alys knew Beatrice
and Margot would not have the self-control to get out of the
keep or even to hide within it, and to get them down that road
and through the forest until they were miles and miles away
from Les Baux and could seek help was out of the question.

It might be feasible later when they were more hardened and
more desperate, or when there was an army encamped in the
plain. Then, if they could get out, there would not be far to go.
Surely Sir Romeo would bargain before any assault was tried.
That would be the time. Alys sighed. It would not be easy with
every man alert, but there was no sense in worrying about that
now.

Oh, yes there was, Alys thought, stopping abruptly as she
began to turn toward the stair. When the siege began, they
might be moved to a more secure place or the upper door might
be barred so that the men could use the lower tower. If there
was anything in the lower room that might be useful, she had
better take it now and try to conceal it.

The lower tower rooms were usually used for storage,
particularly for war supplies—weapons, sand for dousing fires,
barrels of pitch, rope, and such things. Alys was sure all the
weapons had been removed, but sand might be useful to throw
in a man's eyes, and an arrow might have fallen down and
been overlooked; an arrow could stab as well as be shot. It
would be useful, anyway, to see what was there.

Unfortunately, "see" was the wrong word. Alys could not

see anything. A forgotten torch—and flint and tinder—would be useful, too, Alys thought almost merrily. She felt her way to the wall and started around it, reaching out hand and foot and feeling up and down the wall as high and low as she could reach before she took each step. Almost at once, she was rewarded. Her hand, sliding up the wall, came in contact with an instrument that made her cry out softly. A crossbow!

Her first instinct was that the whole thing, the open door, the crossbow hanging so conveniently, was a trap. Then she smiled. No, it must be that they were convinced that a woman would not have the strength to use a crossbow. And, indeed, no woman Alys knew had ever used one, but she was willing to try if she could find some quarrels, or something that could be used as a quarrel. Alys continued her round, discovering that there were tubs of sand and many barrels with closed tops which probably contained pitch or oil.

She made a second round on her hands and knees, feeling between and behind the barrels. Quite near the door, her hand came on something between the barrels and tubs that squished liquidly away from her touch. Alys nearly screamed with horror, and she sat shivering for some minutes trembling with such revulsion that she could not move—and then her brain began to work. When it did, her breath caught with hope, and she advanced her hand eagerly. It was! Miracle of miracles, it was a skin of wine, about half-full. If anything could put heart into those ninnies upstairs, this was it. Alys slung the crossbow over her shoulder, snatched up some straight poles she had found, took the wine, and made her way carefully up the stairs, where she closed the door behind her.

It was now as dark inside the upper chamber as it had been below. With a shock, Alys realized she did not hear Beatrice's and Margot's voices. Almost instantly, however, she heard them breathing. Feeling her way, she found them huddled together on the narrow bed. She stood a moment, biting her lip, regretting the pleasure and relief she had expected her discovery to bring. Then she sighed. It would be a hard, cold night for her. The bed would scarcely hold those two; it was meant for one only.

Tears began to course down Alys's face, not for the discomfort she faced, but because, suddenly, she felt abandoned. She knew it was ridiculous; Beatrice and Margot were only cold, hungry, frightened, and miserable. They had sought

what comfort they could find. But Alys was just as cold and
hungry and miserable and dreadfully tired, yet she knew she
could not even seek the cold comfort of the floor to rest until
she had hidden the things she had brought up from below.

In the living quarters of Les Baux, there was light, food and
drink, and all other comforts; however, Sir Guillaume was not
much happier than his captives. He was, in fact, as much a
prisoner of his own act as they. If it had been possible to
expunge from their minds who had committed the outrage, he
would have been glad to drop the three women on any road that
did not lead to Les Baux and forget they existed. Unfortunately, that was not possible; he had them, and he was stuck
with them.

His doubts had begun soon after his initial fury over
Beatrice's reaction had cooled, and he had naturally expressed
those doubts to his mentor. Master Ernaldus, who had expected this reaction, had pointed out that it was too late for
doubts. To gain anything, the heiress must be married and
made pregnant; merely to save his skin, he must keep the
women as a bargaining counter. To let them go would only
produce utter disaster.

This had made perfect sense, and Guillaume had really
known it before he spoke of his doubts. Although he regretted
plunging in so deep, he realized he must now swim with the
plan to avoid sinking. Seeing the trap he was in made him
furious, but he could not blame Master Ernaldus, who had
warned him again and again of the danger. He did not, of
course, wish to blame himself; thus, his rage fixed on Beatrice.
If she had not agreed with such eagerness to meet him,
Guillaume thought angrily, he would not be in this predica-
ment. It was all her fault. If she had not favored him and led
him on, he would have given up the idea. She deserved to be
cold and hungry. It would be a lesson to her not to play with a
man's affections.

All through the day messengers left Les Baux carrying
letters carefully phrased by Ernaldus. The letters requested
those friends and vassals of des Baux who were bitterly
opposed to the French to come with their men and arms to Sir
Guillaume. Sir Guillaume had a plan he believed could not fail
in preventing Lady Beatrice and Sir Romeo from marrying the

heiress to Charles of Anjou. Those who supported his plan would win high preferment in Provence once it was implemented. If even half of those summoned came, there would be enough men in Les Baux to hold off an army of many thousands, and the keep was stocked for a siege of at least half a year.

Guillaume should have felt happy and confident. In fact, when he reviewed his resources, he discovered he was not worried about the military aspects of his situation. He was ready to fight and not afraid to die—although he could not imagine what that would be like. Still, he was miserably uneasy and, when he went to bed, unable to sleep. It was when he thought of finding a woman to lie with him that the source of his trouble revealed itself. The truth was that now he did not want to marry Beatrice.

The revelation was so startling that he sat up in bed and stared at the faint area of light made by the night candle on the bed curtains. He had been flattered because the heiress of Provence responded to him, but when Guillaume reconsidered the idea of marrying her, he realized that he did not want a wife who had to be wooed and to whom he must humbly bow down. And, even if she agreed to marriage, Guillaume had the distinct feeling that Beatrice would continue to look down on him. Nor, since the land was in her right, would it be easy to control her. If she cried that he mistreated her to her great vassals, especially after she had one or two sons, they could put him aside—or murder him—and declare a regency.

A regency—that thought was not so unpleasant as murder; in fact, it gave him a feeling of relief even while it enraged him —and he had another revelation. He did not want to be count of Provence. Guillaume sighed and lay down again. It was the business that was distasteful. He could find someone else to do that, someone like Ernaldus, but he wished again that he did not have to marry Beatrice. It might be murder rather than a regency.

He woke in the morning no better pleased with the notion. Truthfully, he wished he did not have to see Beatrice at all, but Ernaldus would not allow him to avoid her. No servant, the bailiff pointed out, could bargain with her, not even himself, and she should see no one except Guillaume and the half-witted servant who could not speak that they had decided could serve her without betraying who the prisoner was. Guillaume would not have to stay long, Ernaldus soothed. He need only go with the servant who would carry a large number of delicate and highly fragrant dishes.

"You need not argue with her. Only tell her she may eat if she agrees to the marriage, but if she does agree, do not leave the food. Come away at once and fetch me and the priest. *After* she is married, she will eat. If she does not agree, but weeps and pleads for the food, come away at once. Do not yield to her. A day or two without food does no harm."

"Very well," Guillaume growled ungraciously, "I will go."

"Not now, it is too early. Also, the tray of food is now being prepared. Do you eat yourself, my lord." Ernaldus chuckled ingratiatingly. "A hungry man is too sympathetic to others who are hungry."

Actually, it was not too early; it was too late. The girls in the tower had been awake for hours, even though Alys did not experience the cold, hard night she had expected. Among the furniture in the room was a chest in which the girls had not looked in their distress. Alys remembered it for the sake of hiding the crossbow and wineskin, but when she opened it, she found it full of blankets. Ernaldus did not want the heiress to take a chill and die; he would withhold light and fire, for those give strength to the spirit, which dark weakens, but warmth could be provided with blankets. Despite that warmth, for Alys covered Margot and Beatrice, and the comfort of a pad on the floor, the pangs of hunger banished sleep. With first light, all were awake.

Then Alys heard the outpouring of joy and relief she had expected from them but it did not come immediately. "Is it a trick?" Beatrice asked, looking suspiciously at the wineskin.

"I cannot believe it," Alys replied. "It was well hidden. I am sure it belongs to one of the men-at-arms who either did not wish to share with his fellows or used it to keep warm on nights he stood watch. It is not poisoned. We would be worse than useless dead, and, anyway, I confess I had a small sip last night."

Beatrice was glad to put aside her doubt, and then she surprised and pleased Alys by saying they must all only sip a little to allay the worst of their thirst. Alys endorsed this sentiment heartily—she had thought she would have to fight to get them to agree to it—even Margot consented with no more than a sigh. They were, accordingly, very moderate in their sipping; nonetheless the little they took gave them new life.

Of course, the real strength did not come from the wine, which only took the edge off their thirst. What put life into them was the ebbing of the shock of their capture and the renewal sleep had brought to their bodies. Had Alys not found the wine, hunger and thirst might too soon have brought back their misery. Not that the little sips cured hunger or thirst. It was the delightful feeling of having cheated and outwitted their captor. Temporarily strengthened by this notion, they all felt that if they had done it once, they could do it again.

"You know," Alys said, "Guillaume cannot really mean to starve us, so someone will come today with an offer of food in exchange for compliance. What we must do is get the food brought into the chamber. Then, if there are no more than one or two, perhaps we can wrest the food away from them."

This was agreed to with enthusiasm, and they began to plan. That sent them all down the stairs to feel around in the dark. They came up with several more poles that were intended to push off scaling ladders and a bundle of quarrels that had fallen down in a dark corner as well as anything else they thought would be useful. Some time was spent happily in learning how to use the crossbow, but as the light brightened and Guillaume did not come, the voices of Margot and Beatrice dulled and they began to lose interest in the plan. Alys felt depressed and desperate herself, and was just about to suggest another round of wine when the door opened.

All three girls gasped, and Alys dropped hastily to her knees behind the bed. The crossbow had been hanging from her hand. But Guillaume did not cry out or leap at her; his eyes had found Beatrice. She and Margot clung together instinctively, but, almost at once, Margot began to back away. Alys stifled a sigh of relief. Guillaume looked at Margot and then away, dismissing her movement as a result of fear of him. Beatrice drew herself up proudly but remained silent. Her eyes flicked to the servant who had entered behind Guillaume carrying a large, loaded tray that smelled like heaven. Alys felt like cheering. There was more in Beatrice than she had dreamed.

"Well, mistress," Guillaume said, trying to make his voice

hard when it was more inclined to shake. Why, he wondered, staring at Beatrice's dirty, tear-stained face, her heavy eyes and dry mouth, the hair straggling through her coif and snaking untidily around her face and shoulders, why had he ever thought her beautiful and desirable? How had he let her lead him into this mad adventure? Now he would be stuck with her. But there was wealth and power to be gained, he reminded himself. Ernaldus had devised a speech for him; automatically, he used it.

"I hope you have grown more civil," Guillaume said, "and that you have learned what comes of a too-high stomach. Obedience is the first virtue of a wife, and my wife you will be."

"No, I will not, you low cur," Beatrice responded, her voice cold with disdain and hard with determination. What gave Guillaume hope and kept him from leaving the room was that her hands were fumbling nervously with the tie of the small pouch that hung at her waist. "You have given me little enough reason to change my mind," Beatrice continued, but now her voice trembled a little. "If this is the way you enforce obedience before marriage, I would have no hope for any future."

"I see your stomach is still too high," Guillaume retorted, almost pleased. *Nasty bitch, let her go hungry,* he thought. "No doubt hunger will lower it at last. When you learn to speak me fair, viands will be set for you, but too much pride deserves—"

The measured speech ended suddenly in a cry of pain and shock. Guillaume had been speaking with growing confidence because all three women had been slowly approaching him and the servant. It seemed to him they were being drawn irresistibly closer by the sight and smell of the food. Moreover, Beatrice was raising her hands, which tightly clutched the little pouch. It looked to Guillaume as if she were trying to restrain herself from clasping her hands prayerfully to plead with him.

And then, suddenly, she let go the top of the pouch with one hand and thrust it at his face with the other. He stepped back instinctively, but it was too late. His eyes and mouth were full of sand. Behind him, he heard the servant cry out and then a woman's voice, high and vicious: "I will stick you through the throat! Let go the tray!"

Guillaume was blinking desperately, blinded by tears, reaching out to grab Beatrice in a fury, but a fierce blow struck his hands so hard he gasped with pain, and hands whirled him about from behind and thrust so hard he staggered forward. He heard the servant shriek with terror and the sound of falling, and he opened his mouth to cry out—he knew not what threats or promises—only to choke instead as he was doused with the contents of the chamber pot. The foul stuff blinded him anew, stinging in his sand-scored eyes, and he retched, so disgusted he had no room for fear, as another strong push sent him down the stone stairs to a momentary oblivion.

"Do not throw the pot after him," Alys cried, half choking with laughter, "We will need it."

Beatrice shook the last few drops disdainfully down the stairs, and stepped back into the chamber. "We could get out now," she said, "or we could kill him."

Alys ran back to get a quarrel, but by the time she returned, it was too late; Guillaume was already half-upright, bellowing for help. He had landed atop the servant so that his fall was mostly cushioned. Alys could do nothing but go back into the room quickly, and the girls shut the door and dropped several poles into the bar slots. The poles were too thin to hold the door against a determined assault, but at least they would provide a warning before they gave way. Crowing with laughter, all sank down beside the bed, which would serve as their table. Still, before she reached for the portion that was hers, Alys wound and loaded her bow. Perhaps they would be left to reconsider their sins in peace; perhaps Guillaume would instead return with many men to lesson them more directly than by starvation.

When Arnald got back to Arles with the information the wounded men had given him, he found no one could name the owner of the armorial bearings he described. He had assumed that the abductor would be one of the great lords of the area and that anyone to whom he mentioned the arms would identify them. But ten years had passed since the power of des Baux had been broken, and, being enemies even before that time, they had not frequented the court of Raymond-Berenger.

Once more Arnald tried to speak to Lady Beatrice. It took some time before he found anyone who would even listen to him—but he dared not say he had news of the missing heiress. No one in Arles seemed to know that young Beatrice, Lady Margot, and Lady Alys were missing. Arnald became very frightened when he was told that Lady Beatrice was asleep and no one would wake her for any reason whatsoever.

After a day of desperate anxiety and a sleepless, tear-drenched night, Lady Beatrice had collapsed. But Arnald did not know this. He began to wonder whether Lady Beatrice had done away with her daughter in some scheme to seize the province for herself. In utter desperation he now asked for Lady Jeannette—and she refused to see him, as did Lady Jeanine! Now Arnald was sure they were all involved in a plot and his poor mistress was an innocent victim of it.

Arnald would gladly have risked his life to cry the dreadful crime aloud, but he did not know to whom to complain. Moreover, who would believe a common man-at-arms when the mothers of two of the girls who were missing took quiet naps and pretended nothing was amiss. Nearly insane with grief and anxiety, Arnald rode back once more toward the abbey, seeking along the road for signs of the abduction. Perhaps he could pick up the trail of the men who had seized Lady Alys.

Unfortunately, so much time had been spent in his fruitless attempts to see Lady Beatrice or Lady Jeannette and in even more fruitless worry, that the light failed before Arnald accomplished anything. Hopeless, he turned back. It had started to rain. Arnald did not care that he was wet to the skin and had not eaten all day. Had there been a hope of a moon, he would have searched all night, but the dense clouds made that impossible. Order or no order, he told himself, the next day he would bring out the whole troop to search. And he would send a message with the whole story to Lord Raymond as soon as he entered Arles. Arnald was comforted by that thought and smiled grimly. Ignore him, would they? They would not ignore Lord Raymond. He would set the whole province afire if need be.

It was not until he entered Arles that Arnald remembered an essential omission. He needed a clerk. The story he had to tell was too long and too complex, too important to trust to the memory of a man-at-arms. Besides, even if the best French-speaker among them were sent, he would be sure to garble so involved a tale. Lord Raymond's English, while sufficient for most things, could not be trusted in so desperate a case. In addition, like most illiterate people, Arnald had a superstitious feeling that writing a thing down made it more true and convincing.

Arnald heard the noise before he entered the great hall, and he hesitated slightly, but in the next moment he gave a great cry of relief and joy and ran forward. Whether or not Lord Raymond's rage was going to consume Provence, it had already overset the fat into the fire and ignited the great hall at Arles.

Standing in the middle of the floor, bare sword in hand pointed at Sir Romeo's breast, Raymond was bellowing at the top of his voice, "Where is my wife?"

CHAPTER 24

****

"In God's name, I beg you—" Sir Romeo cried.

But Raymond did not wait to hear the rest. "What foul plot have you hatched?" he roared. "My mother is 'too ill' to speak to me. My sisters are 'attending on her.' Lady Beatrice is 'busy.' Man, you have one minute to bring forth my women-folk—"

"Only come—" Sir Romeo tried again.

Raymond's sword quivered.

"My lord! My lord!" Arnald shouted. "Lady Alys has been stolen away with Lady Beatrice and Lady Margot. I have been trying—"

"Oh, my God," Sir Romeo groaned, his face going grayer. Then he turned to Arnald and roared, "Hold your tongue!"

"I will not!" Arnald shouted back. "I have guarded my mistress since she was a babe, and if she has come to hurt through your henchmen—"

"Raymond, curb your man," Sir Romeo grated.

Raymond put his hand on Arnald's shoulder. "If she has come to harm through Sir Romeo's doing, no man, woman, or child will go out of Arles alive, and I will take down this place stone by stone until there is no more sign of it."

Although this threat obviously could never have been accomplished, and Raymond knew it, he had made it to calm Arnald, for it was obvious that the man was beside himself. Moreover, Raymond knew there would be no need to try to make good any part of that threat. The moment young Beatrice's name was coupled with Alys's, Raymond knew that Sir Romeo could not have had any part in their disappearance. Arnald's ignorance of the political situation had led him to a mistaken conclusion from the true fact that Lady Beatrice and Sir Romeo wished to keep the heiress's abduction a secret.

Raymond's rage had also been caused by a misunderstand-ing. He had arrived in the late afternoon and, on asking for

363

Alys, had been told that she had not yet returned from an expedition into the countryside. Raymond was disappointed, for he had been looking forward to confronting her and having his little joke before loving her soundly; however, for a little while he had pacified himself with the pleasant idea of her coming upon him suddenly in the hall.

He had gone to remove his armor and to change his clothing when it struck him that it had been raining for several hours. That meant that Alys must have gone out quite a while ago. Could she have guessed he was coming and gone out to avoid him? He dismissed the idea; it was ridiculous, but it left a bitter taste in his mouth.

When he had changed and drunk some wine, he sent a servant to announce his arrival to his mother, and was considerably surprised to be told she was too ill to see him. Usually his mother was only too eager to have him come to her when she felt unwell. She loved to complain and have him express concern and sympathy. Even before Alys had opened his eyes, he had often suspected that his mother's illnesses were not nearly as severe as she claimed. Could she really be sick this time? Raymond sat worrying about that until he happened to glance out the window.

Because of the rain, the torches and the central flambeaux had been lit when he first arrived. Thus, he had not noticed the coming of true darkness. Only when he looked out the window did he realize it was night. Then everything seemed to fall together. Alys would surely have returned before dark or sent a message to say where she would spend the night; no matter how sick his mother was—and particularly if she were desperately ill—one of his sisters would have come to speak with him.

Instantly a horrible suspicion gripped Raymond that his wife, mother, and sisters had been seized as hostages to enforce some political action on himself and his father. Before he could think over the idea and realize the flaws in it, Raymond leapt to his feet and demanded audience with Lady Beatrice. He was refused. That, however, was an unfortunate error. Had Lady Beatrice known that Raymond was due to arrive, she would have made an exception in his case to the order that she would see no one except Sir Romeo.

The refusal confirmed Raymond's suspicions. Never in his

life had his grandfather's wife refused to see him. Nonetheless, Raymond would not commit the solecism of invading Lady Beatrice's chamber; besides, his rage and fear required physical expression, and he could not threaten Lady Beatrice with a sword. He had begun to bellow for Sir Romeo, who had not until that moment been aware that Raymond had arrived. This was essentially Alys's error. Since she had not told anyone she had written to summon Raymond, Sir Romeo had not instructed his guards or servants to inform him of Raymond's coming.

The last error, however, was Sir Romeo's. Instead of sending immediately for Lady Jeannette and Jeanine and insisting they appear, he had tried to draw Raymond into his private chamber to explain. This only convinced Raymond that his worst fears were true. It was most fortunate that Arnald had appeared at the moment he did, or this comedy of errors might well have turned into a tragedy. Now, although it could not be said that Raymond was no longer excited, at least he understood why everyone was behaving so oddly.

It was Arnald who unwound the whole tangled skein, for as soon as Sir Romeo had led them into his chamber, Arnald unburdened himself of his whole tale. When he came to the previous day's fiasco, Sir Romeo interrupted with horror.

"My God, man, why did you not come to me?"

"Who are you?" Arnald responded hotly. "All I know of you is that you have long held power here, and I have seen a sprig of your line attending on Lady Beatrice. How should I know whether you desired her for that sprig so that you might continue to hold the power?"

Sir Romeo turned purple, and Raymond, despite his anguish, had to laugh. "No," he said to Arnald, "upon my oath, Sir Romeo is a just and honorable man and, I dare say, loves Beatrice as you love Alys. He would do nothing to harm her."

"I would give my life to have her safely back," Sir Romeo sighed. "Did you not think," he added, "that the child's mother was in agonies of fear and that was why she refused to speak to anyone?"

"No, I did not," Arnald replied sturdily. "Lady Alys does not close herself in her chamber to weep when ill befalls. She *does* something. *She* would have sent out men to search for a missing daughter."

"You do not understand," Sir Romeo groaned. "There are reasons why we did not wish it known that Beatrice is missing. And where were we to search?"

"I can tell you where," Arnald snapped, "if you know who bears these arms." And he described once again the colors and bearings.

"Des Baux!" Sir Romeo roared, bounding to his feet. "Des Baux!"

Raymond's mouth opened in soundless protest; his voice was frozen in his throat with terror. He had done nothing about Ernaldus, and now Alys was a prisoner in his power—or dead.

"I should have known!" Sir Romeo groaned. "When my son told me that a young whelp of that treacherous brood was sniffing around Beatrice, I should have had him killed." Tears came into his eyes. "There is no taking Les Baux. We will have to starve them out, and by then Beatrice . . ."

"But will Lady Alys be safe?" Arnald interrupted anxiously.

Sir Romeo was suddenly aware of Raymond's stricken face. He came forward and gripped Raymond's shoulder hard. "There is nothing to fear for Lady Alys or your sister. Even that young fool would not dare do them any harm if he hopes to rule Provence. To make a bitter enemy of your strongest neighbor would be insane. It is only Beatrice for whom I fear."

Raymond sucked air into his lungs. It was true that des Baux would not permit Alys to be hurt, and des Baux, not Ernaldus, ruled. It was not even certain that Ernaldus was there. Raymond strangled his fear and started to think.

Actually, by then Sir Guillaume would gladly have turned all three women over to his torturers. Since he could not, he had turned on the man who had introduced the scheme to his mind. He came roaring back into the keep after he had washed the sand from his eyes and the filth from his face and body, struck Ernaldus, shook him until his head snapped back and forth, threw him on the floor, and kicked him, all the time screaming, "You brought this on me! Get me out of it! Find me a way to save myself without marriage or I will kill you. I would not marry that bitch to be king of heaven. Find me a way out!"

Again and again Ernaldus shrieked for mercy and promised a resolution to the problem if Guillaume would only cease

from abusing him and let him think. Having relieved the worst
of his fury and frustration, Guillaume snarled that he had better
think quickly and strode away. But there was nothing for
Ernaldus to think about. He knew there was no way to stave off
punishment except for des Baux to marry the heiress and get
her with child. He crawled to his feet, knowing he must escape
and knowing also that there was no way he could save anything
beyond his life. He further realized that if he did escape, he
would soon die of cold and starvation, a penniless outcast.
With that knowledge came hatred and with hatred an answer.

Sir Guillaume and Les Baux could not be saved, but Master
Ernaldus could save himself—save himself and probably
garner a handsome reward. He had only to carry to Arles the
news of who had the heiress and that there was a secret way
into Les Baux. Ernaldus began to hurry, whining with pain but
terrified that Guillaume would return for his answer or remember to tell the castlefolk and guards not to obey him or to keep
him from leaving. All day he scurried from room to room in
the keep and then into and out of a certain tower, always
keeping to dark corners and peering around anxiously to see if
he was noticed.

At dusk, the serfs who owed corvée and were assigned tasks
within Les Baux left to go back to their huts outside the walls.
The keep itself did not cover the entire flat surface of the
strange isolated plateau on which it stood. To the east was an
area large enough to be farmed, and those who attended to the
farms lived on them in huts. Some did day labor in the keep;
some carried in produce and carried out slops for the animals
and manure for the earth. Among these people there was an
extra.

The laborers were tired after a day's work and more
interested in getting out of the rain than in their companions;
no one actually looked at the extra. The casual glance or two
that passed over him recorded a face that was vaguely familiar
—which was not surprising, for almost everyone had seen
Master Ernaldus. Nor was it surprising that no one recognized
him. He was far more portly than natural, what showed of his
face under the hood that shadowed it was puffed and bruised,
and he walked awkwardly and painfully.

Besides, the serfs had only seen Master Ernaldus dressed in
velvets and furs with a fine cap on his head. Now he wore a

coarse, dirty cloak and under it the gown of a clerk. The hood hid more than his face, for he had cut his hair away from the crown of his head in a rude tonsure. It had occurred to Ernaldus that only the most desperate of men would harm a man in holy orders and that he would do well to imitate that condition in life until he was safe.

As soon as he could, Master Ernaldus dropped behind the group and sought shelter between some bushes. He wept with rage and pain and fear as he crouched there, execrating Sir Guillaume for every vice of character and evil, except the ones he truly had: youth, a hasty temper, and a limited understanding. Ernaldus credited himself with extreme cleverness in having eluded his master, but the truth was that Sir Guillaume was no more eager to see the bailiff than the bailiff was to see him.

Guillaume's outburst had been the result of frustration and fear. Once it was over, he was rather ashamed of it and of having misused an elderly man, frailer than himself. Nor did Guillaume want to hear what he knew was the truth—that there was no way out of the tangle except to marry Beatrice or accept whatever punishment would be meted out. Moreover, it had never entered Sir Guillaume's mind to order the servants not to obey Ernaldus or the guards to prevent him from leaving, anyway. As he was essentially an honorable young man, it was impossible for him to believe that Ernaldus would *want* to leave. Sir Guillaume would never have abandoned a man committed to a plan of his making.

A good part of Ernaldus's curses should have been directed against himself. First, there was no need to leave. Ernaldus could have gone to bed and cossetted himself with no opposition from Sir Guillaume. Second, so long as he had not done it directly in front of Sir Guillaume, Ernaldus could have packed all his money and possessions—and a good part of his master's—had the things loaded on horses, and ridden out of the gates without question. Not everyone in Les Baux liked Master Ernaldus, but all accepted his authority. Without a direct order from Sir Guillaume, no one would have questioned Ernaldus's authority to do what he liked.

As soon as it was fully dark, Ernaldus started down the road that wound up the cliff. He was terrified, but he knew that the guards that watched this road were never lax. Even in the dark,

he would be lucky to get down without being noticed—and
even luckier if he did not fall off the road to his death.

In Sir Romeo's chamber in Arles, Sir Romeo and Raymond
were staring at Arnald, who had just said, "Long before a siege
is over, if I know Lady Alys, this des Baux may offer you his
keep free and clear just to be rid of her."

"Are you mad?" Sir Romeo cried.

"Well, if he dare not do her hurt nor keep her in chains,
Lady Alys will find a way to plague out his life," Arnald
answered with simple faith. "She will be *very* angry."

Suddenly, Raymond's face, which had been rigid with
anguish, softened, and he began to laugh. He had to believe
that Sir Romeo was right and that des Baux would not permit
Alys to be harmed. Ernaldus was nothing and nobody; he
would have no power to hurt Alys even if he was in the keep.
Arnald's words had restored Raymond's perspective. It was
ridiculous to think that Ernaldus had anything to do with the
abduction. A common bailiff could have no influence on a
nobleman. None of des Baux's men or servants would help
Ernaldus when their master had decreed that the women not be
harmed. And Alys could protect herself against Ernaldus
alone. She would find a distaff and beat in his brains, or stab
him with a spindle.

"Have you gone mad also?" Sir Romeo snarled. "What is
there to laugh about in this situation?"

Raymond sobered. "Nothing. But Arnald is right. Des Baux
may find his captives less easy to manage than he thought, and
Alys will keep Beatrice steady in refusal. However, if he
separates them, Beatrice's spirit may fail."

"He was courting her, too," Sir Romeo said angrily.

"Courting Alys?" Raymond asked, his voice sharp.

"No, courting Beatrice. My son told me about Lady Alys
breaking up one of those poetical love fests. I spoke rather
sharply to Beatrice about allowing . . . Good God, this whole
thing may be my fault. If that young fool des Baux thought he
was about to win Beatrice with lute songs and she turned him
off sharply because of what I said—"

"It does not matter," Raymond interrupted, with relief.
What Sir Romeo said proved that Beatrice *was* the object of

the abduction, not Alys. "What does matter is getting men out to that keep as soon as possible."

Sir Romeo went gray again. "I tell you it cannot be taken by assault. Do not throw away your life—"

"No, no, I assure you," Raymond interrupted again. "With what do you think I could begin an assault—my ten men and Alys's twenty?" As he said it, Raymond flushed slightly, remembering how Alys always said "our." Assault was impossible, but if there were some way, any way . . . "I intend guile, not force," he went on, keeping his voice steady. "I only wish to support Beatrice's spirit by letting her believe an army has already come for her, and also to prevent allies from entering Les Baux if they are not already in the keep."

This seemed so reasonable a notion that Sir Romeo put aside his doubts and began to discuss practical plans. Only a few hours later, despite the light rain that was still falling, Raymond set out with his troop and another thirty men from Arles, including several older men-at-arms who remembered the road to Les Baux. They made good time, keeping a fast pace until they passed the abbey, slowing until the older men found the sidetrack, and then going quickly again.

On the other hand, Master Ernaldus had made only very slow progress down the winding cliff trail. Because he was afraid of falling off the edge, he clung to the mountainside. But close to the inner edge, the road was less well trodden. More than once Ernaldus's foot caught in a tuft of dead grass or weeds or trod on a stone that rolled. He staggered and tripped and occasionally fell, for he was heavy laden and off balance. The road was steep and pitched him forward. Ernaldus had not walked so far in years. Soon he stopped, crouching against the cliff, sure he could go no farther.

Fear drove him on as soon as his breath no longer tore his lungs with pain. If he were caught, he would die slowly and painfully. Better a plunge off the cliff, he was sure. Exhaustion stopped him again a few hundred feet down the track, and he whimpered that no death could be worse than the suffering he was enduring. However, there was no relief from suffering in crouching on the stony road in the rain. Ernaldus knew there were huts along the road where he could take shelter once he reached the plain. So, alternating between fear and the hope of comfort, he found strength to rise each time he stopped.

Ernaldus was not yet on the plain when he heard the thunder of hooves and, almost at once, thinly, from above, a cry of warning from the guard on the wall of Les Baux. If he had been higher up, Ernaldus might have thrown himself over the cliff in despair. He believed this must be the first detachment of men coming in response to the letters Sir Guillaume had sent out. But he was too far down to jump. He would only break bones and be unable to escape. Not that he would escape anyway. As soon as the men began to ride up the track, they would find him. He ran a little way, but he was so unwieldy with his gold and the stolen goods he had wrapped around his body that he tripped and fell, rolled, and caught himself almost at the edge. Then he lay still, too frozen with too many terrors to move.

He could see the horsemen, dim shadows on the road that was only less black than the brush and stubble of the fields. He could not tell how many—there seemed to be hundreds—but it did not matter; one would be too many for him. But then the miracle occurred. They turned off the path to the keep, veering left off the road toward the band of woods that bordered the grazing fields where they would be sheltered somewhat from the catapults and mangonels of the keep.

Barely suppressing a cry of joy and relief, Ernaldus scrambled to his feet, hope renewing his strength. If the men had turned off the road, they could not be Guillaume's allies. Had they been supporters of des Baux, they would have clustered at the foot of the track up the cliff while one man rode up to identify them. They would not have gone to hide in the woods. Thus, they must be the first group sent out from Arles. That stupid, useless clot Guillaume must have left some clear sign that he was the abductor, Ernaldus thought with vicious satisfaction. Now Sir Romeo would besiege Les Baux before Guillaume's supporters could get to him.

Muffling the laughter he could not contain, Ernaldus staggered down the road. Les Baux would be taken at last; the impregnable fortress would be broached, and all because of a virgin who refused to be broached. Oh, it was exquisitely humorous! And the one man who would come out scatheless and be well rewarded was himself, who had caused all the trouble to begin with. Content with this assessment of the situation, Ernaldus took no special care on the road now. He staggered and swayed, rocked by silent laughter, sure that nothing would come between him and his revenge.

Indeed, he made his way quite safely the rest of the way down and struck out across the fields toward the woods. Good fortune seemed to be his, for he did not need to search for the group. Before he had gone very far, a rider came out and hailed him. Ernaldus said his name was Bernard, a poor clerk, gasping out that he had only that day discovered Lady Beatrice was held prisoner in Les Baux and that he had escaped at great peril to bring word to her mother. Then he did not even have to walk any farther; he was assisted to the croup of the horse and carried pillion to the camp.

"Lord Raymond," the man called. "Here is one from Les Baux who says he has news of Lady Beatrice."

By now Ernaldus knew that Raymond was nearly the most common name in Provence. Then, too, Bordeaux was a very long way from Arles and Les Baux. Nonetheless, for no reason at all, a slight chill of apprehension marred Ernaldus's satisfaction. He could not see the face of the leader; it was dark and Raymond's features were further obscured by the uplifted visor. Besides, Ernaldus remembered, he had never seen the husband of that yellow bitch, Lady Alys. Still, the chill persisted.

"Your name?" Raymond asked.

"Bernard, a poor clerk," the bailiff replied, but his voice shook. For a moment he thought he had heard Rustengo speaking. "I come from Avignon." That was a papal city and likely to be a source of clerks. "I have been in Les Baux only a few weeks, and this morning, to my horror, I learned . . ."

Raymond listened without interrupting, and the tale was perfectly reasonable, but something was bothering him, and the longer he listened, the more it bothered him. At last, it came to him that the uneasy feeling had nothing to do with the actual events this Bernard was describing. There was something familiar—the man's speech. That was it! It was not the speech of Provence. It was of Bordeaux! Rage and fear flashed up in Raymond. Could he be . . . Ernaldus . . . rather than Bernard? Raymond controlled himself with an effort. If Ernaldus was here, he could not hurt Alys, unless . . .

But Raymond dared not simply leap at the man and throttle

him. Revenge was less important than finding out about Alys. "Is Lady Beatrice alone?" Raymond asked sharply.

"No, my lord," Ernaldus answered, startled by this interruption and by Raymond's odd tone of voice.

"Who is with her?"

"That I cannot tell you, my lord," Ernaldus replied truthfully, calm again because he thought the sharp anxiety he had heard in the first question was for Beatrice's situation. It was the truth; Ernaldus had not asked, and Guillaume had not named the women to him. They had been intent on the more important business of getting out the summonses to supporters. "I am not so great that Sir Guillaume would speak to me," he added.

But Raymond had eased his manner even before the clerk finished his answer. Perhaps this Bernard was who he said he was. A person from Bordeaux might easily go to the papal city of Avignon to study, and that was all the man had said. And, Ernaldus or Bernard, it was the truth that this man did not know who was with Beatrice. There was something in his voice that made Raymond certain of it.

Besides, Ernaldus must be sure that no one would think a bailiff from Bordeaux, even if he was a bastard uncle, would be harmed or punished in any way, whatever happened to Les Baux or Sir Guillaume. And, if this *was* the treacherous Ernaldus, the last thing Raymond wanted was that he should think himself suspected until the last grain of information had been leached out of him. Raymond shrugged mentally at the thought; he was not one to think ill of men usually, but Bernard or Ernaldus, there was something about the man he did not like.

"How do you know where the ladies are kept?" Raymond asked.

"I heard by chance from one of the men-at-arms who took part in the abduction. He said they had been carried to the Sow's Tower."

There was a pause while Raymond stared into the dark, trying to see the man's face more clearly. It sounded like the truth, but it was very odd. Why should des Baux have placed the women in a tower when they would have been more comfortable, and more secure, in the keep itself?

"Why?" Raymond asked. "Why in the tower? Why not in the keep?"

"Because Sir Guillaume was too knightly gentle to place so fine a lady in the cells below the keep." Ernaldus stopped abruptly, appalled both at the slip he had made and at the bitter tone in his voice. "Or so I did hear," he added quickly, "and also I do suppose he wished to keep the knowledge of what he had done from his mother. He is young still and much affected by her weeping when she is distressed."

Several ideas collided in Raymond's mind: sudden sympathy for Guillaume des Baux, who seemingly was afflicted with the same kind of mother he had; conviction that Alys, Beatrice, and Margot were truly in the Sow's Tower—the conviction resting on the bitter anger in this Bernard's voice; and from that same cause a second conviction, that whether this man were Bernard or Ernaldus, he was personally and deeply involved in the abduction. Most likely, Raymond thought, this rat, despairing of success in the plot to force Beatrice into marriage because Sir Guillaume would not countenance cruel treatment, had decided to desert his master and make what profit he could from his desertion.

That conclusion pleased Raymond. Although he had no intention of letting the man go until he was sure that he was not Ernaldus, he said, "Very well, I thank you. A clerk has no place in a war camp. You may leave at your will. I suppose you wish to be as far from Les Baux as possible when missiles begin to fly." Raymond began to turn away, sure that his indifference would draw more information in the hopes of a reward.

Ernaldus trembled with fury, but at the core of it was a cold dread. The accent of this Lord Raymond was of Provence, but the voice and manner were too like Rustengo de Soler—and Rustengo was Raymond d'Aix's kinsman. Could God's curse be on him for his murder? Could this be Raymond d'Aix? Could the ghost of the blond bitch have mysteriously driven her husband from Bordeaux to this place and made him turn away the bringer of good news without a suggestion of recompense? Ernaldus wanted desperately to keep the remaining information to himself and give it to a more generous recipient, but he dared not. Any delay would cause dangerous suspicion of both the information and himself.

"My lord!" Ernaldus cried.

Raymond looked back at him, and it was well that Ernaldus could not read the expression on the shadowed face. "Yes?"

"There is more," Ernaldus said, lowering his voice, "but I —I am a poor clerk, and I have lost my place, and . . ."

"If you know something that will save lives and, more especially, save time in freeing Lady Beatrice, you will receive a just reward, I promise."

Deliberately, Raymond had not said "my wife and Lady Beatrice," despite the fact that bringing Alys out of Les Baux was far more important to him than bringing out Beatrice. If this was Ernaldus, he was too likely to make the connection between "Lord Raymond" and Lady Alys, and that would be the end of any voluntary information. More could be extracted by torture, but that would take time and might not be reliable.

There was a perceptible pause. A just reward. Ernaldus did not like that. He would rather have heard "a rich reward," but he had gone too far to turn back. Cursing under his breath, he felt under his robe and held out a key.

"This opens the Sow's Tower in which Lady Beatrice is imprisoned," he said.

He expected a cry of joy, but Raymond only stared at him and then held out his hand for the key. Ernaldus whimpered, seeing his reward diminish to nothing as this foul, dishonest lord took the credit and left him with nothing.

Raymond hefted the key in his hand. "It might be worth its weight in gold—if I were inside Les Baux and had a way out," he said. His voice was low and sounded indifferent, but that was because his heart was up in his throat, pounding.

"There is a postern, a way through the walls," Ernaldus offered, a small hope breaking through because of Raymond's mention of gold.

"So it often is," Raymond remarked, his voice still stifled as excitement grew in him, "but such ways are locked and guarded."

"One is not . . . not now."

Ernaldus forced the words out through his teeth, terrified at Raymond's lack of reaction. But Raymond was only fighting the desire to grab Ernaldus and drag him to the secret entrance without the necessary preparation. Raymond knew this could not be a trap; Guillaume needed no hostages because he already had in his hands the most valuable hostage in Provence. Thus, what Ernaldus offered was truly a path to Alys, now, this very night. To move or speak until he crushed his violent joy and eagerness, Raymond knew, would only lead to failure of the attempt through rash action.

Finally Raymond gained enough control of his voice to ask, "Where is this open door?"

"It is not an easy door," Ernaldus faltered.

"I do not care if it passes through hell," Raymond exclaimed, "so long as it takes me into Les Baux."

The violent intensity of Raymond's desire had broken through that time, and Ernaldus jerked with surprise. It frightened Ernaldus even more. It seemed clear to him that Raymond had not wanted to say what he did say, and the sudden about-face in intention startled Ernaldus. He shivered as Raymond caught his arm.

"Where?" Raymond demanded, his voice shaking.

"On the west, where the cliff is lowest, there is a way up the rock, not a path but a clear way of handholds and footholds," Ernaldus gabbled.

Raymond had leaned closer, and Ernaldus had finally seen his face. That, too, had a look of Rustengo. It *was* Raymond d'Aix! And the pale eyes frightened him. They seemed fixed and blind . . . like the eyes of one possessed. Ernaldus recalled the horrible notion he had had about the ghost of Lady Alys. He shivered again and checked that thought. Could he hope to placate the vengeful spirit?

"But the door is not there," Raymond said.

This was only good sense, a soldier's knowledge of correct tactical precaution, but Ernaldus shuddered violently. To him it seemed like unnatural prescience, a thing only a supernatural being would know. He shook so hard that Raymond noticed and called out for someone to bring a dry blanket or cloak. The creature might be sly and slimy as a snake, but Raymond did not want him too chilled to show the path.

Still, he did not wait for the cloak to come but repeated, "Where is the door?"

"Do you not know?" Ernaldus quavered.

And suddenly Raymond laughed, because in a way he did know. Unless there was some special difficulty, the door should not be visible from the path that led to it. In this case, it would probably be around the corner of a tower or bend in the wall.

"Perhaps I do," Raymond acknowledged, not comprehending at all the terror he was fixing into Ernaldus's mind and soul, "but tell me anyway."

Nothing could be hidden from the spirits of the dead, Ernaldus knew, and Lord Raymond had all but admitted he knew what was impossible for him to know—unless his dead wife possessed him. Ernaldus's eyes rolled up in his head and he dropped unconscious.

CHAPTER 25

****

Raymond was somewhat surprised when the clerk who called himself Bernard fainted dead away, but he attributed it to the man's fear of being harmed now that all his secret had been extracted from him. He could not be troubled with that and merely called the men nearest to him and bade them take Ernaldus to a tent and see if some warm wine would revive him. All Raymond's attention was now concentrated on the practical aspects of entering and leaving Les Baux.

Handholds and footholds were not too bad going up, Raymond knew, for he had done some climbing in the mountains near Gordes. However, they were very dangerous going down, and for Beatrice and Margot, impossible. Alys? Well, Alys might have difficulty, too, Raymond conceded grudgingly—he was rapidly approaching the state of mind in which he resented admitting there was anything Alys could not do. But the area around Marlowe had no mountains, and Alys could have had no experience with cliffs. Accordingly, seven men, all from mountainous areas with climbing experience, were chosen and every piece of rope in the camp was collected.

These orders caused a good deal of grumbling. Arnald and his men came near to insubordination when they were told they could not accompany Raymond. Only the strongest representations of the fact that they would be a great danger to their mistress if they fell quieted their protests. By the time the ropes were tied together safely, the rain had stopped, but the night was considerably advanced. There was some danger that dawn would come before the rescue was complete.

Raymond weighed that danger against the chance that Ernaldus's absence would inspire a thorough search and the discovery of the unbarred secret way. Had he such a rat in his entourage, treachery such as opening a path into the keep would be the first suspicion in his mind, Raymond thought. On those grounds, it seemed the lesser risk to go at once.

When Ernaldus was brought from the tent, he made no more protest than the single cry, "Will it not soon be light?" But he saw Raymond's pale eyes flash, and his mind's eye made out the fixed—possessed—eagerness of the face he could not really see. As he was set upon a horse, Ernaldus heard a command in a language he did not understand but recognized; the voice was familiar, too—it was the voice and language of Lady Alys's master-at-arms. Ernaldus nearly fell off the horse, but the man behind whom he was riding felt him sway and gripped him tight.

Now Ernaldus was so sick and frozen with terror that he could not scream, could not try to wrench himself free. He saw everything that had happened to him since that meeting with Lady Alys under the walls of Blancheforte as one great pattern. Ernaldus knew he was evil. He knew he had not given mercy or *caritas* to his fellows. He had always told himself that there would be time to confess, to repent, to give to the Church and pray. When he had amassed sufficient wealth, when he had reached a position of honor, when he was content —then he would amend his life and make his peace with God.

But he had been given a warning and had not heeded it. When Lady Alys reviled him for his wickedness, instead of taking warning and making restitution, he had arranged for her death. Ernaldus tried to find contrition, but what rose in him was hatred, only hatred, which was beaten down into terror but rose again. The blessed did not walk the earth after death nor possess other bodies. Thus, the blond bitch—Lady Alys—was accursed, too, an emissary of Satan come to fetch him.

Vaguely Ernaldus felt himself removed from the horse and prodded forward. There was brush and loose rock, and he was pushed and pulled, forced to crouch, even to lie down, then pushed and pulled onward. The trek seemed endless. Then there was a steep wall before him. He looked around in a dream. Was this hell already?

"This is the west cliff face," a voice said in his ear. "Where are the climbing holds?"

The clouds had drawn off, and there was a glimmer of moonlight. Ernaldus had never seen this place in the dark, although he had come more than once by daylight. It was instinctive in him to seek a back door. He had not used this path to flee because he had been afraid to climb down, but he had marked the way well—he himself did not realize how well he had marked it.

"Where?" the voice prodded.

Ernaldus went forward, moving aimlessly along the cleft and fractured rock face farther west until he found a dark crevice. "Here," he said. He did not care. They could only kill him, but he knew they would not. Worse was coming.

The best climber came forward, hunchbacked under the great coil of rope. He felt around, grunted with satisfaction, and began to creep upward. Ernaldus watched without surprise. He was quite sure that had he chosen any other crevice, the handholds and footholds would have appeared there. It would be no trouble to God—or to the devil—to order such a thing. There was a profound silence. From the place where he had been pulled and forced to squat, Ernaldus looked out and around. There was soft breathing, but otherwise he would have sworn he was alone. At last there was a sound, a dull, soft, thumping slither. The rope had come down from above.

When it did, Raymond took a half-step, then gritted his teeth and stepped back into the deeper shadow. He was so eager to get up the cliff that his breath would not come evenly. He smiled tautly, thinking that it took more strength and courage to wait, at this moment, than to charge into the set lances of an opposing army. But wait he must, as he was the worst climber and more heavily burdened with steel mail and heavier weapons than his men.

Waiting . . . Raymond's head turned toward the clerk. Was that what was wrong with the man? Raymond knew there had been a change in him, but he hoped he had not exposed his suspicions. Perhaps Bernard either feared entering Les Baux again or feared heights. Or perhaps, Raymond thought, he had given some sign that he did not believe Bernard was an innocent clerk. The last thought made Raymond order that Ernaldus be gagged and bound. If he cried out or got away from them, they would be undone.

Ernaldus submitted without objection to the gagging and having his hands bound, which Raymond thought peculiar, but when the man-at-arms reached around him to fasten the rope that would pull him up the cliff, he began to struggle, kicking and writhing. It was in restraining him that the hard rolls of gold coins fastened around his waist were discovered, and these were stripped away at once. Ernaldus went limp after the gold was gone. His struggles had been instinctive; now he thought he should have expected it. The priests said a man could not take his wealth through death's door, whether it led to heaven or to hell. He felt no fear as he was hauled swiftly up. Not yet. Worse was coming.

The discovery of the gold virtually killed Raymond's suspicions; it was reason enough for all the man's peculiar behavior. Some of the nearly unbearable tension drained out of Raymond. It had been a strain to think he might be so close to the person who had tried to kill Alys and still keep a calm exterior instead of choking the man to death. And if Ernaldus was in Les Baux, they would get him easily when Sir Guillaume surrendered—as he must when his hostages were gone.

Raymond went up directly after Ernaldus, not hauled but helped by the rope, and finally the last man reached the top and drew the rope up after him. Then they crouched and listened. They had not made much noise, and the crevice was in deep shadow. Unfortunately, the moon was out now, very low, but it sent a thin, cold light against the cliffs. That light struck them, and all crouched as close as possible to the foot of the wall. They did not expect to be noticed. Each man hoped the guards' attention was on the woods at the foot of the road where the camp was.

No cry of alarm rang out, and, one at a time, they moved farther west along the wall and then around a sharp bend. Here there was shadow, the moonlight being blocked by the curve of the wall. Not much farther along was the heavy iron grating. One of the men took a pot from his pouch and applied a liberal coating of grease, working it in between the frame and the grating itself with his knife blade. He stuck his hand through and greased the hinges too, breaking his nails as he pushed the grease in and around. Another man joined him, greasing the latch, which was, as promised, unlocked. Satisfied at last, the men pushed cautiously. There was a low groan but no loud screech. They paused to listen, but Raymond gestured impatiently and they pushed the grating open all the way.

Surprisingly, it was not difficult to slide in, although the opening was very small, as long as one went slowly, either hips first or with arms stretched above his head. After that discovery, everything was so easy that everyone, except Ernaldus, began to pray that so much good luck would not lead to bad. Behind the grating was no narrow crawl space but a reasonably commodious tunnel. This was utterly lightless, but feeling along the walls led them to the lower chamber of a tower. In this, the door to the bailey was open, and a thin gray light came in, enough to show the blacker shapes of tubs and barrels and save them from bumping against anything.

Instinctively every man paused and drew weapons. It seemed too easy, as if it had been arranged to accommodate them, to draw them farther in. But it was too late to worry. Cautiously, Raymond stepped out into the bailey, tensed for a shout of alarm and a rush of defenders. But there was nothing. It was not complete silence, but the normal sounds of a nighttime keep—a vague medley of animals moving in pens somewhere, the low rustle of banked fires in the cooksheds, an occasional yap from the kennels. Raymond stepped back into the tower and murmured, "Bernard." A man pushed the bailiff forward. "Which way is the Sow's Tower?"

This important question was the reason Raymond had brought Ernaldus with them. Unlike "square tower" or "north tower," the name of this one gave no indication of shape or position. There was enough light near the doorway for Raymond's eyes, now adjusted to the dark, to make out the blankness of Ernaldus's face. "The Sow's Tower," Raymond repeated. The face remained blank, but the head turned and the dead-looking eyes gazed across the bailey.

At first Raymond did not know whether the gesture was an answer—the only answer a gagged and bound man could make —or whether Ernaldus was looking away as a refusal to answer. A moment later, following the direction Ernaldus had looked, Raymond saw that it was an answer. Between the tower in which they stood and the one at which Ernaldus had looked were two others. Both of those showed black holes where doors stood open. The tower Ernaldus had indicated showed the dull reflection of moonlight from a surface—a closed, doubtless locked door.

Raymond cursed softly under his breath. He was a fool, for he had not needed to bring the clerk after all. He felt foolish, too, about being alarmed by the open tower doors. Naturally those doors would be open. If an attack was expected, they would be left open so that the men could rush up to take their places on the walls without wrestling with heavy doors.

"Take Bernard back to the passage," Raymond said softly to one of the men. "Tie his feet so that he cannot get away—but tie them loosely so he can work himself free in a few hours in case we cannot come back for him." Raymond did not like the clerk, but he would not condemn any man to die slowly and agonizingly of thirst and hunger.

They traversed the bailey without causing any alarm. One of the men shuddered and crossed himself; another mouthed silent prayers. It was easy, too easy. Raymond's hand gripped his sword hilt until the knuckles showed white. Too smooth, too easy. He wondered if perhaps the key would not fit; but it did fit, and it turned without a screech. Raymond ground his teeth and pushed; the door swung back with only the faintest groaning.

It was after the door was closed behind the last man that the signs of the end of the halcyon period began. First, the stench smote them. None of the men had a delicate nose, nor did Raymond himself, but it was rare for a tower to smell like the shaft of a garderobe. Then a man slipped on something and fell, his sword striking a barrel with a loud *thunk*. All froze, listening, but the sound had not betrayed them. Raymond snarled an order to take better care, but he did not ask who had slipped, knowing it could have been he as easily as another.

In the pitch black, they felt for the stair, but Raymond went up alone, thinking it would be less frightening for the women since all knew his voice. The odor was worse as he climbed, and he almost fell off the stair altogether. "Enough," he murmured under his breath, "we have had our ill fortune already. It is enough." But he had a strong suspicion it was not going to be so easy, and, when the inner door would not move upon lifting the latch and pushing, he stood for a moment fighting a sinking heart.

First he cursed Bernard, thinking this door, too, was locked. Then he bethought himself that the same key might easily open both locks, and he began to feel for the lock plate, but the door was smooth from top to bottom. Last he tried throwing his weight against the door in case it was warped and stuck. Still, the door would not open. It moved inward just a little, then sprang back. Raymond stood thinking for a few seconds and realized the door must be barred on the inner side. But that was ridiculous! Prisoners do not lock themselves in! And then Raymond snarled softly. Three young women might indeed have good reasons to lock themselves in.

A shout rose in him, a need to batter at the door and scream for Alys to open it and tell him she was unhurt, unmolested. Until this moment he had known no fear for Alys's safety or inviolability. He had not believed that any man could be so stupid as to insult or assault Alys and Margot d'Aix and Beatrice of Provence. Now Raymond wanted and needed to break down the door, but the fact that the women felt a need to lock themselves in lent a sharp edge to his caution. The barred door changed all expectation of honorable treatment. Raymond leaned his head in despair against the wood. He swallowed hard and tried to think of another way to enter Alys's prison.

Alys, Beatrice, and Margot had had a tense and frustrating day. Once the girls had stopped laughing over their success and Beatrice's brilliant idea about what to do with the near-overflowing contents of the chamber pot, they had begun to worry. It was bad enough to have made a fool of Sir Guillaume by throwing sand in his eyes and pushing him down the stairs; the insult of emptying the chamber pot on him might be the straw that made the ass sit down. Not that Alys or Margot blamed Beatrice. Both burst out laughing anew whenever they thought of it. Still, all of them realized that they needed a defense.

By nightfall, however, they had no more than they had started with. No attempt had been made on them, but that only made the expectation of an assault more acute. Thus, none of them slept deeply, and all woke with a start when Raymond threw himself against the door. Alys was on her feet before either of the others could scream and had a hand over each mouth.

"Quiet," she whispered, "let him think us asleep and easy prey. I have the crossbow. If the door yields, I will shoot the first man in. If that is Guillaume, it will end our troubles."

"But what if it is not?" Margot whimpered.

"Take the extra poles, and stand to each side of the door," Alys urged. "Strike at whoever enters. Try to keep them back until I can wind the bow again."

Margot fell silent but did not move. Beatrice rose from the bed. She did not like this sly attempt to open the door in the middle of the night. It seemed a greater threat to her than a frontal attack during the day. If that idiot Guillaume snatched her away from Alys and Margot, Beatrice was not sure she could continue to be brave. But the noises at the door had stopped.

After a while, Alys went to the door and listened, but without much hope. Its planks were several inches thick and well fitted together, a door designed, when barred, to delay an attacking force with a ram. Alys knew she would hear nothing unless someone was shouting right near the door or if many men were fighting and yelling below. After a few minutes she came back toward the bed and looked anxiously up at the ceiling. The trap door to the topmost chamber was there. She wondered if Guillaume had decided it would be easier to cross the wall from another tower and come down by ladder than to break open the door.

Alys mentioned this possibility, and she and Beatrice discussed in whispers what would be best to do if Guillaume or his men came down from above. Margot sniffled, hardly listening as Alys and Beatrice tried to plan a strategy. Margot regretted bitterly her desire for a more exciting life. She vowed she would try to help Alys and Beatrice, but never, never, never—if they ever reached safety—would she complain about living quietly at Aix.

Margot remained seated on the bed, tense with fear. Because she was frightened while the other two were immersed in plans, difficulties, and possibilities, it was she who heard the faint creak from above as weight came onto an imperfectly flat floorboard. First she was frozen, her instinct for self-preservation bidding her be still. Once Beatrice was isolated, Margot knew that she and Alys would be well treated and might even be freed. But Margot was really fond of Beatrice. When the second creak sounded, she leapt to her feet and rushed to the others.

"They are above! I heard them," she whispered frantically.

Biting back a cry of anger and fear, Alys crawled toward her blanket and grabbed the crossbow. The trap door groaned softly. Alys bit her lip, knowing that the sound meant the trap had been lifted. She felt the bow, fitted the quarrel carefully, and lifted it. She was aware of three things nearly simultaneously: the thump as the ladder came down, the creak as a man's weight came on it, and Beatrice scrabbling on the floor for a pole which had escaped her hand.

"Stop," Alys commanded clearly. "I have a crossbow trained on your back. Do not cry out. Go back up."

"Alys!" Raymond whispered softly. "Are you unhurt, my love?"

Alys was so startled that she almost fired. Her second impulse was to throw the bow away and rush to the ladder. Instead she hissed, "Stand! I warn you."

The man's hoarse whisper was unidentifiable. It was too easy a trick, Alys thought. Both Beatrice and Margot had cried out softly with relief and then drew in gasping breaths when Alys's words implied it was a trick. Now Alys heard Beatrice getting to her feet. Somehow she sensed that Beatrice was raising the pole.

In the same instant, Raymond whispered, *"Hauest noon drede, mi deore, beoth ich!"*

"No!" Alys cried as she heard the pole swish through the air, but she was already turning, already striking Beatrice's hand aside. The pole hit the ladder with a vicious *thwack,* and the crossbow fired, fortunately away from anyone. Beatrice cried out, and Alys dropped her weapon, nearly fainting with relief.

"Stupid slut," Raymond growled, knowing it was not Alys who had struck at him. "Are you trying to brain me?"

"Raymond!" Alys whispered. "Raymond!"

He came down from the ladder and reached out toward the sound of her voice, and they were in each other's arms. Alys clutched at him so fiercely she bruised her hands and her cheek on his mail. He bent his head to kiss her, and then had to lift it to snarl, "Quiet, you fools!" as Margot and Beatrice began to weep aloud. Still, he opened his arms to gather them into his embrace also, for he was very fond of both, and besides, in this moment of triumph, he loved even Bernard.

The way out was no more difficult than the way in. All the attention of the men on the walls was fixed outward on the campfires in the wood. Nor had the keep been roused for fear of attack. When informed that there were enemies in the wood, Sir Guillaume did not order any alert. He trusted his cliff and his walls. All he did was ask how many in the force that had come and, when told some hundred or two, he had actually laughed and gone back to sleep. Oddly, he slept better after the warning, knowing he was committed and no longer wondering whether he could squirm out of the situation without anyone ever knowing. Another thing gave him ease. He had seen a way out himself.

The precious heiress of Provence was unsullied. If Lady Beatrice and Sir Romeo wanted her back, they could have her back—for a price and a swearing of quittance. Otherwise they could spend the blood and lives it would cost to take Les Baux and get back damaged goods withal. Guillaume almost felt content as he slipped asleep again. True, Lady Beatrice and Sir Romeo would not love him for this, but that would be nothing new between des Baux and the counts of Provence.

Thus, Raymond led his womenfolk into the tower with the entrance to the secret way without untoward incident. The only fear Raymond had was that dawn would catch them, and after his brief hug he had not permitted anyone to say a word, threatening to gag Margot and Beatrice if they made one single sound. He did not, of course, threaten Alys.

It was not possible to see the faint light that glimmered on the eastern horizon, but the stars had paled as the sky pearled more gray than black. Still, there was no cause for great alarm. If they made no noise, there was little chance the guards would look down along their own walls. They would look out toward the woods and the area of tumbled rock and low brush that fell away from the cliff toward the wood. That was where the danger was. By the time they were down the cleft, the light would be strong enough for the guards to see them. Most likely they would be shot at from the walls. They could only hope the aim of the crossbowmen would be poor at that distance.

In the tunnel, where voices would not be heard, Raymond warned the women again against making a sound and told them how they would be lowered by rope down the cliff. Again and again he reiterated that they must not cry out, even if the rope hurt them or they were banged against the rock.

"Do you understand me, Margot?" he asked, and when she

whispered a frightened affirmative, he added, "Beatrice, do you understand?"

He did not speak to Alys nor even look at her, although her hand was on his arm. To Raymond's mind there was no need to receive confirmation from Alys. He had told her to be still, and she understood why it was necessary; Raymond was certain that neither fear nor pain would wring any sound from Alys. He wished he were as sure about Margot and Beatrice, even after receiving their promises. Then he described to them and to the men what they must do when they reached the ground.

It was no longer really black where they stood in the tunnel. A faint light filtered in from the grating. Ernaldus sat alongside it, and he could see Raymond's legs, identified by the mail hosen he wore. Beyond him were the skirts of two women; Raymond had spoken to Margot and Beatrice, Ernaldus remembered, but there was another skirt. The bailiff looked up.

Very little light diffused upward, but Ernaldus had been so long in the blackest dark that he could make out something. There was a third woman—or something—blotting out the faint gleam of Raymond's mail. She—it—stood with a hand on Lord Raymond's arm, yet he seemed completely unaware of it. He looked—Ernaldus could see the change in shape of the mail hood as Raymond turned his head—only at the two women in front of him.

Although Margot and Beatrice had been silent as they had been told, Raymond did not quite trust them. He felt an urgent need to see the expressions on their faces. If it seemed to him that either girl was near the limit of her ability to obey him, it would be better to gag her than to have her screaming as she was lowered. A soft word to one of the men-at-arms and he brought a stub of candle, flint, and tinder from his pouch. On the way in, Raymond would not chance a light, but now there was less danger from a stray reflection being seen than from his overestimating Margot and Beatrice.

The man-at-arms passed the lit candle to Raymond, who held it up, illuminating not only Margot's and Beatrice's faces, but Alys's also. Ernaldus screamed behind his gag. The sound was muffled, but he had been nearly forgotten, and everyone was startled. Then, suddenly, before any of the men could get at him, he twisted around and thrust himself forward, pushing hard with his feet against the tunnel wall, squirming, struggling through the grating.

Raymond bent to grab his feet as Alys gasped, "Ernaldus!"

However, one of the men had jumped forward also, and he and Raymond collided. Raymond went staggering back, almost knocking Alys off her feet. They clung together, seeking balance, while the man who had tried to catch Ernaldus threw himself to the ground and started through the opening after him.

Because Ernaldus was a much smaller man and not bulked out with rough ring-sewn armor, he was able to wriggle through. The man behind him stuck fast at the shoulders, managing no more than a futile grab. He had to be hauled in to free the opening, and the men pulling on his legs felt his body suddenly convulse as if he had been injured. They hauled harder, thinking Ernaldus had somehow managed to strike him, but he was shuddering with shock, not hurt, when they got him inside.

"My lord," he whispered, "he went over. With his eyes wide open, he pushed himself right over the ledge."

Raymond stared down at his henchman. "Crawled off? Apurpose?"

"Apurpose—I do not know," the man said, shaking himself as if to throw off something evil clinging to him. "He looked . . . I saw his face. . . . My lord, let us go. There is something evil here. I do not think he crawled off apurpose. He was afraid, so much afraid that he did not see what his eyes looked on."

Raymond shook his head. "No," he said, "there is nothing evil here. The evil was in that one's own heart. What he feared was seeing my wife, whom he believed was dead by his order. There is nothing for us to fear but discovery by des Baux's men." Then he gestured for another of the men to go out.

One after another they crawled onto the ledge, Raymond thrusting Margot and Beatrice out, after four of the men had gone, and sending Alys out with a gesture just before he went himself. It was far too light for his liking, but he told himself that he should be thankful the west wall was more shadowed than any other would have been. Also it seemed a special gift from God that no one had seen Ernaldus fall and that the gag had kept him from screaming.

However, in the supposition that no one had seen Ernaldus fall, Raymond was not quite correct. No one had seen the fall itself, but by a freak occurrence, the body had struck a subsidiary peak of the fractured rock and bounced around so that it finally hit the ground not far from the cleft that had the handholds and footholds. On that side, a guard had noticed the sudden movement. He did not see motion long, for the dead thing came to rest beside a brush-covered rock and was hidden. But that made the guard wary. He scanned the cliffs and was certain nothing moved on them, but the tumbled rock and brush that lay around their feet was another matter. In the half-light, men could move and hide in that cover. He watched the base of the cliffs and listened, cursing the birds that sent up such a tumult of sound at this hour.

The guard had just about given up, believing his eyes had deceived him, when he saw movement again. He shouted for assistance and snatched up his crossbow. Several men darted out from concealment at the foot of the rock and ran zigzagging away from the cliff. The guard sent a bolt after one, feeling a rich satisfaction in having perceived an attempt to enter Les Baux by stealth, but not realizing that the forms he shot at were escaping from the castle, not trying to enter it. His first shot had missed, but he sent another and shouted in triumph as a man fell. However, he got to his feet at once and ran on. Two more guards had run from adjoining sections of the wall and also fired their crossbows.

There were now eight men running away, but three of them looked very strange, as if they were carrying or sheltering huge rolls of loose cloth in front of them. All three guards were attracted and fired at the strange forms. It was not reasonable to hold cloth in front when arrows flew from behind. One arrow struck. The man staggered and fell, and a thin, shrill scream —a scream that sounded remarkably like a woman's—rang out. Two men rushed toward the fallen one; the three guards shot again, but the vagrant breeze of the morning made these tries less true, and then their surprise held them from winding their bows for a few minutes. It was not a bundle of cloth but a woman! One of the men had snatched her up and held her before him; the other helped his companion to his feet.

Now other castle men-at-arms were coming onto the walls, but the running figures were nearly to the woods. A hail of bolts flew outward and then another. It seemed as if several of the running figures were struck, but none fell, and they disappeared into the trees. The three guards who had seen the woman mentioned the fact with surprise, but none of the men who had come onto the wall had been in on the abduction, nor were they aware that there were prisoners in the castle. Thus, the tale was not taken seriously, the others believing that the men had been deceived by the distance and the bad light. Besides, what could they do? They were besieged and could not send out a troop to pursue.

In the woods, Alys wrestled herself from her husband's arms, crying, "You were hit! You were hit!"

"In the flesh by an arrow half-spent," Raymond snapped. "Do not act the fool, Alys! Margot, are you hurt?" She was the one whose protector had fallen on her.

Margot was sobbing, but managed to shake her head. The man had tripped when the arrow struck him, but he had managed to put his hands out, and his full weight had not come down upon her.

"Are there any too hurt to ride?" Raymond asked next. And when he received a chorus of nays, he said sharply, "Alys, what the devil ails you? For what do you weep? Pull that shaft out of me and then see to the other men."

Raymond was in a strange mood, both irritated and elated. He knew he had accomplished what amounted to a miracle, but he was unreasonably annoyed because he had not got away scot-free. Something told him that they had not reached the end of their troubles, and he was in great haste to be gone. However, he was both right and wrong. There were no immediate calamities: The horses were where they had been left, and the short ride to the camp was uneventful. Nor was there any trouble in the camp. Still, the feeling of need for haste persisted, and Raymond snarled at Margot and Beatrice to hold their tongues when they wanted to relate their experiences and at Alys when she begged him to remove his armor so she could tend his wound.

Instead of soothing him, the lack of difficulties nagged at Raymond. His emotional reaction was to order the full troop to ride back with him, but his military instincts opposed that feeling. This, if Sir Romeo wished to take it, was an opportunity to destroy des Baux completely. To achieve that purpose, however, it was necessary to prevent help from reaching Sir Guillaume. Once Les Baux was full of men, it would be too hard a nut to crack, and to starve it out would take a year.

Raymond was certain that Guillaume must have already summoned his friends and vassals. He was equally certain that few or none of them had yet arrived, since there had been no extra tents set up in the bailey and the scouts he had sent out to examine the cliff on all sides reported no sign of tents on the flat land the keep did not occupy. To prevent assistance from reaching Les Baux, it was only necessary to block the one road, but that meant leaving the troop, or most of the troop, where it now was.

With this consideration in mind, Raymond ordered Alys's troop to come with him, leaving Sir Romeo's master-at-arms in charge with orders to do his uttermost to prevent anyone from entering Les Baux and promising that help would be sent as soon as he reached Arles. He then insisted they leave immediately, responding alike to Beatrice's and Margot's moans and laments that they were too bruised and exhausted, and to Alys's tearful pleas to bind up his wound, with threats that he would soon give them something real to weep for if they did not obey him instantly.

The trouble came down behind them as they entered the road that passed the abbey—a troop of men who cried out imprecations at the sight of the arms of d'Aix and charged them. Fortunately the road was narrow so that the larger numbers of the attackers counted for little in the first charge. Then, by a combination of good fortune and ferocity, Raymond wounded the knight who was leading the troop. This recalled that gentleman to the fact that his business was in Les Baux, not in casual encounters on the road, even if d'Aix happened to be an old enemy. Nursing his bleeding arm, he called off the attack.

They met more trouble just a mile or so from Arles. A group of men, either fleeing from the keep or merely leaving it in haste, clashed with Raymond's troop. In a way they were more dangerous, although fewer in number, because there were three knights in the party. However, this time Raymond did not stay to fight. He bade three men surround each woman's horse, spur to a gallop, and charge right through, dealing only such blows as would not slow their speed. Once they were through there could be no pursuit because they were too close to Arles.

Strangely enough, with each encounter Raymond's mood improved, and by the time they thundered through the entrance of the keep, the only shadow on Raymond's bright morning was the question of how to escape the interminable explanations and discussions he saw forthcoming. He did not—at least, not at the present moment—wish to explain how he had got into Les Baux, nor to give any opinion on what, if anything, should be done to punish Beatrice's abductor, nor to discuss whether there would be any advantage in destroying the des Baux.

All Raymond wanted was to get Alys to himself. It had finally dawned upon him that it was extremely unnatural for Alys to have been involved in the abduction. Why in the world did she agree to accompany Margot and Beatrice, and why take only four men? He could not believe Alys had ill intent, and yet he could think of no rational excuse for what she had done.

This irritation of mind, increased by over twenty-four hours without sleep and the nagging pain of the minor flesh wound, expressed itself in anger with his sister and Beatrice. Thus, he seized them both immediately upon dismounting and, dragging each by a wrist, entered the great hall. News of his arrival and of Beatrice's presence having preceded them, Sir Romeo, Lady Beatrice, and even Lady Jeannette were already running from their chambers, calling questions and making joyful exclamations. Raymond flung his two shrieking captives, one at each mother.

"Here, have them back," he roared, "and if you are wise, you will lesson them with a belt for this mischief."

"How? How?" Sir Romeo's bellow rose above the high voices of the women and the wailing of the two girls.

"I will tell you betimes," Raymond said, "but there is no time for it now. Des Baux has summoned men, and troops are already on their way. I bade your master-at-arms keep them from entering the keep, but he has only some forty men. Either recall him or send him help."

"Let me first thank you," Sir Romeo cried.

But Raymond was not interested in thanks. He turned to look behind him, and his lips twitched to refrain from smiling when he saw Alys standing meekly a few feet back as a good wife should. She was filthy and bedraggled, and her eyes lowered when he looked at her. Oddly, that convinced Raymond of her innocence. If Alys had been involved in whatever caused the abduction, she would be defiant. Ignoring his mother's shriek and Sir Romeo's oath when his bloodstained back became visible to them, Raymond took two steps and seized Alys's wrist.

"If you wish to thank me," he said, "let it be with a private chamber where I may deal with my wife."

Alys bit her lips to keep from crying aloud when she heard. She had descended to a pit of despair from a peak of joy when she first realized it was Raymond on the ladder. From the way he had greeted her and the belief that he had come to Arles in response to her request, she had been sure that all was forgiven. But he had not addressed a word to her after that, except to deny her the right to serve him. And when he had seized Margot and Beatrice and left her behind as they entered Arles, Alys had thought she would die. She had followed because she knew not what else to do.

Now, when he seized her wrist so unkindly, Alys had all she could do not to wail aloud like Beatrice and Margot. She was too blinded by tears to see Raymond's face when he slammed the door closed with his heel, so that she was totally surprised to find herself suddenly enveloped in her husband's embrace with passionate kisses being pressed on her lips and cheeks and eyes.

More shocked than pleased, Alys pulled her mouth free. "Oh, do not!" she cried. "You cannot be so cruel as to beat me after you kiss me."

"Why should you think I wish to beat you?" Raymond asked softly. "Do you deserve a beating?"

But the shock had dried Alys's tears, and she stared at him, taking in the quiver at the corner of his mouth, the little lines around his eyes that made them twinkle and indicated not rage, but mirth.

"Oh, you monster!" she cried, flinging her arms around his neck. "How dare you say to a whole hall full of people that you wished to 'deal with me,' frightening me to death—"

"I *am* dealing with you," Raymond said severely, and kissed her again. "Would you say I was having naught to do with you?" Then, when their lips parted, he said, "But you have not answered me. Do you deserve a beating?"

"Yes, indeed," Alys sighed, but her eyes shone with laughter, "for I accused you unjustly, and refused you your rights as a husband, and—and I struck you with—with my riding whip—"

"You devil!" he said. But now he could not be angry with Alys, even though the thing itself was outrageous. "That is something you had better not try again" was all he managed.

"No, but . . ." The merriment disappeared from the clear eyes that had been gazing into his; they became shadowed and dropped, and Alys's grip on him loosened. "I was wrong to deny you," she whispered, "but when—when you forced me, I —I—"

"Never again, dear heart, I swear it," Raymond murmured. "I do not say I will not beat you if you cross me that way, but force you I will not. Nor would I have done so that night, except that I think I was so tired—I had been two days without sleep—that I was not altogether right in my wits."

"Beloved, beloved," Alys cried, her eyes shining anew with joy, "I knew—as soon as you were gone, I knew you were not yourself. I would have followed you, except that I feared you would kill me if I did not let your anger cool. And the next day, when I heard you had taken Lucie away to be married, I vowed I would kiss your hands as you beat me, and so I will, if it will satisfy you to beat me now."

"Oh, you clever little witch," Raymond said, deliberately squeezing her so hard she squeaked with pain, "you know you are safe enough to offer that now when my desire is for a different satisfaction."

"No," Alys said.

Raymond's arms dropped away and his face went hard, and Alys burst into laughter.

"Not until you take off that steel shirt," she went on pertly before the anger that was gathering in Raymond could burst forth. "I am scratched and scraped enough from being snatched up and flung down and climbing mountains—" The bellow drowned her out, but Alys only put her hands over her ears and finished, "And now you are paid for affrighting me half to death in the hall."

Alys then slipped under Raymond's grasp and bent to take hold of his hauberk. She pulled it about halfway up, but Raymond was so much taller than she and the mail so heavy that she could not lift it farther. In fact, she overbalanced and fell against him, and he caught her again, but with the folds of mail between them, his intention was frustrated. Half-laughing, half-irritated, Raymond swung around, backed toward a stool, and sat down on it so Alys could lift off the hauberk. He grunted with pain when it pulled free the clotted blood around the wound, and Alys gasped at the new, sluggish flow of red. Raymond only stood up and pulled off the remainder of his clothing, fending Alys away and murmuring again, "Do not try my patience."

"But Raymond," Alys protested, "only let me—"

"Later," he insisted, seizing her gown at the neck and rending it apart down the center seam.

He expected Alys to be angry, but she had caught fire in a different way at that, and she only stepped out of the remains and hurriedly took off her shift and underdress. Holding out her hand to him, she went to the bed and pushed him gently so that he sat down on it.

"Stay yourself, my lord," she whispered, "or you will be too quick for me."

"Then I will amend it a second time," Raymond said impatiently. "I have been celibate as a walled-in monk since I last had you. If you quarrel with my slaking my thirst with others, then you must accommodate my eagerness."

Whereupon Alys threw herself atop him, crying, "If that is my prize, I will accommodate you any way you desire as often as you desire."

"As you are then, mount me," he muttered, pushing himself back so he would not slip off the bed.

Alys was so inflamed by the idea that she did not even see the smear of blood her husband's back left on the bed. She raised her knees, straddled him, and impaled herself, sighing with delight as she worked herself down. Raymond groaned, which might have boded ill, betokening he was near bursting, but Alys had the upper hand—or, rather, body—and brought them safely home. They both slept afterward, swiftly and deeply, Raymond so deeply that he did not stir when Alys woke and left the bed, nor even later when, having washed and done her hair and obtained fresh clothing, she shifted him and gently cleaned and bandaged the tear on his shoulder.

There were candles lit when Raymond opened his eyes at last. They fell on Alys, sewing beside the bed and singing softly to herself. Passion spent, anxiety allayed, he watched her for a while; then curiosity stirred in him. He asked softly, "Do you deserve a beating, Alys? How came you to allow Beatrice and Margot to fall into such a trap?"

She jumped and blushed, but did not answer until she had brought him food and wine. Then, while he ate, she told him the whole tale. "I am so sorry," she said at last, "not only for the pain I have caused you and the labor to which I have put you, but for Sir Guillaume, also. If only I had not been so selfish, wanting something to do so that I would not think every moment whether you would forgive me and come to me—"

"I cannot object to that," Raymond interrupted, smiling.

"No, but in a way poor Sir Guillaume is the sufferer. And I wonder if he is so guilty, for that treacherous Ernaldus may have planted the idea in his silly head. If I had only looked at Margot and Beatrice and listened to them, I would never have gone or let them go, and Sir Guillaume would not be ruined. Indeed, Raymond, he is only a rather stupid, too-young man."

"Oh, very well, I will see what I can do for him," Raymond conceded. "After all, the fault is really Sir Romeo's. If he had not bespoke Beatrice in such a foolish way . . . or, if you will, the fault goes back to my grandfather, who spoiled the girl."

"But even so," Alys sighed, "it comes back to me. It is as I said from the very first, my lord. In some ways I am truly not fit to be your wife. No one would have bothered to abduct me, the daughter of a simple knight. It was too far outside my knowledge, from not being highbred enough."

"Good God, of all the conceited people!" Raymond exclaimed. "The trouble with you, Alys, is not that you are too lowbred but that you are too proud. You think you make the world go around." And then he began to laugh at her affronted expression. "Do not dare blame yourself for Beatrice's and Margot's mischief," he said seriously. "You are fit to be a queen."

AUTHOR'S NOTE

I wish to point out the mingling of fact and fiction in the tale of the abduction of Beatrice of Provence. The abduction itself, although not mentioned in any of the modern histories I have consulted, has a medieval source. Matthew de Paris (*English History*, 1245. Bohn's Library, London, 1853, vol. II, p. 43.) says:

> . . . a certain knight of small property, but bold and brave in war, incited by the lady's beauty, as well as by the rich inheritance which belonged to her, secretly carried her off, and placed her in safety in a castle near, which belonged to him, considering it quite an excusable offense, according to the saying of the poet, *Genialis praeda puella est*. (Woman is a pleasing prize.)

It must be noted, however, that the young knight who abducted the lady is not named, nor is he identified in any other medieval source available to me. I have chosen to make him a scion of the family who held the castle called Les Baux, a most remarkable place (now a ruin) set atop a precipitous cliff.

This identification of the abductor with Les Baux has no historical basis at all, nor has the existence of Sir Guillaume, who is a fictional character associated with Les Baux only for the purposes of this novel. Thus, Sir Guillaume's actions and his feelings are equally products of the author's imagination.

Finally, no mention at all is made of how Beatrice was rescued. The chronicler implies that there was some fighting, but there is no mention of the terms upon which the lady was recovered, nor of any punishment meted out to the young knight. All that is known is that Beatrice was returned unharmed to her mother, was betrothed to Charles of Anjou shortly thereafter, and married Charles in January 1246.

I must concede that the rescue I described is highly unlikely. Most probably Beatrice was extricated from her too-eager swain's hold by her mother and guardian, either by besieging the knight's castle or by paying a ransom and taking oath that no retribution would be exacted for the abduction. I have, therefore, taken a grave liberty with the true facts in order to produce an exciting and amusing denouement.

In amelioration, I plead that the result, in historical terms, was identical: Beatrice was freed in a condition to marry Charles of Anjou; that is, no marriage contract of which the Church was aware had been made, and she was still a virgin— or, at least not with child. It is the marriage that is of historical significance, because it led eventually to Provence being united with the kingdom of France. How Beatrice was returned to her mother is not relevant in the larger pattern of history, and thus I have felt no great harm would be done by bending the truth to suit my novel.